BY THE SAME AUTHOR

CONTOUR
Hardback ISBN - 978-1906221-447
Paperback ISBN - 978-1906221-430

APPLE GIRL
Hardback ISBN - 978-1905886-715
Paperback ISBN - 978-1905886-623

TWELVE GIRLS
Hardback ISBN - 978-1906510-381
Paperback ISBN - 978-1906510-947

JON BEATTIEY

Trig Point

Matador
9 De Montfort Mews
Leicester LE1 7FW, UK
Tel: (+44) 116 255 9311 / 9312
Email: books@troubador.co.uk
Web: www.troubador.co.uk/matador

This is a work of fiction. Characters, companies and locations are either the product of the
author's imagination or, in the case of locations, if real, used fictitiously without any
intent to describe their actual environment.

ISBN 978-1848761-216 (pb)
ISBN 978-1848761-254 (hb)

A Cataloguing-in-Publication (CIP) catalogue record for this book
is available from the British Library.

Typeset in 11pt Book Antiqua by Troubador Publishing Ltd, Leicester, UK
Printed in the UK by TJ International, Padstow, Cornwall

Matador is an imprint of Troubador Publishing Ltd

do mo chairde go léir in Éirinn

"to all my Irish friends"

TRIG POINT

*A triangulation pillar, set on a hilltop, facilitated map
maker's efforts to work out heights and distances from one
point to another.*

*

*A reference point on high ground used in early
surveying techniques, typically a small concrete pillar
with an instrument mounting facility.*

*

*A magical place on a hill top in remote Southern Ireland
that became the turning point for the life of
a once unloved young girl*

*

*The point where a partnership of souls became rock solid after
a journey through uncharted waters*

*

Water and ground in their Extremity

AUTHOR'S NOTE

As promised when *Contour* emerged as the potential first of a trilogy, the Manor's characters have not faded, *au contraire*, they mature. As in all lives, changes in circumstances bring different perspectives into view. In *Trig Point* the changes may be in time and locations but the concepts are still held in place; vibrancy, colour, emotion, a sense of purpose. Fictional, yes, but with underlying principles to encourage, stimulate and reward. *Bench Mark* will follow in due course.

I acknowledge the tremendous support from all my Irish friends, including the Sheep's Head Way organisation; from Celtic Studies at Queens University, Belfast, from sponsors and from the professional team at Troubador but most of all, the quiet patience and forbearance of Sue, my wife, as she has lived with all these virtual girlfriends during their visualization.

I would also like to place on record the names of the late Tom Whitty for encouraging the placement of the stone seat, and of Seamus Heaney for the words thereon, may their ideals stay with us and be an inspiration into the future.

ONE

Quietly at the kitchen window, looking out into the grey dawn, watching the sway of the wettened branches of the garden trees throw droplets onto the sodden lawn, his mind widened to the greater perspective of the oncoming day. Happily she'd been her normal self last night, doing all the routine things, checking the twins, sliding into bed alongside, picking up her paperback, settling down to await the onset of drowsy eyes; faint snortles and the book slipping onto the covers to show when it was time to switch out the light.

They'd slept; comfortingly back to back as mostly they now did, until the faint fingers of light crept into his sub-conscious; the careful glance at the red figures confirmed the time. Time to start the day. No stir as he eased away from her warmth, slid one leg and another to reach for the cosy thick carpet, the half roll from under the covers to stand and ease his shoulders. Why did it sometimes feel as if he'd slept in a coffin? He'd picked up his clothes, tip-toed away to tread carefully downstairs and dress alongside the warmth of the Aga. So far, so good, if she had woken there'd have been that muffled *'what're you doing?'* or a wee bit later the sound of her going to the bathroom. He didn't want to wake her too early; it was going to be one heck of a day.

He daren't have a coffee, the kettle on the boil made enough noise to rival the power shower, so made do with a glass of fruit juice. Then on with his outdoor shoes, his favourite scarf and the waterproof coat softened with old age; he'd left his stick in the hall. The Aga burbled gently away behind him, a comfortingly familiar sound. Hazel would wake to see to the twins soon. Why did it have to be today? But then,

1

it had been their choice. No going back. He stood for some moments in the comfort of the silent hall, the most vicarious of the Manor's spaces, which had been his first glimpse of Roberta's world, remembering.

Over a year ago.

The twins had changed their lives. Aubrietia, bless her, and lusty Christopher, beautiful babies, both of them, so precious to his darling Roberta, all she'd ever wanted. He acknowledged she'd schemed to make him their father, seduced him, courted him in her own instinctively sexy way, fought tooth and nail to keep him, seen off the opposition. No back tracking, no recriminations, he'd succumbed to her feminine wiles and yes, become a happier, a more rounded sort of guy as a result, despite the huge change in his life. The grey old days long buried in the past, his divorce and the mental upheaval of that time now all but erased. That final day of the old chapter, he'd walked up the hill and had even contemplated whether he should have ended it all and left Roberta to her own life. But June, his beloved daughter, she'd rescued him, pulled him out from that trough of despair. How was ex-wife Samantha faring in her new challenge, the orphanage circuit in Romania a far cry from her first project in Sierra Leone? At least she had the new man in her life behind her, probably much much more than he could have ever been. So many memories.

Last year's wedding, now that *had* been an occasion. Of course, Mary had been in her element, helping to arrange things, proud in the newly declared true role of mother rather than housekeeper to her illegitimate daughter. That no one much bothered any more about that sort of thing he'd told her more than once, and anyway, who could be anything but proud of owning up to such a wonderful girl as her – and his – Roberta? And Roberta had been so stunningly superb, sweeping down the aisle in a cloud of misty silk, bluntly ignoring any tradition that a newly maternal divorcee wasn't expected to wear white. As she had said, it wasn't white, it was cream, and he knew how expensively made it was too. Daughter June had been an equally beautiful bridesmaid – well, matron of honour except she wasn't a matron, not yet. He lived in hope.

The church had been pretty full, what with his crowd and the surprising number of her earlier cronies who had popped out of the woodwork; how many had said *'how luvverly to seeee you darling'* as if they hadn't abandoned her after the errant Michael had scarpered off with young Fiona then flung himself and his Audi off the snowy road in the Alps. He'd have to be ever grateful to the guy really, giving Roberta the perfect excuse to call him in as comforter – and advisor – before encouraging him to get her kit off on the rug in the sitting room. He remembered it *very* well, her yielding up the preciousness of her soul – and body – in more ways than one, to ask him, to allow him, to get involved. And how!

Mary – buxom, motherly Mary, had equally defied tradition that day and given her only daughter away, stood proud and declared *'I do'* in a loud voice when the vicar had asked the routine question, causing some in the congregation to utter suppressed giggles. Good old Mary, what would they do without her or young Hazel, come to that, who they'd almost adopted, poor girl.

Then there was Andrea. They were such very good friends now, with more special memories to share. She still hadn't found a proper partner, sadly, and yes, they did flirt every now and again, likely as much as for old time's sake as for any real need or intention to return to the previous depths of infatuation, though he'd no doubts the smouldering remnants of what they'd had going might be dangerously fanned into flames given the opportunity. Roberta knew, of that he was certain sure and she turned a blind eye. She had her twins, and both she and he knew they'd never split. Too close, too much an indissoluble part of each other.

Across the grass, shrouded in the growing early morning mist, the barn lurked, the core of the business, the backdrop to their success and the setting for this next momentous move. It had certainly taken far longer than anticipated to get off the ground, but here it was, *the day*. He had an hour, maybe an hour and a half, to himself.

The heavy timbered door of the Manor swung shut with no more than the satisfying thud behind him. Standing briefly on the top step, more snippets rolled past; the first day when – hesitantly – he'd come back with her after the tumble she'd taken off that horse, then a few days later the dinner party and the ambience and glow of the place in the warm evening; a couple of weeks or so later *the* evening when she'd seduced him, and later still the time he'd carried her in with a newly plastered arm after that silly tiff, then the day they'd brought the newly born twins home – oh, so many, many magical moments.

He sighed; Samantha, his life with her now a strangely blanketed almost surreal vestige of a former existence. The momentous day when she'd gone to start her new mission in life and left him; cast adrift and not knowing which way to go, he'd vented his desperate personal feelings on Available – his definition – Andrea. Then that night after she'd come back home from her first few months abroad she'd nearly done for him with her reinvigorated ardour. And the difficulties that followed, when his foibles were exposed and she took the brave decision to accept the inevitable.

A tug at his heartstrings; after all, they'd had June and then Peter, both very much part of their lives. Through those difficult years they'd struggled against the odds with little money but had loads of fun, achievements hard won seen so admirable at the time. Dear June, she'd railed at him when she first found out about Roberta then completely gone into reverse once she'd seen the way things had worked out. If she hadn't been around he may not have survived through the emotional chaos. And happily she'd be here at the weekend, all being well.

Crossing the gravel carefully, so as not to produce too much of a crunch noise, he took to the dewed grass, across towards the rustic stile he'd built over the stone wall behind the big old beech. Here it was that he had dragged Roberta out that sunny summer day, given her his signet ring as a token, had promised to exchange it for an engagement ring, not expecting it to happen, but happen it did.

The grass on the field edge was still heavy with the night's rain and dampened his trousers within a hundred yards. He was glad when he reached the meadow beyond and could shake off some of the wet. He climbed the slope of the pasture steadily, reaching the old seat with its slats green mildewed and failing. Another thing, sitting here that time two years and more gone, to unexpectedly see her come off that wayward horse. The start of it all; even now he still wondered what would have happened if Samantha hadn't gone out that particular morning provoking a stiff walk in the country to ease his feelings. Would they still be a staid boring old married couple with no spark of feelings between them? Would his old accountancy business still be dragging on? Academic, because she had, he had, and gone to help a girl and seen those dark brown eyes and fallen for her, as she, and he smiled, often said had fallen *off* for him.

The crest of the hill reached after a fair stiff half hour climb and the wood was ahead of him. The place where much later he'd fatuously wondered if he should have abandoned her, arranged to suffer an accident that would have taken him out of her life. What would she have done? Grieved? Taken the twins and gone back to London? Mary might have been her rock, but it could well have been all too much for her.

The ground was sticky clay round the field edge and his boots were getting heavy, all clarted up with mud. He shook them, one after the other; rubbed them sideways against the tussock edges. The mist swirled around, the cold damp air making him cough. Below, the Manor roof had all but disappeared in the greyness. Through the wood and back, that would be sufficient, maybe another half hour or so. Once into

5

the wood and onto the drier ground he could stride out along the winding path, avoiding the odd thorn sapling and elder brushwood but disturbing some of the bird life, pigeons crashing away through the branches. Then onto the stone track below and an easy jaunt back onto the road, striding out, past the point where the horse had bolted and just there, the spot where she'd fallen and lain, momentarily unconscious, and woken to see him, her future lover. How strange it now seemed after all this time.

He went round the back, through the yard, through the little archway and into the rose garden where they had had such wonderful moments, like the day when Mary had served them chilled Chablis to celebrate their 'engagement' and where Roberta had picked the roses that time he'd come calling. He still had the one she'd given him that day, now brittle dry and brown, lying at the bottom of his pile of handkerchiefs. Sentimental? Well, yes, he was.

She was up and busy in the kitchen, he could see her through the window. No sign of the twins, other than the chairs. Problem with twins, it was two of everything, buggies, chairs and car seats, even bags of clobber to service their every need when out and about.

He slipped out of his tatty Barbour and hung it up, unlaced his boots and laid them on the mat before going through.

'Darling – you were mousey quiet. Had a good walk?' She knew just how much he loved these impromptu excursions, especially as a prelude to what was recognized as a potentially particularly busy day. Indubitably, if he hadn't been a walker, she wouldn't have had him or the twins, at least not as far as she knew. No one else might have aroused her sexual appetite and warmed up all her feelings quite like he did. Okay, she worried every now and again, just as she had the unforgettable day the divorce had come through and he'd cleared off up the hill then, but June had come running, brave girl, and brought him back from the brink.

She pulled him close. 'Yurrgh! You're cold and wet. Not

cuddlable. Go away; get yourself cleaned up. What time did you say they were coming?'

He kissed her, damp nose or no. 'Twelve-ish. Hazel okay with the twins?'

'Sure. They're fine. Mary'll be up before ten. Go on, shoo. Breakfast when you're down.'

The bedroom after his spell outdoors was a haven. He stripped all bar pants and padded through to the shower. Roberta had talked of a makeover, to bring this and their bedroom 'up-to-date', but he'd stalled. Far too memorably redolent of the first time he'd used the facilities, fresh – well, not so fresh, – after that precipitate loving, his instinctive response to her mute cry for help. The mental picture he still had of her beggingly naked on the bed edge that time; no, keep things as they are. The shower was great, stinging hot on goose-pimply skin.

Vigorously towelled and re-dressed, he popped along the corridor to greet his children. Two chubby pink-faced urchins crawling all over Hazel and she managing wonderfully well.

'Morning Hazel. Everything all right?'

She collared Chris, stopping him from sitting on the breakfast tray. 'Yes, Mr Andrew. Do you want Abby?'

Andrew reached across and swept the little girl into his arms. She burbled at him, blowing bubbles, the remnants of breakfast cereal on her chin. She smelt of baby powder and he loved her. Her chubby little hand reached out to finger his still stubbled chin. Hazel looked on, as caringly as always, deeply devoted to her charges. Roberta and he were extremely fortunate in having Hazel around; every day he blessed Mary's foresight in choosing the girl to help. How could anyone have regarded her as a 'difficult child'? Not the brightest perhaps, but when it came to it, there wasn't anyone else they'd rather have looking after the twins. No, she was worth her weight. He kissed the powdered cheek, loved the dimpled smile, the gurgle and the way her eyes – Roberta's eyes – flashed at him. She'd be an unholy little terror amongst the boys in fullness of time.

Hazel put Chris back down onto the floor to scramble unsteadily across the rug and took Abby from him, giving him one of her rare fully-fledged smiles. 'I'll bring them down later, Mr Andrew, if that's all right?'

'Remember we have the film crew starting today, Hazel. We may have to ask you to keep the young ones out of the way to begin with. Sorry if it will mess up the routines a bit, but can't be helped. Do come across when Mary allows?'

'I'd love to, Mr Andrew. I've never seen a film crew before. Will I get to be in the film?'

He smiled at her. She was actually a very pretty person when she tried, though sadly sometimes a wee bit too uncaring about her presentation. Maybe the idea of her being seen on screen wasn't such a bad one. She certainly had come on a long way since those early days and her mother was forever thanking them for 'taking 'er off me hands'; so unfortunate that she'd not ever known a father's care, poor girl.

'We'll see, Hazel. I won't promise, but if there is an opportunity . . . ' She beamed at him again as he blew a kiss at them all and closed the nursery door.

Roberta had his breakfast on the table, 'the full English' as the tourist book had it. Their own bed'n'breakfast worked well for them, geared as it was to the Interior Design courses Roberta still ran every now and again, so such offerings were a tried and tested production. She sat down to her own lesser plateful of scrambled egg and bacon. The coffee percolator stood between them in its sentry box cosy, all ready for action.

He sliced into his egg. 'Hazel wants to be an extra, R. Not a bad idea. Give her an opportunity to preen. After all, she's getting to be quite an eyeful. Good on screen?'

Roberta narrowed her eyes at him. 'Then maybe I'll have to ask Mary if there's a less attractive replacement in the offing. Turning Hazel into a film star might give you wrong ideas, mister. Which reminds me, Andrea hasn't turned up yet.'

He knew what she meant. Andrea was his personable equivalent of a *bete noir*, someone who would always be there to remind him of how he'd kicked over the proverbial traces. Her role as Office Manager now made her indispensable; it was just as well the amicable truce they'd called to her feminine wiles was still very much in place but undoubtedly she still presented a vague threat to Roberta's peace of mind.

'Worry not, R. She'll be here. Probably called in at the supermarket to top up the office coffee supplies in face of the oncoming hordes.'

'Typically thoughtful of her.' She wiped her plate with the remnants of her toast, slurped down the dregs of her coffee and pushed her chair back. 'I'll just check over the Barn, make sure I haven't left anything fragile around. See you over there in a bit?'

'Okay.' Ever his wonderful wife, swirling her skirt as she waltzed out; this was to be her day and certainly the start of another chapter. During the run-up to the twin's birth they'd had that incredible 'Open Day', allowing a snooper from the television company to realise they had the ideal set for another version of the interminable 'makeover' programmes. The oncoming hatching had put the idea on hold at the time, but now it was back with a vengeance and in a far better guise.

He contemplated another slice of toast to go with the remnants of the coffee. So many meetings, so many changes to ideas, the script and the story board, but now it was all raring to go. The production company would be here shortly and after that, no going back. They'd been warned that the place would no longer be theirs, with television crew swarming all over everywhere. Which reminded him, the 'Out of Bounds, Private' notices still had to be put up. Andrea said she'd do it, but time was getting on.

The rear passage door opened in front of Mary. 'Good morning, Andrew. How's yoursen?' The vernacular befitted her status, mother cum housekeeper. She hung her outdoor coat on the peg, dropped her hat on the top. 'Bit wild and woolly out there; not exactly filming weather. Mebbe it'll warm up.'

'Morning, Mary. No, it isn't, I know, I've been up to top o't'hill.' He and his mother-in-law enjoyed some gentle sparring that often included poking harmless fun at her accent.

She glowered. 'So long as 'ee didn't catch cold. Where's my daughter?'

'In the Barn, Mary, where else? Did you see Andrea on your way up?'

'No lad, I dinna.' She changed tack. 'The twins?'

'Down in a minute, I should think. Oh, and Hazel wants – would like – to be seen in the film. I'm happy with that, Mary; do her good, but mebbe you'll have to fill in?'

Her weathered face creased in a happy grin. 'As if you needed to ask. Aye, and it'll be good for the lass, you're right. I'll away up and see what's doing.' She paused before asking 'What's to do about lunch, d'ye know? I've got summat in mind, you ken.'

'Don't know yet. Wait till we see what's in store. I'll be in the Barn myself; when Andrea turns up, ask her to find us?'

It was eleven o'clock. The last phone call from Intrepid Productions suggested they'd be 'on location' by midday. 'On Location' sounded rather grand. He'd had no experience of working with a film crew, though variously he'd been told it could be overwhelming, overstated or plain frustrating. He'd had that idea it might be two blokes and a camera, maybe a girl with a clipboard but a laugh from Alain, the director or producer or whatever he was, at the last meeting suggested otherwise. *'After all, we're making a mini series here, you know, it's not a clip in something else. Hope you have plenty of parking spaces.'* That had sounded ominous, but Andrew was unfazed. They had the paddock if necessary, where the unlamented Bouncer had grazed before he was sold off following Roberta's near demise. Too big a horse for her by far, and to have chucked her off after he'd been spooked by a flappy bit of polythene in the hedge – well, if the horse hadn't, he wouldn't have been here. Picking her up after that fall was listed in the events catalogue as a life changing moment.

Roberta he found standing in the centre aisle of the Barn's

displays, legs spread wide, one hand on her waist and a single tapping finger at her lips, staring at the far bay's curtaining.

'Hi dear.' She was frowning. 'I should have changed that fabric. It's too pink.'

He couldn't see anything wrong with it, but then, he was an accountant, not an instinctive and inspired Interior Designer. Each little display – and there were eight of them – always appeared charming to him, even if he were biased.

'Bit late now. Mary's here, still no sign of Andrea.'

'Give her a ring.' She had that far away look on her face, a familiar expression when she had deep thoughts. 'Are we doing the right thing, love?'

'As I said, bit late now. A challenge? Another chapter and all that?'

'Hmmm,' and she joined him, took his hand. 'So long as we survive, you and I.' She kissed a finger, planted it on his lips. 'Go and phone your lover girl.'

'Roberta!'

'I know. Only joking. I'll stand guard.'

A flash of *déjà vu*, ringing Andrea like this. As clear as clear he recalled the Open day, her failure to appear and the end of the day call when she'd told them of the Brewery's demise which ultimately led to her employment here. Her mobile rang and rang, went into voice box mode. He put the office phone back on its rest, not responding; unlike her not to answer her mobile or not to have thoughtfully phoned in if she was going to be overly late. Now what? Then, just as he turned to rejoin Roberta, the phone rang and he jumped, startled in his reverie.

'The Manor', the standard reply.

'Andrew?' He heaved a sigh of relief. His girl.

'Sorry, didn't catch the mobile, it's on vibrate. Sorry, should have rung. Father's been taken ill. I'm with Mum at the hospital. Be back with you as soon as I can.' She sounded stressed, understandably.

'Andrea! I'm sorry to hear that. What's the problem?'

'Stroke, we think. He's been acting funny for a few days.'

'Oh dear, I'm sorry to hear,' he repeated. 'If you need time off, girl, take it. Just keep us informed. Give me another ring once you know what's what. Love you.'

Inexplicably, he felt his eyes watering. He didn't know the chap well, really only by association and admittedly hadn't had too much time for him or Andrea's mother, come to that, seeing as they'd kept their delicious daughter so much under wraps as to nearly wreck her chances of making a decent relationship. Okay, he'd filled a specific gap at a crucial moment in her life and as things turned out, happily it hadn't hurt either of them. She could have been his daughter, but you didn't make love to your daughter, not even under extreme circumstances. He'd needed solace and she'd needed someone on which to focus her love and her longings. Mutual admiration or something similar; and then Roberta had edged into the situation and straightened things out for the both of them. The trouble was that he cared deeply for these women, both of them. He pushed the intercom button.

'R?' He'd called her 'R' ever since the early days, following in her beloved father's footsteps. No one else would ever be allowed to call her by that mnemonic. 'It seems Andrea's father's suffered a stroke, she's at the hospital with her mother. I've told her to take what time she needs, but to let us know. Any sign?' He knew there wasn't, he'd have heard an approaching vehicle even in the office but it would divert her thoughts.

'Poor girl!' A slight pause and he guessed she'd wipe an eye; much like him, she loved the girl too, in her own way, despite the historically tricky relationship. 'No, no sign . . . hang about, what's this?'

He heard the sound of vehicles too, put the phone down and went out into the yard.

The day was gathering momentum. He crossed his fingers, hoping it wasn't going to prove to be a disaster.

TWO

Alain, a wiry man with a deeply tanned and lined face that suggested some good few years spent in the sun or at least in the open air, with a striking mat of naturally silvery grey hair brushed straight back, climbed out of the equally silver Mercedes. Andrew knew him to be a little older than he, say in his late forties, though maybe prematurely aged, given his features.

'Hi, Alain. Good to see you again. No traffic problems?'

Alain put out a wrinkled hand. 'Nothing to speak of. Where d'we park? There'll be about a dozen vehicles, what with cars, motor caravans and the technical stuff. Gennie and so on, the cater bus as well. I'd like us to have a quick breeze through the schedule in 'bout half an hour?'

Two jean-clad girls had emerged from the back of the second car, stood swinging arms and stretching. There were two more cars in line behind, blocking the gateway, behind them a rather swish looking motorhome; Andrew couldn't see any further down the lane for what else might be in train. He mentally put his best organising hat in place. 'Gennie' had initially thrown him until instinct told him Alain meant a generator truck. Best get that parked nearest the Barn then, together with any other 'technical stuff'. The motorhome would be for the 'stars', presenters and the psuedo clients. He'd suggested 'proper' clients but no, they had to be controllable, camera accustomed, and where appropriate, exude charm, which meant exhibiting some assets. *'You know, have great legs and show a bit of bust'*, which Andrew thought had been a controlled statement. Maybe if Roberta hadn't been party to that particular discussion the description would

13

have been even more colourful. All part of the learning curve.

'Technical trucks can line up on the concrete here, if there's enough length? Motorhome perhaps on the edge of the grass over there and the cars go into the paddock, just inside the gate? The cater bus may have to stay along the wall side. Do you need water?'

Alain nodded. 'The facilities guy will liaise.' He peered down the line. 'That's him, in the red Subaru. He's Barry. Sue!' A long legged blonde in a dark blue puffa jacket detached herself from the group beginning to assemble from the vehicles. 'She's the producer. Took Melanie's place at the last moment. She's okay.'

Andrew wasn't so sure. She looked a tough cookie, in worn jeans, a cowboy shirt under that jacket and now close up, possibly no bra. Wary eyes, but a nice mouth. Lined forehead and the blonde hair went straight back with a scrunchy held ponytail.

She held out a thin hand. 'Hi. You're Andrew, right? Where's the boss girl then?'

'Roberta? Behind you.'

Sue spun round. 'Hi, Roberta,' and advanced on her to present her with a 'wuhhh, wuhhh' smack the air cheek and cheek salutation. No way would he call that a kiss, he thought, and was glad she hadn't treated him that way. 'Luvverly to be here. Great place you have,' she added, swinging her eyes over the surroundings. 'Right, you lot. Briefing ten minutes. Get the vehicles lost. Let's have a walk through.' She took Roberta by the arm and propelled her towards the Barn door, ignoring Andrew.

He turned back to Alain. 'So do you do as you're told?'

Alain laughed. 'Sure. But we get on. She does her job, I do mine. Can we have somewhere to sit round a table?'

Reluctantly he had to suggest the kitchen, the only place large enough and with chairs on tap. The office was too small, and no way would either he or Roberta give up another room in the house to any pushy film makers. He almost wished they'd kitted out the smaller barn tucked away behind the bigger one, so far left to moulder away on its own. 'Unless we can refurbish the small hay barn?' mentioning it only as a vague possibility and gained a surprise bonus.

'Sure. Guess you'd not want us in the house. Given we're here for a couple of weeks, we'll see what we can do. Where?'

Not wishing to seem overly keen, Andrew hesitated. 'It's behind – we've not done anything with it . . .' Roberta had told him, ages ago, that her former husband had considered using it as a workshop allied to his passion for tinkering with cars, but when she'd added '*he tinkered with other passions which took priority*', he'd raised his eyebrows, until at her steady look he'd twigged. Of course, Michael's passion in that context was the one that resulted in his exodus, chasing other skirts and subsequentially his accidental car crash in the Alps that had given Roberta this place. Since then the little barn had lain undisturbed in its dereliction as the abandoned venue for Michael's sexual peccadilloes.

Avoiding the increasing melee as vehicles were being shunted about, he guided Alain around the corner. This was rarely trodden territory and he was rather ashamed of the weed growth. Some of the ship-lapped timbers had come adrift and he wasn't at all sure about the roof; it really was in a parlous state.

'Sorry,' Andrew said. 'I rather think it's past its sell-by date.'

Alain laughed. 'You'd be surprised what our guys can do. Let's have a look inside.'

Between them they exerted enough force on the ramshackle door to make it budge, protestingly, but sufficient to give them access. A flutter of exiting surprised pigeons shook dust down through the shafts of diffuse light from gaps in the timbers.

As eyes grew accustomed to the dim recesses, the abandoned clutter became more apparent. Andrew kept quiet, seeing a grotty mattress bent into a corner.

'Could be worse. If you're happy about this, we'll give it a go. Leave the rubbish outside for you to sort?

'I'd best ask Roberta, Alain, it's more her thing,' wondering if this might disturb a few ghosts of memories best laid to rest. Laid memories, certainly.

'Okay. In the meantime?'

It had to be the kitchen. He hoped Mary was still in good humour. As they walked back across the yard, Roberta joined them. In ebullient mood, she beamed.

'Hi, you two. What are you up to?'

Andrew took her arm to steer her round a pile of aluminium cases. 'Alain's made us an offer. Clear out the small barn and make it usable if he can call it theirs for the duration.' He watched her face, at the impassive acceptance of that old chapter being pulped and was amazed at her strength of mind.

'Don't see why not, do us a good turn. Will it keep you out of the house?'

Alain laughed. 'Sure thing. I'll get the boys onto it overnight; you don't mind, do you?'

'*Overnight?* Do you guys work at night?' Roberta looked as surprised as she sounded. They'd reached the back door. 'Come in, but please mind the twins if they're loose. They can be a little hazardous. Hazel!' she yelled. 'We're coming in!'

Round the kitchen table they had a conference. Not a round table conference because the table was rectangular, Roberta said, making them all laugh. Sue had joined them; as Mary handed coffee mugs round Barry also came in. Alain spread his schedules out.

'Let's go from line one for today. Roberta, you're doing a welcome walk, talking into camera, from gate to Barn door. You smile; twist around so a skirt flares, pat your hair, as though you're preening, look sexy. Gets the viewers' interest on a high. You finish as you open the door. We'll have to have a good pan round the interior, Sue, different angles, floor perspective. Later, p'raps tomorrow, all the boring stuff, customers arriving, shown around, then we'll have our experts doing the critiques – sorry, Rob, there'll be some red faces here – rather like Roadshow parts, lots of arguments over style and so on. This should take us about three days, I've allowed four.

Then we see a set change – I hope that's okay, Rob – another day, possibly two. Trip out for second unit to a customer's house; leave most of the set-up to you, Barry. Same customers back here on the new set, a conference thing while you two argue costings, Andrew, Rob. We need some more talent with you – can you supply or do we import?'

He paused for breath and Roberta leant across the table.

'One more 'Rob', Alain, and you're all off the property. I'm Roberta, all of me. Only my husband has shortened privileges. I don't mind doing sexy walks but you will have to explain set demolition. Not sure about that. Critiques we can put up with, our clients do that all the time. For talent we,' and she looked across at Andrew, 'might have a choice. Let you decide, later.' She sat back.

'Sorry, er, Roberta. Meant well.' He didn't seem at all fazed. 'Right, second week. Another lot of customers, another house visit. Then we had an idea about a fake film shoot.'

'Fake film shoot?' Roberta frowned. Sue laughed. Alain looked almost pleased with himself.

'Like looking in a mirror. Sort of 'this is what we do' thing. Concentrates the viewer's attention on what the fake camera is filming. We've allowed another day for last minute thoughts. Third week,' he paused, looked around but got no reaction, 'we'll use different sets again, so we can run the mini-series. Celebrity week; surprise there, folks, all will be revealed. Then we should be done. Any questions?'

Roberta looked at her husband. He looked bemused. 'Andrew?'

His eyebrows went up and he shook his head. 'So long as we can fit in any genuine clients when – if – they turn up. We'd best talk through the set changes too. Nothing else I can think of.'

'Fine. Right, Barry, your floor.'

The facilities man ran through the logistics, the 'nuts and bolts' as he called it, then Sue produced her far more detailed call sheets. After a further half an hour Roberta had had about enough. It was lunchtime and she was starving.

'Can we have a break? I need some family time.' She'd

17

wondered where the twins were, for it was ominously quiet outside the kitchen. Mary had gone once she'd got coffee mugs spread around, hopefully she and Hazel had them amused either upstairs or, dangerously, in the sitting room. She tried desperately to keep at least one room infant free for sanity's sake.

Alain raised two hands in classic show of surrender. 'Sure. Barry? Is that cater bus working?'

He got a nod. 'Sure thing. Hot dinners all round. You can join us, anytime. No worries. Oh, I've linked water from the yard tap, if that's okay, but give me the nod on the waste, Andrew?'

'Let's have a look.' He stood up and stretched. An hour's conference chat like this hadn't happened since he left his old firm ages ago. Barry followed him out.

Sue picked up her cue sheets. 'Roberta, you can give us the time first thing this afternoon to run through the reveal?' and it sounded very much more like an instruction rather than a hypothetical question. Roberta bristled.

Alain leant back on his chair, tipping the legs; put his hands round the back of his head, sensing her reluctance. 'We'll need to press on now we're here, Roberta.'

She looked from one to the other. Sue raised her eyebrows, Alain smiled, an off-putting cynical smile. 'Okay. Okay, guys, I'm all yours after two. See you then,' and walked out to avoid telling-off that Alain for rocking on his chair. This whole thing had turned rather sour in a matter of an hour or two and now she desperately wished she'd never agreed. All right for Andrew, he didn't have to worry about clients particularly, but to have her carefully arranged, properly thought out designs ripped apart on a whim to satisfy a film producer? And she'd worried about the colour of those pink curtains? Bah! Her instinctive reaction took her in search of the children, her refuge and her loves.

They were upstairs, playing happily on the carpet in Hazel's room, indulgent Granny Mary looking on as Hazel, on her knees, skirt pulled well clear, was trying to persuade them to build the tower of plastic blocks rather than smash them down. At her entry, the two children looked round and instantly scrambled towards her. Despite Hazel's constant attention they still knew their mum. She swept them up; a well practiced all-encompassing motion, an arm round each one. Abby chortled and stroked her mother's nose; Chris found an ear.

'Ouch! You horror!' Roberta couldn't retaliate; her own mother chuckled. 'Mary, these film people are going to be a pain. Here, Chris, give over.' She let him slide down and toddle back to Hazel, swung Abby round to sit more comfortably, a chubby arm round her neck. Moments like these gave her fantastic feelings, *her* children around her. 'I've got to do a 'reveal' or something this afternoon. I hope it rains.'

'Roberta!'

'Well, I don't like being pushed around. That Alain winds me up. Andrew gets on with him, fortunately. I just hope it's going to be worth it. Abby, don't do that.' The little girl was pulling at her pendant. 'Barry, their 'sort-it' bloke, has said we can use their cater van, well, old bus.'

Mary snorted. 'Bangers and mash? Not likely. I've thought we'd have some of those proper ham fritters for lunch, Roberta. Have I got my kitchen back?'

'Hmmm. At least we might get our little old barn cleaned up for free,' and she explained. 'Oh, and there may be a role for our special girl too, Hazel,' turning to see Chris pulling her hair, a favourite pastime. 'Something was said about pretty girls. So there you are! Let's go and have your fritters, Mary.'

She straightened the chairs back to the table; collected the coffee mugs and dropped them onto the draining board. This lot had only been here half a day and now she wished they hadn't succumbed to the production company's blandishments. Andrea was partly to blame, of course, persuading her that it would bring lots of business their way, and Andrew had backed her up. She was losing control.

'Mary? What do you think?'

Her mum, her nanny, governess, housekeeper of old, had the fritters sliding into the big cast iron pan on the Aga. 'Reckon you'll have to grin and bear it, lass. Can't do nought else.'

"Spose not.' All these strange people running amok in what had always been a quiet oasis of calm after her former husband had vanished. Then Andrew had come on the scene, when her life had changed so beautifully and he'd been her salvation. She'd have to lean on him to get her through this ordeal. And speak of the devil.

'Hi, love.' His impression of cheerful control over the happenings didn't help her mood one bit and she couldn't smile back. 'R? What's up?' He put an arm over her shoulders and kissed her neck, feeling her stiffen. 'Not happy?'

'Nope. That guy's only been here barely an hour and he's running the show, do this, do that, you won't mind if we wreck your displays, *Rob,* and what the hell's a reveal?'

Her husband laughed and whispered in her ear. She went bright pink. Mary grinned. 'Actually,' he said, bringing the mood back to sanity, 'it's film maker's slang for introducing, 'revealing', the main character in such a way that gets the audience intrigued. They want you to walk into the frame from the gate, across the yard to the barn door; you'll be great, R, showing off. You'll love it on screen, you'll see.' He patted her bottom.

'Hmmmph,' she wasn't impressed. 'If anyone else calls me *Rob,* Andrew, I'll scream. What do you want me to wear?' His look didn't help. '*No!* I'll wear trousers and a big sweater!'

'Do that, darling, and they'll only make you change again. You've got to look sexy – well, sexy-ish. I want to be proud of you, R, but not too *revealing.'*

She looked at her mum.

'Andrew's right, my girl. Let him decide after lunch. Come on, now, these things are about done. Then I'll go up and let Hazel off.'

'Oh lor, the twins. Hope she's all right with them.'

'If she wasn't, we'd have heard. Don't worry, R. We'll get used to them.'

20

'I won't.' She suddenly had a splendid idea. She'd bargained this one before and it had worked splendidly. 'If I behave, Andrew, dear, can we have another honeymoon? Go back to Ireland, like we said we would?'

Two years ago she'd schemed to have him take her away for a week; they'd gone to Ireland for a lovely week of loving and so far, not managed to take another proper holiday. After this lot was over it would be ideal, apart from the weather. Late summer in Ireland could be wet, though possibly it could also be fine; in any event certainly quiet. They'd take Hazel, if her mother allowed, to help with the children. She knew her own mum wouldn't want to go, so she'd house – and business – sit, and love the responsibility. And Andrea would manage to keep the office going; she was brilliant. Yes, *yes!*

'Andrew?' He'd gone quiet, concentrating on his meal, chewing.

She watched him swallow and he cleared his throat. Maybe he too remembered that gorgeously hot afternoon amongst the trees, high up on the slopes of the hill; such a ravishing ravishing she'd had that day. The little scrap of underwear she'd shed to start him off was still in his hankerchief drawer along with brown crisping rose petals; she'd found those relict knickers by chance and never let on she knew he'd kept them. Proved he really loved her. She kept her eyes on him. He put his fork down.

'Okay. You do as you're told, we'll go to Ireland.'

'Whoopee!' In the background she heard her mum snigger. 'Mum?'

'You're back to school days, Roberta. Whoopee indeed. Get some food inside you, and then let himself get you dressed into something decent. You've less than an hour.'

The twins were still under control but Hazel looked somewhat the worse for wear, no doubt they'd all been rolling around the floor. Never mind, Mary would take over and sanity might then prevail. As soon as she'd finished prancing about in the yard she'd have a good play with them before

21

bedtime. Up in their bedroom, their haven, she stood in front of the long mirror, reflectively, she thought, grinning at her pun, wondering if he still saw her as *that* sexy after all this time. Routines had stolen the edge from their earlier erotic excitements. She preened, imitating a film star, hand on her hair, twirling, her bottom tucked in, her front – less pert but still a good thirty-four – pushed out, and that was how he found her.

Next thing she knew she'd lost not only most of her clothing but also her self-control.

Twenty-five minutes later she came up for air with a pleasurably positive answer to her worries.

'*Andrew!* I'm supposed to be, what do you say, *on set* in five minutes! You haven't changed, have you?'

He rolled onto his back. 'Nope. Neither have you, fortunately. Let's get you dressed,' and slid off the bed. She ran for the bathroom, trailing redundant skirt and blouse with underwear bunched in a hand ready to dump into the laundry basket. He grinned at her departing nudity. Serve her right, reminding him of *that* afternoon.

They agreed, happily; a shorter flaring skirt and low-ish cashmere top worked, emphasised with the very trendy necklace in modern silver and semi-precious stones he'd bought her last birthday and she brushed her hair up into the shape where she could use the matching hairclip.

'Great. You look fab,' he told her, standing back and admiring the view. No complaints about getting her 'on set' if it sparked off a little bit of impromptu connubial activity. Loved her, really really loved her. He'd thump that Alain bloke if he got out of line with R. Calling her *Rob* indeed! He didn't want his girl upset, not for this, not for anything. 'Go on, my lovely one, go down and stun 'em. I'll be with you in a tick.'

'Better be in more than a tick,' she said mischievously, looking at his brevity, 'but I know what you mean.' She dodged him, laughed, and slammed the door behind her. Much more of this and they'd be found out. Almost like the old times, when he'd chased her along the landing to find out if she'd left off the essentials as a prelude to... she bounced down the stairs, much much more on top of the world than she'd been before lunch.

Mary saw her and instinctively knew. Back to his old tricks, she guessed, and she too recalled having to remake the bed before teatime more than once. Better look out, lass, she thought, else you'll fall for another few months off work.

By the time she'd got out to the yard she'd shed some of the foolishness, pulled her shoulders back, and met her fate with the demurest walk on high heels she could muster.

'This do?' The Alain bloke whistled his response, a new face behind a trolley mounted camera made the 'O' for okay sign with his fingers before ducking back behind the viewfinder, and Sue with her clip board gave a thumbs up. Another pair with a sound boom on a different trolley looked far too serious. 'What do you want me to do?'

'From the gate, Roberta, a gentle walk, hips swaying, smile *beyond* the camera, fairly steady pace; we'll track you. Pause at the door, look up at the roofline briefly, then open and step inside. We may have to run it few times before it's okay.'

'What about the light?' The sun having brightened the best parts of the later morning and early afternoon was now tucked behind some fairly solid looking clouds. They had about another three hours before it started to get dark. Autumn was on its way.

'We prefer this, Roberta. No shadows, but we may need to add a bit of reflected light. You'd be surprised what the camera can do. Try it?'

She did five walks in all, listening and learning, and by the end of the fifth take was quite getting used to it. 'Should have been a fashion model,' she said jokingly, after Alain had reviewed the last sequence and nodded his acceptance.

He nodded again. 'I wouldn't disagree. Pardon my comments, Roberta, but you carry that figure well. Come and see,' and beckoned her towards the monitor screen. 'Run it again, Tim.'

Andrew joined her, having watched from the shelter of the back door portico.

They peered into the hooded screen. Roberta watched herself do the walk, the way she glanced up, the way her skirt *had* swung, how she managed to hold the shoulders back and keep her heels straight.

Andrew's hand came over her shoulders and squeezed. 'You'll be getting an offer from Miramax next.'

'Hrmpphh,' though secretly she was pleased with her efforts. She spoke very quietly into his ear. 'Thanks love. For *everything,*' then out loud to Alain, asked 'Will it do?'

'It'll do. A wrap, as some would say. Don't need you until tomorrow. We'll do a few more background shots then call it a day. Back at eight, eight thirty or so tomorrow. Thanks. Oh – and the lads will be in to start on the barn later. If they're too noisy, tell 'em to get lost. Okay, Sue?'

The tall girl was ahead of him. 'Sure, all organised.' She beckoned at another two young men, one with a shoulder-mounted camera. 'Let's go, Phil.'

Roberta and Andrew left them in the yard and rejoined Hazel in the kitchen. Mary was still upstairs. The girl was sitting quietly in the big Windsor chair, reading. The kettle was singing away on the Aga's hob. All very peaceful, all very *Manorish*. Roberta found her husband's hand and squeezed.

'Did we need all this upset in routines to bring us back to sanity, Andrew?'

He knew what she meant. He'd been up to the hilltop this very morning, wondering about their relationship, where it was going, gone over the events that had thrown them together. Latterly, the routines and the pressures of their business had taken them to a state of conveyor belt mentally, sleep, eat, work, eat, watch the television, occasionally they'd go out, later they might have made protected love almost as part of the routine, a sort of physically desirous relief rather than an expression of passion or even togetherness. Sad, really, after the way they'd built up their partnership and overcome the hurdles of another divorce – his, Roberta had already suffered hers – and the side attraction of Available Andrea, gorgeous girl. How many women would have stood for his shenanigans? Not many. Emphasised how much both of them meant to each other. He couldn't properly express his feelings, not with Hazel, bless her, about, not that she would take any *real* notice, but it wasn't fair on her. He took refuge in returning her squeeze; she'd know.

They made a civilised cup of tea, chatted to Hazel, took an interest in her book, listened to the film crew's cars leaving as the evening's light crept into dark. Hazel put the marker between the pages of her book and stood up.

'I'll help Mary put the twins to bed, Miss Roberta.'

Roberta's conscience got the better of her; she'd promised herself an hour with the twins before bedtime, instead of which she'd been dreaming away here in the kitchen.

'No, Hazel, you stay here and keep Andrew company. I'll put the twins to bed. You've had them all day. We'll have a bite of supper together, later, okay?'

'If you're sure, Miss Roberta?'

'Of course I'm sure. Andrew, pop up in half an hour to say goodnight?'

He nodded. If truth were told, he'd fancy an early night and with no innuendos either; after starting the day so energetically and having the stress of the first day's filming, well, half a day in reality, but it was still hard on the nerves, especially with a reluctant Roberta. The inspiring and mutually demanding half hour just after lunch had been truly incredible, a real boost to the ego; exactly as Roberta said, a flash back to their furious love making of that first year together.

As the door closed on his wife, he turned back to Hazel. She'd gone back to her book.

He had to say something, otherwise she'd merely return to her introverted self. Such a quietly pretty girl, and such a shame she hadn't always shown the sparkle or the intelligence that would have taken her into a much better position. As things were, she seemed happy, was very useful, they paid her a realistic wage, she was free to go, but, and he knew it only too well, if they asked her to actually leave for a better job she'd be heart broken, for she deeply loved her role as nursemaid to the twins and helpmate for Mary. How very old fashioned, his constant thought, but selfishness kept both he and Roberta from doing anything drastic to change the life style of this apparently e.s.n. nineteen going twenty year old.

'You okay, Hazel?'

She looked up, a finger in her place. 'Yes, thank you, Mr Andrew,' and smiled at him.

He loved her open unreserved smile, totally without any suggestion or hidden thoughts, and took the plunge.

'Would you like to come with us on holiday? To Ireland?'

There'd always been a chance her reaction might be a strange one but he was totally unprepared for the way the serene smile changed to an expression of such joyful elation. *'Really? Me? On holiday? With you and the twins?'* She jumped up and bounced about like a ten year old.

He nodded. 'There's a catch. You'll still have to look after the twins, without Granny Mary. She'll have to stay here to look after things with Andrea. And your mother will have to agree. You'll come?'

'Oh, yes please!' Her face went from smile to all serious. 'I'll have to learn Irish.'

He chuckled. Such a typically Hazel comment. 'The Irish speak the same language, Hazel. Well, sort of. There is an Irish language, true, but we don't have to learn it, not just for a holiday. They have a lovely lilt, a sort of dialect. You'll be all right.'

'When, Mr Andrew?'

'Once we've got rid of these film people. Three weeks or so. Before it gets too cold and wet. It rains a lot in Ireland.' The heat of *that* day on top of the special hill above their rented cottage over two years ago was an exception and he'd never forget the view. Superb. 'Perhaps you ought to go and help upstairs? Tell Roberta I'll be up in a moment.'

As she made for the door, she paused briefly in front of him, stood on tiptoe and kissed his cheek. The glowing eyes

26

made his heart lurch, emotional man as he was; such a shame she'd no father figure of her own. Then she'd gone, he could hear her light running steps up the stairs.

The die was cast. She'd tell Roberta – say how thrilled she was, how good she'd be, and how happy she was to be able to carry on looking after the twins. They'd be spoilt. He gave her five minutes before going to honour his pleasurable commitment to the twin's goodnight routine.

'You've done it now. No going back.'

'Nope. She's over the moon.'

'Mmmm.'

'So am I.'

'Mmmm?'

She poked him. 'Won't be quite the same.'

'Nope.'

'Not very communicative, are you?'

'Thinking.'

'So?'

''Bout what we'll do, where we'll go. If the weather will be on our side. Rather spur of the moment decision. She certainly liked the idea. Bounced about, gave me a kiss.'

'Did she! Don't tell me, another one for the harem!'

He ran a foot down her bare leg, tickled her with his big toe.

'Give over!' Her elbow dug into his midriff. 'Just as well I know you as well as I do.'

He rolled close and snuggled up. 'How well?' Close enough to kiss, close enough to lay an arm, a hand, across a familiar shape. He watched her eyes close, saw her breathing deepen. 'Love me?'

An eyelid opened, briefly. 'Love you.'

THREE

The programme presenter turned up with the crew at eight in the morning. Roberta squeaked.

'Look! It's . . . '

'So it is. Who else did you expect? She always does these things.'

'Yes, but . . . '

'Roberta, go and introduce yourself. Get her autograph if you're that impressed.'

'Don't you want to meet her? She's your sort of girl, look, shorty skirt . . . ouch!'

'I'm going to phone to see how Andrea's father is, first. Join you in a moment.'

Humbled, she walked off. He returned to the office. The mail had piled up, after two mornings of Andrea's absence the office was suffering and he didn't fancy looking at the e-mail clogged-up inbox either. He tried the girl's mobile first; luckily she answered it before it went into voice box.

'Andrea, dear girl. How is your father?'

'Holding his own at the moment, thanks, Andrew. I'm coming up this morning to get out of Mother's hair. I can't stand her brooding and I daren't leave things too long, not while you've got the telly people around you. Quarter of an hour?'

'Are you sure, I mean . . .?'

'I'm sure. See you shortly.'

She was as good as her word, the little car spun up the drive inside twenty minutes and she dropped it into its accustomed place alongside the main door. He thought her subdued, not the normal sparkly girl who regularly tossed golden curls back and smiled at him before she'd accept a chaste good morning kiss, part of a lovely routine for a lovely lady. She still took his kiss, though likely more as a comfort thing, before he expressed his genuine concern.

'I know, Andrew; and your support really helps. One of those things.' She shrugged. 'Could happen to any of us. Mother's not very clever either, but life goes on. We'll cope.' She changed the subject as they walked through to the office; the old pantry that had been converted when he'd first taken up residence and Roberta shifted her business out of London. 'How're you getting on with the filming? Sorry I missed the first day.' She sat down in front of the computer, hitched her skirt up over those oh so tempting knees and livened up the screen.

'Mixed feelings, Andrea. The director guy knows his stuff, certainly, but sadly he wasted no time in rubbing Roberta up the wrong way, unintentionally of course, talking about demolishing one or two sets to film their replacements, and he called her 'Rob'. She wasn't impressed.'

Andrea laughed, saw where his gaze was directed and ignored it. 'I don't suppose she was. Leave me to it, Andrew, please. I'll pop out and have a look later.'

He tore himself away. At least she was back, had smiled and laughed and that made him feel heaps better. As he reached the back door, the rumble of a heavy truck heralded the unexpected arrival of a rubbish skip. He frowned. He hadn't ordered a skip? Hand held up, he stopped the vehicle.

'Hiya,' said the driver. 'Looking for Intrepid Productions?'

'Well, they're here, but what's this about?'

'Don't know, guv. Ordered late yesterday. Lucky to get it today, mate. We're very busy. Where do you want it?'

'Hang about. I'll go see,' an inspired thought that needed confirmation. He walked round the back of the outbuildings and was suitably surprised. The neglected old barn looked incredibly different. Two blokes were busy fitting a pair of brand new planked doors; another guy was up a ladder refixing shiplap boards and a pile of rubbish lay heaped up on the access track. Staggering, for though Alain had spoken about working overnight he hadn't heard a thing. He spun round, heading for the main attraction.

In front of the main Barn a gaggle of people were hanging round the entrance door. No sign of Roberta.

'Alain?' he asked of one of them.

'Just inside. I'll get him.'

Five minutes and Alain emerged. 'Good morning, Andrew. Seen the little barn?'

'I have. You've worked wonders. It would have taken us weeks to get that done. There's a skip lorry waiting?'

'Ah, right. Shan't be long, Stan,' he said to his gopher. 'We can't afford to have delays, Andrew, not on film work. What has to be done gets done. I thought you might like to see the back of the debris, hence the skip. We'll get it loaded and away later on.' Andrew was treated to a rare grin. 'Sorry if I offended your wife, Andrew, yesterday, I've apologised to her and I promise we'll tread with greater care. Don't want any upsets. She was absolutely great in the walk-through.'

'Thanks. All this is a new experience.' They turned the corner. The skip driver had turned his engine off.

'If we have it dumped back there? It won't be in the way – and we'll get it shifted off site tomorrow?'

Andrew nodded. 'Yes, sure. If there's any room we can add to it?'

'Of course. What about the old mattress?'

The old mattress; there it lay, an old-fashioned spring thing in patterned pale blue, tipped out onto the weed-covered ground. In his mind, he could imagine it, the girl Fiona as he seemed to remember her name, knees in the air, her head sideways, taking a pounding. Michael, Roberta's then husband, would be grunting and heaving away at her, he likely all the while listening with half an ear for discovery, adding spice to the assignation. Or perhaps they only went at it when Roberta was out, away in London, who knows. He felt disgusted, as sickened as the mattress looked with its torn fabric and its stains. Okay, he wasn't perfect but he would never have subjected any girl to that, not in a crummy old barn with dirt and spiders' webs, rat droppings and decaying straw. No woman deserved such indignity, not if there was any modicum of affection.

'Burn it,' he said, without thinking.

Alain looked at him sharply. 'We can't *burn* it. I'll get them to put it in the bottom, first. What's it to you? Memories?' and gave half a grin.

'Not me, mate,' Andrew replied. 'Before my time. Get rid before Roberta sees it.'

'She wouldn't . . . ' but Andrew stopped him.

'No, never. *Never!* Her former husband and the flighty girl he employed as a secretary.'

'Ah. Bit grim, out here, on that.'

'Yes.'

The lorry unloaded its skip and the mattress went in first, soon covered by a layer of detritus from the barn floor, followed by a miscellany of old boxes, rusting pieces of ancient farm machinery, rotten timbers, broken furniture and an ancient cream enamelled washing machine. He heaved a sigh of satisfaction and went on a tour of inspection. The new plank doors swung easily on new iron hinges, all the shiplap boards were back in place and the lights worked. The traditional redbrick floor had been swept and didn't look too bad. As he turned to go out a robin flew past him having scavenged for spiders, a good omen. Two of Alain's lot were approaching with a new table from a furniture van. This was scarce believable.

He stepped to one side and let them past. There was a stack of chairs in the open van and another smaller table. No doubt they'd take it all away when they went, but certainly it smacked of good organisation. He was impressed. At the Barn the door was open, through which a number of cables snaked from the recording van and the lighting truck, the generator quietly humming away within its well sound insulated box. He

31

could hear the presenter girl talking away, interspersed with questions from a couple, obviously the 'imported' clients. He hadn't seen them come. Roberta stood to one side and he could tell she wasn't too unhappy from the way she had her head on one side, a typical Roberta trait he'd come to know and love. And as if she'd felt his thought waves, she turned to catch his eye, smiled and moved quietly towards him.

She took his hand. 'You've missed the best bit. Marilynn had to change – no inhibitions, just did it. And the sound guy had his hand in her knickers fixing the radio mike's transmitter. No running for cover. I gather we've a renovated barn?'

'Very good job too. Overnight, I can't believe it. The skip will take a bit more rubbish.'

'Quiet please!' A voice from the little group in front of the set and as heads turned Andrew all but blushed. He should have known better. He whispered at her and they tiptoed out.

'Got rid of the mattress?'

Eyebrows raised, he nodded. She knew?

'I knew.' came her answer to his unspoken query. 'Good riddance. Let's go see what other rubbish we can unearth.'

That said, they could only find an old carpet and a collection of all but empty paint cans, some large dilapidated boxes full of old plastic plant pots and a well-past its sell by date rusty and blunt lawn mower from the gardener's hut, half hidden behind the big laurels at the back of the lawn.

Roberta looked around the near empty little shed with its potting bench 'Poor Albert. He would have hated us chucking these out. Such a shame he's given up. No mistletoe this Christmas.' She pulled a face. 'Come on, dear, else I'll get over-sentimental. I'm back into the frame this afternoon, being the expert, apparently. You can always be a client!' and she laughed. 'Kiss me?'

'Smacks of an illicit rendezvous, R. Snogging in the shed. Bit like . . . '

'No room for a mattress, dear.' A ripple of anticipatory

excitation shivered down her spine, for that image of the past had triggered the imp in her. She held her face up and he obliged, kissed her again, welcoming her softening mouth. 'Don't . . .' He covered her lips once more and her arms went round him as she moved back against the bench.

'You're late for lunch, you two. Where've you been?' Mary looked her daughter up and down. She was flushed, dishevelled and her skirt was covered in peat dust. Andrew coughed, covered his confusion by going to wash his hands in the small sink. Quite like old times.

'Been putting rubbish into the skip, Mary.'

'Hmmm, is that right? Well, your soup's cold. I'll have to put it back on the stove.'

Roberta caught Andrew's eye. He winked and she blushed. Like two errant school kids, they were.

Mary wasn't fooled but she'd not say; instead, 'the twin's will need a walk this afternoon, while it's fine. Is it all right for Hazel to take them up the lane?'

'I'd rather it was just round the garden, Mary, there may be too much traffic on the lane while we've got this lot here. Unless you go with them, sorry, but we're 'on set' this afternoon.'

'You should have taken them out this morning then, instead of . . .' and stopped.

Roberta ignored the comment and went up to change. She'd have to make it up to the twins later. In the mean time she was hungry. Surprising how one's appetite was heightened under certain circumstances.

The afternoon's shoot was tedious; take after take until Alain was satisfied. Every time she'd looked at Andrew in his 'client' role she had to control her expression. Teach her to encourage him to have his wicked way in the gardener's shed, but it had done wonders to her ego. Two weeks ago it wouldn't have happened; she wondered what had involuntarily inspired them both in such a fashion; had it been the buzz of the filming? Concentrate, girl! Ultimately the producer girl Sue agreed with Alain they had what they needed and they were able to relax.

'Tomorrow, Roberta, we need a few more people about. Rather than import extras, have you anyone in house?'

Roberta looked at Andrew. '*Hazel?*' she mouthed.

He nodded and bethought of Andrea too. Even Mary, if she'd play ball.

'Our au pair, our office manageress, and maybe Mary – though she may not want to.'

'Well ask, would you? From ten o'clock? We might draft in a couple of the crew as well, just enough to give us the right impression of more people.'

After the last car had departed, the Barn and the estate yard fell silent. Before they finally retreated indoors, Andrew took Roberta round to the little barn.

'What do you think?'

'Lovely job they've done. Real bonus.' She walked round, peering at the rafters and the way the support pillars rose from the old brickwork piers, all brushed down and looking far more respectable. 'It's all very traditional. Good job it isn't listed though. What we'll use it for now it's lost its ghost? When they've gone?'

For 'ghost' read 'mattress' he knew she meant; 'Tea room,' he replied, inspired. 'Or a craft shop. I'm sure we'll think of something.'

'Glutton for punishment, aren't you? Never satisfied. Wonder what Michael would have thought of his trysting place now. Or Fiona, come to that. Probably not as romantic without the spiders.'

'Gardener's potting sheds have spiders, and dust.'

She gave him an old fashioned look. 'At least I didn't get bits of twig on my backside. Or grass stains.' He knew to what she was referring, their afternoon lost in rapture on an Irish hillside in amongst the trees.

'True. We're going back, you know.'

Their eyes met. 'I know. I wonder if we'll find Ken and Sheila again.'

'Maybe.' The couple they'd met who lived out doors in the summer months and who had blessed their unborn – "*all the love in the land*". Lovely people.

At ten o'clock the next morning Andrew introduced a shy Hazel to Alain. He gave her a quick up and down appraisal, nodded his head. 'She'll do. Hazel, have you ever been on camera before?'

'No, sir, I haven't.'

'Well, nothing to worry about. Just do as you're told, *don't* look at the camera, and you'll be fine.' He turned, sidetracked, for at that point Andrea came across the yard and into his peripheral vision.

She'd got through the office routines and this would be a welcome diversion. Having been tipped off by Andrew she'd glammed herself up more than usual, just in case. She'd phoned the hospital, her father was still holding his own and the initial worry was subsiding; she was trying not to think about him or her mother and what they'd do, if. If – when, she'd said to herself but suppressed the thought. This would take her mind off things.

Andrew noticed Alain's reaction and grinned inwardly. The girl at her most provocative, a dress that he'd been introduced to before, though no doubt this time complete with all the appropriate underlying accompaniments that had been missing the last time he'd seen it in action, a couple of years ago. Surprised that she'd kept it and still thought to wear something she'd had so long – at least she could still get into it, though he was glad she'd got that cardigan thing over the top,. It didn't seem at all out of fashion either, surprisingly.

She caught his eye and winked. She knew he'd recognise it. She'd left it in her wardrobe as a keepsake, a reminder, and decided to give it an airing to gauge his reaction, just for fun. Roberta wouldn't know the significance.

The next scene in the schedule went like the proverbial dream. Both girls did exactly as they were told and though Hazel played her role well enough, he felt Andrea got more attention than the rest of them. Maybe it was the way she walked, or the play of the dress fabric, or the natural way her cheeks dimpled when she was asked to smile. Whatever, the end result got them off early. For a change, they took advantage of the standing invite to share the location catering and Andrew was pleasantly surprised. Good food, a choice, and hot.

'Very competitive market,' Alain explained. 'So many companies out there and reputations travel fast, both good and bad. The ability to turn out decent grub in any place and at any time to suit classy people is the key. You don't get a second chance if you foul things up in front of a snobbish actress. Quite a few of the guys used to be in the Army Catering Corps. I've known some interesting people turn their hands to this. Like it?'

'Mmmm,' he could only nod with a mouthful of lasagne, moist, flavoursome and hot.

'Yon Andrea,' Alain nodded in her direction. 'She your secretary?'

'Office manager. And no, you can't poach her. She's too valuable.'

'And decorative. A beautiful girl. She'll show up well on screen. If she ever wants to change roles, let me know.'

Andrew held his breath. He'd half expected this, the way Alain's eyes had followed the girl about, but the guy seemed too professional to do more than express mild interest – at the moment. 'What about Hazel?' he asked, to divert attention.

'Oh, yes. She's very quiet. Pretty, though, as you said. Meekly does as she'd told, which makes a pleasant change for a girl her age,' and he pulled a wry face. 'Is she . . .?'

'Fraid so. Not so you'd really notice; she's a lot better than she used to be. Very good with our children. We're very lucky in having her about.'

'Your children, Andrew, what ages are they?'

'Coming two in December. Christmas day, actually.'

'Oh dear, poor things. Both of them? Twins?'

'Yes. Aubrietia and Christopher. Lovely kids. Roberta adores them. All she'd ever wanted.'

'You're a lucky man, Andrew. She's a charming person. I can quite see why you're so protective of her, that mattress thing. How come the girl's called Aubrietia? Nice name, though isn't it a flower?'

'We were in the garden when we discussed names; I came up with the name as a joke, along with begonia and cincineria, as I recall. Before twins were diagnosed.'

'Diagnosed! I like it!' Alain laughed. 'Well, two for the . . . '

Andrew stopped him. 'The number of times we've heard that. A quid in my pocket for each time, we'd go out to dinner on the proceeds. Do you want us this afternoon?'

'Only Roberta for a while, in a discussion with Marilynn. Nothing tomorrow, if you remember we're looking at a completed project – the one Roberta recommended, the Old Rectory at Barfield, Karen and Chris's place. We went to see them early on. A very photogenic pair and the setting's fabulous. Your wife did a very good job on the design there. We won't be changing a thing.'

'Glad to hear it,' Andrew responded, dryly. 'Which reminds me, you know she's not happy about the demolition of any of the barn sets? Do you have to?'

'If we don't, it won't hang together. Surely you can see that? All I can promise is it'll all go back as good as new, or better. You've seen us at work on your little barn?'

'I'll try and convince her.'

'Good man. Now, we'd best be getting on. We're going to have a review of progress at four, in the aforesaid barn. You can see what used to be called rushes if you want.'

'Rushes?'

'When we were into proper filming. Exposed film was processed and prints 'rushed' back for the director to see if it was okay. Nowadays we're spoilt. Digitally filmed, transmitted, edited and ready to screen within minutes, let alone hours. Mind you, gives us different headaches. Almost too good. Lets so many use computer generated images; you can lose a lot of the true artistic effect. Anyway, must get on. See you at four?'

He spent an hour with his children, crawling all over the floor and having his hair pulled. Mary was cooking. The Manor slumbered on into the late summer afternoon.

'Where's Hazel?' With a child on each arm, he'd gone back into the kitchen, looking for a cup of tea.

'She not in her room?'

'No. I looked earlier.'

'P'raps she's over in the Barn.'

'No reason to be. Can you keep an eye on these two?'

'I'd rather you take one with you, lad.'

'Okay,' a sensible suggestion. Abby was nearly asleep so he took Chris. The usual little huddle of people were round the back of the camera, the big lights on, with Roberta in animated conversation with the presenter, Marilynn. He tapped Alain on the shoulder, whispered his question.

'No, not seen her since this morning. Your Roberta's good, Andrew.'

'It's her thing. Are you about done?'

'Ten minutes. See you in the conference barn?'

'Sure. But I need to find Hazel.'

'If I see her, and I'll ask around.' He turned back to the action.

Andrew retreated, Chris on his shoulder. He was puzzled. The girl normally said if she was going out and they certainly didn't keep her chained up, metaphorically speaking. She was a free agent. Nevertheless, he felt responsible for her and if she'd not been within Mary's purlieu this afternoon, where had she gone? Concern was mounting. He went back to Mary and handed Chris over. Abby was asleep in her buggy.

'Nay, lad. I've no idea. Unlike her.'

'I know, which is what I'm worried about.'

'Wait until Roberta's done, then we'll see. Andrea all right?'

He'd had no thoughts about her since lunch, assumed she'd go back into the office; she normally surfaced for a cup of tea about now. He'd go and look. As he approached down the little corridor, he heard voices. He pushed open the door and there the missing girl was, sitting alongside Andrea, absorbed in the screen.

The two girls looked round at his entrance.

'Hi, Andrew,' Andrea pushed her chair back. 'This girl's taken to the job. She's pretty good, too. If I'm not about, she'll make a good stand in once she's had a bit more practice, eh, Hazel?'

He swallowed his potentially crushing comment about absence and so on. The girl's expression, enthralled and so evidently happy was a revelation. Andrea wasn't to blame either; it was good of her to take the girl under her wing. Why hadn't he thought of this himself?

'I'm glad to hear it. Hazel, will you go and see Mary? Tell her where you've been?'

The girl, still smiling, got up from her chair. 'Thank you ever so much for showing me the computer, Andrea.' So polite, so charmingly biddable, almost too good to be true.

When she'd gone and he heard her light footsteps echoing down the corridor despite closing the office door behind her, he said his piece about being concerned and so on.

'Sorry, Andrew, didn't realise,' Andrea was only mildly apologetic. 'Something she said while we were together this morning. Asked me what I did, so I said I'd show her. Didn't realise,' she repeated, 'that you'd miss her.'

'No harm done. Is she as bright as that?'

'Took to it like quoted duck etcetera. Yes, not bad at all. Can I carry on with the tuition?'

With a subtle change of tone she was becoming less her usual discreet self, another minute and she'd not resist flirting with him again and in this dress not wise. Time for tea – and then there was that call to see the completed film so far. She stood up and did a single twirl.

'Remember the dress, Andrew?'

'Only too well, Andrea,' and the added *darling* had a particular emphasis. 'I recall it had a tendency to fall off those shoulders of yours.'

She laughed, of course. 'So it did. Perhaps it's better trained now. Shall we go and have tea?'

Sensible girl. 'We'd better. And yes, I think it's a good idea to offer Hazel a chance to do more. Thank you, Andrea. That was a good move.'

She curtsied, acknowledging his gratitude. 'Thank you, kind sir.'

'Not at all.' In the same jokingly formal way, he carried on. 'Please be more circumspect about your choice of office attire, Miss Andrea. I wouldn't like to, well, er. . . .'

'Send me home to change? Or rip it off me? Come, come, Mr Andrew. In this day and age, one can't be too careful. Sexual harassment and all that nonsense. You mustn't say such things!'

They were sparring with each other, as usual. All good fun. Time to go. 'Tea, Andrea, come on.'

In the kitchen all was serene. Two small people asleep in their buggies, Hazel washing up Mary's cooking utensils, Roberta sipping tea.

'Your mug's over there, Andrew. Andrea, grab another from the cupboard. Ten minutes then we go and see how well we've behaved.'

'Day off tomorrow.'

'Good.'

'But there's a couple coming at eleven.'

'Andrea! You didn't say!'

'I'm sure I did. Anyway, we'll all be here.'

'Hmmm. Oh well. Shall we go?'

The whole party traipsed over to the 'conference' barn, as it was becoming known, except Mary, quite happy to continue in role as baby sitter. A large flat plasma screen television had been set up on another table and the chairs ranged around. Marilynn and Sue were in close conversation, Alain perusing his shooting schedule. No one else there other than a technician.

Alain got up. 'Thanks for coming. Tim, when you're ready. Sue?'

They all sat down and Tim set the recording running. Roberta did her walk, the camera panned inside the barn, the 'clients' came in, inspected the sets with Marilynn; it flowed almost seamlessly. After a quarter hour or so, the screen went black.

'What do you think?'

Roberta was thrilled. 'Marvellous. But just fifteen minutes after all that time?'

'Fact of life, dear girl,' Alain responded. 'Sometimes we can film all day and get twenty seconds. Why it's so expensive. We've done well. Hazel,' as he looked straight at her, 'you're very good. So were you, Andrea. Better than some professional extras. Well done.'

Tim had covered the screen and unplugged his recorder. 'I'm off, Alain.'

'As we are. See you all the day after tomorrow. Leave you in peace for the day. Of course, you're welcome to come and see what's what at the Old Rectory if you wish.' He slung his jacket over his shoulder, joined the other two girls at the door and the conversation fading away into the darkening evening sounded all very technical.

Roberta took her husband's arm. 'I feel a good deal happier about this than I did, Andrew. And you girls were awfully good, even if you didn't have to say anything as set lines. And that Marilynn certainly knows her stuff.'

Across the dark yard, the external lights of the Manor suddenly sprung into life. Mary had heard them coming, bless her. They trooped into the kitchen. Both little people were awake and about to start a competition, the loudest one to cry, or scream in Abby's case; she had recently learnt how to make a splendid noise. Hazel swept into action.

'I'd better be off, guys.' Andrea picked up her coat. 'Take this dress home and me in it. See you tomorrow.'

41

'You can stay for supper if you want, Andrea,' Roberta said. 'You've earnt it.'

'Thanks, Roberta, but I'd better get back. Mother's on her own.'

'Of course, silly of me. Give her our best wishes and your father as well.'

'He doesn't appear to understand much, Roberta.'

'No, I suppose not. We're all so sorry.'

'I know. I'm very glad I'm here, with such supportive people. Night night.'

Her little car's headlights disappeared into the dark. Roberta busied herself laying plates round the table as Mary finished the dish off under the grill. Andrew sat in his chair, elbows on the table, head in his hands. 'Shame,' he said.

'Yes.' She put the mats out. 'That girl should have had a place of her own before now. And a proper boyfriend. Not that I think it would have changed things over her father, of course.'

'No.'

'What'll she do if he dies?'

He looked at her. 'If? When, R.'

She sat down beside him. 'Oh, Andrew! Poor girl!' She took one of his hands, rubbed it between her own. 'I'm so lucky, having you. She's got no . . .' and stopped. 'You still carry a flame for her, don't you? Is that why she hasn't found someone else?'

Mary slid her competitive version of a lasagne from under the grill and put it on the big cork mat. 'You two, dissecting the poor girl's life, leave her be. She's old enough to sort matters hersen. Hazel, can you take the twins upstairs now?'

The girl, dextrously keeping both Abby amused with her small grey bear and Chris with a plastic soldier, looked at Roberta for confirmation and getting a nod, eased them out of their respective buggies and encouraged them out of the room.

'I'll serve up then go and help the lass, but I reckons you should be more careful discussing Andrea in front o' her. Put ours in the oven to keep warm.'

'She's right.'

He nodded. 'We should realise Hazel's a lot brighter than we give credit. I found her in front of the computer with Andrea and getting on very well, so Andrea said. I've agreed she can carry on – if that's okay with you?'

Roberta blinked. 'Hazel, on the computer? She might . . . oh,' realised she would be falling into the same trap and shut up.

Between mouthfuls Andrew talked it through. No, she should know he didn't carry a flame for the girl in the way it could be construed by another party, though yes, he had a lot of affection for her and also rather sorry the way life had dealt her such a peculiar hand, no, he didn't think he could ever be accused of standing in the way of any other relationship; it just hadn't materialised.

'Then you don't think we can do anything for her?' meaning Andrea.

'We can carry on being as supportive as possible, I think it would be good for both her and Hazel for her to do some form of training, and we should encourage her to take her proper holiday entitlement. And when we go to Ireland she'll have an increased feeling of responsibility. She had far more at the Brewery than she has had here, you know.'

Roberta laid her fork down. 'Phew. That's better, I didn't realise how hungry I was. You're right, as usual. Perhaps we should have seen all this before?'

'Too busy being busy. We've not exactly stopped for breath since the Open day, now have we? It's taken this filming thing to bring it in the open. Seeing the girls strutting their stuff on screen. Hazel's some lady, seen like that.'

She saw his expression. It wasn't the time to pull his leg about flirting as she could have done and had done frequently before, possibly too often. He was serious. The caring bit of him that she had loved – did love – and that had brought them close. She agreed with him. Hazel had developed as a woman, was shapely, and had an enviable clear skin and a lovely head of hair. She also managed to hold a good posture, always kept

43

herself clean and tidy, though admittedly her dress sense was a trifle weird. That they could sort, diplomatically.

'Andrew, darling, you're a lovely man. I'm *so* glad I married you. Look after our other girls, love. I trust you.'

'Thanks for the vote of confidence, sweetheart. I will, look after them, I mean. Of course I will. We both will. Now, shouldn't we let Mary and Hazel have their supper? We'll call it a day. I fancy an early night.'

'Euphemism?'

He pushed his chair back. 'You know me. Always a sucker for a pretty girl.'

FOUR

Roberta awoke to find her man in reflective mood, hands linked behind his head, staring at the ceiling. She rolled sideways and cuddled up with an arm across his chest, fully expecting a 'good morning' salutation, instead, disappointingly, merely got an absentminded peck. Hey, not good enough, no, no way, not after she felt she'd been so collaborative last night; she deserved far more appreciation and slid a full leg's length over him before pulling one arm out from his pose.

'Remember meee? Lover girl? She who responds? Come *on*, Andrew. We've a whole day off from that lot. Whatcha thinking?'

He tucked the one freed arm round her shoulders and pulled her tight, dragged the other arm back and instinctively caressed some curves.

She purred. 'That's a bit better. Whatcha thinking?' she repeated, trying to catch his eyes.

'Bout Hazel. We've underestimated her, R. Don't you agree?'

She wriggled to get comfy. Being cuddled was nice but she had to breathe and not suffer from loss of circulation. What was going on in her man's mind? One aspect of his manifold attractions was this *frisson* of emotional excitement, a sort of incipient *liaisons dangerouse* that kept her very very much on her toes. His play with Andrea, way back, had certainly given her some strange sort of goose bumps at the time, knowing what he'd done, even the last battle with ex wife Samantha had added spice to things. Was there something so wrong with her that she'd fed her own emotions on these foibles? And now there was another female bringing her – probably totally unintentional – attractions into the arena and all the vibes were telling her the danger threshold was approaching again. Yes, she had underestimated Hazel's budding potential.

'Andrew, are you telling me something?'

'She's a lot more woman than she was. Like a hatching butterfly. Spreading wings and all that. Is it right we should hang on to her?'

She eased herself up, letting his hands slide down her front. 'If this filming thing has caused such philosophical thoughts, Andrew dear, I don't know that I'm all that impressed. I preferred things as they were. Or some of them at least,' not forgetting the sexy interlude in the gardener's shed after *that* mattress's disposal. 'On the face of things she's still mentally a youngster and *very* vulnerable. And I don't want you upsetting the status quo. She'll fly when she's ready. I know that you care for her – we've been through all that – but I think that care should be *very* carefully applied.' A little of the cosy comfort of their drowsy morning had evaporated. 'Sorry, darling, but I have to pay a call.'

He pulled the covers back over once she'd gone into the bathroom and closed his ears to the morning ritual. He'd shower once she was dressed.

'It's Friday today?' a rhetorical question over the breakfast cereal.

'Yes, dear,' Roberta replied, indulgently. 'Now go and say good morning to your children. And Hazel.'

He pushed his chair back. 'I'll have coffee later.'

'Okay.' She cleared their dishes away and started to wash up. Was it right to have the twins looked after so well by Hazel? Shouldn't they be more involved, like ordinary parents? Instead of having this admittedly comfortable regime of 'visitation on demand', like keeping pets? They'd slipped into these habits unconsciously, these routines, so ably supported by beloved mum Mary and her disciple, Hazel. Hazel, dear girl, and yes, Andrew had a point. The butterfly was flexing within her chrysalis. She sighed, a deep deep sigh, just as Mary slipped through the rear door into the kitchen.

'That bad, Roberta, lass?'

Roberta hadn't heard her come and jumped. 'Mum! You startled me!'

'Evidently. Why the sigh?'

She dried her hands and sat on Andrew's chair. 'I . . .' and stopped. Was it right to burden her mum with worries about Hazel, because the girl was like a substitute younger daughter to her?

'Out with it, my girl,' Mary insisted as she hung her outdoor coat on the peg and wrapped her full apron round. 'I can read 'ee like the proverbial. You're bothered.'

'It's our Hazel, mum. Andrew says she's flexing her wings and *he's* bothered. In case we're being too protective. Seeing her on the film set pulling her shoulders back and reacting so well, then Andrea's report on the way she took to the computer. He reckons we're holding her back.' Elbows on the table, she propped her head on her hands. 'I don't want to lose her, mum.' Strangely, she felt tears coming and buried her head in her arms.

'Ah.' Mary pulled out the carver chair and settled her matronly bulk into it. 'She'll have to fly the nest sooner or later, love. She's near coming out of her teens now and been here o'er two year. Reckon we've done a goodly job o' bringing 'er up, out o' 'er shell. Don't fret love. It'll work out. Now, what's to do?' She reached out a comforting hand. 'Tell 'ee what; you two take the day off. Take the twins out. Do you good.' She stood up and Roberta nodded.

'Okay mum. If Andrew agrees, but Hazel . . .?'

'Leave her wi' me for now. Or give her the day off too; drop her down to her mother on your way out. I'll cope. Be proper parents, like.'

Andrea swung her little car into the accustomed slot. A far more suitable dress for today, which could even be classed as old fashioned, she mused as the pleats fell round her calves,

47

but it was because she'd taken pity on him. Yesterday had been rather too o.t.t. though admittedly she'd rather enjoyed the experience, showing off like that and it had certainly given her ego a good old fillip but seeing Andrew's reaction pulled her up sharp. Watching the old flame flicker. She'd felt rather cheap, so had happily taken refuge in Hazel's adoration then seen his response to the younger girl. Oh, shucks. Men!

He was in the office and her senses did a flip. 'Morning, Andrea,' was all she got before he spun round in the chair, looked her up and down and added his compliment, 'That's a nice dress.'

'Glad you like it. Sorry about yesterday.'

He shook his head. 'Images of past misdeeds. Alters the pulse rate. Worry not. Thanks for looking after Hazel. Will you . . .?'

She put out her hand, stroked his cheek, stooped down and brushed a kiss. 'Of course, glad to. She's brighter than you know.'

'I do know. Look after her. Roberta's worried about losing her.'

'Ummm. I can't comment, Andrew. Not my place.'

He swung back to the screen. 'You're right. But I value your support and your advice, Andrea, dear girl. Let me know? We're going to go out for the day, *en famille*. Look after the shop. Mary's about. We'll drop Hazel off at her mum's. Should be back mid afternoon. I've looked at the e-mails. Nothing you can't deal with. Leave you to it.'

He'd gone; minutes later she heard the car go, crunching over the gravel before the silence dropped in. He'd not asked about her dad so she'd been unable to express her deep concern that all was not well. How did she feel? Her body relaxed after the brief energetic rush from home to car, from car to office. She stretched, pushing her chest out and pulling in her tummy, took three deep diaphragm pulling breaths and shook her curls free before keying into the invoices. Boring stuff but had to be done. After ten minutes she'd found a cross totalling error and had to do a re-run, straightening out a silly mistake.

Why was it that she felt so comfortable with him yet at the same time so on edge? Here she was, near thirty and still single, still living at home, not unhappy with her lot but at the same time aware of the annoyance over a continuing niggle of inner what, dissatisfaction or was it need? Inexplicably a cutting pang of pain, she thought perhaps jealousy, sliced into her mood; jealous of Roberta, her ownership of Andrew and those two adorable children, when all she had was a second hand and, let's face it, tatty association, a worried mother and a father who was hovering at the edge of life. Or death.

She pushed the chair away from the desk, swung it round, and vividly recalled the stupid time she'd experienced that weird and virtually mechanical sex with him on this very chair and all the waves of anxiety and trepidation that followed. Something wasn't right; her brain was not connecting. He'd not sought her since, not in that way, and quite rightly so, despite she'd idiotically sent out 'come hither' signals – especially the day after the twin's arrival and she'd seen the look in his eyes. The agony of his pulling away from her she'd thought had long gone; replaced by this far deeper friendship, back to a father/elder daughter relationship, or perhaps even a brother/younger sister one. But was the old wound starting to pull apart again like some ancient ulcerous canker? And why now, after well over a year? Something was wrong, as though a piece of her had dropped off, worse still, she'd no concept of why – unless it was Hazel taking some of his attention, for he'd never appeared to bother about her before. The girl shouldn't have strutted her stuff before the camera like that and taken his eye.

She needed some air, to get away from the office and the ghosts. She flung her shorty coat over her shoulders, pushed the door to behind her, went the length of the corridor and out of the back door, crossed over the gravel and paused, undecided.

Mary heard the footsteps and the door close, looked out of the kitchen window and saw her standing on the edge of the lawn, staring at the shrubs. *Whatever's possessed the girl?* It looked like rain, no time to gallivant round the garden.

Andrea walked across the grass, heels sinking into soft turf, heading instinctively for the big old beech at the other end of the garden. There she leant against the rough silver grey bark, looking back at the old house, feeling the knurled scars of years against her back in a strangely comforting way. That's what she needed now, someone to hold her, hold her close, possess her, own her. Andrew had, once. Possessed her. Held her. Made her his own then rejected her in favour of another. Roberta. An upsurge of irrational anger shook her.

She screamed, endeavouring to vent her sudden build of frustration or desperate sense of loss, turned and hit her clenched hands on the unresponsive beech bole. He should have made her pregnant and then she'd have had a chance, and a child. Someone to hold, to love. She screamed again and sagged to her knees, sobbing, feeling an agony of welling emotion unknown ever before. She curled up, foetus like, scenting the damp smell of earth and decaying leaf mould for all the world like some raw sexual odour.

Mary heard the phone go in the office, knew Andrea was still outside although she'd walked out of view, and hurried to answer the insistent ring.

'The Manor, Mary Tower speaking.' Though Tower wasn't really her surname but Roberta's maiden name she'd happily adopted it to save her daughter any embarrassment.

She listened to the steady tone of voice as the girl at the Hospital explained. It was not any good news, but more the somewhat impersonal statement of finality. 'I'm sorry; she's out of the office at the moment. I'll get her to call you. No, on second thoughts, I'll tell her. Better that way.' Oh deary me; and Andrew was out when she most needed support. The handset replaced, she returned to the kitchen, put her coat on and went in search.

It was quite like old times, in Andrew's mind, this family

50

outing. A flashback to the time when he and Samantha had struggled to make day trips to the seaside with their two, to walk along the sands, to eat gritty sandwiches in a less drafty nook amongst the rocks; trying to get Peter as toddler to walk in the edge of the waves, stopping June from sitting down and getting her knickers soaked; being the traditional parents.

The twins, firmly ensconced in their ever-so-safe car seats, were trying desperately hard to reach out and hit each other and giggling fit to burst. Roberta kept turning round to try and distract them but to no avail. They were on their way to the Safari Park; somewhere they could at least make the excuse or pretend that it was educational. Neither of them had done anything quite like this together, a brand new experience and strange. Get used to it, Andrew thought, 'cos Ireland beckons and the twins would inevitably influence their choice of days out. No strenuous hikes up steep slopes and rolling around in the long grass. Well, perhaps, but it depends very much on their girl. Hazel, bless her.

Roberta looked at her husband, at the set of his jaw, the confident way he handled the new Volvo and as she thought yet again how lucky she'd been, got that increasingly familiar comfortable feeling deep down inside. 'Luv you,' she said, unthinkingly.

His glance across, be it ever so briefly and his grin. 'Luv you too. Even though I've inherited a couple of gremlins,' trying hard to close his ears to their racket.

She thumped his thigh. 'Gremlins indeed. You wait. I'll wind them up and set them onto you!'

'Yeah. You would too. Stop it, Chris!' By stretching his belt Chris had just managed to connect with Abby's arm and she cried, flailing her own arm in a strenuous attempt to retaliate. Roberta laughed. Gremlins. Lovable gremlins.

They were through the first gate and slowing to join the queue. Suddenly, down there in the depths of her bag, she became aware of her mobile whirring and bleating. She struggled to fish it out before it went into voice box as Andrew frowned. Couldn't they get away from the place for an hour before someone needed them? She flipped the lid and saw the number, nodded at him. The Manor. Mary or Andrea?

'Hi? Mary, what's up?'

Andrew watched her face change and a cold shiver ran down his back. He'd not seen her look so grim for ages. What was up indeed?

'Pull round, Andrew. We're going home. Sorry, twins.'

Mary had Andrea in the carver chair in the kitchen, close to the warmth of the Aga, with a big mug of strong sugared tea within reach. The girl was shivering and had a strange look on her that Mary'd not seen afore and she was worried, though trying hard not to show it. Finding the girl all hunched up against the beech, it had taken her all her strength to pull her up and get her walked back across the grass, into the house and some semblance of life into those staring eyes. Now the girl was apparently in shock, but for why was anyone's guess, 'cos she'd not had the news afore. Almost as though she'd suddenly flipped into a mental state. Just as well Hazel was spending the day with her mother. She'd not have been o'er helpful and it would not have done her any good, seeing Andrea like this.

Phoning Roberta wasn't what she'd wanted to do, but didn't see there was a choice. They'd be back within the hour. Sad do, curtailing their day out like this.

'Andrea, lass, have 'nother sup o' tea.'

The girl shook her head.

'Do you good, lass. Ye hae to have summat! Here.' She lifted the mug and offered it up. With a conscious effort, the girl seemed to obey, took a tentative sip, then suddenly she put the mug down, convulsed and was violently sick, gasped and retched, doubling up with her head between her knees. She heaved, face screwed up, retched again. *'Maryee!'*

'Aye lass, let it come. Here.' She stretched across and managed to collect the bowl from the sink, really too late but better the girl had something to hold. With the damage done, the only other thing she could do was fetch an old blanket for the girl's shoulders, try and keep the warmth in her. Lordy, what a mess!

When she returned, the girl was sitting upright with mebbe a trifle bit more colour and gave a wan smile. 'Sorry.'

'Not a lot ye could do, lass. If it had to come, it did. Hae ye eaten summat? Best if I can help 'ee to the shower. Reckon ye can stand?'

Just as well the recent refurbishing of the sizeable downstairs toilet had included a basic shower, Andrew's splendid idea to improve the facilities. Mary helped Andrea shed her ruined dress and the rest of her things to get her into the warming stream.

'There, lass. Just you get yoursen sluiced down. I'll be back in a mo', ye'll be all right?'

Andrea nodded. She wasn't sure if her suddenly errant stomach was going to behave, but she did feel reasonably confident. She let the water cascade over her and emptied her mind just as she'd emptied her tummy.

Mary did as a rapid and effective clear up of the kitchen as she could. Nothing she could do about the smell immediately, but she didn't want Roberta coming back to a mess and she'd have to catch them so the twins went straight upstairs. She desperately hoped it wasn't the virus bug, else they'd all be down wi' it, and that no help to anyone. At least it probably accounted for the girl's strange behaviour. When your stomach's going to revolt it could do strange things to your mind, she knew that only too well. The distant sound of the shower stopped. At least there's some life returning. She went to check.

The girl was standing on the shower mat, vigorously towelling herself down, actually looking rather beautiful in a Grecian goddess sort of way, despite her wettened hair draped over her shoulders. She caught sight of her saviour and gave a wry grin.

'Sorry,' she said again. 'I don't know what came over me.'

'Best not think about it, lass. D'ye feel better?'

An emphatic nodding head, 'Yes thanks, apart from feeling stupid. Rather messed up the kitchen too. I'm so awfully sorry. I'll have to help you clear up.'

'Nae, lass, I've coped. But ye canna put that dress back on. Can I sluice it through? Won't damage it?'

Again a shake of her head, 'Shouldn't think so, it's acrylic or something. Can I borrow something of Roberta's?'

'Aye, reckon. She'll be back in a jiff.'

Andrea stopped rubbing her foot, up on the stool. 'You didn't call her?'

Mary nodded in turn. 'You were acting so queer, I reckon I had to.'

'Oh, *Mary!* She'll be ever so cross!'

'We'll see. Now, are you dry? Wrap yoursen in this,' and she held out the blanket. 'Then we'd best look at what we can borrow out her wardrobe for 'ee afore they gets back.' The news she had to impart would have to wait.

Up in Roberta's room, Andrea felt like an interloper. This was where Andrew slept, and and . . . she couldn't bring herself to think any more. Mary was riffling through the wardrobe.

'Here, try this 'un.'

'This' was a sheer woollen dress in mid grey, not unlike the one she'd put on this morning, but an awful lot more expensive. She'd best not ruin it, thinking carefully as she stepped into and pulled it up. It actually fitted quite well. 'She won't mind?'

'Nae, not 'er. Best brush your hair though, it's a wee bit straggled.'

Which was an understatement, she thought, looking critically in the mirror and tried to remember what her brain had been at before she'd collapsed. She remembered screaming and thumping the tree. Her knuckles were sore. She'd wanted to be held, cuddled. Stupid.

'Right, Andrea love. You look a good deal better. Fair canny in fact. We'd best go down?'

With a weak smile, she agreed. Her tummy was also sore and she daren't nod. How was she going to explain all this to Roberta – and Andrew?

Mary heard the car and waited on the top step. Before she unstrapped the twins, Roberta got out and went to her. 'Mary?'

'Andrea's been rather ill, I'm afraid. You'd best keep the twins out of the kitchen.'

She went on to explain the circumstances, having quite forgotten the other problem in the adrenalin rush of sorting out Andrea being ill.

'By the beech? In a heap?'

'Then when I tried to get her to drink . . .'

'Oh lor. Poor old you.'

'Poor Andrea.'

Roberta nodded. 'Wonder what got into her? How is she now?'

'Better. I got her showered and lent her your grey woollen dress. She's by the Aga, keeping warm.'

'Right. I'll get the twins back upstairs, Mary. Is she infectious, do you think?'

Mary grimaced. 'Hope not. I think she started to hallucinate before she collapsed. The nausea would follow. Something triggered it.' Then she remembered the phone call and her hand went to her mouth. 'Oh lordy, poor girl! Roberta, I near clean forgot. I had a phone call before all this, why I went to find her. The Hospital. 'Bout her father. She won't handle it. Better tell Andrew, he'd be best to break the news.'

Andrew, having tucked the Volvo estate back into the garage, returned to the house, mind churning. What had been intended as a pleasant day out had gone sour on them, but paramount was this uncertainty over Andrea. She had seemed perfectly okay when they left so what ever had gone wrong? Now he was faced with sorting her out and finding a way to break the news without precipitating any further trauma than was unavoidable. Roberta had said she'd keep out of the way and Mary would keep the twins amused. He squared his shoulders and went to find her.

She sat on a stool, hands in her lap, back to the Aga. Her hair was down; the dress clinging as only a woollen dress could cling. He knew that dress too.

'Andrea, my dear girl, what have you been up to?' He heaved himself up to sit on the table, hands under his thighs, legs swinging, facing her.

She shook her head but there were no curls to bounce; her hair was all straggled and limp. 'Sorry to have spoilt your day, Andrew. I'm not really sure. Something my mind wasn't happy with, I guess. I felt rather weird.' She daren't say too much more.

'Hmmm. How are you feeling now?'

'Loads better. Mary's been great. The shower helped too. And this is a lovely dress.' She blushed. 'Not a lot else I could do, I'm afraid.'

'So I can see. Or not, as the case is. Tempting!' Anything to keep her mind off reality.

He got a thin smile and she crossed her legs. 'Better not, Andrew.'

'No. Though given the chance . . .,' and he grinned. He must keep things light-hearted, for her sake. This was not going to be easy.

She stood up and let the fabric flow down. He slid off the table and took her in his arms; let her fold herself close, warm and soft. Her head went back so he could nuzzle her neck. She smelt clean and womanly, happily. '*Andrew, oh, Andrew.*'

'I know. And I've something to tell you, Andrea. I'm so so sorry.'

He felt her stiffen, heard her sigh and then soften closer to him.

'Hold me, Andrew. Hold me.'

He tightened his arms around and held her firmly as the tears came. Unwittingly his hold shifted down to her waist, only the woollen fabric betwixt her and a magic feel of her fullness against his chest. It must have been some moments before she stirred.

'I knew, Andrew. I think that's what my sub conscious mind was telling me. I knew. Only . . .'

'I wasn't around.'

'No.'

'I'm sorry.'

'You weren't to know.' She eased herself to stand up straight and he reluctantly relinquished his armful. 'I'll be okay. Just so long as I can ask for a cuddle every now and again.'

'Any time. I'm quite good at the comforting bit.'

'So long as I don't get you into trouble.'

He chuckled despite the sombre intelligence he'd imparted. He guessed she'd already come to terms with the probable outcome, perhaps in a strange way some weird telepathy had precipitated things, though this reaction could not have been anticipated. 'Any more than you already have managed to do in the past? I'll be honest with you; I wouldn't have missed out on our experiences.' Well, he had to boost her morale somehow. Was it wrong?

She looked up at him, sharply, eyes narrowed. 'Really?'

'Really.'

'Heavens. What about Roberta?'

He took a deep breath. 'I think . . .' paused, thought, put his faith in his wife and went on. 'She didn't *really* mind, it sort of gave her some sort of superior feelings, a bit of a weird exhilaration.' What made him put these thoughts into words he wasn't sure, only that she'd put up with Andrea's proximity for so long, then it was the look in her eyes when they'd dumped that old mattress and twenty minutes later they'd been at it in the gardener's shed. Almost as though she needed her kicks, as some would have said.

'Oh. You mean, I was an inspiration?'

'I didn't say that.' She may have been right, none the less. She leant forward into his arms. 'I'd better go home.

Mother will be waiting for me. Can I give you a ring tomorrow?'

'You can't go home in just that dress. Are you sure you'll be all right?'

He felt her nod. 'I have a coat. I've worn less before now. In better circumstances.'

Amazing, this girl; a couple of hours earlier she'd reportedly been a total wreck, then she'd taken the sad news of her father's death on board, and now she was flirting again. He loved the warmth of the feel of her.

'Hold me?'

His hands slipped down and up and felt the lovely soft sveltness of bare flesh as the dress rode clear of warm thighs and more. She accepted his kisses, left, right, before the fabric slipped back. Just enough. A gesture, a gift of acknowledgement, and just enough.

'She's going to be all right?' Roberta was sitting on the edge of the bed, easing her leg muscles by rubbing her hands up and down. They'd had a strange day. A sad day certainly, a very confused day. After Andrea had driven away and they'd had a late lunch, they'd spent a couple of hours with the twins, playing hide and seek as best they could with two energetic little ones who didn't *quite* comprehend what was expected. Then they'd all got rather excessively wet at bath time. Finally they had a solemn dinner, the three of them before Mary had gone back to her little house. She'd bring Hazel back with her in the morning, Saturday, and Andrew was reminded June would be coming. They'd retreated to bed early, hoping the twins would sleep through. The wireless Baby Alert was checked.

'I think so.' He waited for her to stand before sliding under the duvet. 'There's something about her.'

'Don't think I don't know.'

'I'm sure you know. Do you mind, my darling?'

She fluffed her hair up, straightened her nightdress and very decorously lifted the cover, sat on the edge, slid legs around and sank into the mattress. Lying straight, on her back, she stared at the ceiling. 'You and your girls.'

'I wouldn't be me otherwise, R.'

'No, I don't suppose you would.' Then she said what had been in her mind for some time. 'It's what makes you so exciting. Don't ask me why, 'cos I don't know myself, but sharing something of you gives me shivers. Probably what started this all off, finding out about Andrea? Except I got it wrong the first time,' she added as she massaged her wrist. 'I broke this, remember; served me right.'

They lay in silence for a long moment.

'You're not saying a lot,' she said.

'Not a lot to say. Strange day.'

'Very. Disappointing for Abby and Chris.'

'They wouldn't know any different.'

'True. Did you kiss her?'

'Andrea? Mmmm.'

'You did. Do you love her?'

He rolled over and stared at her. 'Love?'

'Yes, love. You know, as in palpitations, hot flushes, deep inner yearnings, can't keep your sticky hands off her.' She didn't move, her hands were straight down by her side, like lying to attention. 'And fulfilling natural urges. As you did.'

'As I did. Long time ago. Am I on trial?'

'Nope. Would you yield to natural urges again?'

'With her?'

'Who else, Hazel?'

'Roberta!'

'Well, you admitted she's pretty and shapely.'

He rolled over again and buried his head in the pillow. Women! As if! He couldn't say the obvious things, like Hazel wasn't yet twenty, years younger than Andrea had been and their age difference was great enough. Was she winding him up, 'cos if she was . . .?

She pulled an arm up and stroked his back, running

fingers down his spine. 'Only teasing. You're mine, really. All mine?' but she still couldn't keep the query out of her voice.

'Roberta, don't.'

'If you have to be kind to her, Andrew, I won't mind. Just take care.'

He lifted his head and stared at her. 'You're serious, aren't you?'

'I know how much she means to you. And I know how much you mean to me. So long as we don't hurt each other.'

'I wouldn't hurt you, Roberta. Not ever.' He pulled her over and sought her mouth to silence these silly, foolish, remarks. 'I love you.'

She reached out an arm and shut the lights off. 'I know. Prove it, again, please. Then think of establishing how we can re-orientate ourselves.'

'What?'

'Well, I think we've lost a sense of where we are. You need to do some map reading, mate, get us back on track. Think about it, love. You're the one who likes maps. And put Andrea back on track too. How, I don't mind. Just do it.' Her hand strayed. 'But me first.'

FIVE

She shouldn't really have been too surprised to find him gone when she woke up. He was very good at sliding out of bed without waking her, but it was Saturday and not normally a day for early rising. Jumbled thoughts took a moment to rationalise, like, is the film crew going to appear at a weekend, was there anything she needed to do, apart from be a mum and a wife and . . . oh lor, Andrea's lost her father . . . and June's coming today. Where's he gone? Surely not *another* walk up the hill? Remnants of last night's conversation crept back and she had a sharp stab of unease, had she been too forthright about his evident concern for Andrea? And she'd mentioned Hazel in the same breath, oh, stupid, *stupid!* Something about getting them back on track? Only because she'd felt they'd drifted into far too boring a day-to-day existence and that's what had killed off his relationship with Samantha, wasn't it? So get your bearings, girl. Get *yourself* back on track. Though there *was* something about Hazel and she had a sudden brilliant idea.

She swung out of bed and headed for the shower.

Actually, he had thought about another walk but the incipient rain clouds had denied him that let out. She'd troubled him with her chat last night and his thoughts were all jumbled up. Not that it had produced any deep feelings of unease because they were far too interwoven a couple for problems of *that* sort. It was only her comments about getting bearings or something. And sorting Andrea out. These women! Chris was still asleep, but Abby was sucking a thumb and kicking chubby legs around her cot blanket. When she saw him her face lit up, her thumb came out and she held out both arms,

61

a *'pick me up Daddy'* gesture. He lifted her warm nappy swaddled body out of the cot, held her to give her a smoochy kiss and tucked her onto his shoulder. Her thumb went back in as he returned to Roberta. She was fresh out of the shower.

'Darling! Who've you got there then?' Still wet and towelling but willing and able to tickle her daughter under her chin. 'Who's daddy's little girl then? I thought you might have gone out, dear.'

'Too grey and horrible. No, I've been in the nursery.'

'So I see. Is Chris all right?'

'Still asleep, hopefully.'

'Give me a moment, then we'll breakfast them in the kitchen. Should be all right, Mary did another clean up. I'm sure Andrea's problem was purely emotional, nothing else.' She hung the towel up and padded into the bedroom. As he followed her she added a surprise. 'That girl instinctively knew her father had died, or rather her sub-conscious did. Her loss and her inability to express that loss caused the problem. I think she's emotionally unstable at the moment, Andrew. Be careful with her.'

He put Abby down on the bed to crawl around. 'Is that what you said last night?'

'Sort of. You're the replacement father figure in the girl's mind, as she hasn't anyone else.' Underwear in place, she was sorting through the wardrobe. 'And she's got my Balenciaga. Hope she doesn't ruin it.'

'Where do we go from here, R?'

She paused, about to drop another clingy woollen dress in mid blue over her head.

'I think, dear, she needs a holiday or at least a bit of a change. She only had those few days off last year to go walking. Nothing happened then.'

'We can't take her to Ireland, it wouldn't be right.'

The dress emphasised her maturing figure as she smoothed it down and he was fascinated by the way she reached under the hem to tug her slip into place. 'Stop ogling me. No, it wouldn't be right and she can't be away at the same time as us. Right. That's better. Hoi, Abby, don't fall off. Catch her, Andrew. I'll go and fish Chris out.' She eyed Abby thoughtfully. 'And change her before you come down!'

Andrew spent quite some time in the office after breakfast to catch up on residual accountancy work, neglected during the run-up to the filming. He still kept his old clients going, had even added one or two new ones as the older businesses faded away. It would have been easy to abandon his old occupation but common sense told him he needed to keep that string to his bow in good order. Just in case. Half way through the morning he heard a car and looked up to the welcome sight of June's Polo driving into the yard. He saved the spreadsheet and shut the programme down. Coffee time.

He met her in the yard, took her in his arms and hugged her tight, reciprocated her continental welcome, took her little holdall and with an arm round her shoulder brought her through into the kitchen. They'd not spoken, just happy to be together.

The kitchen was empty; Mary and the returned Hazel presumably up with the twins and Roberta in the Barn. June eased out of her coat. Andrew waited until she'd hung it on the back door peg.

'I'm so very glad you're here. William all right?'

She nodded. 'Sort of. What's amiss, dad? Nothing wrong with the family?'

He shook his head. 'No, not with Roberta or the twins. They're fine. It's Andrea. Poor girl's lost her father. Yesterday. Took it hard, collapsed on us. Not sure what's going to happen.'

'Oh, I'm so sorry for her. How's her mother?'

'Not sure. She still lives at home, as you know.'

June knew. She certainly felt for her, without a life of her own and stuck out here in what had to be a claustrophobic environment with precious little chance of stretching her wings; it was enough to make any girl flip after a while. 'Any coffee going?'

'Oh, yes, sorry. I'll buzz Roberta.' He pressed the key on the intercom phone and moved the kettle back onto the Aga's hob. 'Mary'll be upstairs.' He looked at the clock. Eleven. 'She'll be down directly.'

'So when's the funeral?'

'Early days, June. End of the week probably, I don't know. She ought to have a break, but we're thinking of taking ten days or so across to Ireland once the film crew have finished. I promised Roberta, as a sort of reward. She doesn't much care for all this now it's started. Despite that she's very good on camera, as are the other two girls. You'll be impressed.'

'Other *two* girls?'

'Hmm. Andrea and Hazel.'

'*Hazel?*'

'Do you have to repeat everything? Yes, Hazel. Not noticed how grown up she is? Nearly twenty, you know.'

'*Twenty?*'

'There you go again. Yes, twenty. Old enough to get married. Like you did.'

'Umm.' She changed the subject. 'So the film crew don't work weekends then?'

'So it seems. One other good thing – we've had the small barn refurbed. You didn't see it in its abandoned state, but it's very usable now. When we've had coffee I'll show you.'

The twins fell all over June. They always did, they loved her and she them. Hazel gladly surrendered Chris because he'd managed to undo her blouse buttons twice so far. Mary laughed at her face and welcomed June with a matronly hug.

'Lovely to see you again, lass. Staying overnight?'

'If I may. Anything I can do?'

'Just keep them twins amused. Take 'em into the garden if you like. While it's fine.'

'After. Dad's promised to show me the small barn.'

Roberta gave Andrew a look, as if to say don't let on, then

shrugged. Up to him. 'I want to go into town this afternoon, love. A bit of retail therapy. If June will look after the twins, maybe Hazel would like to come too. If you'd like to that is, Hazel?'

'Oh *yes please!*'

Mary had a shrewd idea of what the expedition could be all about and approved whole-heartedly. 'June and I will cope, won't we, lass?' and not waiting for an answer, carried on, 'we'll have a nice dinner tonight. One or two things you might add to your shopping list, Roberta. I'll write 'em down.'

Andrew got up. 'June?'

'Coming, dad.' She declutched from a clinging little girl. 'Go with Granny, Abby. I'll be back in a wee while.'

'I've not been round here before.'

'Didn't think you had. It's been abandoned for quite a while. A monument to past misdeeds.'

'Whatever do you mean, dad?' She waited as he unlocked the new door and swung it open. She instinctively stooped her head as she entered, though had no need to. Her father clicked the light on. 'Oh my, how cosy! Is this the film company's?' The big monitor was still in place, the piles of the aluminium cases and now he noticed a small filing cabinet.

'Uh huh. Quite a usable place now. We've some idea we'll turn it into a tearoom or craft shop when we get it back. Spread our wings a bit. Speaking of which, did you take another glance at Hazel?'

'Yes, dad, and I see what you mean. She certainly is becoming rather grown up, I agree, and has a nice figure on her. Good-looking too. Shame she's not as bright.'

'You say that, but Andrea had her on the computer the other day and apparently she cottoned on rather well. And she also did a good job in front of the cameras last Wednesday, so maybe this 'little girl lost' front she puts on isn't quite true. More to her than meets the proverbial eye. Anyway, what do you think?'

'About her or the barn? The barn's fine. Why didn't you sort it before?'

'Ah. I could say ask Roberta but I won't. If you promise not to tell.' He gave her a sideways glance and she grinned, put a finger to her nose and tapped. 'This is where Roberta's former husband had his wicked way with the servant girl. On a dodgy mattress in the corner. We binned it. I rather think it caught a raw nerve. She'd sort of pretended it didn't exist and consequently ignored it until now.'

'I can imagine. Rather like airing dirty underwear in public. Or lack of. She okay about it now?'

'I don't know, June. She's said some odd things the last day or two.'

His daughter pulled out one of the new chairs. 'Sit down, dad. Tell me about it. No good bottling it up and who else knows you as well as I do? Apart from mum, but she's not in the frame. Come on, tell.'

He did as he was told, sitting opposite her. It smacked of that time when he'd gone to find her that first time she'd come to the Manor and she'd walked out in the rain. They'd had a heart to heart then and it had helped him sort out his feelings at what had been a particularly crucial time.

'Seems she's always had a thing about these indiscretions, June. Maybe one reason why Michael was an attraction in the first place, knowing he ran after other girls and they let him play. He spoilt it when he actually left her.'

Her eyes opened wide. 'His playing away turned her *on?*'

'It's a theory. Why she and I first started. Sort of in reverse, all the excitement, the risk. Seeing that old mattress again had an effect on her. As some might say, yes, it turned her on, not that I like the expression, June, but it did.'

Her face was a picture. 'Dad! Is this something you really want to share?'

He ignored her, almost as though he was in a confessional and had to get it off his chest. 'In the old gardener's shed. Really wild, she was. Anyway, we're a staid old married couple now and boredom's setting in. We tend to sleep back to back mostly. I mentioned about Hazel growing into a woman and then yesterday we had the upset with Andrea and I sort of got the impression she expected me to . . .' He stopped. He couldn't quite believe what he was saying.

'She's looking to you to get her all excited over your . . .' June had the same problem, trying to take it on board.

'I'm not sure. Then she started talking about re-orientation and getting back on track. Oh, and getting Andrea back on track too. What does she mean, June?'

'If she means what I think she means, dad, it's a bit dangerous. All sorts of things could go wrong. You don't want to lose her, do you?'

'She said *so long as we don't hurt each other* and *she knows how much we mean to each other*.'

'Sounds to me she's offering you a licence to play away. She's getting her gratification in the idea you have a yen for younger girls.' She didn't much like what she was saying but this was her dad. With her mum in the arms of another man, however good he was to her, she'd begun to lose touch so her father meant a lot more to her. 'Did you say you were going away for a few days?'

'Yep. Ten days away into Ireland. A re-run of a lovely week we had two years ago, though this time with the twins so we'd take Hazel to help. Andrea needs a holiday too, but we can't take her as well. Someone's got to run the office.'

'I would.'

'What? Run the office?' his look must have shown his surprise. 'June, you have your own job. You wouldn't want to be stuck out here, all on your own.'

'Two things, dad. Well, three, really. I didn't tell you. I've handed in my notice at the printers, 'cos I'm bored with it, so after next week I'm unemployed. Mary will be here, wouldn't she? And I'm not sure where William and I are going.'

'Oh, *June!* No!'

'Fraid so. He's far too wrapped up in his job. That's not your problem. The problem is you, if I hear you right, or maybe it's Andrea. But I thought you two were all happy lovey dovey?'

'We are, June.' He drew breath. 'Well, yes, we are. It's the others. If I could – she could, Andrea, I mean – find herself a caring partner it would be a great help. Then maybe Hazel should have another job – a different job, with more people around her. I don't know. What do you think?'

'She'd hate it. And she might be quite vulnerable elsewhere. No, dad, Not an option.' She couldn't comment on Andrea's ability to raise a new partner.

'So you'd look after things here if Andrea came with us?' He had a rational thought. Four adults and two children – would they all fit into the Volvo? Well, it was big, and an estate. Have to ration the luggage. Enough of this. 'We'll discuss it later. We'd best get back.'

They put the chairs back and stepped out into the light. June tucked her arm into her father's. 'Lucky old you. All these ladies around you. Make the most of it, dad.'

'Hmmmph.'

She squeezed. 'Go on, you know you find it fun. Roberta loves you; she'd not have it any other way. You'll see.'

After a light lunch, Roberta collected Hazel and with a slight degree of trepidation, set out for town in the new Volvo. It was a much larger car than she'd been used to but necessary with the advent of the growing family. Andrew's old staid car wasn't of much use and she'd regretfully given up her MGF in face of the increasing costs of running two cars, but as the business focussed more and more on the Manor, the trips into London had, sadly, diminished. The flat conversion of the old family house there, completed some few months back, was now bringing in good rents, so only the occasional pleasure trips took them to spend a night or two in the retained top flat. All change. Change at the London end and the sacrifice of space, memories, and a way of life, so change in car also reflected the sacrifices she'd wittingly made, after discussion and agreement, true, but still changes. Now other changes were inevitable. She desperately hoped her machinations would have the right outcome. Risky, but her gut feeling told her it had to be done.

'When was the last time you went shopping, Hazel? For clothes, I mean?'

Hazel settled onto the smooth grey leather. This was a lovely car. 'My mum bought all my clothes, Miss Roberta. She never took me.'

'I thought not. Well, I'm taking you shopping, Hazel, for a new dress or two. Will she mind?'

'Not sure, miss. Depends on what it is. She doesn't think I should show too much.'

'Quite right too. But you're nearing twenty, Hazel, and it's grown up dresses you need.' Not those old-fashioned youth club style blouses and pleated skirts. And a decent bra for the girl wouldn't come amiss either. She was going to enjoy this. And if Andrew didn't open his eyes when she'd done her job, she'd wear jeans for a week. She knew just the place. The big car purred down the drive. Quiet, smooth, and so light to steer. Mmmm. She was *certainly* going to enjoy this, especially if she'd got her suspicions correct and the girl accepted the *fait accompli*.

June played with the two little people most of the afternoon though keeping their attention on one thing for more than ten minutes at a time proved, as usual, exhausting. Her father – and theirs, as she had to keep reminding herself, helped them play a sort of odd cricket for a while until the phone went and took him away (much to his relief, she thought). Finally, she took them back indoors and Mary fed them jam fingers and milk before she started their bath time. By the time she had been splashed for the nth time she did wonder whether parenthood was all it was cracked out to be. But then, it didn't look as though she was destined to try it for herself. The door to the bathroom eased open.

'June, dear. Are you coping?'

With soap up to her elbows and bubbles in her hair she had to smile grimly and say 'yes, of course'. Her father laughed. She scowled at him. 'Bring back Hazel, all is forgiven.'

'What did we say, there's more to her than a pretty face, eh? Do you want a hand?'

'Grab a towel, dad, and take Abby. I'll dry Chris.'

'Fine.' He lifted the little girl out and smothered her in the towel, tickling her fat little tummy until giggles turned into loud happy screams. Then he rubbed her dry, back and front, liberally dosed her with baby powder and carried her off to her cot. June was doing the same with Chris when she became aware of another observer.

'Shall I take him now, Miss June?' offered Hazel, back home, ready and happy to resume her duties.

'Oh, yes please, Hazel, if you would. I've had a fair old basinful. Not that I mind, but he is a handful,' and on adding 'Oh, and skip the 'Miss June' bit. Just 'June' will be fine,' she was rewarded with a charming smile.

'Sure, June. Let me have him.' The girl's voice had changed.

A tired Chris with thumb in mouth was handed over and June escaped. She forgot to ask Hazel about the afternoon but no doubt she'd hear later. On her way back to her room she met Roberta so asked her instead.

Roberta's eyes sparkled. 'You'll have to wait till later. Surprise. A dress-up dinner, my girl. You have something smart to wear?'

'Nothing new, but I do have a long dress, a pale pink thing.'

'So long as it'll impress. Eight o'clock. Dining room. Proper dinner. Have a shower if you want, there's plenty of hot water. See you then.' She skipped off and June wondered what had got into her, for she certainly was a lot livelier than before lunch. Shoppatherapy must have worked. A proper dinner? Pity that it would be, what, four ladies and only her dad? Oh well.

The dining room was rarely used, for most evening meals were either in the kitchen (work-a-day) or sitting room (weekends when in the mood) despite Roberta inevitably having an occasional niggle about the casualness of the affair, having been brought up in an environment with a far stricter social code. Occasionally she got her own way and they pushed the boat out, sitting in regal splendour at the dining table with Mary presiding.

This evening would bring its use back close to Mary's heart, a return to the traditional London style, days when almost *every* night was a 'dine-in' night. She'd had her instructions, welcomed, from her daughter and was busy setting the table with the silver cutlery, the cut glasses from the cabinet and the Minton that had come out from the sideboard. The menu was easy; she'd done the prawn and haddock bake, a sure-fire winner. Roberta had let her into the secret as soon as they'd returned and she hummed as she worked. Her only concern was how the girl herself would perform. She had high hopes.

'Everything okay?' Roberta appeared, as yet unchanged. 'And have you seen Andrew?'

'I think he's in the small barn, lass. Said summat about planning. Came in for a cup o'tea then went off again. Shall I put the water glasses out?'

'Yes please. The full works, Mary. We'll see how she does. Anything else, before I go and rescue the man?'

'I'll manage. Quite like old times, this.'

Roberta grinned. 'Yes, it is, isn't it? Except you get to sit down! See you in a bit,' and left her to finish dressing the table.

She found her husband poring over a strew of papers and maps on the film maker's table. 'Time to come in, Andrew. Dinner in an hour, dress up job. What are you doing?'

'Planning the Irish trip. Thought it was easier out here than moving things about in the office.'

'Good idea. Finish it tomorrow?'

'Provided the crew don't come back. Why the dress up? It's not my birthday. What're we celebrating?' He straightened up and studied her. She had that mischievous look about her he treasured. 'What have you got up your sleeve, R?'

'Ah. Wait and see. Dinner in the dining room. We've June as a guest?'

'Not just for her, surely?' for as he regarded her as part of the family he'd not have expected too much formality on her behalf.

'As I said, wait and see. Do you want the shower first, or shall I go?'

'You go. I'll just tidy up.'

She left him to it. Upstairs, Hazel and June had already managed the twins safely asleep and Roberta found Hazel in her room. 'Thanks for seeing to them.' She felt guilty she hadn't said good night, especially as she'd been out all afternoon. Tomorrow, she'd spend lots more time with them tomorrow. 'Which one, Hazel?'

The girl pointed at her bed. 'I love that colour.'

Roberta smiled. The one she'd have chosen. 'I'll leave you to it. Three quarters of an hour?' Hazel nodded. She was inwardly nervous, but she'd be ready.

Roberta collided with Andrew at the head of the stairs. He tucked an arm round her and swept her into their bedroom, pushing the door shut behind them with his foot. 'Share the shower?'

The narrowed eye look before an affirmative grin; this was getting much more like the old times. 'We've not got much time.'

'Enough.'

Mary was satisfied. The candles were lit, the starters in place. The wine she'd leave to Andrew. The bake would hold, the rest would be ready nicely in time. The afters were in the big fridge. All she'd got to do was a quick wash and a change.

June came down the stairs, swishing her flimsy hem and glad she'd had the foresight to bring her heels. She had a shrewd and intuitive idea about what Roberta had in mind, just that sneaking feeling and hoped, for all their sakes, she was right. With no one else around, she went into the sitting room and dropped into an armchair. The fire was laid and ready to light but it was too early for that. Relaxed now, she let her mind wander. How her father's life had changed, so different from three years ago! Three years since she'd been so shocked at his behaviour and the revelation of her mother's decision to move abroad and work for that Charity. Since then, the twins, the Brewery's closure and Andrea entering the scene but not in that order, but nothing much had happened to move her own life forward. William seemed as committed to his IT consultancy as ever, excluding her from so much of his life and had as good as openly said he didn't want kids to clutter up the place. Her resignation from her admin job at the printers had come as a shock to him, but he'd shrugged and said *'whatever, do what you want'* so she had a jolly good mind to do just that. Like her dad and mum, but in reverse.

Roberta and Andrew came downstairs hand in hand. She was glowing inwardly and he was, well, contented. He'd chosen her dress, the memorable misty beautiful blue one from ages ago that still just about fitted her, for having children inevitably had taken its toll. There was June, apparently wrapped in thought, or staring into space, in a brown study or whatever.

'June?'

'Oh, sorry, miles away. My goodness, that's a stunning dress, Roberta. And you look smart too, dad.'

'Not too often we get dressed for dinner, my girl, but we can when we want to. Come on through.'

They grouped together in the dining room and Mary marshalled them. 'June, dear, over there? I'll stay here, easier to nip into the kitchen. Roberta, here. So Andrew, this is your place.' Which left the chair on the right for Hazel.

The steady steps were heard down the stair treads and she appeared in the doorway. Roberta wasn't disappointed. Her afternoon had been well spent and she felt her eyes pricking.

Andrew stood up again, overwhelmed. A transformation – was this their *au pair*? Heavens! 'Hazel; my dear girl. You're beautiful. Absolutely stunning.' Which she was; the dress

Roberta had chosen fitted her superbly, the deep green with the lighter reveals in the skirt, the low cut vee emphasising her maturing cleavage and the wide belt of darker fabric as a fashionable belt pulling in her waist. Her hair was back, piled a fraction to one side and Roberta's borrowed clip sparkling. She'd not ever needed make-up, but tonight, lip-gloss and a trace of blush, a darkening of eyebrows, all showed she'd got the knack. She was on two-inch heels and preening. He took in the amazing sight of her, gorgeous from top to toe, and loved what he saw.

'Roberta, this afternoon?' So this is what she'd been up to, his ever-thoughtful wife. Bringing the girl out, making her a woman. He couldn't help himself; stepped forward, took her hands, leant forward and meant to offer her a cheek to cheek kiss, not thinking she'd do more than accept with a conventional light pressure back. Surprised, he felt her lift on her toes, lean towards him and her lips were soft, warm and searching; her dark grey eyes deep and mysterious and also from somewhere she'd accessed a very subtle perfume. This girl had changed, become someone for whom he could feel some real affection.

Roberta coughed, ever so quietly and broke the spell. 'Hazel dear, you look wonderful. Come and sit here.'

The girl demurely smoothed her skirt as she sat and accepted Andrew's help at easing the chair into the table. 'Thank you so much, Roberta. And Andrew. It's magical, all this, and so unexpected. I really am a very lucky girl.' There was no trace of awkwardness, no hint she felt anything other than being perfectly at home. The dim and self-conscious teenager had gone; a very confident young lady had taken her place.

Her serviette she shook out and placed perfectly. Andrew offered the water jug around and June started the ball rolling.

'So you enjoyed your afternoon out, Hazel?'

'Oh, very much so.' She turned back to Roberta. 'I'm flattered that you should place so much confidence in me, with both the children and now all this. I hope I won't let you all down,' and the light laugh accompanied her charming smile around the table.

Mary was clearly very pleased with her protégé. 'Nay lass, that you'll never do. My, but you put us all to shame. Now come on, I hope you'll like my special starters.' She picked up her little knife and fork and started them all off. Andrew knew this as a Mary special and hadn't forgotten she'd produced the same for that very first dinner when Roberta had invited him and Samantha after his rescuing act. Avocado and chilli. He started pouring the chilled wine out.

An occasion they'd all remember, this coming out party for Hazel. In a few weeks time she'd be twenty. Roberta caught his eye and winked. Her idea had worked, risky though it had been. She'd schemed. She'd won, too. She'd been her old seductive self and here they were, to echo her words, beginning to get back on track.

They didn't make bed until gone midnight. The evening had rolled; one way or another it had all gone perfectly. The conversation spun pleasantly around and Andrew could not believe how different the girl had become. No diffidence, no cast down eyes, but her quick and lively responses, even the occasional turn of phrase that caught him staring at her. This couldn't be the same girl, not the one who had been more stolid than demure and so slow and backward, who had merely stood around and not said a word? Incredible.

He voiced his opinions as they prepared for bed. 'She's incredible, R. How, just how, did you manage to get her like that in such a short time? And so beautifully turned out? Remarkable. She's lovely!' He was sitting in the little tub chair and easing shoes and socks off.

Roberta grinned; having shed her dress she was putting it carefully back on its hanger. 'Fancy her, do you? After all this time under your feet now you've woken up to her? So Andrea's got competition? Oh, darling, you're so transparent! I can see your enthusiasm standing out a mile! Down boy!'

Her comment was so embarrassing and he felt far too

warm. He stood up and shed the next layer. June had given him a light good night kiss before she went into her room and whispered about Roberta and her quirky need for this emotional tangle, quoting the *liaison dangereuse* thing again Had Hazel been manipulated in the direction of this display, so he would edge towards her?

'Have you been probing, R? Is there something else you've discovered? Has she been fooling us? Not that I'm upset, far from it, I'm glad, very pleased if she's decided to drop any pretence. Has she been pretending? She couldn't have behaved so well on set otherwise, could she?' Suddenly it all fell into place and the odd feeling he'd had about her was now confirmed. She'd been fooling them all? And his clever wife had cracked it?

Roberta took up her nightdress in preparation to drop it over her head but paused. He'd twigged. 'Why I took her out, Andrew. Gave her an ultimatum. She did actually cry and I felt absolutely rotten. She almost got out of the car and ran off, so I had to grab hold.'

'You *what*? Roberta, how *could* you?'

'I saw her change, same as you did when she got in front of those cameras. She's been making a fool of us, Andrew, but not with any malice aforethought. And for some time, I guess, since well before she came here. Oh, yes, she was dim at school, and so on, but *appearing* to be dim was her self defence, with a difficult home and being bullied. And with practice eventually I guess her mind got to believe instinctively what she wanted – appearing to be stupid.'

The nightdress fell over her head. She struggled a little and reappeared.

'So what happened?' She was amazing, this wife of his.

'A deal. I took her shopping – which was what I've yearning to do for ages – and she did her best to drop her 'little girl lost' act. If she didn't do as she was told, I threatened to sack her.'

'Roberta! You didn't!' Hard to believe she could have ever gone that far.

She pulled and wriggled at the lacy hem. 'I did. I gave her half an hour on her own. Left her in the Costa shop. She stood up when I came back and I got a wry grin. So we went shopping. She's rather sexy, husband mine. We had a lovely time. Spent somewhat too much money, but had loads of fun. You like the result, I think. Good kisser?'

'Roberta – you're mischievous. Wicked, trying to wind me up. What do you want me to do, shag her?' The word dropped into the quiet and he felt appalled at his lapse.

She slipped under the cover, grinning. 'You wouldn't dare. She might not want to play either, so it'd be rape. Serve you right!'

He finished undressing and got in alongside her. A toe began to work its way up his leg. He lay on his back and reflected.

'Roberta?'

'Yes, dear?'

'Why tempt me with something I wouldn't want to do, because I love you, not a beautiful twenty year old virgin?'

'How do you know she's virginal?'

He blinked. 'An assumption, I guess. We've been looking after her for nigh on two years or so, and there's been no one else about.'

'True. Well, let's keep her that way. But she'll be a different lass from now on in.'

'Won't affect the twins, will it?'

'No, no, not at all. She loves them. Made that abundantly clear. No, she does not want to leave us. But she did ask for a pay rise.' She chuckled. 'Proves the point, dearest. No flies on her. Do you mind?' Her foot had gone as far as it physically could and she wriggled her toes. 'Darling?'

'Hmmm. How much?'

'Told her you'd talk to her. Sorry.'

He rolled over and flattened her, pushing her into the pillow, wallowing in her response. When they came up for air, he simply murmured 'okay' and the nightdress seemed to be getting in the way.

SIX

She got up early, leaving him comatose. Testing moment, as much for her as anyone and was she going to wreck things or sort them? She tiptoed into the warm nursery. Abby still eyes closed and beatific. Chris opened his eyes and attempted to stand so she lifted him up and pretended not to notice the damp. Would he cry? It was cruel, really. She put him back and stood a few paces away against the wall. A moment's reflection before the precipitated yell and it was as much as she could do, not to give in. She waited, hugging her dressing gown close to her.

Another minute, probably less, and she came in, swathed in pink chenille, straight across to Chris and the racket stopped, miraculously. No hesitation, she picked him up, cuddled and whispered and Roberta almost, almost, felt jealous. The girl turned, and saw her standing behind the door. What ever would she think?

'Oh, lor, sorry, Roberta, I didn't see you. Shall I change him?' No malice, no suggestion of any thought of connivance, just an open happy grin. 'Shall we leave Abby for a bit?'

'Yes, do that. Bring Chris through to us when he's dry.' She left her to it, slipped back down the passageway to their bedroom.

Andrew was awake and reading. He looked up. 'Morning, darling. Twins okay? Was that Chris yelling?'

She slipped back under the duvet and nestled close. 'Yes. Hazel will bring him through in a moment.'

'*Bring him through? Here?*' They'd had an unspoken agreement not to encourage the children into their bed.

'Just this once, Andrew. Humour me.'

78

He shrugged, went back to his book but put an arm round her shoulders. Two minutes later and at the tentative tap on the door he removed his arm.

'Come in, Hazel.'

The girl slowly pushed the door open with Chris, all fresh and smiley in her arms.

'Let me have him. No, don't go, have a perch on the bed. I – we – want to talk to you, Hazel.' Roberta watched her carefully for any trace of untoward emotion.

The girl sat unselfconsciously on the end of the bed, crossed her legs and adjusted the dressing gown despite which it still flopped open again over her thighs. She ignored it. One hand kept her upright, the other fell into the gap between her knees; her eyes were on Chris. Andrew put his book down the better to take in the vision.

'We wanted to say how pleased we were with the dinner party, Hazel. Came up to expectations and we loved having you with us. Did you enjoy it?'

The girl first looked at her knees and then idly scratched a kneecap, seemingly to consider her reply. Then a sensible and honest response, 'Yes, I did, but I was pretty nervous. It was a very nice evening though, thank you both very much. Did I . . . ?' Her gaze shifted up towards Andrew and she changed tack. 'I'm very sorry, Andrew, if I've misled you about my, er, level of comprehension.' She pulled at the gown's hem with her free hand as though she was still nervous. 'I guess you've every right to be cross.' Her fingers twitched at the fabric to pull it tighter. 'The only thing I can say in my defence is I never really set out to mislead either of you. It just sort of happened that way,' and now uncrossed her legs, smoothing the dressing gown out, 'but I'm a lot happier in my mind now it's all out in the open. I promise you, I'll be a good girl from now on,' and her otherwise straight face began to dimple at the edges as an indicator of her mischievous side. She stood up.

'Go and get dressed, Hazel, but check on Abby as you go, there's a love. We won't say any more on the subject. Thank you for what you've said. Oh, and better let me know if there's anything else you need, in the dress line, I mean. Now we've got you out of servant girl mentality there's some catching up to do on your dress allowance.' Roberta smiled, with Chris bouncing on her knees. 'But how's your mother going to take to the new you?'

Hazel grimaced. 'Guess I'll have to still do some play-acting for a while, sort of gradually change. Mind you, she may not notice. There's a new man in her life.'

'You didn't say?'

'Not my sort of person, Roberta. He doesn't rate me either, doesn't like me around. So it's all for the best.' She shrugged. 'I'm better off here, and very grateful.'

Andrew nodded his head. 'As we are. Roberta,' and he put his arm back round her, 'says we owe you a pay rise. How about another five hundred a year?'

Roberta snorted. 'He's an old skinflint, Hazel. Let's call it a thousand. But maybe some more time working with Andrea?'

'Oh, yes, surely. And thank you very much. It's what I had in mind, actually,' and her grin couldn't be contained any longer. 'It's a strange feeling, this, but almost as though I'm a sort of adopted daughter.' Then a serious look as she added, 'June won't mind, will she?'

'Heavens, no. She'll be pleased for you. Now, Abby?'

'Yes, sure. See you downstairs for breakfast with her? Leave Chris with you?'

Roberta nodded. As Hazel moved to go, she added, 'Well done. You're a great girl, Hazel. Keep it up.'

The door closed behind her. Andrew let out an expellation of breath. 'Phew. That's more than a bit of a strange start to the morning than I bargained for, R. And in case you get the wrong impression, I was going to go to the thou, 'cos I was sure she'd haggle. She will have to do a few more hours, though, to compensate. Now, do you think I can get out of bed safely?'

'Well, if you will insist on sleeping in the buff. She won't come back without knocking anyway. She sure has changed, hasn't she?'

'Yep. Sure,' and he chuckled. 'That's her word, sure; and don't you dare suggest anything, my darling girl.'

'Wouldn't dream of it,' but was going to pull his leg. She grinned. 'You know she *sure* hadn't got anything . . . '

Andrew interrupted her. 'I know. I saw. She *sure* didn't seem to have a care, either. One aspect to consider rectifying, R, in your 'let's make her a lady' scheme. Now, I bags the bathroom.'

With the pleasant Sunday breakfast in the nicely cosy kitchen alongside the slumbering Aga no more than conserve smeared plates and dregs of coffee, Andrew wiped his mouth with the linen serviette, pushed his chair back, stood up and stretched. 'I'd best finish planning the Irish trip, I think. Roberta?'

'I'll stay with the twins this morning. Light lunch and dinner later. We could all go out this afternoon if you like. Stretch the Volvo's capacity?'

'Don't include me, Roberta. I'll be happy doing some baking and then I can start the dinner off.' Mary started collecting the washing up. 'You're quiet, June?'

'Didn't sleep too well last night, I'm afraid. I'll curl up in the sitting room with my book if you don't mind, folks. And I ought to be getting back this afternoon, so count me out for dinner.'

'That's a shame, June. Sure you need to go back today, not in the morning?'

'Too much traffic on a Monday morning. No, this afternoon's fine. I can take my time.'

'Okay. If you're sure. What about you, Hazel?'

'I'll help Roberta with Abby and Chris.'

Andrew returned to the small barn. He'd got most of the ideas in place so all he had to do was book a cottage and the ferry on the Internet, probably tomorrow after he'd run all the ideas past Roberta. The last hurdle was finding somewhere, just for bed and breakfast, in between Rosslare and the Beara for a night or maybe two, somewhere interesting for them all. All! And up came the vision of Andrea, his former *bete noir*, he'd almost forgotten about her during all the upheaval over Hazel. How on earth had that happened? Poor girl, after that catastrophic Friday; he should have rung her yesterday. His special girl. Abandoning his task, he returned to the office and called her at home, with a strange feeling of peculiar inner excitement. The phone rang and rang. Reluctantly he tried her mobile. She answered, 'Andrea Chaney.'

'Andrea, my love. It's Andrew. How are you?'

'Andrew, hi, thanks for calling. I'm okay. Well, sort of.' She went quiet.

'I should have rung yesterday.' That soft voice, it often gave him the shivers.

'It would have been nice.'

'Yes, sorry. Can I do anything?' Had he kept the old desire out of his voice?

'Come and see me?'

'At home?' That wouldn't do, not with her widowed mother there.

'No. I'll walk up to the Post Office. Twenty minutes?'

He thought. His special girl. Was this a good idea? Well, he owed her, he wanted to see the reality of her and it was only ten o'clock. 'Okay. Twenty minutes.'

'Thanks.'

He left them all doing their planned activities, merely said 'I'm popping out for an hour – see how Andrea's getting on,' got a nod from Roberta on her knees in the nursery, and went. On the corner by the group of sycamores at the edge of the green, he spotted her; there she stood alongside the post box, all snuggled up in her *faux* fur trimmed coat, hands thrust deep in pockets, with high heels and shorty skirt. A beautiful picture, one he'd never tire of admiring. He pulled up alongside, leant across and opened the door. He couldn't help it.

'You looking for business?' and grinned.

'Do I look that cheap, Andrew?' She sat in, skirt riding high.

'With lovely legs like that? I doubt I could afford you! Where shall we go?'

'Onto the old airfield?'

'We could go back to the Manor. Lunch in the offing?'

'Later. Just you and me please, Andrew, for a while. Do you mind?' Would he guess there was now a gap in her life that only his presence would currently fill? He'd been too much a part of her for so long a time. She sat quiet as he drove the quiet car into the country, watching the trees and hedges slip by.

He pulled up in the dead-end access road, now gated and derelict. The tall hedges shielded them from the main road but they still had a view over the valley. The Manor was the other side of the hill. The watery morning sun flickered through the moving branches above them, bright and shade alternately. With the engine off, the quiet was no more than the rustle of the trees. She certainly felt far more at peace here than sitting at home, with the emptiness of her parent's life shattered and grey. She wanted to be loved, taken into someone's arms, no, *his* arms. She'd known his loving and yearned for the awakening of those feelings once more. How else could she cope with moving on? No father, a desolate mother, living in an old fashioned home that wasn't a home. The Manor was her home but it wasn't. She bit her lip, aware that her mental ramblings were doing her no good, no good at all. She'd have to get away, make a clean break, unless . . .

'It's a nice car, Andrew. Good heater; I'm rather too warm.' She leant forward and eased her coat off her shoulders and he helped her pull arms from the sleeves . . . oh, *Andrew!*

He took her back with him for lunch. Roberta saw him help her out of the car and wondered. He looked different, introverted; she worried, wondered what impact the girl had had on him within those less than two hours he'd been away.

'Andrew, my darling, how is she?' Andrea had gone to the

downstairs cloakroom. She seized the opportunity, took and held his hands and looked at him. Not a glimmer of a smile and he scarce met her eyes. 'There's a problem isn't there? Tell me?'

He pulled a hand away and putting that arm round her waist, gently propelled her into the sitting room and shut the door behind them.

'Sit down, Roberta.' She sank into an armchair as he stood in front of her. *Oh no, not again.* 'Two things, dear. Actually, one I don't really want to talk about but she gets to me every now and again. I could have nearly given in to temptation. The other, well, now she's talking about wanting to leave us. She's suddenly made up her mind and I don't seem to be able to budge it.'

His beloved dark-eyed girl's face looked up at him, full of concern and disbelief. She reached up to take back a hand.

'Darling? *Leaving us?* Why?'

'Two things. Like I said, I nearly gave in and she knows how close we can get all too readily. Secondly, she reckons now is as good a time as any to make the break, with the loss of her father. And she's sure; almost confident, that Hazel would manage to learn those office routines that would keep us afloat. She'll work out a couple of month's notice, to be fair to us, she said. I'm sorry, Roberta, truly, truly sorry.'

Her look said it all, with the concern, sadness, a touch of resignation. 'It wasn't you, Andrew?'

He shook his head. 'No, I don't think so. Egotistically, I could say if I had yielded to her temptations she may have stayed; I don't know. She's been with us two years, R. Two years. Seems like yesterday. I shall miss her.' He turned away to walk to the window and Roberta saw, or thought she saw, incipient tears, knew how much he loved the girl in his own special way and felt for him. She loved him more than he knew; his yen for the other girl's affections she understood, and understood too that he'd never desert her, his wife, not even for an Andrea. Or a Hazel. She rose from the chair, crossed over and wrapped herself round him, resting her head on his shoulder.

'She's part of you, isn't she?' She felt his answer in the move of his head. 'And part of the man I love, Andrew. You are who you are. I'd feel her loss as well, maybe not as much, but I would.'

Her half turn allowed him to hold her tight. *'Roberta.'* Was that a sob of emotion?

'I know.'

Through the window, across the garden with the brown tinged grass of the end of summer and the ragged remnants of the herbaceous border still showing echoes of its former glory, the branches of the big old beech swayed gently against the cloud flecked noon-past greyish blue sky. They stood entwined for some little while, each wrapped in their own thoughts. This was their place in life, what they had made between them.

The door opened behind them and they turned as one. Andrea.

'I'm sorry,' she said, and made to leave.

'Don't go, Andrea.' Roberta turned to her husband. 'Spare me moment, dear?'

As he passed her, he touched her shoulder below the mass of golden hair. 'Andrea,' he said, looked at the mystery of her and shut the door behind him. The two girls were on their own.

She stood there, uncertain. Roberta hadn't bargained for this but she had to make the best of it. One part of her was saying good, she'll no longer be a threat, the other was telling her that without Andrea Andrew might change and she would not know how or why or even if the special things she shared with him might also alter beyond recovery.

'Andrew tells me you want to leave us.' She paced back to the window and sought inspiration from the ghosts of the garden's former summer days. 'You don't need to, not on our behalf. We'll be hard put to replace you, you know.'

Behind her she heard the rustle of the girl's skirt as she moved nearer and started to speak. 'My father's death has made me think, Roberta. When I came here, you asked me about a career progression.' Her voice sounded low and emotional. 'I'm sure we both know I could stay here for as long as you wanted me to. But if I don't make a move, sooner or later something might go wrong. I don't want that. So I'd best go. Believe me, it's a hard decision. Andrew hasn't made it any easier.' She faced up to it. 'He and I seem to have a problem. I . . . .' Her voice gave way and as Roberta turned to face her, she sat down. Her short skirt rode up naturally and Roberta could again see how eye-catchingly provocative she could be.

'Nothing new in that, Andrea. You've both done well do stay apart over the past year or two. What's so different now?'

The girl was struggling. She shrugged but still couldn't speak. How could she admit she wanted him the way she'd never felt before? Not for sex on its own, but love. The love she knew she couldn't ever have, not with Roberta loving him and him loving Roberta. It was ironic her father's death had triggered this emotion.

'You haven't . . .?'

An emphatic headshake, wishing but not wishing.

'So why now, Andrea? Surely we can still let things stay on an even keel?'

Another headshake, another deep breath, and a hiccup. *'We might.'*

'What, you think *my husband* would succumb?' She placed the emphasis to ensure this girl knew where she stood.

Andrea's head went down as she looked at her knees. She had to be honest though it hurt; it hurt a lot. She nodded. It had happened; ages ago, true, and not since, but today it had been a close shave. She'd needed solace and he so responsive to a girl's emotions.

'Hmmmph.' Roberta thought a brief moment. The girl was right, of course. In certain circumstances her Andrew was far too easily seduced, poor man, as she knew all too well with her eyes on the fireplace rug where she'd done just that. 'And if he did, what then?'

'You'd hate me. Andrew would hate me afterwards, and himself. It would never be the same, would it? No use for anyone.'

'What if I said, go ahead?'

'*What!*' Andrea was startled beyond belief. 'You don't, can't mean it! No woman would willingly allow her partner that licence!'

Roberta turned back to the window, the better to speak her mind. This situation was getting perilously close to where finally, after all this time, she could lose her temper. 'Andrea, think on. Let's be frank. If you *seduced* my husband, how would *you* feel? Would you want him to leave me and the twins, the business, his self-esteem gone, all for the sake of the chance of a few minutes stroking those gorgeous thighs of yours – and tits – and maybe exploring your hidden depths, *again;* giving you a thrill and the chance of having a child? If I suggested you borrowed our bed and went for an all-out bonking session *now,* would you? Would it satisfy all those inner yearnings, make you feel deeply passionate and sexy and *in control*? And do you think he'd feel anything different up yours than in mine?'

Andrea sat silent. Roberta had a wonderful way of setting out the raw basics, but she hadn't finished as she spun round and faced her.

'Did you flash your knickers at him this morning? Did he fancy you? Or did he fidget, maybe stroke the curvy bits then pull away? You didn't fall out of the car into the hedgerow, or crawl into the back with your knees up, did you? No. No, you didn't. So why do you think you – or he – would at any time in the future? So why run for cover, girl? Maybe it's because you know it wouldn't have happened, even if you hadn't all your underwear in place? You *are* wearing knickers, aren't you?' She was tempted to be rather coarser.

Andrea moved her legs sideways and tugged at her skirt hem.

'So there you are. Find another man, Andrea. A red-blooded, testosterone fuelled nice man who'd *really* go for it. But stay here, Andrea. Please, for a while, anyway.' The tenor of her voice changed as the crude outburst of her emotions brought a strange relief. 'We need you, at least until Hazel finds her feet.' Yes, despite the danger, she still wanted her around, maybe she'd ultimately regret the ploy, but for the moment, no. To change the mood of the moment, she added, 'You know she was play acting?'

Roberta walked around the room, fingered the bowl of bronze chrysanthemums, stopped at the window again and waited.

Andrea deliberated, trying to understand her own earlier reasoning, that she'd said she'd go merely to help them stay together, or maybe because she'd felt spurned and was going in a fit of pique rather than the logical career move; now, however, the very woman who'd suffer most from any infidelity was now asking her to stay? And, if she asked her inner girl, she was truly afraid to go out into the unknown. Here was secure and comfortable, like a cosy cosy bed – oh why choose that simile? The giggle had to be suppressed.

'Okay,' she said. 'You've not pulled any punches, have you, Roberta? Bit basic?' she added feelingly and then picked up on Roberta's curious comment. 'Hazel? Play acting?'

Thank heavens; Roberta relaxed as Andrea widened her thoughts. 'Mmm. Yes,' and explained, anything to get away from the drama. 'She was so used to being the simpleton girl at school, self protectionism against being bullied; she couldn't get out of the habit and grew into the role. Then what with the filming and, thanks to you, a session on the computer, it gave us – actually me – the clue that she was a lot brighter than we thought. I had it out with her yesterday afternoon while we were out shopping. Then I thought, show her off. We had a dinner party last night to give her the opportunity to shine; you should have seen her. A *lovely* lady. So you've got competition, my girl. And just so you know, if, *if*, a very big *if*, he does stray, which I'm pretty damn sure he won't, I am *not* going to throw a wobbly, because *I* seduced him first and he's mine, *mine*, you understand, but I'll jolly well make the other girl's life a misery, whoever she is. Anyway, I still have my moments.' She thought back to the gardener's shed episode and grinned. 'So what's the answer, Miss Chaney?'

'I'll stay then. For the time being.' Despite her emotional roller coaster, her mind had cleared. 'I like it here, but I'd also like to expand a bit if it's possible. Especially if Hazel is in the frame.'

'Atta girl. Let's go and tell the boss.'

Andrew had returned to the office, to sit and contemplate. Far too introvert, that was his problem. *I can't get her out of my head. I've loved her; she's always been there, available, lively, golden haired, cheeky, adorable shape. Her very closeness under R's constant gaze a challenge, when I know I shouldn't want her, but I do. Better than looking at sexy magazines. Forbidden fruit and all that. If we had succumbed out there, would it have burst the bubble? Would I have given in? Would she have? What would I have felt like when we got back? Or would she have gone home alone?* He heard footsteps in the corridor, and jerked upright, quickly livened up the computer screen and swallowed. *Oh, women!*

Roberta caught his look. She knew that look all too well, and wondered how she was going to get round the problem. She'd persuaded the girl to stay, to remain within the danger zone, maybe foolishly. Andrea was behind her.

'I've persuaded her. She's going to stay, Andrew. At least until we get Hazel trained up. Aren't you pleased?'

Roberta, oh, Roberta! Do you know what you've done, my love? Instead, he said fervently 'Thank goodness!' and meant it.

'So can we have lunch now? I'm starving after all this play-acting.' She led the way back to the kitchen. Andrea dragged her feet a trifle so she could gently brush her hand against him and whisper, dangerously, stupidly, thoughtlessly, *'another time'.*

He pretended not to hear but allowed himself the luxury of a smile. Who had been the most devious? Andrea in knowing how he'd react, Roberta in keeping her *bete noir* under surveillance, or had he, in playing hard to get and containing his foolish occasional desire for the girl in check? All this, in just a few hours?

Lunch came and went. June packed her little bag, embraced them all in turn and promised she'd come back next weekend, though if he could phone her and let her know about running the office? Sure, he said, once we've sorted things out. He held her tight, told her not to worry, kissed her and let her go. Her little car purred away and he felt a sense of loss, like he'd been left entirely alone. He turned and walked back up the steps into the arms of his family. His family, a lovely loving wife, a lively pair of children, a sensible mother in law and with a pretty and as effective an *au pair* as they could possibly ever have.

'Take Andrea home, Andrew, and then come back for us. We'll go for a walk in the Country Park. Just for a while, to get some air.' Roberta wanted a change of scenery; tomorrow they'd be back in the thick of it again, dratted film company. 'I'll get Abby and Chris ready while you've gone. Take Hazel with you for the ride.'

To keep an eye on me, she means, he thought. I don't blame her, either. Why was it she was so amenable over his unfathomable attachment? Another woman would have thrown him out a long time ago if either he or Andrea had messed around with each other since his marriage. That's one reason why he loved her so much; she tolerated the way his hormones reacted. But how much would she tolerate? And for how long?

The two girls climbed into the back of the car, laughing and giggling over some thing. Perhaps Hazel was regaling Andrea with how she'd been so clever in staying dumb for so long. Well, she had been clever. Devious as well, but she'd done no harm. No meanness in her whatsoever, on the contrary, she was so friendly and open and loving to them all, especially the twins. Bless her. He eased the big car down the drive and took Andrea home. She leant back into the window once out, outside her house.

'Thanks, Andrew. It's been a long morning,' and she gave a wry grin, 'but we've survived. See you tomorrow, then?'

He nodded, took her kiss on his cheek as the most natural

thing and was about to drive on when Hazel opened her door, hopped out and joined him in the front. Andrea had swayed her shorty skirt up the path and merely waved. He watched her go with extremely mixed emotions.

'Don't mind, Andrew? I can call you Andrew, can't I?'

'What?' blinking, he brought his mind back to reality. 'Sure, Hazel. As the films have it,' lowering the pitch of his voice to a sexy drag to add *you're a big girl now* and narrowed his eyes as he leered at her in fun and very nearly put his hand out to stroke her knee. But didn't.

She giggled. 'Not too big, I hope,' pushing her chest out in a harmless return gesture.

'Stop it, Hazel.'

'Sorry,' and her faced dimpled in a smile. 'Guess it's like being let out of school early.'

He chuckled in return. 'Let's go and pick up the family,' and he pulled away. Was Andrea watching him go?

'I feel like one of the family, Andrew. You've been very kind.'

He looked sideways at her. The bouncy dark curls, the enigmatically grey eyes, the dimples below her cheekbones and the smooth line of her neck down to the crisp cream blouse. She also seemed to have the Andrea knack of showing her knees. How come girls' knees below a skirt line with that mysterious dark space between were so provocative?

'You've been the kind one, looking after our two so well. We'd have been hard pushed to find a better nanny, Hazel.'

'Thanks. I mean it. I love them both, Andrew. As I also love you and Roberta, for being so understanding and . . . supportive. And Mary, too, 'cos she's the one who really looked after me when . . .' her voice trailed off.

It must have been a desperate time for her, he realised that; thank goodness it was all behind her. Great shame she had no father in the frame and as if she'd mind read, she said, 'you're almost like a dad.'

'Not a sugar daddy I hope?'

Her head turned sharply. 'No.'

91

Back into the Manor driveway, to swing round with a spurt of gravel to face the way out again and she hopped out like a cricket, ran across to sweep up a waiting Chris from the steps while Roberta carried Abby down and across to the car. He went and collected the twin's buggy to put it into the back. Lovely to have all this space in the new estate car, it made such a difference. A positive indication to show how well the business was going.

They waited while Hazel clipped the booster seats into the car, fastened the twins in and squashed herself between them which had an added advantage of keeping the peace. She certainly had the knack. Roberta envied her; it would have taken her about an hour. She slipped into the front alongside her husband.

'Got her home safely?'

'Yep. Hazel bears witness.'

Roberta laughed. 'Come on, let's go.'

SEVEN

Bright and early the first vehicles of the film crew contingent rolled into the yard well before any of the Manor's dwellers had come to terms with a Monday morning, largely because they'd had another extravagant dinner, the second in one weekend. Andrew rolled over and looked at the clock.

'Lord, R, it's half past seven! Hey, come on, lazy love. Time we was up.' He threw the duvet off his side and streaked for the bathroom. Roberta rubbed her eyes and tried to ginger up some enthusiasm.

'Can't a girl enjoy her beauty sleep?' she muttered, to herself because the bathroom door was shut. 'Bloody film crew. Roll on whenever.' Start of the second week, possibly even another week after this. She resolved to be as good as she could be, merely to get them off the premises and get life back to normality, then remembering Ireland beckoned she cheered up. Andrew had run through his plans last night to her complete satisfaction for he'd organised a few days back near the Beara where they'd had that super week, three years ago. Was it three years? No, two. She'd found out she was pregnant not long after their return and the twins were into their second year. Logical maths. While Andrew was still bathroom bound, she went to see her babies. Two-year-old babies, come Christmas. Children then, and from the noise they were making it was a wonder they hadn't woken her earlier.

Hazel was already ahead of her, bless the girl.

'Morning, Roberta. Sleep well? I did. So did these horrors, by the look of them.' The 'horrors' were both standing up in their cots, bouncing up and down in competition and screaming fit to bust. The girl put her fingers to her mouth and made 'shushing' noises; Abby responded but Chris didn't. Roberta went to pick him up.

'I did too, especially after last night's supper.' She answered Hazel's query as she hefted Chris onto her arm. 'Shall I sort him while you deal with Abby?' A rhetorical question that, for Hazel already the little girl on her knee and was unravelling.

'Do you know what we're doing today?' Hazel asked as she dextrously removed the night's disasters and headed for the nursery's small bathroom, a giggling little female tucked under her arm.

'Not yet. You okay with being an extra?' Roberta was close behind with her struggling armful.

'Sure,' the reply muted with a safety pin in her teeth. 'Love it. Will your mum cope with these two if I'm called for? Or are you on standby?'

Glory be, thought Roberta, is this the same girl? Bright and cheerful, vivacious and very with it. Not quite a million miles from the subdued, though eager to please, diffident lass of last week, but not far off. How would she affect Alain and his mates? Sparks may fly.

'Don't know. Take it as it comes. Come on, let dog see rabbit, or more appropriately, bare bottom see the sponge.' She heaved Chris onto the plastic and cork topped changing stand as Hazel carried Abby out to dress her. 'Better put her into dungarees today. Just in case.'

Ten minutes later she retreated to get dressed. Andrew had already cleared off downstairs. She threw off her nightdress. What would she do if – more like when, inevitably – Hazel moved on? Hopefully the twins would then be reasonably self-sufficient and able to look after their basic requirements by themselves. The thought prompted her about the concept of nursery school – more expense, more time spent running a taxi service. She'd wanted the children, she had to put up with the inconveniences, not that she'd renege on her obligations, oh no, she was really very comfortable with them. The reflected figure in the mirror showed no sign of sagging, happily, still sexy and she wiggled her bottom as she pulled her pants on. No more though, two little people were quite enough. Another thought went drifting through her mind as she struggled with her bra, a visit to Doc Mac and see what could be done more permanently in that department, especially if they'd gone back to excitingly different impromptu ravishments. As they had, oh lor! Next layer. A flirty skirt and that warm woollen sweater in case she had to stand around. That one clung quite well too and now she'd got competition in the looks department she wasn't going to go frumpish. No way. She eased feet into comfortable shoes and headed cheerfully downstairs.

Mary had come up early, rather thoughtfully even after a late night last night, and was about to sort the washing. Really, she didn't need to run home to her little cottage every night. Hazel was stuck into the twins' 'let's throw breakfast cereal at daddy' routine, but at least she had put on a full size pinafore to guard against the worst excesses. Andrew was immersed in the paper, a large mug of coffee and an empty plate apart from crumbs at his elbow

'So you lot have had breakfast then? Where's mine?'

Mary put down her basket and reached into the Aga. A plateful of streaky bacon and tomatoes was slid onto her mat. 'Should keep you going 'till lunch, my lass. 'Less you want cereal first?'

'No, no, this is fine, thanks. Any coffee left after guzzler there has had his fill?'

Andrew peered over the paper and moved the cafetiere her way. 'Still some left, love. Or we can make another?'

She tipped it. 'Ugh. More grounds than coffee. Mary?'

'All right lass. Just let me get this lot into the machine.'

Hazel slipped off her stool. 'I'll do it. Let the monsters take a breath.'

In the middle of the happy carefree breakfast routine came a knock on the kitchen's outside door and Alain poked a head round. 'Hiya, folks. Ready for the fray? We've a briefing meeting in the small barn in ten minutes?' He caught sight of

Hazel. 'And can Miss Hazel spare some time today? I'd like your Andrea girl as well, Andrew, if you can bear to let her out of the office. See you round there?' and he'd gone.

Roberta frowned at his departing figure. 'Bloody man. *Briefing meeting in ten!*' she mimicked. '*Your* Andrea girl, Andrew. Remember she's *yours!*'

Hazel caught her look. There was something going on there, she knew, but couldn't be sure what. Not her place to worry but none the less it was intriguing. At least she'd be on set again today. 'Mary, is it all right if I spend some time out there?'

Mary looked at her daughter for guidance. This new Hazel was a mite too forward for her own good. More mature she may be, more adult and no bad thing but she should not forget her place.

Roberta nodded. 'So long as we don't neglect their routines between us. I don't want them to get lost in the mêlée. Yes, Hazel, it's all right, but only when Mary says. And when we've found out what's in store. Do we all have to go, Andrew?'

He'd kept his head down. Alain he could cope with, a bolshie Roberta less so, especially after a fraught weekend. He'd go and get out of the domestic fracas. And shortly Andrea would be here and she would brighten his day, that was certain sure.

'I'll go and report back, girls.' The paper folded up and dropped onto the re-cycle pile; he leant over to give his beloved a kiss and went to the door. 'Shan't be too long.'

Roberta sniffed. 'Do you know, Mary, that's the first kiss of the day? Once upon a time I'd have a struggle to get out of bed.'

'Shush, girl. That'll do.' Mary, old-fashioned Mary, did not think Hazel should be treated to such suggestive comments. 'If I'm to look after the twins, then Hazel should give me a hand with beds, and sharpish, whilst you keep eye on these two. We won't be gone o'er long. Come on, lass.'

She was left on her own. Well, not really. She rose and got

the flannel dampened to wipe well plastered fronts, knowing full well there'd be yells and wriggles because neither young person liked soggy flannels round their chops. Tough.

'In good voice, aren't they?' A louder than normal familiar voice behind her announced Andrea's welcome arrival.

'You can say that again.' She flung the flannel into the sink and grabbed the towel. 'And how are things with you today, Andrea?' Maybe there was more in her inflexion than she'd intended because the girl coloured up.

'I'm all right, Roberta, thank you, after a good night's sleep. Sorry about yesterday. I'll try and keep my head down for a while.'

Roberta pulled a face. 'Maybe I should apologise too. I went a bit too far yesterday.'

Andrea's eyebrows rose in polite query. 'In what way, Roberta? I probably deserved it.'

'Well, er, asking about underwear and so on.'

The girl chuckled. 'Serve me right. I suppose I was at a bit of low ebb, what with father's death and mother taking it so hard. Got to me.'

Roberta considered this; thinking that she'd been a bit of a cow, not taking Andrea's emotional state into account in quite the right way. At least it didn't seem that she was bearing a grudge.

'Sorry,' she said, rather inadequately.

'Then we're quits?'

'More than that, dear.' Mischievously she added, 'equals.'

'Equals?'

'So long as you don't take it the wrong way. Who's been in whose bed?'

Andrea twigged and coloured up once more. 'Oh dear. You'll never let me forget, will you?' and in the mood of the moment she added, 'I'm not claiming squatter's rights.'

Roberta laughed. 'Just as well. I think there's some rent owing, isn't there, if we're staying on that track?'

'Stop it, Roberta. I don't think the – er – land lady wants to renew the tenancy, does she? Even if the . . ., ' and she stopped.

'Enough. More than enough. Don't even think about it.' Amazingly the twins were pre-occupied with their fingers, playing a sort of peek-a-boo. Time to get them out and about.

She lifted Abby. 'Grab Chris, Andrea, there's a dear. Follow me.'

The two women went out into the yard, into the conglomeration of milling technicians or whatever they were. An incomprehensible quantity of people to produce a simple programme, Roberta thought, no wonder it cost so much. She weaved her way round to the small barn with a wriggling Abby. She wanted down, with all these exciting things going on around her.

'Stop it, Abby.' She looked round for Andrea, bringing up the rear but slowly with an unsteady toddling Chris. *Heavens, the girl is doing well.* They reached the door, just as it opened.

'Why, hello!' Alain looked from one to the other. 'Two charming ladies and two equally charming little people! Roberta, you're to be congratulated. And Miss Andrea, so nice to see you again. Andrew will put you in the picture, if you'll pardon the pun. Excuse me,' and he hurried off down the path. Andrew ducked out from the dimness of the barn with the producer girl Sue behind him. He looked from the one to the other, unsure of what to say.

'We've made up our differences, Andrew,' Andrea said, still holding firmly onto Chris's chubby hand. 'Would you like to take him, if I get back to the office?'

'Yes, sure.' Being greeted with the little group round the door unbalanced his equilibrium.

Sue pushed past, clutching her clipboard. 'I'll see you in the barn in half an hour?'

'Okay,' he replied, abstractedly. 'Roberta, is it right to bring the twins out here with this lot about?'

'Is it right to abandon them while we play film stars?'

'Ah. No, 'spose not. Andrea, it's good to see you this morning.' He meant it, in all sincerity, aware of how easily the day could have had a totally different outlook. The picture of her holding Chris's hand, a girl grown into more of a woman, with a child. Which was how she should look, happy, contented, smiling, at ease. What was it Roberta had said about getting back on track? Map reading? He'd take a bearing on her hill any time of day, her looking like that.

They walked back to the Manor, round the Barn and across the yard, avoiding two guys pulling out more lighting cables. Back in the kitchen, with Mary having stripped all beds and got the washing machine going, the twins were handed over to her and she took them off upstairs, out of the way.

'So what's going on?' Roberta sat down.

Andrea was about to excuse herself and get to the office but Andrew put out a hand. 'Hang on. Hazel?'

'In the loo.'

He waited a minute until she rejoined them. 'Right. Alain wants a beauty parade – his words – a sort of crowd scene, us lot milling round, before Marilynn appears and starts a conversation. We're also to be graced with an appearance from Steven. This starts them off on the second programme apparently. They're doing another discussion on a display now, so about eleven or so for us. Alain's asked for different dresses from last time, not too jazzy but still, er, sexy-ish.'

Roberta groaned. 'This is getting silly. Sexy dresses indeed. Still,' and she brightened, 'Hazel's all right. We'll put her into a new dress. You wait. Andrea, if you don't feel happy in that you can borrow one of mine. We know you and I fit – except you've a bigger top. What will you wear, husband mine, a dee-jay?'

'A decent sweatshirt and ordinary trousers. I wouldn't want to outshine you lot.'

'Huh. Fat chance. Come on, girls. We've been set a challenge. You stay down here, mister. No gawping.' Roberta jumped up. Anything to get this filming over.

Within the half hour they'd reappeared. Needless to say they were all splendidly dolled up to the nines, straight out of some style magazine. Roberta he had seen in the light linen thing before, but seeing Andrea in the emerald green and with a rather tight bust line would set any bloke's pulse going. Then Hazel in her lemon yellow shift dress, a perfect fit tightening into her waist and emphasising her shape, not too low a bust, but that look she gave him. She knew her worth, that one.

The crowd scene went well. Other extras joined them; within five minutes the two presenters edged in and the cameras focused onto them, taking the scene forward. Roberta, as lead, was walked out with the two presenters and Alain shouted 'Cut!' It was over.

'No second take?'

'Nope; that was fine, eh, Sue?'

'Perfect. Those girls of yours, Andrew, admirable. Lovely dresses. If we can pick up on the approach to the selected design next? That's you again, Roberta, I'm afraid. Not for long. Then we go into more discussion with a client, that's with Marilynn and Steven. That'll be it for today. Demolition of a set tonight and the re-hash. If you can advise us in the morning, Roberta, please. Shouldn't take more than an hour or two.'

She cringed. Set demolition. Teeth gritted job. 'Which one do you want to demolish?'

'You tell us, Roberta. Whichever one you want to lose. Doesn't matter particularly, so long as it's not in a corner, 'cos we need visuals. Tell Barry. Right. Are we clear for the next scene? Can we walk you through first, please?'

Andrew took the two girls indoors. Roberta would be better on her own. 'You don't want to stay in those dresses. I'll brew coffee. See you in a bit.' and moved the kettle back onto the Aga's hob.

They returned to Hazel's bedroom, after Hazel had peeped in on Mary. No problem there.

'All went well?' Mary had asked, as if it wouldn't.

'Remarkably. We're off to change.'

As Andrea slipped off her borrowed dress and commenced putting day wear back on, Hazel plucked up courage as she watched, enviously. 'How long have you known Andrew, Andrea?'

Andrea pulled up her zip. 'Before Roberta,' she answered shortly.

'Did you go out with him?'

Typical girly question, she thought. 'Not in so many words, no. We met purely professionally. But he did express a care for me when I got attacked. Good friends ever since,' – *what an understatement* – 'especially when the Brewery closed and he and Roberta gave me this job. They've been very good to me.' She slipped her low shoes back on. How happily coincidental she and Roberta were broadly the same size. She had to say it, to confirm her mindset. 'I think a lot of Andrew, and Roberta, of course.'

'Thought you did. It shows, the way you look at him. He's rather dishy, isn't he? I think Roberta's awfully lucky.'

'You know how they met?'

'Something about a horse?'

'Hmmm. Get him to tell you.' She put her foot back down and wriggled her slip round. 'Best get on with the job. See you at lunchtime,' and left Hazel still loath to change.

Hazel looked down at the lemon dress. A year ago she'd not have dreamed of owning something like this. She owed them, both of them. Andrea hadn't been all that forthcoming, almost as though she had something to hide. She flounced round, enjoying the feel of new fabric on her skin. All these years as a dimwit, but now, well she'd shine. Reluctantly, she undid her zip and stepped out of *her* dress.

At the end of the day they looked at the 'rushes' in the small barn, much more accustomed to the scheme of things. Andrew watched Hazel's face as she saw herself on screen. Riveted, her expression in a sort of ecstasy, the lemon dress fitting her so well and her poise, amazing. He felt very proud of her. Andrea, well, she was a natural. Roberta reached for his hand, as she did, and squeezed; whispered a promise in his ear.

'*Elegant, aren't we?*'

He nodded. '*Proud of you.*'

'*So you should be. To the Manor born . . . I owe you, my love.*'

They both chuckled at the borrowed phrase, aping the role. A good day's acting.

Alain seemed pleased. Sue ticked boxes on her clipboard. Tim switched the thing off and draped his cloth over the screen. The day was complete.

Andrea smiled at him. 'I'll go. Done my bit, Andrew.'

'Thanks, Andrea,' then he had to ask. 'Have you a date?'

Her face clouded. 'I was going to say. Friday. Eleven in the morning.'

'Right. Anything we can do?'

'Be there?'

'Of course. See you tomorrow?'

'Of course.' She smiled at him again, a slightly sad smile.

Later that night, Roberta honoured her promise. He loved her, body and soul. Andrea or no, she was his passion. She purred. Rolling over, she murmured her question. *'What would you say if we added to the twins, Andrew?'*

He went quiet and still.

'Andrew?' She pushed herself above him, up on her elbows.

'Is that a question or a statement, R?'

'Question. No malice aforethought. I need guidance, beloved.'

'Ah, beloved is it? Feminine wiles? Or are you going broody?'

She flung herself down alongside him, elbows too much under strain. 'Don't think so. I wondered if I should have some knots tied. Save us any embarrassment. Wanted to know what you thought.'

'I'm happy with just the twins, R. If – and I'm not being silly – you became pregnant again, then you should already know I'd be as supportive as ever. But not seeking any additions, not specifically; do you know something I don't?'

'Not at the moment, dear, mind you... ' and she rummaged.

'You're a glutton for punishment.'

'Hmmm mmm.'

The rest of the week's filming passed uneventfully.

102

Andrew discussed Friday with Alain and the schedule was adjusted accordingly. On the Wednesday Hazel was asked to do a solo performance and acquitted herself with merit. Andrea pulled a face. Competition! Becoming blasé with it all, or even well practised, the Manor team responded to all demands and rose to each and every one.

'Well done, you lot. Couldn't have wished for a better set of local stars. It's a wrap. We've everything we need, unless the edit throws up something but there are quite a few excess shots to play with. You happy?' Alain had asked them all into the small barn for the Thursday evening run-through, fairly sure of the reaction. They'd not disappointed him, with all the 'wows' and 'ooh, yes, I like it' noises. Even Roberta had smiled at him. Now he could reveal the surprise up his sleeve. 'I've arranged for a specific edit, Andrew, Roberta, of footage we won't be using in the screening version that we'll be happy to let you have on a disc. Something you can use as a promotional thing. Website home page or whatever. We'll send it on to you as an additional thank you, because your cooperation and professionalism has saved us at least two if not three days filming. Great team, all of you.' He turned to Andrea. 'Would you object if I showed some people I know some of the takes that show you doing the walks? It might not come to anything, but you never know. New talent is always welcome and you have flair. So has Hazel, in a different way.' He couldn't leave her out, but she lacked some of the bouncy confidence the blonde girl had shown. 'We may come calling, girls.'

Hazel coloured up, Andrea pursed her lips, and Roberta, being the nearest, gave him a peck on the cheek. She'd had to forgive him some of his pushiness, for everyone's sake.

'Our guys will come and clear up tomorrow, Andrew, you don't need to be about. Give me a call if there's anything left undone. The Barn's film set we built – if you don't want to keep it, Roberta, we'll take it away and build you another one.'

'The studio run through and the voice overs?' Sue reminded him.

'Oh, yes. When we've done the final edit, we'll invite you to a preview. About a month's time, okay?'

They'd packed up the technical kit, heaved the filing cabinet and the other furniture into a van and gone. The other members of the crew had already disappeared and the yard was echoingly empty. Andrea wanted to go too; she had tomorrow to deal with and needed time on her own.

'We'll be there, Andrea,' Andrew reassured her. 'Roberta and I. Whatever you need, anything, just ask,' as he walked her across to her car.

She touched his arm, 'Thank you,' and sat into the driving seat, pulled up her skirt and swung her legs in. Looking up and towards him as he leant down, she closed her eyes to his kiss, then her enigmatic parting comment, 'Thanks merely said are inadequate, Andrew. Thanks can be expressed in other ways. I'll see you tomorrow.'

He stood back, wondering at what she'd said and let her go, watching the little car until it was out of sight.

'Celebration. It's all over, so let's get drunk, or at the very least, merry. Mary, what's for dinner?

'Beef bourguignon, with plenty of red wine, Roberta. Boiled potatoes, carrots, red cabbage. As you should know, asking me about using the farm shop.'

'So I should. Sorry. Well, another bottle, or two. Go and sort the twins, Hazel, then take your time. Half seven – ish ?'

Mary nodded. 'In here ?'

'Cosier. Yes.' She went to the door and yelled. 'Andrew!' He was somewhere out there, but blowed if she was going to search. He'd come in soon enough.

He was sitting on the old cast iron bench in the rose garden, to watch the remaining glimmer of daylight ebb away over the hill and listen to the last few moments of the blackbird's song that were so elegiac, echoing into the stillness and the quiet. Peace, peace and quiet. The film project was finally at an end, come what may, all over bar the odds and ends. Thank goodness; though some considerably remarkable changes had occurred as a result and possibly even for the better. Hazel's renaissance was probably by far the best thing, for she'd be more of an asset than ever. Andrea, well, it was more than likely her poor father's death would have triggered all the turmoil rather than Alain's lot, though if she got a chance of some further exposure to the film or telly world as a result it may not do her any harm. But, selfishly, he did not want to lose her, not his Andrea. His darling Roberta, now, she'll be glad to have seen the back of the film crew. What a fortnight!

Tomorrow, well, they'd manage. The day would come and go. The healing process had all ready begun for Andrea; she'd survive. Her mother, perhaps only time would tell. He couldn't possibly ask the girl to come with them to Ireland, not now. Anyway, not even the big car would take four adults and the two exuberant children; it would be squeeze with three. A far cry from their last trip across the Irish Sea! Time to go in, his tummy was rumbling. Hope Mary had a good meal on the go. The bird had flown off to its roost and silence settled in, then he heard Roberta's call.

He stood up and stretched, and headed indoors.

EIGHT

It had been a long time since he'd seen Roberta in a two piece costume; most work days she would be in a swirly dress down to her calves, occasionally in slacks if she was expecting to go clambering about in the Barn; on the not infrequent occasions when they had an evening out on the town she'd be in one of her bespoke fashion dresses, courtesy of her late father's connections amongst the *fashionistas*. With a formal event ahead of them she dressed accordingly and insisted Andrew wore his darker suit.

'It's not going to be all *that* formal, dear,' he protested, thinking about what Andrea would be wearing. He couldn't see her in black.

'Better be seen properly turned out than become a talking point, my darling,' she replied, looking critically at him and stepping forward to straighten his tie. 'You'll be the envy of anyone less suitably dressed. There, you'll do. Make sure you don't scuff those shoes.' She reached up and pecked his cheek then turned to collect her little bag and miniscule hat from off the bed. 'Shall we stay out for lunch?'

'Isn't it expected to get an invite to a meal or something from the family?'

She shrugged. 'Possibly. And if we do get an invite I suppose we'll have to go, show solidarity with your girl.'

'Roberta, she's not *my girl*. She's our *employee!*'

'She's your girl,' Roberta responded emphatically. 'And I don't mind. We both employ her, I like her a lot but *you* look after her and I've no quarrel with that. Nor with you, dear. Come on, else we'll be late. And you shouldn't be late . . . '

'. . . For a funeral. Okay, love. If she's my girl, can I do what

106

I like with her?' he asked, in joking mood.

'Now now, don't take things too literally,' she gave him a grin. 'Or else.'

'Else what?'

He didn't have a reply; she'd walked off down the stairs, bottom swaying in the shapely dark grey costume skirt. Getting her into the car in that tight skirt would be a slightly interestingly problem, or so he thought.

'Just as well we're not going in the old MGF, R, not with that skirt,' his comment as he opened the door for her. She grinned, sat down sideways, swung legs in and he had to admit, she had the knack. Real debutante training and he said so. An old-fashioned look came back with the comment, '*I was trained, Andrew. My world.*' So it was, he'd forgotten and not very sensible to have shown his forgetfulness.

'You look lovely, darling. I'm proud of you.'

'So you should be, and if it's any consolation, Andrew, I'm proud of me too.'

She got a surprised return glance followed by a grin. 'You egotist!'

'Proud of having you as a husband.'

There was no answer to that. He eased the accelerator pedal down and the big car rolled across the gravel, smooth and effortlessly. Very pleasant at long last to have a sensible vehicle, even though initially it did seem too large; surprisingly it wasn't too much of a thirsty beast either. Roberta pulled the sun visor down to use the in-built mirror to position her little hat onto her specially arranged curls and pinned it in place. How many times had he seen her wearing a hat? Twice, three times? She wasn't a hat person, but this really set her off. Great girl.

'Love you,' he said, out of the blue, as he turned onto the main road.

Neither of them had been in the big brick church at the end of the town High Street before. Their wedding and the twin's christenings had been in the traditional parish church in their village and where Roberta 'did' the flowers every month as part of the arranger's rota. This was new territory. Andrew slid the big Volvo into a convenient space on the side road and did his chauffeur act, going round to open the passenger door for Roberta to reverse her proper deb's performance. Then together, hand in hand, they walked back to the grey stone steps and up into the gloomy recesses of the Victorian building redolent of pitch pine and ancient dust. What light there was came from dim lamps on iron and brass chandeliers and filtered daylight through red and blue stained glass. Was that a slight shudder from his love?

Dark suited, a steward offered them an order of service and gestured at his colleague indicating the entrance to a pew. A few strange glances from others already seated, though surely one or two would recognise them? Cautiously, he looked around as Roberta bent her head and estimated about fifty or so, maybe more. The organ started playing softly, an emotive piece he recognised and Roberta reached for his hand, she'd know what he was thinking. Minutes passed and more mourners arrived before a white cassocked cleric appeared from the side to raise his hands. They stood as the procession entered and moved slowly towards the front. There she was, walking with her mother, blonde hair sombrely crowned with black ribbons, as composed a picture as he could have anticipated. She'd seen them, acknowledged their presence with an ever so slight smile and a little nod.

A man's life ended; a brief soliloquy from presumably a former colleague, a couple of hymns, a few prayers; that's all it was. How did he feel? Saddened for the girl who'd stood so straight alongside her mother, now pacing back towards them behind the coffin? For her loss or for the way she'd been cosseted? Her mother's eyes were reddened, her face grey and lined; this was a long-term partnership dissolved by human frailty. It could happen to any of them, at any time. Unconsciously his grip of Roberta's hand tightened. Their eyes met and she knew his thoughts. *Que sera, sera.*

Later, in the schoolroom behind the church they sipped

weak tea and nibbled on scones during their wait for the party to return from the crematorium, engaged in desultory conversation that Roberta was brilliant in keeping going. He marvelled at her skill; social occasions were not normally his scene but he did his best. Then Andrea was back and heading straight for them.

'Roberta, Andrew,' her acknowledgement with acceptable cheek kisses apiece, 'Thank you for coming.' She was, amazingly, still dry-eyed.

Roberta opened her arms. 'Andrea, love. We're with you,' taking the girl into an embrace. 'Whatever you need, you know...' and Andrew patted her gently on the back in empathy.

'I know. Without you both, I might not have survived.' Released from her hug, she turned back to him. 'Especially you, dear Andrew,' and now he saw incipient tears. What could he do but hug her himself, feel the warmth and the shape of her as he had so many times before. This love for her would not go away. It was far too deep. She disengaged herself. 'I must circulate.'

As he let her go, watching her, her figure, her poise, his mind rushed back to that first time they'd met in the old Brewery and he'd watched her walk away down a corridor with that same poise, the start of an association which had seen all manner of emotional strengths and weaknesses develop.

Roberta was shaking her captive curls at him. 'Don't stare, love. It's rude.' Her smile, that cheeky grin, defused the moment. 'We'd best go, leave her to it. Her family's friends, not ours. We've done our bit. Come on,' and she led the way through the scattered little groups, throwing a give-away smile here and there to see them towards the door and fresh air.

'Phew,' she unpinned her hat and shook those curls free, took a deep breath as she did from habit once away from social constriction. 'Well done, you.' She tiptoed and pecked his cheek. 'Proper lunch? I'm starving.'

They undertook a reprise of a former occasion. The Royal George had changed hands recently and was smartening itself up, though happily and sensibly the new owners had kept on the established restaurant manager.

At the same table where ages ago he'd first offered lunch and then taken her away to bed her in an afternoon, they sat and giggled. Her shoeless foot crept up his leg in exactly the same way.

'You remember?'

'I remember. The word was wanton.'

'Ah. But you were the wanting one . . .'

With a half head on one side shake, he corrected her, 'we both were, my love.'

'Except you had a distraction. Didn't you?'

Was she ever going to cease to be part of them? 'I couldn't help myself then.'

'And now?'

'Older. Sadder. A lot wiser. And more in love with a beautiful girl who happens to be the mother of our two beautiful children.'

Her foot stroked. 'You say all the nicest things, boy. I believe you. You'll always love Andrea, too.' A realist, his Roberta.

'Love covers many facets, R. None of us can destroy our feelings unless we cease to be human.' He thought back. 'Andrea's father must have loved her in his own way. She may not have experienced the best childhood but it's the only one she had.' A moment's pause to gain courage, then: 'I gave her affection when she needed it, and yes, made her a woman in her own right, perhaps it was just sex, maybe that's just what she wanted at the time. It's done *us* no harm?'

The subtle slight shake of her head indicated agreement. 'No, Andrew, it's done us no harm, not now we both understand the reasons and the limits. I'm sure we're the stronger for it, too, and a lesson we both learnt.' She reached across the table for his hand. 'You'll never leave me for her or anyone else, will you?'

'You sacked the guy who used the mattress.'

'He didn't love me. Nor poor Fiona or whatever her name was. You love me and I can *feel* that love all the time. Maybe not in the same sexy way we used to, but in our togetherness, the

110

way you look at me, the touches, the caring, the everyday caring.' Her deep brown eyes, the ones with the familiar amber glints, fixed and held his with the mystery and the depth of her soul. This was a mission statement.

'I'll never leave you.' The re-iteration of a firm held belief. 'Not while we live,' he added, not able to get the picture of another girl walking up the aisle in the earlier funereal procession out of his mind.

'Ah. Poor Andrea.' Intuitive guesswork and so straight back to reality. 'What will she do, do you think?' his lovely girl asked.

'As we've – you have – persuaded her to stay with us for the time being, she'll carry on as normal for a while, at least until something else happens. Then she might get a call from Alain? She'll stay with her mother anyway. Perhaps we should pray for some hunky bloke to show up who'll sweep her off her proverbial feet.'

'Who we allow to so do?'

He laughed at her and her instinctive thoughts. 'Possibly. Your meal is cold. I thought you were starving?'

She pushed it away. 'I'm suddenly not hungry. Not for that anyway. Take me home, Andrew. Please.'

Mary had the twins in the kitchen, standing on chairs, pudgy hands all covered in dough with evidence of some chaotic attempts at making biscuits or something. Hilarity must have been the order of the day, judging from the screams of delight when their mother appeared; she risking irreparable damage to her costume by hugging the one then the other.

'Where's Hazel?'

'I let her go for a walk, Roberta. She'll be back soon, ne're fret,' and her look went interrogative, eyebrows raised. 'All go well?'

Roberta nodded. 'As these things go. Glad we went, eh, Andrew?'

111

'A strain for her. Held up well.' He changed the subject. 'The Royal George's improved since we last went but neither of us had much appetite, not then. What's on the menu tonight, Mary?'

His mother-in-law nodded at the Aga. The large Le Creuset casserole was simmering away. 'Beef stew and dumplings.'

Yet another classic piece of *déjà vu* and a flash back to the *'beef stew, your favourite'* from Samantha that night after he'd returned from his assignation with this lovely girl who was now his wife and mother of his second family. And former wife Sam, currently in a new and very different life and with a new partner, bearing no regrets or recriminations, was now only a distant part of his submerged history and son Peter with her. Would Andrea ever sink into those grey recesses of a buried past?

'How long?'

'Until we eat? However long, it'll keep. Say another hour and a half, 'bout sixish?'

'Suits me, Mary,' said her daughter. 'Shall I take these two urchins upstairs?'

'Reckon you'd better. Afore we get the whole place plastered!'

That night she melted into his arms in the same magical way he'd always loved, a supremely wonderful surrender of body and soul that was her, especially her. *'Love me,'* she'd whispered as their togetherness spun the world away and away, and it was though they lay on the top of that world, above them only the stars, for they had climbed their metaphoric hill and stood at the point where all senses merged, peaked and flowed. She was his centre, the centre of his world. His own cardinal point, a point where he knew he'd always be.

NINE

After a traditional family style weekend, Monday came as an anticlimax. Andrea appeared for the start of a working week all bright and breezy with no suggestion that last Friday gone had impacted on her status quo, casually answering Andrew's concerned query with a nonchalant 'fine, *I'm fine,*' but half way through the morning after she'd had a lengthy telephone conversation with a prospective client over how contracts were worded, she swung her chair round and caught him on the hop.

'You weren't expecting me to come with you to Ireland, were you?'

Startled, Andrew looked up from his pencilled figure doodling. Occasionally he had to indulge in some more creative accounting than normal, especially for the less clued-up elderly clients in his accountancy business and this one especially so, hence his mind was elsewhere.

'Sorry, Andrea, what did you say?' He tried to focus in.

'You weren't thinking of including me in your Irish jaunt?'

'Um, er,' his hesitation coming from two counts, of surprise and of concern. 'It had been talked about.' He had to come clean. 'Principally, my dear girl, because you haven't had a decent holiday. Not that I'm pushing you, but you haven't.'

She stood up and stretched. Her blouse popped out of her skirt's waistband and showed an inch of bare flesh. 'Sorry,' she said and started tucking it back in. 'Not wise.'

What did she mean, not wise to show flesh or come with them?

She caught his look and the dimples appeared. 'Neither, Andrew,' reading his mind. 'No, I won't come with you to

Ireland. You're taking Hazel, I guess, so I'll stay put and look after things with Mary. Then I'll go and find the sun somewhere when you get back. You go for coffee break, I'll hold the fort.' The phone rang again; she sat back down to the desk to answer it, eased her skirt's tightness and ignored him.

He stood in turn, touched her briefly on the shoulder and closed the door behind him.

Roberta was taking her coffee break with Mary; Hazel was walking the children round the garden. The kitchen was warm and cosy, familiar and a safe haven.

'Andrea won't be coming with us to Ireland.' He pulled out a chair and sat down to the table; a coffee mug came his way as if by magic. 'Thank you, Mary.'

'Ah. Umm.' His wife thought a moment, comprehending his thoughts. 'It would have been a bit of a squash, dear. Yes, I know we talked about it,' she added, seeing his look, 'but she's taking a commonsense approach. We'll manage with Hazel. That'll be all right, won't it, Mary?'

'Reckon. Her mum's taken up wi' this new man in her life, she won't worry. And wi' the lass now more openly *compos mentis* it'll be a good thing. Yon Andrea and I will cope, never fret.'

'Okay.' He just had to accept it, whatever he thought. 'Then I'll confirm the bookings?'

'Please.'

Settled then. They'd leave tomorrow week, take the overnight ferry and be in Ireland first thing Wednesday morning. Roberta's reward for keeping her cool, as the expression had it, and his welcomed promise to her in response for the agreed cooperation over the filming. Secretly, he was looking forward to the reprise of that sublime week three years ago, except it was going to be an autumnal reprise. Never mind, it would be good for them; offer different surroundings, different challenges, take them into another perspective.

He rang June from the privacy of the bedroom phone.

'Hi, dad. How's things?'

'Okay. And with you?'

The ever so slight pause put him on edge. 'Jobless,' she replied, as if that covered everything.

'Hmmm. Silly girl.' He heard her breathing, her wondering what to say next; he knew her so very well now. 'Still want to come here, and if so, what will William do?'

'He's talking of doing a six month course in the States, something new in the Internet line the whizz kids have dreamt up. I think,' she said after a pause and he sensed her emotion building, 'I'd love to come to the Manor, if that's a possibility, dad.'

'Of course it is, June. You shouldn't need to ask. We'd all love to have you here, but . . .'

'You don't want a "like father like daughter scenario", that it?'

'I didn't say that. What I was going to say was Andrea's looking after the office, she won't come to Ireland, and maybe very sensibly, but with only Mary she'll be a wee bit lost, no disrespects to mother-in-law, and I don't want her moping. She wanted to leave us, but Roberta persuaded her otherwise, thank goodness. So I'd be a lot happier if you were here, but not at the expense of your marriage, June.'

A deep sigh, then the expression he dreaded. 'What marriage, dad? I was too young, and too gullible. Seeing you and mum break up got me thinking.'

There wasn't anything to say. So desperately sad, looking at a partnership dissolving into stultifying apathy and knowing there wasn't a lot anyone could do about it; once those cracks appeared it was only a matter of time, or otherwise endure a grim soul destroying determination to hold onto a failure for appearance's sake and hope for a turn-around His separation from Samantha had initially been triggered from boredom but happily the consequences had worked in their favour so neither felt the loss. Without doubt his subsequent marriage to Roberta was the best thing ever to have

115

happened, despite the complications of Andrea. As darling Roberta had said, so understandingly and not realising a certain Princess had uttered similar words, she'd almost married Andrea as part of the deal. Wow!

'Dad?'

'Sorry, love. I was thinking too.'

'Funny thing to do on the phone, isn't it? Can I come?'

'Yes. Yes, do that. It'd be good. The twins will be pleased, having so many Aunts about. When?'

'Tomorrow. Mid-morning.' She coughed, as though to disguise her breaking voice. 'And thanks, dad, I love you.'

He put the phone down and brushed at his eyes. Daughters!

'What can we do, R?'

'Not a lot, dear. Sad, though.' A small poignant smile, knowing exactly what was going through his mind. 'Would you have stuck with Sam if I hadn't happened?'

He shrugged. Hypothetical question, though deep inside, yes, he probably would have, in a strange admixture of loyalty, indecision, reluctance to lose face and best of all, a treasure of lots of memories and lovely ones at that. Even now some recollections pulled at him. He had to hold her, hug her tight, kiss her lovely hair and on down to her neck and as she twisted around, her lips. *I love you.*

'Thank heavens for that. Luv you too, darling. Don't go and get maudlin, my love. Think positive.'

'Positive that June's losing interest in William or positive that she's coming here?'

Roberta's lovely deep brown eyes narrowed. 'I have an idea. Don't quiz me just yet, dear boy, let me work it out. In the meantime, go and have a tumble with your kids. That'll cheer you up. I'll call you when lunch's ready. And send Hazel down, I want to talk to her.'

As Hazel entered the sitting room, Roberta mentally swelled in pride seeing the bright, confident, well dressed young lady now with her sparkling eyes and dimply smile, a far cry from the dowdy little sparrow of a girl that had come to them a couple of years ago. Groomed, inspired and cultivated, a lovely, lovely person.

'Hazel, sit down, love,' she'd nearly said 'lass' in a Mary like way, 'I want to have a discussion.'

'Discussion as in serious, Roberta?'

Roberta laughed. 'Don't panic, dear girl. I ain't about to fire you, or tell you off. No, nothing like that. You're coming with us to Ireland and I gather your mum has no objection, which is great. No,' she repeated, 'Ground rules. You are, and you don't need telling, a very attractive young lady. If you come with us, I need you to agree, to promise even, not to be distracted by any nice young men. Or any less than nice ones either. In other words, Hazel, preserve your dignity. And your virginity. That's not to say someone might not heave up over the horizon who may just sweep you off those delicious legs but as long as I have a vested interest, it has to be someone who deserves you. I speak from experience, Hazel, bitter and hard won. My father, of blessed memory, was blinkered when it came to my marriage, but dearest mum Mary wasn't and sadly couldn't interfere, 'cos at the time it wasn't her place. And so I suffered.'

Hazel was wide eyed. Roberta, telling her all this? Now she'd shed her 'little girl lost' exterior, she felt infinitely more of an adult woman but had to admit to herself, there were bits missing she still had to learn. No qualms about letting Roberta educate her either; she owed her heaps.

'Don't tell me if you don't want to, please, Roberta.'

The only response was a slight frown and a shake of the head as she carried on, 'but my life changed so dramatically when I met Andrew. He and I *clicked,* to use that ugly expression. If only I'd met him first! At least when I did I was a lot wiser. I'd like to spare you the sadness of falling into bad relationships if I can,' and she moved round the little table, brushing the surface as if it hadn't been dusted. 'If you'll let me, though there's many a girl who'd run a mile if any old married woman started to interfere in their love life as probably I would have when I was your age, too.' She caught Hazel's look. 'You can tell me to shut up and mind my own business if you like, but whilst on holiday with us you do as we say.'

'You're not an *old* married woman, Roberta.'

'There's some who would disagree. However, thanks for the compliment.'

The girl uncrossed her legs and stood up. 'You've been good to me, probably far more than I deserve, playing games as I did. Sorry, sorry.'

Roberta held her arms wide, and Hazel skipped the three yards to be hugged tight. 'For all the love you've given to my two kids, how can I be cross? So pleased you've come out of the shell at last.'

The girl pulled back. 'When did you guess?'

'Ah. That would be telling.'

'Please, Roberta?'

'Then it was that walk in front of the camera, my girl. Too confident by far. No, don't say anything. Shove it in the 'File Thirteen' bin. Past history. Now go and let my husband off twins duty before they wreck him.' She gave an encouraging smile. 'No more lectures. Well, not unless you step over the line.'

'I'll try not to. Thanks for all your confidence in me. I promise.'

'Good girl. Now hop it.'

'Andrew, what's 'File Thirteen'?'

'Pardon?'

'Roberta told me to 'shove it in file thirteen' when we were talking about my silly way of pretending to be stupid.'

He unravelled Abby's fingers out of his hair and let her slide carefully onto the floor. She wasted no time in attacking Chris, trying to build a tower out of plastic cups and Hazel grabbed a handful of mini-jeans to hoink her away. 'Stop that, Abby!'

'Search me. An expression she picked up from somewhere.

I'd guess it meant bury it out of any possible recall. Sensible. You are all right?' He laughed at her look. 'Silly question. Will they go down okay?'

'After wrestling with their dad? Another silly question. I'll be down for lunch in half an hour.'

Such a treasure, their Hazel. He left her to ensuring they curled up for a lunchtime sleep and returned to the kitchen.

'Been giving her the third degree, R?'

Roberta grinned. 'Sort of. Told her not to play away.'

'And File Thirteen?'

She pulled a face. 'Blast from the past, Andrew. One of Michael's ex-services expressions. Means losing something permanently.' She changed the subject. 'I'm in the barn this afternoon but I'd like your help if you can spare the time.'

'Sure.' The interrupted accountancy work from the morning would have to be tomorrow's job.

'Give Andrea a yell, Andrew. Lunch's ready.' Mary gave the pan another stir. 'So June's coming over?'

'Tomorrow. And staying a while, to help out whilst we're away.'

The meaningful look from his mother-in-law said it all. Nothing further would be mentioned about his daughter's situation unless he raised the matter. Soul of discretion, that was their Mary. She wouldn't lightly dismiss her help either; thank goodness.

As the remaining few days before the holiday ebbed away, fragile tempers came more into evidence; any little upset in routines, any problem not readily resolved and voices embrittled and rose in tenor; fortunately Mary's commonsense and implacable character saw them through. June said little about her home life, other than a brief session with her father when the office was opportunely vacant.

'He's off to the States on Monday, Dad. Didn't seem to

bother either of us. See what happens when we both eventually get home.'

'Have you said anything to your mother?'

'Not in so many words. Wait and see. I'll be better off here anyway, keep my mind off things. Andrea and I are getting on fine. She's a charming girl, dad.'

'Hmmm. Yes, she is.'

His daughter looked at him curiously. 'You still hold a torch for her, don't you?'

'June, the ripples of the past have mostly been smoothed out. Don't muddy the waters, there's a good girl. Suffice to say Roberta's not unhappy, okay?'

'Okay.'

Finally he got the car loaded to his satisfaction, though the fragility of their individual truces came perilously close to explosive point over what was packed and what was abandoned. The twin's requirements seemed paramount and he couldn't argue too much over that; luckily Hazel was a good deal more realistic than her employer which helped his relations with his wife. A far cry from the last time they'd gone down this route, with just the two of them and blinded to most things other than their infatuation. Infatuation? He'd lusted after her then. And she him, too.

'R?'

'Hmmm?'

'Happy?'

'Mmmm.'

'What you thinking?' he asked in abbreviated format. 'You're not very communicative.'

She put her book down and half rolled towards him. 'Sorry, love. Got to a juicy bit. You don't read much nowadays.'

There really wasn't any point in saying anything, not worth an argument, sorry, discussion. He didn't often read in bed, believing in a simplistic view that going horizontal was for sleep or . . .

Her hand was exploring, provocative wench. 'Last night in our own bed, darling. Nice?'

'Hmm Mmmm.' She was a clever girl, his wife, and experienced. 'On or off?'

'You're a beautiful girl, R.'

She was warm, soft and cosy to cuddle. The duvet slipped sideways and the light stayed on.

TEN

It had been a risk, planning to take the overnight ferry, being unsure of how little people would cope; on balance they'd assumed they would sleep through and the crossing less traumatic for them all as a result. Of course the experience came as completely new to Hazel, heightening her delight of travelling through different countryside.

'I've never seen hills like these!' she'd exclaimed as the route to Pembroke had taken them past the Malverns and on into Wales.

Roberta gave her body a little shake down into the seat cushions. Another of those odd little things that gave her such pleasure, watching and listening to this girl's happiness. She'd shared the driving, the journey thankfully not too tiring on the whole and now they could curl up. Hazel would now appreciate the benefit of having to carry extra pillows up the stairs from the car deck.

'Can you get comfy, Hazel?'

The girl wriggled sideways. 'I'll try. Sure you'll be all right with them?' The twins had zonked out, wedged into the couch with the pillows. Roberta had promised to stand first watch, Andrew when she started to wilt. 'I'll do my share,' she'd said, but as a youngster, far more likely to doze off so they'd told her to sleep. And within ten minutes of the ferry's sailing, she duly was asleep, showing the clear relaxed expression of a carefree existence.

Andrew nodded at her, still upright in his armchair. 'Happy girl. Does well. Sure you're okay?'

Roberta nodded. 'I'm okay. At the moment. You kip, darling, if you can.'

The ferry's deck swayed gently beneath his feet. An hour to go, the dawn was edging into day. Roberta snored gently but he daren't tell her. Hazel had scarcely moved in the sleep of the innocent. Abby had thrown herself about and nearly fallen off the cushions, had cried once, briefly; Chris never moved. At least tonight they should sleep soundly. He stretched, eased his shoulders and risked a walk over to the forrard windows. Grey skies, grey sea streaming past. A fishing boat was heading outward, a tanker way over to the east emphasised the horizon. It didn't look too bad a day. Hands on the back of chair, he let his body relax to the slow rise and fall as the vessel pitched gently into the tide. Nothing to worry anyone. Across to the south the wind turbines below Rosslare came more into focus and the odd shape of the water tower. Memories.

The tannoy burst into life with that irritating *Ding Dong*. *"Would all car drivers and passengers please . . . "*

The rattle of the steel sheeting of the ramp, the slow edge of the traffic queue down the slope, the stare and scrutiny of officialdom and then free to go. Ireland here we come.

Andrea swung the chair round and round, hands tucked below her thighs. They'd be in Ireland by now. The place was hers for all of the ten days. June was in the barn, Mary in the kitchen. Half nine, strange feeling not having Andrew about, or Roberta for that matter. So now she was the resident boss. Well, sort of. What would she do first? E-mails, as normal. The screen burst into life on the brilliant new home page she'd devised, slowly dissolving pictures of rooms changing before your eyes, thanks to Alain's expertise loaded from the disc he'd sent as promised. Click onto 'Messages' and see who wants what.

June walked around the displays in the Barn, straightened out some cushions, adjusted the fall of sample curtains, flicked dust off the chairs and picked up a sweet wrapper some idiot had dropped. Beautifully quiet at this time of day. She sank into an upholstered chair and let her body relax. There were two appointments today, quite sufficient to cope with, one this morning at eleven, another just after lunch. Was she up to it? Yes, of course she was. Roberta had given her a very good grounding in the patter, told her to follow her instincts, but if all else failed, well, she could get her on the mobile . . .

'Wouldn't dream of it,' she'd said, but Roberta had insisted. *'My clients, June – don't let me down.'* Her father had smiled. *'As if!'* And here she was, in charge of sales, well sort of. A very brief thought about William, boarding his plane to the States, quickly suppressed in favour of another thought about her mum, who'd done a William. Better, for actually Mum had used her instinctive talents to advantage, using her caring skills for little people out of luck. Bless her.

William merely wanted to be number one geek. Sad. Sad for her too. Where was her longed-for version of her father? He'd ridden to Roberta's rescue, made lives around him a lot more bearable. Even Andrea's, though that was one heck of a complication. Just as well she didn't get to go to Ireland.

Mary, mother Mary, pillar of steadfastness in her devotion to her girl and all that she did, wiped down the draining board, polished the work tops and topped up the Aga kettle. The girls would be in for mid-morning coffee break soon and she had some new apricot-preserve filled flaky pastry cakes for them to try, less crumbly than croissants. Her thoughts were also over the water, wondering about the twins and how they were coping with their journey. Good that Hazel was with them, that girl's a star and such an unpretentious one. Yes, Roberta was a good mother, but she did place a lot of reliance on the girl. Not like her day when . . . but there had been similarities. Henrietta had lent on her for everything, she'd done all the baby things even though in the eyes of the world the little girl had technically been Henrietta's, instead of her husband's love child. With her. Roberta was *hers*.

Hazel wasn't the twin's mum. Mind you, she'd make a splendid one.

The kettle was singing; that hadn't taken long. She went to the passage door and called.

Andrea hit the send button on the last message and reverted to the home page, swung the chair round and standing up, stretched. Her skirt's zip fastener top button popped. Was she getting fat? Mary's call was timely. She pressed the intercom button, *'Coffee, June!'* and walked down the corridor towards the kitchen.

June heard the bleep and Andrea's tinny voice, came out of her introspective dreaming and shutting the Barn door firmly behind her, crossed the yard. They had half an hour before the first of the day's visitors.

Hazel was wide-eyed, taking it all in; the strange road signs, interrupted yellow lines at the road edge, different number plates on most vehicles. After the steady half hour drive away from the coast, Andrew pulled into a fuel station. Roberta had dozed after her less than restful night and woke up with a jerk. *'What?'*

'Breakfast?'

'Mmm, what a brilliant idea. Where are we?'

He laughed. 'Ireland?'

She thumped him. 'I'm starving. Hazel, how's the rear contingent?' and turned her head round. 'Still comatose?'

Abby stirred and stretched, her brown eyes blinked and then she smiled, gorgeously. *'Mamm – am.'* Roberta beamed, 'Hello darling. You're on holiday!' and got another wide smile back and a gurgle. Chris was still fast asleep with his mouth open.

'They're fine, Roberta.' Hazel used a delicate finger and carefully attempted to push Chris's chin to close his mouth. He stirred but didn't wake.

'You'd best wake him, Hazel, please.' She opened her door. 'Do these places have toilets? I'm bursting.'

'This one does. The sign's over there.' Andrew knew he'd have to follow her, but first things first. He got out and rescued Chris from his seat as Hazel unstrapped him. 'I'll explore. Got the twin's rations?'

Oh, the complications of family travel. Much as he loved his little brood, the maintenance logistics could be trying, bags, buggies and finding suitable spaces to park them all. With quiet efficiency Hazel sorted it all out and the multi-resourced outlet, fuel for cars and fuel for people, far and away the best place she'd ever seen, had high chairs organised in the 'eat-in' area. Roberta returned to duty in far better shape – she'd managed a little wash as well.

'Your turn, darling. You okay, Hazel?'

'I'll go after we've fed them, Roberta. I'm fine at the moment.'

Amazing. It took over an hour but well worth it and he just couldn't fault the service. Smiles all round, nothing too much trouble. Ireland. He was glad to be back.

Mary had the apricot filled Danish cakes on the plates and freshly made coffee. If himself and his wife, her daughter, could live it up abroad, well, they wouldn't stint things here either. Keeping the business going, indeed. And these two girls deserved some molly-coddling.

Andrea sat on a stool, June pulled up her favourite chair, Mary sat on the other stool and there they all were, the home team. An unexpected silent moment as they all looked at each other and suddenly smiles turned to giggles.

'Three musketeers?'

'Wrong sex. Try the Three Graces, June. Except that we're not nude and all in a huddle.'

Mary frowned at her. 'I'm not going on down that route,

126

Andrea. You can if you like but I'm past them sorts of antics.'

Andrea laughed. 'June?'

A sort of devilish concept, that. Going nude. No males around. No, not sensible, but a weirdly arousing thought. She reached for an interesting looking cake as Mary started pouring the coffee. She bit into it and apricot jam squeezed onto her chin.

'Yum. These are good, Mary.'

Andrea took one and cautiously took a far more lady-like nibble. 'You'll have us putting on weight, Mary, tempting us like this, but June's right. Lettuce for lunch?'

The 'clients' at eleven o'clock were a middle aged well-to-do couple.

'We've decided to have a complete make-over now Adrian's retired, haven't we, dear?'

The woman's idea, June thought, but he seemed pleased to go along with it. Money to burn. Without letting on this was her debut, she took them through the Barn, introduced them to different concepts, showed them the samples books and left them to browse for a while. Roberta had told her most clients took between thirty minutes and an hour to get bored and look for help and directions, so she went for a prowl around. The small barn, empty of all its film crew's appurtenances, echoed in a strange way, solid packed brick floor or no. She had a funny feeling, sombre, brooding and a touch melancholic, as though the place kept ghostly secrets. Perhaps it had. What was it her father had said? A monument to past misdeeds? She shuddered. No girl in her right mind would have willingly given herself in this place – unless she was blind to everything but her body's passion. Maybe that was it, mere passion. Not her scene.

She went back to the couple and fixed her 'I'd love to help you' expression in place. Quite a challenge, this selling business. Better than sorting out accounts at the printers.

Andrea returned to her routines, checking on outstanding

accounts to run the invoices through. It shouldn't take long and then she'd have a prowl round the gardens before lunch.

Roberta felt an awful lot better after the breakfast interlude and much more prepared to do her map reading thing while Andrew drove.

'How long will it take, d'you reckon?'

He'd decided early on in the planning that they'd not follow the same route as last time, but swing north and head for the mid point of the west coast, to touch Limerick before reaching the cottage.

'Early afternoon, allowing for stops.'

'Did you say Jerpoint?'

'Yep.'

'Any specific reason you chose that place?'

He shook his head. 'Not really, other than it wasn't too far and yet would give us a good start in the morning. Just below Thomastown,' and pointed at the place on the map. 'Through New Ross and north towards Kilkenny.'

'Where the cats come from.'

'If you say so. News to me.' He thumbed through the papers in the 'planning file' and pulled out the B & B details. 'There, all yours. Now, shall we press on before the backseat crew get bored?'

She was a lot better at directions this time and it took less than three hours to reach their destination, allowing for the three quarters of an hour they spent in a grassy picnic lay-by well back from the road for the twins to let off steam. The large bungalow well set back from the road and easy to find, fronted a collection of glasshouses, the gardens smiling a welcome at them as Andrew swung the Volvo into the drive.

'You're very welcome now, come along in. My my, what a bright pair of little people you have there! I've the two rooms for you on the front with the cots as you asked, not a problem at all. My daughter's lent the one, we had the other anyway. Now, will you be wanting a cup of tea? I have the kettle on ready.'

Their hostess was broad and cheerful, absolutely what Roberta needed, cosseting; and completely on top of her hospitality. The large rooms were ideal, the cots neatly placed end on end against the wall of the larger one.

'You'll be taking this one, the young lass in here?'

Roberta opened her mouth to explain, but Hazel was ahead of her. 'No, I look after the twins, that's my job.'

Eyebrows were raised. Mothers were expected to look after their children, not young lassies. Still, if that was the way of it, who was she to object? Just as well both rooms were doubles. She merely nodded and would leave her guests to organise themselves.

'Tea in the front in ten minutes then,' she said and bustled off.

Hazel was unflappable, just grinned at Roberta and took the twin's bags from Andrew.

Roberta sagged onto their bed, swung her legs up and stretched out. Bliss.

Andrea walked slowly across the grass. Last time she'd done this her thoughts had been all over the place. Today, day one of this strange arrangement, she had a much clearer idea of where she was going. The old beech stood guardian. Avoiding the place where she'd collapsed; she crossed to the stile and used the bottom step as a seat. Just as well it was dry. She sat still, hands under her, let thoughts run free.

June saw her couple away. Yes, they'd had a wonderful morning, no, they weren't sure at the moment, could they take the sketches away and have a think? They'd phone her in a day or two. Thank you very much. Not at all, my pleasure, hope we can help further. Yes I'm sure you can. Goodbye.

She saw Andrea way across the length of the garden.

Mary looked out of the kitchen window. Two girls, sitting close on Andrew's stile, talking away, heads together, and as she watched, saw June's arm go round the older girl. Two girls with emotional upheavals comforting each other. The one with a marriage of sorts, the other with nothing, except Andrew's care, dangerously too caring. What could she do? Nothing, other than keep an eye and soothe things down where she could.

Lunch was subdued. Mary couldn't raise the tone; both girls had gone quiet and introspective.

'I'm leaving early, Mary. Not a lot more I can do today and it'll give mum a surprise. I might take her out to see a film tonight, for a change. That all right?'

'Of course, lass, whatever you think. We'll be all right, won't we, June?'

June nodded. She'd love to have gone to the pictures too, but daren't say. At least she had a nice dinner to look forward to; she'd seen the preparations. Mary was obviously in experimental mood while Roberta's back was turned. The next couple were due in half an hour.

At the end of the afternoon, she shut the Barn up, slid the key into her jacket pocket and returned to the house. Andrea had gone. Mary had the kitchen warm and smelling of newly baked cakes again.

'What's the lovely smell, Mary?'

'Ginger cakes, lass. My favourite, crunchy topped, lovely with Earl Grey tea. Want to try?'

'Sure. Great.' She sat on the stool, swinging her legs, like a twelve year old. 'Mary?'

'Yes, lass?'

'Did you know about Andrea and my father? Before he . . . ' what, gave Roberta the twins, agreed to marry her, or before her mother left? She couldn't define her question fully.

Mary eyed her over the mug of tea she held with both hands.

'I had an inkling, lass, no more. Thems two hae played games a while, reckon. Their business, not ours.'

'But she's – Roberta's your daughter, didn't you care?'

The mug went carefully down onto the table. 'Aye, lass, I cared, but what's a body to do? I couldna' tell Roberta to gie him up, not when she'd fallen for the man. Sorry, lass, I ken he's your da, but . . .' Mary's broadened speech came over in such a comforting way.

'Are you glad she married my father? Even if Andrea's so obviously and admittedly still in love with him and I know he's got a deep affection for her.' She couldn't say 'he loves her' because it didn't sit right. The conversation they'd had, out there on the stile, had cleared the air but hadn't produced a solution.

'It's the best thing that could have happened to my daughter, him and the twins. Andrea keeps them on their toes. He'll not forsake my lass, despite the attractions, nay.' She changed the subject by asking her own question, 'and yoursen, where do you see your marriage going, eh?'

June coloured up. Serve her right. 'Don't know, Mary. We married too young and my mum was right. We should have waited.' She'd known their relationship was dodgy for some time but at least it wasn't because of other emotional attachments, merely what they called 'incompatibility' in the jargon. 'Maybe it'll work out when he comes back.' *If he comes back.*

'Aye, lass. As Roberta first married too soon. Pity she didn't meet your father . . .' and stopped.

June had to smile. If he had, she wouldn't have been here, or anywhere. At least that was something. She *was* here, and happy with the truth of it.

'I'm going to have a shower, change into a decent dress, Mary. Then we'll have a lovely dinner, I know. Two grass widows.'

'Hmmmph.'

They couldn't have wished for a better welcome on their first night in Ireland.

'You go on now. They'll be all right with me. I've three lovely little grand children of my own. Two little darlings they are, as good as gold, that I know. Have a good time now, the three of you.'

Their hostess had insisted, telling them of the best pub in Thomastown and that they should have the evening to themselves. Hazel had been all for staying, but she wouldn't hear of it. 'No, you take the chance, lass. There's always another night you'll be needed.' She'd come to terms with this 'au pair' business once she'd chatted to them all over a good cup of tea, for this Hazel was no twitchy brainless girl but a real godsend for the parents.

Andrew wasn't too sure whether Hazel should be allowed to sample the Guinness. Roberta had gone straight for it, ignoring his suggestion of a white wine.

'Nope. When in Ireland, go with the flow. Pint, please.'

'Are you sure? Hazel?'

'Why not? And I am over eighteen.'

'And don't I know it! All right. Another two pints then.'

And there they sat, poring over the menu, creamy frothed glasses of the black stuff in front of each of them.

'Smoked salmon.'

'Smoked salmon.'

'Oh, all right then. Three please.'

The little dark haired waitress in her jeans grinned. 'And for main course?'

Roberta closed her eyes and let her finger run down the menu, found it opposite the Irish stew when she opened them. 'Oh well.'

'Beef and ale pie. Hazel?'

'I'll go with Roberta's choice.'

'That's fine. Won't be a tick.' Their waitress scribbled on her pad and disappeared.

'She's a slim one. Great smile.' Perhaps he could have said 'great figure' but that would be frowned on. He was right.

'Andrew, please don't comment on all the girls you see.'

Hazel sipped at her glass, inwardly grinning. Roberta was all too conscious of her thickening waistline, heading towards her forty.

They enjoyed the evening, relaxing more as the meals vanished and plates left clean. Floater coffees topped it off.

'What d'you think to Guinness then, Hazel?'

'I could get used to it, though one pint's enough.' She'd struggled a bit with the last half, but careful sips completed the task. Would she feel drunk? No, perhaps not. Once back in the house – bungalow – and the twins still happily asleep, she took no time at all to get into her pyjamas and into the soft bed, double though it may be. Bliss.

'Hazel took to the change of action well?'

Roberta raised eyebrows. 'Yes. Why shouldn't she?'

He pulled a face. 'No reason,' and changed the topic. 'Tomorrow I thought we'd have a look at the local sights.'

'Which are?'

'There's a glass blowing place and the old Abbey.'

'Fine. As long as we keep the little people amused and under control.'

'I'm sure we will.' He flicked the bedside lamp switch off and nestled close.

She put an arm round him. 'I love you, husband.'

'I love you too, wife.'

'Wife? Anything else?'

'You know as well as I do. Sleep well.'

The morning of the second day. At least she was in a proper bed, not all creased up on a shipboard settee thing, but she did have a struggle to remember exactly where she was, her mind was swirling about in an unusually strange way. At least it was quiet. No twins type racket. Were they all right? Andrew was still asleep, judging by the breathing noise. She would have poked him, but other things were paramount.

Once comfortable, she slid quietly next door to find Abby playing peek-a-boo with Hazel in her bed and Chris still asleep like his father. Hazel looked up.

'Morning. Roberta. Sleep well? I did. So did the twins, I think.'

'I did. Had a problem waking up. Shall I help you get them dressed?'

'Can I use the loo first?'

Breakfast was absolutely splendid. Everything, the works, including proper coffee and Irish soda bread. The twins had a whale of a time, plastering faces and dropping crumbs 'as they do,' said their hostess (Betty, she said to call her). It took an hour, probably more, but she hadn't timed the start.

Ultimately they were in the car and heading out. 'Glass works or Abbey?'

'Glass works sounds fun, but we may have to keep the urchins in the car?'

They were there nearly an hour and a half, watching the looks-so-easy skill that produced wonderful pieces and bought a set of four lovely glasses with deep purply stems.

'Remember we have to cram everything in the car, Roberta,' Andrew reminded her as she was fingering a large decanter. 'Nice, but impractical. Bottles work fine.' He got a grin in response.

'You're right. And this is day one. Where next?'

'The Abbey?'

Theirs was the only visitor car in the car park. Tickets obtained from the information building and with a promise from the girl on duty to give them a guided tour in another ten minutes or so, they crossed the grass through the collection of tombstones towards the entrance. Roberta suddenly shivered, with a chilling feeling of something peculiar as though she'd crossed through an invisible or spiritual barrier, and clutched at Andrew's arm.

'R?'

'Weird feeling, Andrew. I expect it's nothing,' but she kept hold for a moment.

Hazel was ahead of them, a toddling youngster in each hand, seen as though in an old newsreel, as though the children were Andrew's and the girl an image of his wife . . .

'She's good, isn't she?' her vision was blurring. No, not her. Please, no oh no o o . . .

'Brilliant. R. What would we do without her?' A hypothetical question, that. She heard him from an echoey distance but she couldn't respond. The world was fading away, going grey, fading, fading . . .

Roberta took another few steps towards the archway entrance to the Abbey and collapsed onto the turf, as silently as though she was a fallen doll.

ELEVEN

The guide, Bernice, shrugged into her comfy navy blue woolly coat. First tour of the day and it wasn't overly warm out there. Not many more weeks to go before they closed the site to visitors and she could go back to her degree work. She stepped out of the door to be greeted by a problem.

The man was helping the dark haired girl to her feet; presumably he was her partner, husband, whatever. Had she tripped? . . . *I sincerely hope not, think of all the Health & Safety questions* . . . The two tiny children were being held by the younger girl. She ran.

'Are you all right?' Foolish question, of someone who'd fallen over – or was it?

The man was as white as the proverbial, almost like his partner. She didn't look at all well, pale to almost sickly grey but at least she had the vague flicker of a smile.

'Sorry,' she said. 'I don't know what happened. My eyes went all blurry and then everything seemed to go black.'

Her husband had his arm round her shoulders. 'Do you think we could let her sit down inside somewhere?'

'Of course. Can you walk?'

The wan smile came back. 'I hope so.'

Hazel was scared stiff. Never having seen Roberta in the slightest way ill, to have her role model subjected to such an indignity frightened her. Whatever had happened to cause her to collapse like that? The twins wouldn't understand either, not that they could grasp the seriousness of why their mum had fallen over. Both had gone silent, staringly silent, poor mites.

She gently urged them to toddle on with her, following

Andrew and Roberta as they walked quietly back between the tombstones to the information building.

Bernice let them into the mess room, to offer Roberta the only armed chair. 'Would you like a drink?'

'Thank you. Perhaps a tea?'

'For you?' Bernice first turned to Andrew and then on towards Hazel, widening her question, 'and the little people?'

'They're all right,' Hazel was quite sure. She didn't really want anything either, not this side of lunch.

'You're very kind. Sorry about all this.' Roberta's colour was slowly coming back and she was grateful for both Andrew's firm handhold and his obvious deep concern. Her mind was actively scanning through the reasons why she'd felt so odd, worrying about any possible deep seated problems; none that she knew of . . . what had she been thinking about, the twins and Hazel? Surely that wasn't it? No, not unless . . . she wasn't pregnant, was she? Um. Yes, she'd had a *very* decent breakfast. She hadn't got a headache, just weirdly dizzy and then the blackout, though there were some thoughts coming to the surface . . . Surreptitiously she moved her hand held by Andrew across to rest it on her other wrist. As far as she could feel, her pulse was okay. She looked up at him. 'Darling, do I look all right now?'

He too was trying to explain to himself why she'd fallen, a very perturbing situation especially as it had come out of the blue. The last time he'd picked her up – so long ago – she'd fallen off that horse and therefore a logical accident; then that time they'd had a row she'd crashed into the chair and broken a wrist, but just to *fall over*?

'Your colours back, love. How do you feel?'

She shrugged. 'Okay. Shaken up but okay.' How could she tell him of the weird and surprising mental lock-in of thoughts that were surfacing? That her worries and concerns over their personal uncertainties had been swept away as though she'd had her mind re-booted like some computer's hard disc? She would need to mull over this strange revelation, establish the veracity.

The trayful of mugs Bernice brought across were steaming. 'Sugar?' She poised a spoonful over the pink stripy one.

Roberta pulled a face, she wasn't one for sugar but maybe that's what she needed. 'Just one, thanks.' She sipped. Ooh, but it was hot. Another careful sip. She put the mug down. 'Let the twins loose, Hazel.'

'Sure?'

Slightly cross, she repeated, 'let them loose.'

Abby looked up at Hazel as if for reassurance then toddled carefully across to her mum's knee to be hoisted up and cuddled. Chris followed and Andrew swept him up.

'They're lovely little people. Twins?' Bernice watched the byplay, much relieved the problem was diminished. Hypothetical question, but anything to get conversation going.

Roberta nodded. 'Little horrors too, sometimes.' Abby was sucking away on her thumb, content now she was back in familiar territory, whereas Chris was protesting. He wasn't keen on being held and Andrew lifted him over towards the pictures on the walls to keep his interest.

'Maybe we'll carry on with the tour?'

'Sure, if you think . . .'

'Pity not to, bit of an anticlimax otherwise. If that's all right?'

'Let me look after Abby and Chris, Roberta, while you two look round,' Hazel piped up; historic monuments didn't figure high in her list of things to do, not having been brought up in an academic world.

Roberta shook her head. 'I'd rather keep them in sight, Hazel. You don't need to tag along if you don't want to. I'm sure we won't be all that long.'

'It usually takes about three quarters of an hour. Unless I get a lot of questions.' Bernice wasn't going to shirk her role, not even for the reluctant Hazel. The Abbey deserved respect.

Andrew kept the momentum going. 'Come on, Hazel. It can't be too bad.'

She didn't reply. She couldn't argue; she was being paid to be here after all. A smile returned and their eyes met and held just for the moment in a very understanding way. He was growing on her, this man of Roberta's.

Bernice did her job well; the Abbey's history came alive for them, the seamier aspects of monastic life titillating as retold – Andrew could imagine the scenario vividly. Stark contrasts were explained, between a life of dedicated service to a religious order on the one hand and the use of privilege position and authority to pander to all creature comforts on the other – for the few. No wonder the Abbey had aspects of its architecture designed for defence. But the detailing of that architecture was, as Bernice pointed out, a credit to the craftsman of the age. The carvings were so full of symbolism and she had it all off pat. Extremely interesting, and ultimately even Hazel, doing her best to swallow her disinterest, was fully drawn into the story telling. The twins behaved themselves too, almost believable they had become equally overawed by the *presence* of the place.

Roberta held herself in check, controlling her walk, her head movements, her breathing, nervous to a degree, doing her best to diminish any internal worry. She couldn't fault the guide, Bernice did her job superbly, she was just so sorry she'd let her family down with that silly black-out and given this girl cause for concern. As they recrossed the grass and the point where she'd fallen she apologised.

'I'm sorry for the inconvenience. I hope it hasn't upset your day. Thank you ever so much for looking after me – us,' gave her polite smile and moved on, back towards the car with Hazel and the twins in tow.

Andrew added his thanks to the girl, expressing his praise for the way in which she had brought the Abbey's history alive. 'You sure you hadn't lived here in a previous existence?'

She laughed. 'Not likely. If I had, it would hardly have been a virtuous one. The usual perception of the *monastic* life doesn't take in some aspects; from all accounts if they could, they would.' The smile turned saucy, and she winked. 'I wouldn't have made a very good nun. Take that which way you like.' Abruptly, she turned away. 'Sorry, I'd better let my colleague off. Glad you appreciated the tour. Hope your wife will be all right.'

'Nice girl, that,' was his comment, sliding behind the wheel. 'She said she wouldn't have made a very good nun.'

'Nor you a monk, dear, especially if there were nuns like her within grabbing distance. And from all accounts, from what she said, religious orders didn't always mean total abstinence.'

'Abstinence from what?' He was teasing her, knowing full well what was in her mind.

'Well, you know, er . . .' Roberta stopped. She didn't want to embarrass the girl in the back.

Andrew changed the subject. 'Let's go and find a late lunch. Then somewhere else where we can let these two romp about.'

Andrea settled herself back behind the desk, having given herself a good talking to before she left home. Become your own person, she'd thought. Do not think Andrew; do not think silly foolish girly things. Let him go. Before the screen livened up her reflection showed a strange ghost of a face and that was what she was. A ghost of a woman, living in a shadow land, a dream world of vain hope and make believe. Believing that she'd make it with Andrew again one of these days when he needed her and she at her potent best, oozing availability. Not to hurt Roberta, no *no* NO; merely to get that sublime sense of fulfilment, the jazz of her sex. Merely? To reach a pinnacle, the top of her hill. Reach an achievement; accomplish an objective, like tracking across a wasteland of deserted countryside towards a potential goal. Would she have been satisfied if they had come together? She loved him. Did she? What was love, in this context? A biological need to become a fulfilled woman with a potential pregnancy, or

140

simply – simply – have her feminity stimulated for momentary ecstasy? Or the depth of want to become enveloped in the embrace of another soul?

She felt an itch, pulled at the fabric of her skirt the better to gain access to scratch, and was again vividly reminded that he *had* had her, on this very chair, ages ago, and no pleasure in that memory of either feelings or action. *Not* to be repeated, not in that way. *Or in any other, Andrea. You told yourself to become your own person, remember?* The screen saver was drifting in its aimless way in front of her; she moved the mouse and yesterday's spreadsheet reappeared. Back to work.

June's day started badly. She'd come down to breakfast with a headache not helped by knowing she'd a few days of tummy pain ahead, just one of those crosses even a stay in these surroundings didn't totally overcome in the bearing, though the aggro ameliorated to some extent given she at least had a bathroom to herself. An idle thought about William, dismissed. Andrea would let her know the moment when she had an e-mail from the States. When? If, even given what he did.

Mary's sympathy was instinctive, a knowing smile as the plate of lightly scrambled egg was set down in front of her.

'Won't hurt you, lass. Got to keep body and soul together. Stay in the warm.'

'Thanks, Mary. I think we've someone coming mid-morning. Maybe I'll stay and read until then, if that's all right?'

Mary nodded her approval. Leastways the lass wasn't flogging herself, trying to prove a point. She was a good 'un. 'I'll be out later on, doing the shopping. Andrea's in the office. We'll have a late lunch. Coffee?'

'A small mug. And another slice of toast, not too burnt. Have we heard from Roberta?'

'Not since. They won't be thinking too much of home, I don't suppose.'

They'd been back to Thomastown to eat, all of them, though the twin's presence rather complicated the event this time round. Their last night's waitress doted on them, especially Abby, Andrew was sure she had been given a bigger portion of ice cream. He kept a close eye on Roberta, her little unheralded 'funny turn' this morning had put him on edge. Way back in their very early days he remembered she'd asked him if he'd nurse her if she was ill and, dismissive of any suggestion that she'd ever be ill, had said *of course*. She couldn't be ill. It wasn't her, to be ill. She caught his glance and smiled, slid a hand along the bench seat and laid it on his thigh. *'I'm fine,'* she was saying. He moved his spare hand to cover hers and squeezed, gently, mouthed *'Love you.'*

Both eyes closed briefly, an acknowledgement and an affirmation. 'It's time to go, you lot,' she said, pulling her hand away. Andrew rose and stepped across to pay the bill, Hazel helped Roberta to ease the twins to the floor. Tomorrow they'd be in their cottage.

'Thanks a million,' the girl beamed at him, 'Enjoy your stay. Take care of those little ones.'

He'd happily given her a few euros over the top for the way she'd looked after them, pleasant girl. Maybe they'd be back. Who knows? He picked up his receipt, gave her another smile and followed his family out into the growing dark.

The Volvo swallowed them and Andrew's emotions got the better of him.

'Darling?' Roberta's quizzical glance saw and recognised the look. He could get quite oddly sentimental at times, so much part of *him*.

He shook his head, reached forward and started the car.

'No, tell me.'

He took a deep breath. 'Gets to me, now and again. How lucky I am. With all of us, here, close together, miles from home but so close.'

She nodded. 'I know. Don't think I don't know, love. Let's go.' She wanted to get horizontal; it had been a long day. Hazel heard him too and her heart gave a funny little leap.

With the twins settled and Hazel happy to curl up with her book, they were on their own and quiet. She stretched out on the bed, letting all her muscles relax. Since the scare this morning she'd felt fine, not a single twinge in her head or anywhere else and her mind had settled down.. Now she'd perhaps explain – no, suggest the cause of the upset. Or maybe it wasn't an upset but a re-programming occurring in a special place – a sanctuary of sorts, that Abbey. Having thought things through and realised she'd dismissed a lapse as a quirk, her intuition couldn't stay silent, not for another week before she could seek professional confirmation.

'That thing this morning.'

'Mmmm?' He was refreshing his memory about the onward journey tomorrow, studying the map. 'I think we'll go round Cork. Shouldn't take us too long. We'll eat in that Glengarriff pub again if you like. See if they remember us. Sorry dear, what about it? You still okay?'

'Oh yes, I'm okay. More than okay.' She did a little flick with her legs to gain the momentum to sit up, and rubbed both hands down her thighs. 'I'm sorry, dear,' and waited. Would he cotton on?

'Sorry? For passing out? You couldn't help it, could you? So long as there's nothing sinister in the background. We'll have to have you checked out once we're back.' He folded the map and stood up from the dressing table stool, glanced at his watch. 'I'll look in on the twins and we'll call it a day. Unless you want to – perhaps better, in case Hazel's . . .'

She grinned. '. . . getting undressed. I'll go.' He'd missed her cue. It'd wait.

The journey across to the west was smooth and uneventful, and Andrew once more blessed their decision to move to the bigger car. Now they were back on familiar terrain, almost as if they were coming home, driving up the wide central street towards the hills and their hide-away cottage. All as she remembered, all so so familiar. There was the pub where she had her first ever Guinness and they'd had a crazy go at Irish dancing.

'Stop!'

'What's up?' Andrew eased the car into the side and turned the ignition off. 'Want an early pint, girl?'

'No. Look!' She pointed at the couple walking away from them on the other side of the road. 'Aren't they our friends – you know, the ones who lived outdoors during the summer?'

'Could be.' He restarted the car and drove slowly onwards to pass them. They certainly looked familiar. He powered the window down, leant out and tentatively called. 'Ken?'

A brief hesitation before the smile broke out and the reply came back. 'Andrew!' and the couple crossed over. 'How y're doing? 'Tis good to see you – and a family? My, this is great, eh Sheila?' His partner, with her bronzed skin and long dark hair had the outdoor gypsy look on her, her long skirt in patchwork fashion matching Ken's long cord jacket and curly locks.

Sheila stooped down and peered into the car. 'Two wee souls! And who's the lovely lass between them? You're a beautiful colleen and no mistake! Roberta – ye've done a good job here. Did we not say all the love in the land? My, but it does us good to see you two again, and with the young ones. Ye'll not want to be in the pub tonight, but we're playing late. T'would be good?'

Roberta nearly replied in the vernacular style, the accent was catching, so melodic and somehow so right but she'd not do it justice. She got out of the car and walked round to give her wonderful friend of that idyllic week two plus years ago an embrace and gain a strong grasp of hands from Ken. 'We had to come back, Sheila. To show off the twins and . . .'

'To where they started?'

She blushed. 'I think I brought them here, embryonically, Sheila, but it would have been a lovely idea,' and added, more in hope than expectation, 'Why don't you two come up to the cottage later, before you start at the music, if you can?'

Ken looked at Sheila, no speech needed, they appeared to be telepathic. 'Sure. In about an hour? Give you enough time to sort yourselves out?'

'Lovely. We'll get the kettle going.'

It was almost, not quite but as good as, as though they'd never been away. The same view and the same sun sinking redly behind the same stately trees. Well worth the effort to come back. She sank onto the big bed, kicked her shoes off and closed her eyes. Last time the overwhelming thought was that they'd been playing truant – from Andrew's failing marriage and from her past misdeeds. Misdeeds? Ummm. Seducing him, having no thought about the death of her former husband and relying on dear Mary, mum Mary, to keep a fledgling business going. Worth it? 'Course it was. Now, well, she was properly married and she had two loyal people back home running the business as well as a mum. A lucky girl, a very very lucky girl.

'Andrew?' She sat up and called. Where was he?

'Darling?' A head appeared round the door. 'Showing the twins where they'll be sleeping. The owners were as good as their word. Two cots. Don't you want to come and see?'

She should have, and not left it to Andrew and Hazel. 'Of course, dear. Sorry. Is she all right?'

'Yes. Quite at home, but we need to sort some sustenance for them. Come on, 'cos we'll have Ken and Sheila here ere long.'

'Coming.' She stood up, carefully, but no, she was okay. False alarm?

Abby was as good as gold, once tucked up, she popped a thumb where a thumb should always be and within minutes was fast asleep. Chris, a different matter, different place, different humour and he shouted loud and clear to voice his disapproval. It took the combined efforts of the two women to placate him and – probably – his own fatigue to finally send him off. Just in time, footsteps along the path.

'So how you're doing?' Being settled into the lounge area in front of the log fire with mugs of tea all round, the daylight just about gone and the low light of the table lamp by the fireplace adding some extra to the glow from the flickering flames, it was cosy.

Andrew led off. 'As you saw, two little people and a wonderful girl to help us look after them and I've made an honest woman of the lady I love. Mind you, we do have a fairly hectic life back home.' He went on to explain about the filming and the way the business had grown since their inceptive open day. 'We're indebted to this young lady. Without her we'd have had a hard time.' Hazel had changed and was looking a true picture in her new pale linen skirt and the Irish woollen sweater.

Sheila had taken the sofa seat next to the girl and now reached out to lift and hold her nearest hand, feeling the back with her fingers. 'Sure, she has an honest spirit, this one. Have you been under a cloud until recently? Perhaps less sprightly earlier?' Hazel felt a shiver down her back; was this Sheila psychic?

Roberta took the strain, aware Hazel might not be too happy revealing her past, er, deception. 'Hazel didn't enjoy a very happy schoolhood, Sheila. She had to keep her head down to avoid being bullied. It became addictive, I think, this attitude. That right?'

Hazel nodded. 'Until Roberta brought me out of my shell.' and laughed, lightly, musically. 'The twins helped.'

'They would. Mind you, you have a way with them, I think. You'll be a very good mother in your due time, Hazel. And make a handsome lad a very happy one when you find him, though he may be closer than you think. You're a pretty lass.' Sheila looked across at Andrew. 'If you find one like Roberta's man, as I believe you may and soon, you'll do well,' and turning to Roberta, smiled a knowing smile. 'He's been good to you, I think,' and winked.

The conversation moved away, to weather, tourists, the way the village had been 'improved' as Ken had said in a disapproving way – and inevitably it was time for him and Sheila to meet their musical obligations in the pub.

'What do you play?' Hazel asked.

'The bodhran, the whistle, and Sheila the fiddle. Sure and 'tis a grand noise. Come and hear us some time.'

'Another time.' Andrew stood up as the two moved to the door. 'We'd best have an early night; we've travelled a fair old way.'

Ken nodded. 'Till then,' and the two were gone.

'Nice people,' Hazel said. 'What's a *bo-rrun?*'

'Very. A *bodhran* is an Irish drum.' Roberta curtailed her explanation until another time, wondering about Sheila's perception over Hazel's mental attitude. 'She has what the Irish call second sight. She told me I was pregnant before I was even sure myself.' And immediately realised the implication in Sheila's words, *good to you,* and that wink. Oh, no, not another sign? How old was she now? Was this a good idea? Not a lot she could do about it.

'Turn in?'

'Yes. Hazel?'

'I'd like to get some fresh air, just for a minute. A short walk.'

'I'll keep you company. You get to bed, R.'

They walked up the road and along the grass slope overlooking the valley. There wasn't a sound or a breath of wind. The near full moon had crested the hills opposite to offer just enough light to see the outline of the trees and the silver shine of the waters in the bay below.

'I love this place, Andrew. I feel so at home, even though I've only just come.'

He turned to look at her, at the beauty she was, put an arm round the warmth of her and hugged her tight. 'So do I, my girl, so do I.'

'That Sheila. She knew about what I pretended I was, sort of simple? Roberta said she had a sort of second sight?'

'I know what you *are*, Hazel,' not wanting to debate Sheila's powers. 'A pretty young girl who's lately become a lovely young woman. You've been acting as nursemaid to our two far too long. You'll have to spread your wings, my girl.'

'No!'

'What?'

'I don't want to, not yet. And anyway, you may need me more soon.'

'Whatever do you mean, Hazel?'

'Er,' and she realised he *didn't* know, but then it was only an assumption, an intuitive guess on her part after the day's event's. 'Well, as the twins get more mobile and so on,' she added rather lamely to cover up her confusion. It wasn't for her to suggest what her instinct was telling her. She liked his arm round her, it felt nice and comforting but she tactfully eased away. 'Hadn't we better go in?'

He reached for her hand instead and she didn't object.

Roberta was tucked up, scarce a vestige showing, the bedside lamp the only light. He wasn't sure if she was asleep and slid very gently alongside her, reached back handedly to turn the lamp off. She stirred, merely to snuggle closer. With care he eased an arm across and held her.

'Mmmmm,' a murmur, 'that's nice. She all right?'

'Think so. Said she loved the place. Go to sleep, love.'

'Mmmmm.'

June said goodnight and wandered slowly towards the staircase, leaving Mary to her cosy little room off the downstairs corridor. On a whim she turned into the sitting room, not putting the light on, for the moon showed through the window to give a velvety blue glow. They hadn't bothered with a fire, not because it wasn't all that cold but she and Mary tended to stay ensconced in the kitchen, somehow it felt so much cosier and anyway, the sitting room was more Roberta's province, even in *absentia*. She dropped into an armchair, let her body relax. It hadn't been too bad a day even if Andrea had seemed preoccupied and gone home early. Her clients had been nice people with a genuine interest and no worries about a spend. At least she was earning her keep and definitely heaps better and more satisfying than the printer's office. Sleeping alone had been strange at first, despite the accustomed marital bed not having had any built-in comforts lately. A drift of cloud across the moon dimmed the room briefly; the shadows of the furniture on the carpet vanished and reappeared, the view out of the window showed more clouds building. Perhaps it would rain tomorrow. How were they getting on in Ireland? Would her father think to ring tomorrow? Would William phone in? Unlikely. She had to come to terms with it; he wasn't going to be her future. Like father, like daughter. How had Roberta worked her way through the problem of a divorce?

. . .in this room, she had risked her soul in offering temptation. Exploited a vulnerable being; seen a chink in another relationship and exercised her feminine wiles to the full. . .

June wondered at the strange thoughts. How had Roberta persuaded her father to move across into her arms, away from her mother? And should she follow suit or would William precipitate matters on his own? Did she need another man in her life? At the moment there were no urges within her to seek out any other partner, after all she was still only twenty-four. Plenty of time. Roberta was a lot older and she'd craved a family. Which she now had, though sometimes gave the impression the twins were like a fashion accessory. If it wasn't for Hazel she'd have had to be a lot more hands-on, even with Mary about. About time Hazel moved on if she was going to get anywhere, otherwise she'd be out of things. Time for bed. This wasn't getting her anywhere either. She stood, went to the window, watched the moving clouds against the big tree for a while, shivered, drew her cardigan close, turned and left the room.

During the course of the night she had a strange dream, involving Roberta in a garbled incomprehensible way, Hazel running through the garden, her father holding the twins' hands,

Andrea standing under the big tree with another man. *Another man?* She woke up, blinked at the clock. Nearly five. She turned on her side, pulled the duvet close and brought her knees up, prayed that she'd have someone cosset her, appreciate her, *love* her to bits and went back to sleep.

Andrea had a long discussion with her mother that evening after they'd eaten. Prompted by a casual comment from her mum about the imminent opening of the new Supermarket on the old Brewery site and the inference she would have been in a different job, a far better job, by now if the Brewery had stayed working, she rose to the challenge only to regret it.

'Don't think so, mum. That lot were set in their ways. The only job would have been Mrs Rollason's, and that not a lot better than what I did. I've no regrets, not now, working for Andrew.' Inadvisably, she added, 'he's been great.'

'So it seems,' her mother replied, dryly. 'Something tells me in more ways than one. Those eyes of yours are too expressive, my girl.'

'Oh.' She felt herself colouring up and climbed out of her chair to top up her glass. 'More wine, mum?'

'You did, didn't you?' ignoring her daughter's question. 'Sleep with him? I knew when you came back that time you had. You can't disguise the look. I didn't say anything to your father. Just as well you didn't get pregnant.'

Andrea nodded slowly. She wouldn't deny it, because it just wasn't something she'd do, not deny the best experience she'd ever had. 'Only the once, mum.' – *Liar* – 'When Samantha had just gone. He needed me, well, someone.'

'And how do you think he felt afterwards and what about his new wife, now?'

'He wasn't married to her then. He's said he loves me, mum . . . and Roberta knows that. She's a very understanding woman. Andrew's a very lucky man, having her.'

'Lucky having you about, too, An. Would you sleep with him again?'

Andrea's blush deepened. 'Really, mum!'

'Well, don't. *Don't!* I know you. You wear your heart too clearly on your sleeve sometimes. Find another man and get Andrew out of your system. Roberta doesn't deserve to have her relationship threatened, not even by you. And from all accounts, her Andrew's a bit weak in that way otherwise he'd still be with Samantha.'

'But she didn't . . . ' and stopped as her mother raised a wagging finger.

'Not for you to say, madam. There's more to her than you know.' She reflected briefly and went on, 'though I won't deny things had cooled off. She loved him despite he got boring.'

'Boring? Andrew? I know he hadn't got that much spark when I first met him, but when I got to know him properly he was okay. Very caring, actually,' and she remembered his concern when she'd had that brush with a former college contemporary who'd been looking for something she wasn't prepared to give. 'They parted amicably, didn't they?'

'Only because it was obvious what each other needed to do. All right, An, I don't deny it's all worked out for them, but I wouldn't want to think it's my daughter that's going to upset things. Leave him alone. Now, I'm ready for bed.' She moved to the lounge door. 'Just you take heed, now. Good night, dear.'

'Good night, mum.' The door closed behind her mother and she sank deeper into the large leather armchair, tucked her legs under her and let her mind roam.

Sleep with him again? She longed to, her inner woman craved for his loving, and although he'd only had her, what, three times, she'd welcome him again, any old how . . . As the feelings worked into her brain, the stimulus, the automatic reaction, began to work; she could feel the swell and the flow and cried, tears dampening her cheeks as elsewhere; cried for him, for her need, her womanhood and her stupidity.

He woke with a puzzled feeling, as if he'd heard his name being called from a long way off.

He eased his neck, feeling some stiffness but managed to turn his head to look at Roberta. Still sound asleep, by the way she was breathing. It wouldn't have been Hazel; she'd have tapped on the door and looked for Roberta if there was a problem with the twins. Proverbially with ears pinned back, he listened; apart from the regular noise from the sleeping Roberta and the faint windage in the trees outside, nothing.

TWELVE

'You didn't call for me last night, did you, Hazel?'

The girl looked up from her breakfast cereal, surprised. 'No, why would I?'

Roberta looked from one to the other, eyebrows raised. 'Is there something I should know about, *husband?*' and grinned. 'Nothing you two cooked up between you on that late night stroll?'

'Lord, no. Heaven forbid, dear. It's just that I woke up around four o'clock and could have sworn I heard someone call my name. Strange!'

'Strange indeed. Not crying in your sleep, Hazel?'

She shook her head. 'I slept very well, thank you.'

Andrew dug into his bowlful. 'Sorry, folks. Down to imagination then. What shall we do today?'

Roberta looked through the window at the clearing clouds and inwardly wished for a reprise of the clear sunny day two years ago, still vividly present in her memory. Too soon to dare propose what was deep in her mind.

'If, sez she, it's going to be a fine day, how about going over to that island, you know, the one with the garden?'

'Garanish?'

'Think that's the name. The twin's first boat trip?'

Andrew's raised eyebrows and the repeated 'first?' comment, made her pull a face.

'You know what I mean. Boat, not ferry. You know, trail fingers in the water, splash splash of oars, picnics in big wicker baskets, straw hats, flouncy cotton skirts, cool white wine, etcetera.'

'Very evocative, dear. Not sure that a commercial boatman

would fall in line, not a guy making his money from tourists, but you never know. Fine with me. Hazel?'

'Anything. I'm a new girl to all this. A boat trip to an island sounds very adventurous.'

'Right then. Get 'em organised. I'll go check the car.'

He didn't need to, not really, but they'd done a fair few miles. The oil level was fine; the tyre pressures okay, the visual check on reservoirs, water, steering, all in order. He dropped the bonnet and walked onto the lawn, watching the red squirrels dash for cover in the pine trees. No horrid greys here. The clouds were wisping away over the top of the northerly run of hills. That was where he and Roberta had climbed, that sublimely warm day two plus years ago, up there, past the woodland, up the side of the stream, onto the high peat hags and taken in the three sixty degrees panoramic views. Then gone back through that cool woodland, found the grassy bank in amongst the trees and . . .

'Darling!' the cry from indoors shattered the dream.

'Coming!'

Rather than go into the village and take the bigger boat, he'd remembered and aimed at the smaller one-man affair run from the little quay out on the Castletownbere road, thinking that might be the better bet. As indeed it was. Yes, of course he'd take the little ones, no problem, yes; he'd love to give them a bit of a trip round so they could see the seals afore landing them on the island. No, he didn't use oars unless the outboard motor packed up.

Shame, said Roberta, 'cos the sound of the oars and the splash, splash, splash would remind her of boating trips on the Thames when she was a little girl.

'For you, my lovely lady, I'll do some rowing,' he'd said and was as true to his word, coming into the landing stage perfectly after the last half mile under oars.

'Thanks so much. It's been great. What time do we have?'

'Just stand on the quay, lady. I'll see you. Last trip back

154

usually at the half past five. The island shuts at half six.'

'How can you shut an island?' Andrew was puzzled.

'The access is fenced and there's no one living on the place, not now. Difficult to land elsewhere.'

'Ah.'

From the entrance where they paid and the little ones had their chins tickled by a welcoming lady receptionist the path led through some large overhanging shrubs, to open out onto a vast mown lawn.

'Wow!' Hazel was impressed. 'You could have a cricket match in here!' Across to the right a sort of pagoda presided over the scene, its roof smothered in leafy climbers.

Roberta became enthralled at the size and scale of the place, fascinated at how such a project could have been engineered given the materials and the work involved. 'It's beautiful.' she said as she wandered off towards the building on her own.

'Leave her,' Andrew caught Hazel's arm. 'Let her have time on her own. She deserves it. We'll catch up in a moment. Let the twins loose.'

After ten minutes or so, Roberta re-appeared. 'Awesome.' she said. 'Lovely place. What it must have been like in its heyday, secluded and serene. Nice views from the end of the terrace, but you can go on up the hill, there's another path. Best keep the twins with us, 'cos there's a pond. Come this way,' and she shepherded them along the route she'd found.

A set of magnificent steps between the huge shrubs climbed impressively upwards and eventually opened up onto a huge rock surrounded by the mature trees rooted below. In front was a magnificent view around the bay, behind the old Martello tower that had originally formed part of the defences against invaders.

'What's that for?'

'Let's go see. If mum will look after the little ones.'

Roberta waved an arm. 'You go. Castles aren't my thing, not after Jerpoint.'

155

Inside, the place seemed claustrophobic, but the lure of the upper floors took them to the foot of a narrow winding staircase. Hazel wasted no time, Andrew was forced to follow and the revelations brought about by the angle of upward vision didn't help his *sang froid*.

'Sorry,' she said, reaching for his hand as he struggled up the last few steps.

'For what?'

She blushed, to give her credit. 'I guess I did a reveal?'

He laughed. She'd remembered the definition from the filming. 'Perhaps I should say I didn't look.'

'Then you wouldn't have seen where you were going. Sorry,' she said again. 'But then, it's you and I don't mind.'

There was nothing to be gained by pursuing this any further. Andrew did his best to answer Hazel's queries, but admitted history was not his strong point and they spent the next ten minutes taking in the fantastic views the height of the tower afforded before descending. They sat on the rock for some time, letting the twins scramble about amongst the vestiges of heather and get thoroughly grubby. The day was warming up, the waters of the bay below turning blue and sparkling.

Roberta lay back and closed her eyes. 'Perfect.'

'Hmmm.'

'Expressive, that.'

'What?'

'Hmmm. Could mean anything.' She opened one eye at him. 'Hmmm, happy; hmmm, not sure; hmmm, don't be a silly girl. Am I a silly girl, Andrew dear?'

He checked that Hazel had the twins under control across the other side of the rock and itched across to join her and let a mischievous hand explore, egged on by earlier revelations from the other girl. The eye closed, she moved ever so slightly but enough.

'Don't,' she said, not meaning it. 'We're not up in that wood now.'

'Just checking. No, you're not a silly girl.'

'That's all right then. Up a bit. Hmmmmm.'

'Hmmm, happy?' He saw the smile appear, eyes closed or no, and let his instinct take over.

'Happy. There, yes. Gently,' and within a few moments her back stiffened, 'Glory be, Andrew. That was quick. You haven't lost the knack, have you?'

'Keep you quiet until . . .?'

'It might. It might not. Depends. Where's Hazel?'

He looked across. They'd disappeared. 'Better take a look. You okay?'

'Silly question. Of course I am, dear boy. Glowing. How about you?'

'Don't ask. Don't look either.' He carefully rolled over and scrambled to his feet. 'They'd probably gone down the path. You coming?'

She raised an eyebrow. 'Coming or have come? Grammatical error? Give me a minute, minor adjustments to underwear. Remind me to wear looser pants.'

'Or none at all.'

'Randy!'

'We're on holiday. That's what holidays are for.'

'Last time was a honeymoon. This is different.'

'No it's not. I still love you and we're not over the hill yet.'

'Nor ever will be, with your stamina, but I'd rather be up *the* hill. Go on, go and see where they are. I won't be a minute.'

He walked over the mound of the rock and down the other side onto the path between the tall bushes of heather, down into the resinous scented pinewood. Where had they gone?'

'Hazel?' Silence.

Louder. 'Hazel?'

'Down here!' Her answering call came from the right, from behind a rhododendron bush.

'They're okay, Andrew.' She knew; bless her for understanding his anxiety.

They were sitting in a row, on a log, throwing pine cones into the water below and both Abby and Chris were giggling fit to burst. Well done, that girl.

'Hitch up,' said as he joined them, 'let me have a go.'

Two minutes later Roberta swung down the path, all bright and breezy. 'Well well, you lot! Shall we go on and see what else there is?' She stood, hands on hips, smiling down at them.

Her family, her husband who hadn't lost his touch and the twin's he'd given her, and how! And if she was right, what would it be like this time next year? Would she manage? So long as she didn't lose Hazel.

The rest of the gardens were thoroughly explored with twins alternately carried and encouraged to toddle, surprisingly staying in good humour though Roberta had grim visions of a struggle at bedtime. Eventually they made their way back to the pier where their boatman was already waiting. Very perceptive.

'Did you guess or were you fetching someone else across?' Roberta asked.

He tapped his nose. 'Experience. Five hours, give or take. Ready to go?'

'Thanks, yes. Great place.'

'Tis that. On a good day. Not much of the season left, have to make the best. Shall I row or can we use the motor?'

'Motor, thanks. It's getting close to tea time.'

He laughed. 'Aye, 'tis that.'

'Stock phrase, 'tis that.'

'Don't be unkind. He was nice, very friendly. We all have our quirky phrases.

'Like 'Hmmmm?'

She poked him. 'Don't.'

'That's what you said earlier, but . . .'

If looks could kill. He laughed. She was back on form and he loved her. Hazel sat back and watched, learning. Abby had a thumb in; Chris was already sagging to one side of his car seat, fast asleep. He did the three-point turn and headed back into the village.

'We need to shop, Andrew, or do we eat out?'

'I don't think I can manage an eat-out tonight, R. The usual place?'

They stopped at the grocery store cum post office to shop and as Andrew was about to get out with Roberta, Hazel piped up. 'Let me cook tonight, Roberta. If I can help shop?'

Surprised, but pleasantly so, she concurred. 'Fine, Hazel. Andrew, you stay put.'

The two girls came back to the car all smiles, carrying a big cardboard box.

'Remind me, Andrew, to take a bag when I go shopping. Ireland's plastic bag free, and has been for some time. I'd all but forgotten. They don't pussyfoot about like in the UK; they just get on with it. Anyway, we have enough. Let's go.'

He got landed with putting Abby and Chris to bed, fortunately, contrary to Roberta's fears, with no tantrums. They must have had a happily tiring day, and Abby was asleep on his knee before he knew what was what. Chris didn't demur either, just curled up and closed his eyes. With both quiet he went to change, stretched out on the bed and let his muscles relax. And fell asleep.

The girls, with Hazel in charge, brewed up a lovely fishy paella, Roberta popped the cork on a bottle of white taken out of the fridge (placed there yesterday from the half-dozen they'd brought with them) and called up the stairs.

'Dinner!' And got no answer. 'Androoo! Dinner!' She had to go and see. 'Darling, it's supper time,' putting a hand on his forehead to gently wake him. There was no point in Hazel cooking up a decent meal if he was going to sleep, none whatsoever. 'Come on!'

His face puckered up as if frowning, shook his head from side to side. 'Andrea, don't,' she heard him say and quailed. Oh, no, no, *no*, not her again! She nearly slapped him.

Suddenly he woke up. 'Roberta, thank the lord. I must have been dreaming. Nightmare.' He rubbed his eyes and struggled to sit up. 'Supper ready?'

'That's what I've been sent to tell you. You know what you just said?'

Puzzled, he shook his head, 'No, but I shouldn't have slept. Not sensible. What did I say?'

'*Andrea, don't.* So what was she doing to you that you asked her to stop?'

'Oh lord. Not sure. Sorry, love, maybe something out the past. I can't remember.'

'I should hope so.' She wasn't going to delve further, not at the moment, 'It's on the table. Come on,' and she marched off downstairs.

But he was sure and would not tell her. A cross he'd have to bear, that girl's antics and could but hope Roberta wouldn't flip. Before he joined them he sluiced his face to freshen up, having a half hour nap wasn't at all a good idea at this time of day.

The meal was brilliant and he said so. 'This is good, very good, Hazel. Well done. You'll be in charge of cooking at this rate.'

She preened. 'Glad you like it. Mary's a good teacher. I quite like cooking.'

Roberta caught his eye and gently shook her head. She knew what he might say and it would not be a good idea, not yet. *Make someone a good wife,* yes, very true but not just yet.

'You do the washing up. Cooks don't wash up. I'm going to put my feet up.'

'Up, up, up? Well, all right. Well worth it. Could do with a coffee, though.'

'I'll make it.' Hazel flicked the switch on the kettle and reached for the mugs. 'Roberta?'

'Yes, okay. Not too strong. And open a packet of those better biscuits.'

It didn't take long to clear the decks, put things back into place and collapse into the welcomingly soft armchairs with a steaming mug and two interesting and original biscuits each.

'Good day?'

That flick of eyebrows and the 'yes' said it all before Roberta leant back and let her psyche unravel. She couldn't cope with any more drama tonight. Let the other girl take the strain.

'I've enjoyed it. The twins were fine too, I'm sure they appreciated the open air.' Hazel stretched, arms up and back, her breasts moved upwards to strain her blouse buttons and showed her lace edged bra beneath. Andrew's instinctive polite reaction to look away was sublimated by what, curiosity or unforgivable desire? To compound the felony, she lifted a knee to tuck a leg under her and her skirt slid all too revealingly. Then her eyes caught his and she straightened the hem.

I want to show off. If you have it, flaunt it, someone had said. I know I have it, so I will. Give him another treat, 'cos after we went up those stairs I know he'd looked. He put his arm round me last night. Roberta won't notice and I'm sure she won't mind. After all, Andrea flirts and she's still there. He's a really lovely man. That dark curly hair. Smashing eyes. Ummm.

Roberta still had her eyes closed, Andrew was sure another few minutes and she'd be asleep.

'Darling?'

She started. 'Hmmm, what?'

'You're falling asleep. Go to bed if you want.'

Her eyes closed again. Two minutes later and she started to snortle. He got up, rescued the mug from the arm of the chair and would have picked her up but knew he'd never get her up the stairs, at least not gracefully. *'Darling!'*

A louder snortle and she woke up. 'Yes. All right. You're right. All this fresh air. And a good supper. Give me a pull?'

He helped her out of the chair, made sure she was steady, and let her go. 'I'll be up in a short while.'

He collapsed back into the chair, listening to her moving about upstairs, then the silence.

Hazel had closed her eyes as though she, too, was drifting into slumber. A few more minutes and he'd be following suit.

She looked through slit eyes across at him with his legs splayed out and was fascinated. Being the sheltered, unadventurous sort of girl for so long and without the chance to mix and socialise with her peers, she'd had no opportunities to become familiar with 'things' let alone become exploratory. Every aspect of her puberty, her adolescence and her strange yearnings had been suppressed as though she'd been corseted or kept in a convent style atmosphere; formerly it hadn't bothered her but since the day when Roberta had pulled away her veneer of protectional dimwittedness to bring her out into the sunlight and beauty of being a proper and appreciated girl, well, she wanted to fill in the gaps. Who better than Andrew, acting *in loco parentis?* Would he be prepared to educate her about matters, er, below the belt? She had mulled it over several times and now the question was churning away inside her, accentuated by the circumstances, his close proximity and knowing she'd shown him everything. Well nearly everything.

Would he? Likely not, and the concept flew around her mind like a demented captured bird. No, it wouldn't do at all. She'd earlier thought of asking Mary, but decided she'd not be too happy to talk about – er – sex. Andrea – again there was a possible problem because of the feeling that something was going on between her and Andrew, asking her might be dodgy; she might also be painfully scornful over her lack of knowledge. June, no, as Andrew's daughter she was out of the question. Roberta, well, that didn't seem totally right either. She had to do something. When she'd stretched and her boobs had all but popped out he'd noticed, of course he had. His eyes were closed. She gently undid the top button of her blouse. Not much difference, so she unfastened the next one. Then she eased up and let her skirt hem become less tight. And gently cleared her throat.

After she'd gone up stairs with that skirt flouncing around, he relaxed. She'd suddenly become extremely dangerous, flirting with him like that. She was still a youngster, relatively speaking, an employee, and under his and Roberta's roof. How was he going to handle this change in her? He couldn't be too hard on the girl. Showing her underwear had been provocatively obvious, silly girl, and letting her blouse to open up more so. He'd had to put an arm round her as a sort of fatherly goodnight thing and kiss her – on the cheek – before he sent her to bed. There was something on her mind, certainly, a strange mute appeal in her eyes, as though he was expected to say or ask something. She'd not come out with anything meaningful other than a comment about repeating how good she felt in his – their – company and wasn't she a lucky person. Had she pressed too hard against him in their comforting 'goodnight' embrace, accidentally or meaningfully? Whatever, it hadn't helped his status quo. He waited ten minutes or so until he was sure she was in her room with the twins before padding quietly up. The little bedside lamp was still on, casting a warming glow round the room. He undressed, quickly, quietly.

Roberta stirred, opened her arms.

'Darling, you awake?'

'Sufficiently.' Her nightdress top wasn't fastened at all, an open invitation.

He slid alongside her, took her in his arms as she wrapped hers round him, and nuzzled at her neck. 'Love you?' He felt her move beneath him.

'Love you too. Darling, gently, gently. . . ' he didn't need any encouragement, for, and she wasn't to know, his inspiration had already come from a vision elsewhere; from downstairs, a vision seared into his mind and it wasn't Roberta's, it was irrepressibly another's.

Her eyes stayed closed, her head on one side, savouring the feeling within her, still firm, an incredible sensation. Usually he'd slip away within a minute or two, sometimes leaving her with mission unfulfilled. Not tonight. In her soft movements to maximise the effect, abruptly she came in a good old-fashioned way and bit her lip to stifle an expressive expletive.

Instead she whispered 'Darling!'

He eased away and rolled onto his back. 'How's that?' He'd not known her as soft and cuddly for ages, so fully aware of him and sublime, really, truly, sublime.

163

A soft whisper back, 'gorgeous, gorgeous.' A quiet few precious moments before another whisper, 'Like old times?' as she relived the days before Samantha had gone when their loving had been stolen bliss. That's what had made it so special, not routine, and tonight some of the old magic had come back. Why now? Jerpoint?

'Like old times? When so?' He could be curious but not really thinking, having let his mind relax into the mood of the moment.

The glow was gradually fading. She propped her chin on her elbowed hand, looking down at his closed eyes, tousled hair and perspiration moist brow. Had they been *that* energetic?

'Before Sam left. Around the time you tumbled Andrea. While I was still a secret lover. You know, *an affaire*. What turns you on so effectively, darling? Another girl's hidden assets?'

A silly thought came into her head and it startled her. No, more than startled, shocked. He hadn't? Had he? He wouldn't! He hadn't really answered her question. She couldn't bring herself to even casually suggest anything, so maybe it wasn't so silly. He'd been a while and there hadn't been any chatting, just the odd few words she couldn't make out. And the girl was, to use that modern hideous expression, gagging for it, even if she didn't actually understand the phrase or the longing every adolescent had, not that she was still in that particular time frame but her situation would have depressed the urges until now. So had he? They'd been a while, long enough for him. Not now, hope for the best and tackle the girl tomorrow. Did she care? Yes, she blooming well did and collapsed back on her pillow, rolled to turn her back on him, whispering her 'goodnight', but he'd fallen asleep anyway. Despite their achievements, the effect had soured under her suspicions.

She'd programmed her mind, *'Wake up early'* and it managed to obey her. Barely seven, and the morning light brought the clarity. *Cause and effect.* He was still sleeping, had scarcely stirred, but, as a presumably satisfied, happy and unworried male had slept the proverbial. Just? How just? What was she going to do? Grin; grin and bear it, tax him with the situation and risk an upset or what? Tip toe through the scenery? Live with it, for she did enjoy what had happened, yeah? Ouch, but the floor was cold. Oh, for the comfort of the deep carpeted floors of home! Without worrying about the flimsies she pulled on jeans and the big woolly sweater and eased the door open mousey quiet.

Hazel woke him. 'Andrew? I can't find Roberta!' The girl's dressing gown wasn't doing her modesty any favours. Her smile was a mixture of worry and pride and her hand was still firm on his shoulder. He sat up, mind now well into gear. Roberta certainly wasn't there, her side of the bed cool. Her hand fell away and she pulled the gown closer over her frontage. The twins mattered, now was not the time to flirt.

'You've looked downstairs?'

'The car's gone.'

'*Gone?*' Thoroughly alarmed, he forgot. She quickly turned her head, some vestige of her manners giving him and his nudity opportunity to salvage some sanity. 'Give me a moment, Hazel. Get the twins dressed.' Where could she have gone, and why, for heavens sake, this early in the morning? She'd never done anything like this before. He dressed quickly; worrying, not appreciating he'd behaved exactly the same way in the past.

Glad that she'd found the keys, glad the car was facing outward, glad it was quiet and they'd left the gate open. Would he wake? Didn't matter, she was away. She drove, very carefully, down the narrow winding road towards the village and the coastal road. The mobile was on the seat beside her.

June heard the phone going as she was on her way downstairs, looking for an early cup of tea, puzzled at the early hour. Logically she took the call in the kitchen.

'Roberta! Hi, good to hear you. Anything the matter?' She glanced at the clock. Not quite eight. The girl's voice sounded tinny, echoey, but then she would be on a mobile and from Ireland. She wanted to speak to her mother? 'Are you sure I can't help? Your mother's still in her room. No? So give me a moment.' She put the phone down and reluctantly went to do as she was asked.

Mary had replaced the receiver and sat down heavily into the armchair.

'Is everything all right?'

Mary appeared to weigh the question in her mind. Then: 'Nothing that won't work its'sen out. Don't 'ee worry your pretty head about the matter, lass. If she rings again, find me. Now, how's about that cup o'tea?'

Mary back into vernacular was a sure sign that *the matter* did matter, but evidently not something she was going to share. Was it something to do with her father? She took the mug back up to her room, to allow Mary space. She'd find out in due time.

Roberta flipped the lid shut on the phone, replaced it on the seat and sat watching the bright orange pink of the sun's early rays turn the wine dark sea a gorgeous kaleidoscope of shimmering colour. Her mother hadn't said very much; she got the impression June had stayed within earshot. Would she ring back? She couldn't be away much longer; Hazel would manage the twins fine, but it was *her* job. And Andrew would panic because she'd taken the car for no explained reason. Tough.

A fishing vessel appeared from behind the island and she marvelled at the straight creaming white wake following. It would be pretty cold and breezy out there, but no doubt ultra refreshing. The little phone chirruped. She listened carefully to her mother's measured thoughts.

166

'You think? . . . I shouldn't . . . but what about . . . *what?*'
That she could not believe.

'You think I should? Won't it be dangerous? . . . yes, I know.
Bye, mum. Thanks.'

The phone tossed back onto its seat, Roberta restarted the
car. She'd love to stay and watch the oncoming day across the
water, but she had two little people to look after and a husband
to deal with. And a girl delicately poised on the brink of proper
womanhood. Was unmasking that lady's character as good an
idea as she'd first imagined? Before she turned the car round
she drove onwards, up the wide road heading west, with a yen
to see right down the bay towards the open sea and the
Atlantic. Space and quiet. How she'd love to be out here for
ever, but it was no good, for she had responsibilities and those
all of her own making. Ten minutes of longing and resolution
before pulling out of the lay-by, an easy three point turn on a
wide empty road and a return.

Hearing the welcome sound of the car crunching onto the
stone chipped driveway, Hazel swept the two little ones up, a
strong arm round each, and carried them down the wide
staircase, out onto the path to meet their mum. She'd gathered
Roberta had been upset about something and hoped, hoped very
sincerely, that it hadn't had anything to do with her and the
stupid way she'd behaved last night. She'd tossed and turned all
night, wishing she'd not been so cheap, so exhibitionist,
desperately wanting to return to the father/daughter concept
without any sexy overtones. Okay, she knew that he knew that
she was feeling her wants an awful lot more, but he really should
behave like a proper husband and not like a, what was the
phrase, a Lothario. She'd seen the word somewhere. Abby was
wriggling and about to get dropped. Chris, surprisingly, was
placid. She let them both slide down and toddle towards Roberta,
walking slowly toward her. That expression boded no good.

'Morning, Hazel. Where's my husband?'

'Gone for a walk.' She made no comment on how he'd
reacted.

'I need to talk to you. Which way did he go?'

'Up the hill road. Said he needed to think, he'd be back in half an hour or so, and not to worry if you returned. When you returned, sorry.'

'Come inside. Let the terrors crawl about. No, second thoughts, I'll cuddle Abby. You keep Chris.'

She wasted no time, with Hazel inescapably pinned down on the settee by a restless Chris. Abby she bounced on her knee while she talked.

Hazel felt like a ten year old caught doing something really naughty. She knew she'd gone red and her feminine reactions were kicking in. How on earth had Roberta worked out what she'd done last night, for she'd gone to bed by then and nothing had been said for her to overhear, so how? She knew she'd been foolish; her more adult mind had worked that out overnight and, as she'd already concluded, it could have ruined her standing with both of them. Her emotions welled up and the tears came. 'I'm sorry, Roberta.' What more could she say?

'The only thing in your defence, Hazel, is your delayed adolescence. Hormones are weird things and now yours are running away with you. I know my husband is the only male within reach and he, poor man, is far too susceptible. You did wrong, my girl, to flutter your wings in the way you obviously did. You must learn to control your own emotions. Any more mistakes and you'll have to find another position. I'm sorry, Hazel, but remember I did warn you, though I didn't expect my husband to be in your sights.'

'How did you guess, Roberta?' Her curiosity overcame her emotions, she had to know.

'Masculine reactions, my girl. Once wound up they take time to wear off. Any available female sending out 'come hither' signals stands a fair chance of getting laid, and I would certainly not like to think you become classified as available. It would do you no good at all, and possibly a lot of harm. Stay well back from that start line, Hazel, for all our sakes. I thought I'd gone through it all before we came.'

'Sorry,' she said again, rather pathetically, and wondered if she should now take the opportunity to ask about all these things she knew nothing about, other than from her inbuilt feminine instinct. 'I don't know a lot, Roberta. My mum wouldn't tell me anything. The girls at school excluded me from their chattering. The nurse explained about the monthlies but nothing else, said it wasn't her job. I'd have read things but I didn't know where to go. And I've never used computers or the Internet until Andrea showed me that time.'

So mum Mary had been right. The poor girl must have been left well and truly in the dark. 'When Andrew comes back, we'll leave him in charge and we'll go for a walk. Breakfast first, I'm ravenous.'

'Where did you go?'

Roberta smiled. 'I did an Andrew. Went off to think, and anyway, I can't use the mobile from up here, no signal. Mary needed to know we were all right. Don't worry, I won't do a runner.' She wasn't going to expand on her other problem.

To Andrew, she played it cool. 'Had to phone Mary, the phone doesn't work up here, you were fast asleep. So what's the problem?' She could tell he didn't like the idea she'd gone off with the 'new' car, without telling him – asking him – but the car was as much hers as his. 'I've cooked some bacon – it's in the oven. Keep an eye on the twins. Hazel and I are going up the hill – girly talk. See you in a bit.'

To give him his due, she thought he'd accepted the situation rather well, with a wry grin and an 'okay, dear'. She couldn't help giving him a kiss, dear man; it wasn't his fault that he was surrounded by temptation. What he'd say when – if – she laid Mary's suggestion at his door was anyone's guess. First she had to mount her own concept of how to sort Hazel out.

The day was warming up. By the time she and Hazel had gone the distance at a brisk walk they were both fair puffed, though being no more so than the younger girl gave her some satisfaction.

'Let's go down this track a ways. You okay?'

Hazel was all a-glow, her heart going at a fair old pace. Just as well the ground was dry because neither had seen fit to change shoes, not that fashion footwear was the order of the day, rather the more comfortable old flats. Amazing how they both had similar ideas on things to wear.

'Uh huh. You don't hang about do you? Is this a route march?'

Roberta laughed. 'No. A means to an end. For me, that is. Making sure there are no gremlins lurking in my metabolism anywhere. Having that blackout the other day was scary, I can tell you – but I reckon I know what caused it. Come on, let's go and park on that log.'

The track, used to haul out harvested timber, although deeply rutted, allowed them to reach a point where the treeline gave way to open views. The valley rolled out below them, the autumnal tints beginning to tinge the close canopy of the dense lower woods. Roberta took several lungfuls of the pine-scented air. Myriad deep pink spires of foxgloves edged the roughly heaped piles of stone and earth bulldozed to fashion the trackway and straggled lines of blackberry thorn strayed across their path. She picked her way across the ruts and reached the decaying bole discarded by the foresters. Just as well she'd worn an old skirt. Jeans may have been a better idea but she still detested them. Hazel she'd never ever seen in trousers, not once. Strange, that, until it clicked – she'd likely have been used as a role model.

Hazel was still coming, equally tentatively; her hair was all over the place but still looking great. Would that there was some lusty lad in the offing who'd love to take her deeper into the trees and do some educating. Birds and bees, etcetera. Until that day, she was *in loco parentis*. How much did the girl know? The said girl reached her, flounced her skirts, brushed them carefully under her to sit on the other flatter dry bit of the log, left her hands clasped in her lap and started to swing her legs. So wonderfully and oddly refreshingly old fashioned.

'Lovely up here. Never known anything like this before. So

quiet. And still. How far are we from the lake?'

'It's not a lake. It's the bay. Goes away to the right behind the hills and out to sea. The Atlantic; I gather they even get cruise ships in here. And we're about eight miles or so, more by road. I've been up here before. Two years ago.'

Hazel looked sharply round at her. 'With Andrew?'

'With Andrew. Before he and Sam were divorced. A naughty week. Great fun, though. We walked – scrambled – all the way up there.' Roberta waved her hand towards the high tops behind them. 'On a very hot day. I – er – we . . . ' She stopped, aware she might be going stupidly and unnecessarily red. No, she *wouldn't* give Hazel a blow-by-blow account. That memory was far too precious.

But Hazel was ahead of her. 'You made love in the open air? I'm envious.' She stopped swinging her legs, pulled her skirt hem up and studied her thighs. 'Do you think I'd tempt anyone?' She knew she could, but wanted someone else to tell her.

Crunch time, Roberta. Give me strength, Mum. 'You're far too tempting, miss. You have a figure, lucky girl, to die for. A pretty face, lovely legs and gorgeous hair. Any red-blooded bloke would have you on your back in no time. Is that all you want, to be fucked?'

Hazel went bright red. *Fucked?* She knew the word, of course, but had never had it thrust into her face in this way before. 'I –er – '

Roberta kept her eyes firmly and determinedly on the view down the valley. 'And if – when – you do get inadvisably and unprotectively bounced, you may get pregnant. That means a baby, with all that that entails – and which you know very well takes a lot of time and effort – and money to support. The man who takes you may not care any more afterwards, 'cos all he wanted was to get inside and take his pleasure without concerning himself about *you*. *Bad move,* Hazel. It could be – though not necessarily – messy, sordid, unpleasant, potentially infectious and likely painful.'

Hazel smoothed her hem back down and unconsciously

171

moved her legs closer together. This she couldn't understand. Roberta and Andrew never gave the impression that their sex life was anything but lovely – from what she'd seen or overheard, which granted wasn't all that much, but even Andrea gave out 'I love being loved' signals – and she wasn't in a relationship that she knew about, other than the obvious wishful thinking one.

She had to be honest. 'I don't really know what happens. I can guess, and what with everything you see on the telly and so on, but no-one's actually explained. Properly, basically.'

'Ah. I thought not. Who, then, were you going to ask? And when? The first male who tears your knickers off? Far too late after that.' She thought back to her first time and shuddered. She would not wish that on anyone, least of all this precious young girl. Her mum had made a rash suggestion and that was disturbing, not to mention an intrusion into her relationship. 'You want *me* to tell you – in basic terms – what happens? What you should feel, if everything happens right?'

Hazel nodded. Her pulse was racing. She would know! How it happened, how she'd feel, what was expected of her. She'd be a *knowing* woman. *Yes!*

Roberta took a deep breath. Mary, mum Mary, had done her best at the time, but she'd learnt a lot since. Especially since Andrew. They'd loved because they did *love* each other, despite their faults and his wandering thoughts. That had just been the male in him, not the husband. His care did not diminish, nor his regard, not really; nor his ability to rouse her merely because his eyes wandered. Or his hands. Or, well, maybe not since. And they'd started from a different baseline, she his seducer, and he the seduced. She kept her eyes down, swung her legs just like Hazel had and started speaking like a college lecturer. It took her ten minutes, slowly, keeping the emotion and the tone as non–provocatively as she could. When she finished, she looked sideways at her listener. Hazel was still flushed.

'Well?'

'Is that why I get damp?'

Roberta raised her eyebrows and eyes to the skies above. Damp, this girl, already? Heavens. She continued, to expand far more than she'd intended, feeling a trifle jealous. She had to be *properly* involved before her system got going. 'Trigger point, Hazel. Once your body gets the idea that something – you know what – might happen, then the reflexes take over to make it easier all round. If it doesn't then you could be in for a hard and painful time and all the medical complications in train. Do you feel sort of dissatisfied when you dampen and you know nothing is going to ensue?'

The girl nodded. That's why she had messed things up last night, 'cos she wanted something to happen, though now Roberta had explained, she wasn't sure she'd have let him anywhere near her, whether he was an Andrew or just any other bloke.

'You can – er – sort yourself out.'

'Oh?'

'Mmmm. You really want to know? It's a rather life changing thing. Bit like a drug. Once you start it's difficult to stop. Not that it matters if you do or don't, but you have to remember to keep yourself very clean.' And she went on to explain with far more courage than she'd ever thought she could manage. 'And if you have a problem getting to the right place I may have to show you. Rather intimately.'

Hazel stood up. This was a lot to absorb. Rather exciting though. 'Thanks, Roberta. You're being a rather nice useful sort of surrogate mum.' She took a few careful steps across the track and stood on the top of the shallow bank to gaze out over the valley below seeing and not seeing. The peculiar sensation she was experiencing, deep down inside, was a mixture of impatience, of a longing, and more timely, an awareness of a now clearly defined urge. She turned back and her wistful questing look at Roberta spelt it out.

They walked back down the road hand in hand, in silence, each with their thoughts; a new level of relationship had been fashioned.

Andrew greeted them. 'You've been a long time. It's nearly lunchtime. These two are hungry. You all right, Hazel? You look somewhat flushed. Has Roberta been overdoing things for you?'

'I'm fine, thanks Andrew.' She caught Roberta's thoughtful eyes and gave an ever so slight nod with a bit of a grin. Overdoing things? No, she didn't think so. She'd be okay now she knew what she knew.

'Ham salad?'

Roberta very nearly giggled. After the morning's weirdly stressful experience she could do with something more substantial. 'Would you take the twins upstairs and give them a spring clean, please, Hazel – and yourself too, perhaps? Take your time. Lunch in half an hour.'

When the girl had taken the twins slowly upstairs and they heard the water running, Roberta pushed her husband into one of the big soft armchairs and sat on his knee. He wasted no time in an attempt at gentle and undemanding exploration, but she kept access difficult.

'Don't, Andrew, and I mean it. Not the time or the place. *No!* Listen carefully, darling, for I ain't ever going to repeat this, for her sake,' and ran through the gist of the reason for taking the girl up the hill, without going into the intimate details. She wouldn't want to stir his imagination; it was lively enough already as far as Hazel was concerned. 'Please, please, dear, keep her at a safe distance – like you always used to.' She thought of her early morning conversation with her mother but now totally dismissed the proffered suggestion. No way would she risk it. Not now. With the experience given and taken, the girl should be content for a while and with the ever far more evident commonsense she was displaying, unlikely that particular problem would rear its head again – and even if it did, well, she wouldn't really mind. Quite fun, actually, especially out in the wild because there was that *frisson* of excitement, for who knew if other eyes were about.

'You're taking a lot on yourself, R. Shouldn't her mum have . . .' but he had to stop, as her fingers came up to rest on his lips.

'Sshh; remember her mum's still unaware of her daughter's new status, love. I don't think she would anyway. Some mums' relationships with their offspring ain't going to be like mine and their daughters can't understand how beautiful it can be if their mothers pass on the proper thoughts. Sadly,' and she slid off his knee, stood up and pulled him after her. 'We've a lunch to make. No more to be said. Right?'

With a wry grimace, he nodded. This woman of his; how she managed to put such an interestingly different complexion on things!

THIRTEEN

Andrea was getting used to having the place entirely to herself. She'd even re-organised the filing system more to her taste – and re-labelled all the client folders to give a better indication of their status. What Roberta would think to the new colour coded stickers idea she wasn't sure – red was understandable, so was the grey, but pink and yellow? And green should be obvious too. The phone rang as she dropped the last one back into the file drawer.

'The Manor, Smiley Interior Designs, Andrea speaking, how can I help?' Technically of course, Smiley had given way to Hailsworthy but who would know that?

'By coming out to lunch with me.'

She thought she recognised the voice, however much time had passed and she'd all but forgotten. 'Alain?'

'The same. Can you spare a couple of hours at lunchtime? I'm in the patch and want to run an idea past you. Say half twelve in the Royal? I know it's not up to much but is nearby and we won't be disturbed. What do you say?'

She blinked. *Alain the film producer guy!* Wanted to see her? Why, for heaven's sake? Could she take a couple of hours? What was June doing, would she cover the phones? The prospect was both pleasing and daunting at the same time.

'Andrea?'

'Sorry, Alain. Thinking. Yes, probably okay. Give me a number; I'll give you a call inside half an hour. I'm on my own here and I need to get June to cover. How's the make-over programme coming on – we haven't heard from you?'

'Nearly there. Just a few voice-overs and some background shots. On your own? Where are all the others?'

'Ireland. On holiday. Back end of the week. Surely you remember Roberta had to be bribed to be nice to you?'

She heard his laugh; it sent shivers somewhere deep and, foolishly, she told herself, sounded rather sexy. Ridiculous girl; but he had left an impression in her mind.

'Half an hour. Please say yes.' The phone went dead.

June was fine with the idea. 'No problem; it's not as though we're overwhelmed with work, is it? Maybe it'll bring a few more clients rushing to the door out of sheer bloody mindedness! Take your time – oh, and do find out when it's going to be screened.'

'Don't worry, top of the agenda. Text me if you're desperate. It's less than quarter of an hour away.'

Alain was leaning on the bar in very relaxed fashion with a tonic water, elegant and groomed in light grey slacks, pale pink shirt, startling deep maroon neckerchief and the curly grey hair she remembered so well, combed straight back. The weather beaten look suited his features, all crinkly and smiling.

'*Andrea, darling girl!*' he was giving her a cheek-to-cheek kiss and holding her hand before she scarcely knew it. '*Luvverly to see you again!*'

She extricated herself carefully. 'Nice to see you again, too,' she answered, politely. 'On your own?'

'Good Lord yes. Don't have an entourage. Can't afford it. They don't know where I am anyway. This is quasi personal. Shall we go through? I've a table organised by the window. What would you like to drink – or shall we have a bottle at the table?'

'Bottle at the table', she replied, rather faintly. Quasi personal? Whatever did he mean?

'Good girl. My ideal.'

She found an arm round her waist and being propelled rather proprietarily into the dining room before she had a chance to breathe, and somehow wished she'd had a chance to change into something a bit more *him* than the office two piece

177

and simple blouse. He waited until she'd sat and made the gentlemanly gesture of helping her ease the chair forward before taking his seat opposite. Serviettes in place and menus studied, quick fire choices aimed at the waitress girl, wine ordered and then the bombshell.

'I want you to come and work for me, Andrea. Get you out of the doldrums; give you a chance to flex those lover-erly assets of yours. My P.A has gone all maternal and I need someone effective – and pretty. Much easier working alongside someone with a nice face and figure. And I know what you can do, because your Andrew didn't want to part with you. Told me to keep off. So I won't. What do you say, eh?'

He had a rather wicked look, mixed up with mischief, stern-ness and a hint of longing. Um. How old would he be? Why did she ask herself that? She leant back in her chair, took a full lungful of air and saw his eyes acknowledge the way her chest expansion pushed her boobs out under that stupidly formal office style blouse. Whatever would Andrew say – or Roberta, come to that, if she considered such an amazing bolt-out-of-blue offer? And the way her thoughts were running it wasn't as if she'd rejected the idea out of hand, was it?

'Why me?'

'Because I like you and, as I said, you're a looker and pleasant with it. And evidently efficient. And I want to give you a chance to become known. Reckon there might be an opportunity of some more screen work coming your way if you are seen.' The waitress was approaching with two large plates and a bowl cleverly balanced on her arm. The starters – which gave her a chance to think as Alain got stuck into his *moules marinière*. She toyed with her mixed *pâte* salad and wondered. The way her emotions had run her around since Andrew first appeared in her life hadn't exactly given her a chance – or a desire – to look around. But this wasn't a *relationship* he'd offered. Just a job with sexy undertones which was all part of the way these people behaved, all luvvy dovey. It would be fun, exciting, challenging. And she could always . . . no, if she left the Manor that would be it. They wouldn't want her back, would they? Especially if June was going to become a semi-permanent fixture, and young Hazel would be able to deal with most of the routines, of that she was sure. Whatever would Andrew say?

Alain wiped his chin for the umpteenth time and the pile of discarded shells grew higher. She took another polite mouthful then pushed her plate to one side; her appetite just wasn't there.

'I've floored you, have I? Sorry. No point in pussy footing about. Want some time to think on? Don't blame you.' He reached for the wine bottle in its chiller and eyebrowed his query. She nodded and he splashed a half glassful into her goblet. 'I need an answer within a week, ten days outside. Now, how about arranging the 'cast n'crew' showing of the thing we've done on the Manor for starters? Put an evening together for when the motley come back from the Emerald Isle? You can do that. I'll give you a budget, a guest list, the contacts on the technical side and leave it with you.' He pushed a card across the table. 'Ring Steph. She's the one you're replacing. She'll fill you in.'

'Where?' she faintly heard herself ask, as if she hadn't guessed.

'The little barn, where else? We don't need the Odeon at Leicester Square for this one!' and laughed. 'Oh, Andrea! You're made for this. Try it. It'll be fun.'

The rest of the meal went in a blur. She did manage to do some sensible justice to her lasagne and the rather nicely put together salad, stopped herself from drinking a full second – or was it a third – glass of the decent chardonnay and giggled at his comment about 'puddings' versus 'sweets'. She wouldn't have either. A coffee, yes, and a couple of those thin 'mess-up-your fingers if you weren't careful' mints, then it was time to go. A gentle hand on her back this time to see her out to the car park, another kiss on the cheek and untidy legs were swung into her little car.

'Nice legs, Andrea.' That cheeky smile again and she knew

179

he was honest and truly forthright and not a 'let's try it on' guy even if the innuendos were titillating.

'Thanks. And thank you. Forgive me if I'm a bit dazed. I'll ring.'

'You'd better, or I'll be back at the Manor telling them all how you behaved. Naughtily.'

He grinned at her again, shut her door and strode off towards his slinky pale grey metallic low-slung thing with scarcely any tyres. She hadn't a clue what it was, Porsche, Mercedes, Alfa Romeo, whatever.

She drove out of the car park very carefully, knowing how totally irresponsible she actually was. She should really have left the car there and got him to run her back.

'He *what?*'

'Offered me a job. Sort of P.A. The current model's got herself pregnant.'

June's eyebrows went up a notch or two and she frowned. 'Not his?'

'Lord, no. Happily wed, apparently. And she won't be coming back, 'cos she believes in being a proper mum, so she's said, according to him. So it's not just a temporary thing.' Andrea supported her muzzy head on her hands, propped up elbows on the desk. 'I don't know what to do, one part of me says go for it, another's telling me not to be stupid, being tempted by the glamour thing. It's all a bit sudden.'

'You're worried what my father will say, aren't you? That you owe him – and Roberta – and . . . '

'And that I'll miss him? You *know*, don't you?'

'That you've had a fling with him? Yes, I do. Bloody obvious. Just surprises me how amazingly accommodating Roberta's been all this time. If it had been me I might have seen him off ages ago. Dodgy, very dodgy.'

Andrea laughed at June's face. 'You're right.' Then she went all quiet and serious. 'Yes, I'll miss him. Of course I will. I ... ' She swallowed and tried again. 'If Roberta hadn't happened ... '

June said nothing. If Roberta hadn't happened and Andrea

had been her father's only bit on the side, her mum might still be married to him, though what the relationship would have been like goodness only knows.

' . . . I might have been unavailable. And pregnant.'

Her confidante shook her head. 'Is that what you want, a family?'

'I don't know what I want,' she replied somewhat hesitantly, and then remembered the day her father had died and she'd collapsed by the old beech tree. She'd wanted to be cuddled, held, *wanted,* and the hesitation vanished. Far more positively she went on to say 'Yes. I want a family, June. A husband, partner, whatever, someone who cares for me, hugs me, takes me to bed, looks after me. Is that too much to ask? I'm knocking on thirty.'

'I don't think I'm the right person to proffer advice, Andrea. I may be married, but that's about the long and short of it. Not much cuddling let alone caring. Heaven knows why I married him.' The wry grin, thinking 'like father, like daughter' again, before suppressing the thought almost as soon as it had come. She – and Peter – were the living proof that her father and her mum had gone a fair old way down the road before they'd run out of steam. Idly, she wondered how her younger brother was – Peter had followed his mother out to Romania to help on the orphan front.

'Seems your father and Roberta are the only stable ones around here, then. P'raps it's the second time round version that succeeds. Maybe if I get a crush on someone else it'll work better.' She spun round on the office chair and looked up at June, propped up against the doorjamb looking terribly Andrew-ish. She swallowed, if only to try and quell the sudden lurching overly familiar wrench in her gut she got when reminded of him and his absence. 'Do you think I should talk to him?'

'My father? Yes, of course I think you should. When he gets back, Andrea. It's just a few days. Give yourself time to think it through. It's the only fair and right thing to do. One other thing though.'

'Hmmm?'

'If you do go, it'll mean Hazel stands a fair chance of being promoted. And I'll have to seriously consider staying on permanently, too.'

'An ill wind, June. Let's go and have a cuppa. I'm parched. Far too much alcohol at lunchtime. And no doubt Mary will have words on the subject.'

'You'll tell her?'

'Of course. After all, she is the power behind the throne.'

June giggled. 'Some throne. But you're right.' She pushed herself off her support and held out her arms. 'Andrea, come. Luv you.'

'Leave the Manor?'

Andrea nodded. 'I've not said yes, Mary. It's just an offer.'

'Hmmphh.'

'That's a very expressive reaction, Mary.' June grinned at Andrea across the table. 'I told her you'd express an opinion.'

'Hmmphh. I'd say nought, but seeing as you asked. Best thing, lass. You can't stay here all your life and high time you was wed. No, don't go on, I knows how Mr Andrew . . .' and she stopped. No, she would not demean her daughter's reputation, not even to these two girls, precious though they were in their own individual rights. 'If this Alain has seen fit to offer you a position after the filming thing, then he must ha' seen summat in you. Best wait till himself gets back.'

'I'm not leaving on the presumption I need to in order to marry, Mary.' She got a sharply turned head and a very old fashioned look and grinned. 'But I guess there may be more of an opportunity out there than amongst what clients come our way.' They were still staring at her. 'Oh, all right, then. I'm minded to take him up on his offer. And oh, I nearly forgot. He wants me to organise a cast and crew preview of the filming we did – back here, in the little barn.'

All the response she got to that announcement was an awed silence, but then she hadn't properly worked out how she was going to tell them nor therefore anticipated what reaction she could expect; it came out as a spur of the moment thing.

Finally Mary frowned. 'It's up to Roberta to say. Not yoursen.'

June agreed. 'He shouldn't presume, Andrea. Nor you. You told me how Roberta reacted to him calling her '*Rob*' and that display set demolition idea. If you set about organising something behind their backs you won't need to think about leaving. You'd be pushed. Ho hum. You'll have to stall, unless you ring, then you'll have to say why and the cat will be let loose. Oh dear.'

Another silence and Andrea buried her head in her folded arms on the table, trying hard not to let emotion get the better of her. June walked round to stand behind her and started to massage the girl's shoulder blades, feeling the tautness of her neck muscles gradually subside.

'You don't have to respond immediately, love. Do you?'

Andrea lifted her head. 'S'pose not. I've got to ring this Steph girl he wants me to replace. I can leave it until tomorrow. Oh, bloody hell!'

'I know. Life's a bitch. Could be worse.' June slackened her pressure. 'There, that better?'

A deep sigh. 'Mmmm. Thanks, June. I'd best get back to the office. Can't let the business go to the dogs just because I'm being childish.' She moved to get up and June stepped back.

Mary, impassive expression in place, had her arms folded and had kept her own counsel after telling the Andrea girl what was what. It was up to the lass to work things out. She reached for the mugs to clear the table as the two girls left the kitchen and shook her head as she wondered. Would it work out for Andrea? Interesting times ahead. Had Roberta sorted out young Hazel's problems? And had she talked through her condition with Andrew? The twins, too, were they properly managing with this holiday jaunt?

183

Alain had watched her go, suddenly conscience struck – in the realisation she was very probably over the limit and he should have insisted he took her back, not that she would have been very co-operative. He deadened his concern by telling himself she didn't have far to go, that it was unlikely there were any bored traffic police around at this time of day and anyway, she gave the impression of being a steady sort of driver. His mobile purred at him. Stephanie.

'Hi girl. . . . yep. Be right back. . . no, don't say. . . Good girl.' Now she was going on a bit. 'Can't be sure, Steph. Tell you when I return. Oh, and cancel Suzie, there's a dear. I can't cope with her this afternoon. Some other time. I'll ring her. . . yes, sorry, but you're better at saying these things than me. See you in fifteen, twenty.'

Would Andrea do all these essential things as well as darling Steph? He shrugged, clipped his belt and spun the Mercedes thoughtlessly out of the car park in a shower of loose gravel. As he headed out towards the M40 en route for Slough his mind had to home in on the picture of her across the table, that bouncy gold head of curls, the steady eyes, the dimples as she smiled, the shape of her under those drab work-a-day clothes. If she accepted his offer he'd take her shopping. Why was he doing this? There were half-a-dozen women in the system who'd leap at the chance of being his p.a. and were infinitely better qualified than an Andrea. There'd be some snide glances if his plan succeeded. Was he being honest in believing a new face and new ideas, new habits, fresh thinking would be worth the hassle? Or was it because she'd grabbed at his emotions with her haughty stance and that *je ne sais quoi* approach? Beautiful girl. At least he was honest in saying someone would – might – see her and look to cast her in some role or other. Even him. He kept the car at a steady sixty, closing his mind to the boy-racer types trying to goad him to excess speed and saw Hazel, the other younger girl in his wandering mind's eye.

Another looker, though ever so slightly odd. Something about her suggested she wasn't fully with it, though she'd brightened up remarkably quickly in front of the camera. Too young. He dismissed her from his thoughts and saw his side turn-off coming up. Steph would give him a knowing look when he got in. *'Business lunch, hah,'* she'd said before he left. *'I know you.'* When he'd explained she'd been slightly mollified. *'Make sure I get a chance to vet her before the ink dries on her contract,'* she'd suggested. *'Don't want some amateur looking after my boss.'* He'd given her a peck on the cheek and thought, weirdly, of the Bond sequences where Moneypenny had been just as proprietorial. He grinned as he turned in through the big iron gates, got a hand waved acknowledgement from the security guy, drove carefully down the tree lined drive to the Art Deco office block and slid the car gently to a stop in his space. Moneypenny. He'd tell her, which would make her day. Had Andrea got back safe and sound? Of course she had. He'd ring her later on.

June wasn't at all sure. Not that she knew this Alain guy or what had gone on, or not as the case may be, during the filming thing, though she could well imagine how any proper male would react if the Andreas – or Hazels, come to that, strutted their stuff in front of a camera lens. Was this offer Andrea had had flung at her a 'must have her' follow-up or, hopefully, for her sake, a meaningful thing? And how would her dad react? Logic said both he and Roberta would see it as a good move and accept matters, especially as they'd got Hazel in the frame, and she, the daughter and step daughter of the 'business partners', was quite prepared to buckle down to a proper role. She also guessed Roberta would secretly be pleased to see the back of an ever-present temptation. On the other hand, would her dad become grumpy and a pain without the side attraction? There was always Hazel. In the meantime, she had the customers – sorry, clients, – to see to. Business came first.

Andrea settled into her chair, wriggled her bottom, peered at the screen and attempted to come to terms with the prospect that all she'd become so used to over the past months might well be history if she said yes. Everything she'd dreamt of after the Brewery's collapse, striven for, sacrificed her virginity for, all the stress and emotion; the strange push-pull relationship with Roberta, all to become a thing of the past. All the carefully thought out filing system worthless, the *rapport* she'd built up with their suppliers and the business clients no longer hers. A completely new environment, new contacts, new systems, and the thought she'd be responsible for organising the day-to-day arrangements of a guy like Alain? The prospect he'd been so upbeat over, that she'd be back in front of a camera lens? Her? An office girl from the back street Brewery running the life of a mainstream film, well television, actually, producer, director, whatever? The screen blanked. She moved the mouse again and tried to concentrate.

Mary wiped the work surfaces down automatically. These girls. And just as she'd thought they'd got life pretty well sorted, Andrea thinking of leaving? Time to get the dinner on. Just as well Hazel had turned out the way she had. Of course she was proud the way her Roberta had worked out why the girl had been backward; mind you, them problems she'd spoke of on the phone would take some sorting, seeing as how she'd not had the chance to learn about things naturally, like. Should have seen that coming. T'was really the girl's mother's job, but that one wasn't well blessed with much common sense. Hope Andrew kept his head. Only a few days to go. 'Bout time, much longer and the place wouldn't be the same. Too many bosses.

FOURTEEN

This was too good to be true. Bright sunshine, blue blue sky seen through the Ventolux and she felt absolutely on top of the world. 'Andrew?'

All she got in response was a muffled grunt-like noise that could have been interpreted as anything, from a 'morning' to a 'leave me alone'. She wriggled up and took a better look through the big window. Marvellous. She ruffled his hair, the only bit visible.

'Wake up, darling. It's a super day out there. I've got plans,' and used her toe to advantage. 'That is, if you want to.'

'Want to what?' His head came off the pillow and he twisted about to look at her. 'What are you scheming now? And mind what you're doing down there.'

'Why, are you fragile? Come on, dear. Too good a day to waste,' and she totally abandoned the foolish fleeting idea of encouraging his baser instincts, flinging herself out of bed at the same time burying him in the duvet and padded into the bathroom, slipping the bolt. Sometimes he was getting to be a real old stick-in-the mud. The early days of constant flirtaceous preludes to a sexy romp seemed to have ebbed away, apart from the occasional randomly inspired moments. Like out on the island, although that wasn't anything near like the full-blown orgy they used to have. Too many distractions. So would her idea work? The shower on full blast nearly scalded her; the swift reaction to turn it down brought a contrastingly cold douche that stung and made her cross. '*Damn!*'

The door rattled. 'Roberta? I need the loo!' She heard him, just, and was minded to pretend she hadn't. The early morning euphoria was evaporating.

'Won't be a moment!' Now the imagined quarter hour of bliss under the shower had been blown away all she could do was pretend she was clean, towel down and let him have the benefit of the steamy warm place. He'd be an age; he always took far longer than her for some inexplicable reason. Once they used to mostly shower together, a mutual back lathering session often ending up in a slippery gymnastic conjoining more fun than . . .

At least she got a kiss, sort of.

'So what was this plan of yours?' She was dressed, he finalising his towel-down with special attention to his toes, foot up on the bed. She smoothed her hair back, critically inspecting the result in the mirror. Why hadn't he suggested it? Surely he hadn't forgotten?

'Hazel will look after the twins. We'd have the day on our own. It's a pretty good day for a scramble up the hill. *Our* hill. For old time's sake?'

'Ah.'

Was that all, for heaven's sake? A mere 'ah' as a reaction to the best day ever in their – her – memory bank? He didn't even look pleased, let alone romantically inspired. Was there still something wrong with them? Her heart skipped a beat, or was that a figment of novelistic imagination? This would not do, no, not at all, and she thought she'd got her mind straight after the Jerpoint incident?

'Sure she can cope? It's quite a hike up there, and if anything goes wrong . . .'

'The girl's twenty, for heaven's sake, Andrew, and a good deal saner than she ever was. If we can't trust her now . . . we shan't get another opportunity. Don't you want to?'

She watched him, watched him look out of the window at the challenge of the climb, the allure of the hill. It was what he always had wanted to do, long walks through rough country; what had initially brought them together and nothing she wanted more than to share the challenge with him and seek her reward up there, lying on her back in the warmth of the sun on long soft grass with the sky above . . . just as Sheila had said that time, ages ago.

'Okay. If you're sure.'

She took a long deep breath. Would it be the same? She could but try.

They said goodbye to the twins who didn't seem at all bothered now that Hazel had the large rug out on the lawn with interesting things spread all over it for them to build, knock down, throw about or even try and eat.

'You'll be all right with them? I mean, we're not sure how long we'll be, maybe several hours?'

'Surely,' Hazel came back at her with a relaxing smile, 'it's not as though it's anything new – and I can always wave a red towel or something – you said you can see the house and garden from up there, didn't you? No, I'll be fine. You have a lovely day.' She turned back to the improvised play area in time to stop Abby from hitting Chris with a small plastic spade. 'Hoi, that's not what it's for! Give it here! Go on, Roberta. Enjoy yourselves.'

Andrew shouldered the small rucksack, picked up his stick and opened the gate. He had mixed feelings, liking the day and the prospect of stretching his legs on the hill, not liking the risk of something happening that would cause them to regret leaving Hazel with the responsibility. Roberta caught up with him and took his free hand, hoping.

'As she said, darling, it's not as though she hasn't looked after them before. Don't worry. Just let's make the best of the day. It may rain tomorrow.'

He had to grin. That was what was known as stating the obvious. He swung her hand in his, 'True,' he said and turned his head to look at her. Still the same Roberta, sparklingly mischievous eyes with the glinting amber specks above the deep brown, still the bouncing shining hair, still the dimples when she smiled her beautiful smile. Still the same schemer. They strode on, round the bend in the narrow lane where the incline grew steeper. The house roof had disappeared below the trees.

She seemed preoccupied, eyes fixed on the road way and the need to avoid the occasional dangling or trailing bit of hedgerow vegetation, concentrating on getting her breathing into tempo with their striding pace. Still a fair bit of this road to do before they took to the hill and the climb to the wood began. They strode on, in silence, absorbing the peace and the gentle warmth of the morning, allowing the steady rhythm to bring muscles into tone. It was going to be a glorious day and she was so so right to have suggested this. A return to the old feeling, something of the heady recklessness that had been akin to a drug. He squeezed the handhold a little, caught her glance and the grin and knew it was going to be fine.

Hazel lay back on the rug, knees up, and let the twins crawl over her. Chris loved pulling and twisting her hair, little monster, but Abby was content to curl up against her arm and suck her thumb. That's what she did best. Her mind drifted, into the way her life had changed, become more, what, rounder, fuller, more demanding? Given her new challenges, certainly, and opened up new horizons. She still loved the job and these two little infants, reaching round to stop Chris pulling at her ear. She loved the twin's parents too, and especially Roberta's mum. Without her none of this would have happened and she'd have been stuck in some menial job in a shop or something. She certainly wouldn't have been in a TV programme, or been able to wear what she did. No, life was fine. No regrets, well, not really. Others of her age would have – might have – done all sorts of other things, like been to all the groovy nightclubs, had dates with six boys in as many days, experimented with drugs, had their hair dyed three colours in a month. Worn skimpy skirts or super tight jeans. Walked about on four-inch heels. Started to worry about where the next tenner was coming from. Lived in crummy back-street smelly houses, thinking about her mum's place. Or not, thinking about Roberta's background. Some would be brainy, go to university, land well paid jobs. They may even have had loads of sex and started a baby either accidentally or on purpose. It's what girls did. Even Roberta – and her mum. Would she? Chris, fed up with his hand being held firmly to stop him from hair twisting, pulled at her and she let him go, watched him crawl over and start stacking the plastic tubs in a row. He was going to be one bright kiddo. If she had a baby of her own, would it feel different? Was that what she wanted? Roberta had, and had these two – 'Hey, Chris, don't!' Her Andrew must have been all she wanted – given her happiness – 'No. *No!* Leave it!' – and now she had a yearning all of her own. 'Come on you two; let's give you some more breakfast.' She sat up, disturbing Abby's quiet doze, struggled to her feet and taking Chris by the hand, Abby rather haphazardly under the other arm, managed to get them into the kitchen and safely into their chairs before escaping to the loo.

The lane was petering out. The hill access would be the other side of the rough pasture with its mini hills and hollows, and the gate defied all sane attempts to open it, given there was no proper latch but a tangled knot of old baler twine; the hinges had long since given up.

'Up and over, R.'

She hitched up her old skirt and took a tentative step onto the second bar. The gate sagged but held as she swung a lovely thigh up and over as ordered, sat briefly on the top and dropped. Andrew did a successful vault.

'Show off.'

'You could have if you'd worn trousers.'

She wrinkled her nose at him. 'Far too hot and sticky. Why don't you wear shorts?'

'With my legs? I'm no Adonis. Anyway, trousers protect against stings, scratches and bites.'

'True. Did you bring the cream?'

'I did. Now come on.' He led the way through the gap in the overgrown grass and nettles, heading for the far corner. Amazing how it was all coming back, even after all this time. It could have been last week.

She plodded after him, picking her way. Perhaps

lightweight trousers weren't such a bad idea. At least she had decent socks and better boots, but trousers weren't as sexy, now were they? How was Hazel coping?

The twin's second breakfast wasn't going too well. She guessed she had overdone it a bit, so maybe she'd skip a lunch for them. So long as they kept up the liquid levels and she rinsed the plastic beakers out and refilled them with cool water. Better that than sugary stuff; if she had anything to do with it, these two would be the healthiest pair out. The beakers handed over, the said pair appeared to have a 'who can drink it first' competition, with two hands per beaker and rude slurping noises. Great kids, both of them. Would they go down and have a mid morning nap? Then she could have a spot of sunbathing and read more of her intriguing novel. Better than scrambling over rocks in this heat, wondering how they were getting on up on the hill.

The hill rose steeply before them, the horizon suddenly close up and meaningful and they had to scramble. Had it really been as precipitous before? A clump of rocks appeared to the right, the ground levelled off in front of them as they struggled on and the next chunk of terrain hove into view, a sort of valley, though the highest point was still not apparent.
'Looks like a boggy bit. We'll keep to the edge, love.'
She eyed the bright green area with the sludgy orange mottled bits and nodded. 'I don't fancy being up to my knees in that lot. Round to the left?'
'Reckon.' He glanced at his watch. They'd been going just over the hour and nowhere near the crest as far as he could remember. The wooded area was way over to their right, the route they'd take on the return. 'You okay?'
'Yep. Fine.'
It wasn't bad going now, a lot less of a slope with more surface rock and smoother grass that may well have been sheep or rabbit nibbled. A small brown bird appeared, flew off to sit on a stunted thorn bush and chirp at them.
'Skylark?'

'Or linnet?'

'Don't know. Have to buy a bird book. I thought skylarks were always up top and singing.'

'Like that one?'

She craned her neck, squinted into the sun with hand shielding her eyes and saw a speck, the trilling noise registering for the first time. 'Could be. Hope we don't tread on a nest.'

'Not much chance. Far too late on.' He viewed the next bit and strode on up.

With a heave, she stepped up onto the rock, hopped across to next one and followed his lead. Still okay, thank heavens. Hope Hazel's all right with the twins.

Happily, they were being as good as gold. Fast asleep on the couch, bless 'em. She'd give them an hour. Back out into the sunlight, thought of and acquired a cushion, stretched out on the rug and pushed a plastic cup out of the way so she could tuck the cushion under her head. She picked up the book and found her place. This was the life. The sun was jolly hot now; perhaps she'd get some tan. She pulled her skirt right up one handedly, other thumb in her place, but it didn't want to stay bunched. 'Pain,' she said out loud, put the book down, stood up, unfastened the zip and shed it, lying back down on top as an extra cushion. Bare legged now, she could feel the warmth. Great. Ten minutes later the book slid and she didn't feel it go.

The terrain certainly had become more hill-like, far rockier and a lot easier. They'd avoided two more boggy areas, peered curiously into the absolutely clear waters of a pond, wanting to see some sign of other life but nothing, not even a tadpole.

'Wrong time of year,' said Andrew, feeling incredibly knowledgeable. 'But look, there's a frog!'

'Well spotted! Isn't he gorgeous?' She bent down to see if she could catch it but no, it hopped out of reach into a patch of reeds. 'Oh well, I guess he doesn't appreciate the chance of being turned into a prince.'

'Or princess?'

She did her narrowed eyes look at him. 'You'd like that, wouldn't you? Instant sexy princess on a mountain top?'

He laughed. 'Competition? Wonder what she'd be wearing?'

'By the look of that, turdy green top and mottled brown trousers. Ve-reey fetching! Betcha she'd have a slimy kiss, too.'

'Hmmm.' There really wasn't an answer to that. He hopped across onto the next rock in line and she shrugged and followed him.

It took them the best part of another hour to finally achieve what was conceivably the highest point. Another hill across a fair old depth of a valley could have been higher but impossible to gauge. It could have been where they'd got to last time but he couldn't be sure. One rock much like another, but the view hadn't changed. Marvellous. Roberta chose her spot carefully and equally carefully lowered herself down, smoothing skirt fabric under her, lay back and let her head rest on her hands.

'Wake me up in half an hour.'

Andrew sat down, pulled his knees up and studied the view. The glimpse of the bay below the tree line and the run of the smaller hills across the south shimmered, totally out of focus in the haze. Worth it? Most definitely. And neither of them out of puff either. He fished in the rucksack for the water bottle.

'Drink?'

'Hmmm?' She sat up, one hand supporting her as she turned. 'Oh, yes. And an apple, please.' He passed her the bottle, dug deeper into the bag and found her an apple. He took one himself, bit deeply as she slurped.

'Don't drink it all, R. Leave some for later.'

She wiped her mouth on the back of her hand and passed the bottle back. 'That's good. Still cool. Thanks,' and bit into her apple too.

They sat, biting, nibbling and chewing as the heat built up around them. 'You realise this is totally abnormal for Ireland?'

'Is it? We've been up here twice and it's been hot both times.'

'Lucky old us. Wouldn't like to be up here when it rains.'

'Which it does. Frequently. Why Ireland's so green.'

''Spose so.' She heaved her apple core away.

'Litter lout.'

'Bio-degradable. Not litter. Anyway, some bird or other will find it. Not as though it's a drink tin or bottle, or orange peel. Or a cigarette packet.' She thought of something else but didn't add that to the list. Far too suggestive and indicative of the way her mind was playing up. She lay down again, shielding the sun with her eyes.

'Where's your hat, dear?'

'Oh yes. I'd forgotten. In the rucksack.'

He dug it out and gave it to her. She straightened the flimsy linen to suit and let it rest over her forehead. Within a couple of minutes he swore he heard her snore.

. . . Hazel woke up with an itch, lifted her head and peered at her legs; saw a horrible big black hairy fly sitting on her thigh. 'Gettorff!' she nearly screamed, and kicked. The fly took off and she leant forward to look. Yes, a big blotchy red mark, as best she could see with sun-glazed eyes. She rubbed at the swelling; she'd not ever had anything like this happen to her before, the odd little bite maybe, nothing like this. It was horrid, *horrid.* In her annoyance and confusion she forgot about the twins until she heard a yell. The twins! Oh, no!

. . . This was all very well but time was moseying on. 'Roberta!' She'd have red bits above her socks, that was for sure, the rest of her was covered. His arms were beginning to feel sore, so no doubt he'd got them burnt too. What a pain! 'We'd best get on, darling.' She didn't stir.

He got up off his perch on the rock to move her hat. Her eyes were still closed. 'Roberta!' He shook her gently, but got no response.

195

. . . Oh, lord, whatever would Roberta say! The bruise was beginning to show and the little girl was screaming her head off. Chris's face was puckering up, as if he was going to follow suit. Had she damaged anything else? Tenderly, Hazel undid her buttoned up top, and began to check, arms, legs, no, nothing else, everything moved properly. Just her forehead then, where she'd landed on the floor. Why hadn't she woken earlier? Why hadn't she wedged her in securely? Why hadn't she put the old duvet on the floor, in case? Roberta would kill her, if Mr Andrew didn't. A careful look at Chris, no, he wouldn't roll out, not while he was awake anyway; she carried a tearful Abby into the bathroom, sat on the bath stool, laid her across her lap, reached for the tissues, moistened one and started to brush her forehead, letting the damp cool her off. Gradually the tears abated, the hiccups came instead of the cry. 'Oh Abby, Abby darling, I'm so so sorry. I wouldn't have had this happen for the world!' How could she have been so careless, so stupidly confident? Abby's eyes, full of tears, caught at her, at her emotions, and her eyes, too, started to water.

. . . Up on the hill, Andrew was panicking; it seemed she'd gone unconscious like that time at Jerpoint. He'd felt for her pulse, found it after a struggle, he never had been overly good at that, however it seemed to be there, if not very strong. She'd not stirred and he resisted the temptation to shake her again. Finally he resorted to wetting his hankerchief and laying it on her forehead. No way could he carry her, not all the way down the hill, and to call someone out on the mobile – assuming he had a signal – would be terrible. *'Roberta! Roberta, darling, wake up!'* The first ever moment he'd seen her, in a heap on the grass after that horse had tipped her off swum vividly back into his mind. Was this scenario never going to go away? How long had she been in this state? Covered by her hat, he'd not have known.

. . . Abby's little hands rubbed at her eyes, before the

vestige of a smile, an Abby smile. Hazel picked her up off her lap, cradled her, rocked her, and kissed at the swelling bruise. Then she remembered bruises needed a cold compress or something and found the flannel, wet it with one hand, laid it carefully on the bruise, waited for another yell, which didn't come, and hoped for the best.

. . . What on earth was the matter with her? He should have had her checked out after that collapse at Jerpoint, though she'd seemed to be perfectly normal afterwards and they'd put it down to a tummy thing. *'Roberta!'* He dampened the hankerchief again and stroked her brow, brushed the hair back. It seemed so desperately silly, up here on the top of a goddamned hill with his most precious girl in a seeming coma. He'd have to call for help and fished the mobile out of his pocket. The wretched thing was flat, no screen light, no anything. How could he have been so bloody effing stupid!

. . . Hazel carried her through, back to the cot this time instead of the couch, kissed the bruise again, laid her down, prayed for the best, and thought Chris was marvellous, just lying there watching. *'Mama,'* he said, *'Want mama.'*

'Yes, darling, I'm sure you do.' *So do I,* she thought. To sooth him she picked him and hugged him, then laid him down in his cot in turn. She didn't want any more accidents, thank you. How long before the parents returned? It was lunchtime and though the twins weren't going to need anything other than another drink, she did. A sandwich perhaps. Gosh, but it was getting warm. Wonder what it's like up on the hill? She would have loved to have gone as well; she'd never done any proper walking, not that sort. Perhaps she could get Andrew to take her if Roberta would let him and the weather stayed good . . .

. . . He turned back to her, lying so peaceful and still, hair spread around, as though she was asleep. Which she was, but unconscious – whatever could he do? His eyes pricked, his heart pounded, his tummy was all squeezed up and suddenly nauseous. He couldn't lose her; whatever was happening – if the worst came to it he'd just have to get back down to raise help.

'*Roberta!*' he dropped down on his knees beside her, felt her forehead, – not hot, – laid anxious lips on hers.

Andrea shut the system down. Enough. Time to go home. The afternoon's concentration on the routines hadn't stopped the lunchtime revelation from going round and round her brain to the detriment of her usual efficiency; she'd had to re-do the accounts three times – which would have made Andrew hoot, he always managed to do these things effortlessly. Andrew – oh lor – what would he say? The hard disk's whir subsided, she pushed the chair – the chair – *oh, stop it, Andrea* – back, stood up, stretched, smoothed her skirt down, picked up her little bag and shut the office door behind her. How many more times?

'I'm off, Mary! Say 'bye to June for me.'

'All right, lass. Take care. Regards to your mum.'

Routine, the oft repeated words. Familiar. Comforting. How many more times? She went out to her little car, thankful the afternoon had lessened her chances of having over much lunchtime alcohol left in her system, especially after two mugs of tea. She drove home in a very steady fashion, unlike her usual dash down the country lanes.

Her mother was in the front room, doing the ironing. As though her father was still out at work, not just the memory and a photo on the fireplace; despite they'd never been close she still mourned the emptiness in their lives. How would her mum react to the momentous news – and why wasn't she rushing to tell her? Because she didn't know whether she had made up her mind to accept the offer, or what?

'Hi, mum! Mary sends her regards.' *As usual.*

'Had a good day, An?' The iron went *thud*, down onto the rest. 'Cup of tea?'

198

'Might as well.' *The usual things.* 'I've been out to lunch.'

'That's nice, dear. By yourself?' Her mother's voice rose in a curious way. Well, girls didn't usually go to lunch by themselves, now did they? Andrea put the kettle on as her mum came through into the kitchen.

'No, mum, not by myself.' She reached up for the mugs and the teabags. 'Went to the pub. With Alain.'

'Who?'

'Alain. He's the producer – sorry, director, – of the telly programme.' The kettle was starting to sing and she had to raise her voice. 'He's offered me a job.'

Her mother reached forward and flicked the switch. The kettle's noise stopped. *'Offered you a job? What, in television?'*

She could tell by the tone of voice disapproval was in there somewhere. Oh, dear. 'Not really, well, sort of. His P.A. is leaving to have a baby and he's asked me to take her place.' She put the switch back down. 'You did say I had to think about moving on, mum.'

'A *P.A.?*'

Andrea had to grin. 'Yes. Personal assistant. Sort of Girl Friday.'

'Girl Friday?'

'Yes. You know, super secretary. Thinks for him, organises. Tells him what to do. He said it'd be fun. I think it would be, too. And I might get noticed for another telly role or something.' The kettle had boiled and she poured water into the two mugs. 'He's a nice guy. Not at all pushy or pawing.'

'So you'll accept?'

'I might. What do you think?' Andrea reached for the fridge door to abstract the milk jug. 'Could be the lucky break.'

Her mum picked up her mug and cautiously sipped, 'Ouch. That's hot,' took the proffered jug and splashed milk into the steaming tea. Andrea eyed her mother – this confusion was telling, normally she was so precise, tea bag out, milk, sip, more milk; sipping without milk unheard of.

'Mum! Take the tea bag out!'

'What? Oh, yes.' She fished around with the spoon. 'How will your Andrew react?'

'He's not my Andrew; he's Roberta's. He'll have to get used to it – and anyway, there's Hazel.'

'Hazel?'

'Yes. You know, the girl they took in to help Mary with the B & B and so on. She turned out to be far more intelligent than they gave her credit for – I tried her out on the computer at work and she surprised me. So I don't feel too bad about leaving.' Curiously and maybe inconsequentially she added, 'Of course, she's a very pretty girl as well.'

Her mother sniffed. 'Essential qualification for the Manor's office?'

'You could say that,' Andrea replied, dryly. 'But a lot younger than me. Well, eight or ten years, I guess. And very much Mary's protégée. And then there's June as well, you know, his daughter.'

'I thought she had a job back home. She wouldn't travel, surely?'

'I think she's got a relationship problem. Bit like her father, only in reverse. Her William's gone off to the States on some computer course. So she gave in her notice and – you know, I told you!'

'So you did. Sorry. Well, if you want to move on, you do, my girl. You're old enough to make up your own mind. But you'd have to find digs or something, wouldn't you? I mean, this job isn't around here?'

'No, it isn't.' Rather weirdly she hadn't asked and he hadn't said either. P'raps he thought she'd know. 'Would you mind, mum? Being left on your own?' Something she knew might make the world of difference to her ultimate decision; if her mum couldn't cope then it was a non-starter.

Her mother shrugged. 'I'd manage. You should have gone long since, not that either your father or I wanted you to. No, An, you want the job, you take it.'

He'd been so surprised and at first extremely cross with her, putting him through the entire gamut of trauma, all that heart stopping worrying concern for her before the huge relief that left him all weak-kneed and then the humour of her play-acting, followed by the joy of knowing it was only an act and finally the unstoppable passion in her. And now the reality setting in as it eventually had to even after the mind-blowing way they'd loved.

'Perhaps we'd better be sensible, my love. Cover up so we don't get sunburnt in places where the sun doesn't normally get to?'

'*Now* you suggest it. What was wrong with the wood, then?'

'Oh, I don't know. Too much like a record stuck its groove. Had to be different. Wasn't it different?'

Oh, yes, it was different. Wonderfully frenetically different and he had the bruises to prove it; what she'd look like once he got to inspect her back was another thing. The arms had come up and captured him, those mischievous suddenly opened eyes bored so closely into his and the whisper, once lips had been released, which explained it all. Of course he'd been cross, but once she'd explained, how could he not react as she obviously had planned he should react?

'You planned all this, didn't you, you scheming little madam!'

'Uh huh,' she wriggled, said 'ouch' as a stone or something interacted with a less soft bit; he rolled off and she managed to stand up, completely unabashed at her state. 'Even the place. Perfect. Distant views, otherwise hidden. Top of the hill. Soft –ish – ground, blue sky as a blanket. What more could a ravishing male require, boy?'

The embarrassment of the situation paled in comparison with her evident pride in their achievement but the common sense aspect dictated action. 'Put your top on, R.'

She sparkled back at him. 'What about the rest?'

'You're a beautiful girl. And so, so sexy.'

'Even after twins?'

'More so.' True, she'd filled out but not lost the essential

201

shape. Stretch marks? Spoils of war, nothing to be ashamed of; womanly.

Now was the time. 'So you won't mind if I tell you I'm pregnant again?' and she watched his reaction with mild amusement. Rather unusual, but then, it was responsible.

That night he'd take her out to celebrate. Hazel had no option but to carry on in the baby-sitting role, for it wouldn't have been fair to the little people to keep them up that late, and anyway, it was a sort of penance, for when they'd got back off the hill she'd met them with a woe-begone long face, explaining tearfully how Abby had rolled off the couch and banged her forehead. Roberta, immediately concerned, swept in and collected her young daughter from the floor where she was happily playing and subjected her to a thorough inspection. Abby jerked her head away from probing fingers and laid it tight to her mum's breasts, a thumb heading for the obvious place.

'Darling! You've been in the wars, haven't you? Does it hurt?' She moved her to kiss the dull red patch. 'Naughty Hazel! Letting you fall off!'

'I'm so sorry, Roberta. I didn't put the cushions on the floor. I should have.'

She was in a very forgiving mood. It could have happened to anyone. 'Well, let it be a lesson. You're only as safe as you think, my girl. You didn't think. Take more care in future please. Now, tea?'

Hazel inwardly felt undeniable relief that she hadn't been castigated quite as much as she knew she could have been and resorted to a change in topic to ask about their day.

Roberta airily dismissed her tentative comment about being away a long time by saying it had been far too wonderful a view up there merely to turn round and come straight back.

'We wanted to make the most of it, Hazel. Who knows when we'll be back again? Andrew'll take you up there tomorrow if you like.'

'Really? Would you? Sure you don't mind? And after I've been a naughty girl?'

Andrew had no choice in the matter. If Roberta said, he'd have to, provided it didn't turn to rain. A nice idea for her, a sort of 'thank-you' for being who she was, co-operative, diligent and caring, well, most of the time.

'You deserve it, Hazel, despite the lapse.' Then he had another idea. 'We could try the simpler walk along the Sheep's Head Way,' – he'd read about it and studied the maps – 'and we'd get pretty good views across the water of both the Beara and the Mizen.' That way he'd get to explore different ground and keep *their* hill sacred.

Roberta dug out the only dress-up frock she'd packed. The pale blue one. The one she'd worn that very first night after Andrew had moved in with her. Why had she brought it with her, when it was so obviously impractical? Because she had that sixth sense? As a lucky charm? Or as a last resort if all else failed, for she'd been so uncertain in her mind that he was still as continually and deeply attracted to her as then, and with the unexpected but not unwelcome state within her she had unwittingly needed the comfort and reassurance. She showered, luxuriating in the master bedroom en-suite that was so much a wonderful bonus in a rented cottage, washing away the detritus of the afternoon. He'd taken the news very well, considering. Perhaps it was the way in which she'd play acted and anything was better than being, well, say, in a coma or something. Like he was only too glad that she was *not* ill. Didn't quite explain the fainting fit and the oddness of thought at Jerpoint, except she'd maybe had too much breakfast that day. Blood gone from head to tummy to aid digestion, or was it the aura of the place? The water was running cold, yugh, time to get out. Hope he doesn't have a different view tomorrow.

She dressed with care, spent some time on her hair, added the tiny touch of perfume, slid her feet into the other luxury, her only pair of Jimmy Choos, and went to find him.

FIFTEEN

Andrea knew he'd phone. She'd not contacted his Stephanie as she should have done. June hadn't tried to influence matters, to her credit, neither had Mary. Okay, her own mum had taken the situation on board and had been all very calm and rational over how it would affect them both, which helped her in one way but still left her with the bigger problem, how Andrew would react and how she would feel if she did say she'd go and hence burnt her boats.

'Dear girl, I hope I haven't offended you? You're not ill or anything? Or has the idea gone sour? If I buy you another lunch will it help?' The timbre of his voice down the phone sent odd shivers down her spine.

Despite her nervy reaction to his call, she had to laugh. 'Alain, this smacks of bribery. I'm sorry I haven't got back to you. The truth is I really feel I must talk to Andrew first. I owe him – and Roberta – for so much, it's only fair. Organising the preview thing, yes, I'd certainly like to do if only for experience, but again, if we're going to use the little barn here we do need the proper say-so. Can you leave it until they get back? I'm sure you appreciate my position?'

The brief silence was mind blowing. Would he reject her reasoning, abandon his quest?

Then she heard his chuckle and in her mind's eye imagined his face crinkle into a smile.

'That's just what I'd expect from you, Andrea, honesty and loyalty. Two extra good reasons why I know you'll make a great P.A. Sure thing, my girl, take your time. Just let me know as soon as you can. Give me the nod and we'll go out for lunch again – to celebrate or to commiserate if we have to. Either way, I'd enjoy your company. Okay?'

'I am *not* 'your girl' yet, Alain. We'll see about lunch as and when, but thank you very much for the offer.'

Another chuckle. 'Sorry, Andrea, habit of mine, being too familiar to the ladies; gets me into trouble. Even with Steph. Call me. 'Bye.'

She drew breath. Well, she'd obviously said the right thing, but the decision wasn't going to become any easier. She shoved the chair back and went to find June.

The little restaurant was tucked away, up a slope behind a fuel filling station, the most unlikely place – until they'd parked the car and walked up the shrub-girt path into the single story wooden building and into a revelation. Seen through the wide windows the upper stretches of Bantry Bay lay quietly still and mysterious with the brooding grey-blue shadows of the hills of the Beara as a distant ethereal backdrop. Two palm trees stood sentinel beyond the wide glass panes – it felt as if they were in a tropical conservatory, lush and intriguing. The place felt warm and welcoming, intimate, cosy, discreet good taste amongst the white clothed tables and a select collection of photographic art on the back walls.

'Good evening, welcome! Would you like to take this table?'

Seated close to the windows, pampered with iced water, freshly prepared breads, a superb choice of menu and an eclectic wine list, smiling attention from the accomplished waitress and well worth the twenty odd kilometres to find this place, Roberta and Andrew relaxed.

They smiled at each other across the table; the telepathy working in complete accord for the harmony of their relationship had been subtly re-defined. Roberta sensible to her condition, Andrew aware his beloved had risen to a remarkable challenge and now it was up to them both to build on the situation. Tonight's occasion might, just might, mark another milestone along the way where they were going in their marriage. Ireland definitively the catalyst; the chance to experience this state of affairs at home virtually non-existent, for there they would have been far too involved with on-going scenarios to warrant time and expense on such a different dine-out location. And, of course, they had the afternoon's memories still fresh and unsullied. The challenge of the hill, its climb; the experience of the view, the splendid scenery; the acceptance of the necessity to invest time and passion in each other's needs despite Roberta's admittedly frightening ploy to get him to display his depth of concern; to arouse his desire.

Inspirational, this place, nowhere else they knew would have given them this and they wouldn't have been here if it hadn't have been for the filming. . .

'Here's to Hazel. And absent friends.'

'Hazel and absent friends!' He happily concurred as they clinked glasses, for certainly without their young *protégé*, life might have been chaotically problematical. She'd absorbed so much of the worry and strain of living with two young lives. And so pretty with it. So dedicated, too.

Over the rim of the glass, her eyes, and the amber glints. Oh, those eyes! The mischievous look with the complete awareness of the way his mind worked. Her expression.

'Still room in the harem for another?'

'Too pretty, that one.'

She shook her head. 'Not at all. It's her personality, the way she carries herself and manages to organise everything. A lot better than I could most of the time. Actually,' and she took another sip of the delicate red, 'we're extremely fortunate and I'd love to reward her for all she's doing. Not financially, because that's not what she'd want. She's short of some proper emotional experiences. And I don't want her to learn about – things – without some form of oversight.'

'So what are you suggesting?'

The starters were arriving. Large plates, works of art, superb. Discussion was suspended. Outside the light was changing, the still waters of the bay deepening into pewter grey, the hills merging into the evening sky. A delicate tinge of orange contrasted in the softness. Roberta was captivated, her empty plate showing mere traces of its former glory and with chin on an elbow propped hand she stared at the vision across the bay. '*Magical!*'

Andrew could only agree wholeheartedly. A splendid end to a momentous day – and not over yet, not by far. He repeated his earlier question, his stimulated curiosity now way beyond abandoning the subject.

'Oh, well, er. . .' Should she, or shouldn't she? 'I've told her – explained, because I had to, – what makes us females behave the way we do. I'm not sure it was such a good idea, but I thought she needed to know; otherwise you might have been caught up in her experimentation. Now she knows she may seek to experiment anyway, just to try things out. She needs same age companionship now. Preferably of the right sort.'

'Boyfriend?'

A nod. 'Better that than some unhealthy introvert goings on.'

'She's not likely to get out and about while she's working for us, now is she?'

'That's the difficulty. A no-win situation for us. Heads we lose her to love, tails she loses the twins.'

'Same difference. You mean she has a choice, the love of the twins or the love – possibly lust – of some uncertain male.' He looked around. This conversation could be an intriguing sideshow for the other diners, but no, the half dozen other occupied tables were far too wrapped up in their own affairs, happily. The main course plates appeared from the kitchen. A chance to let the thoughts settle. The considerate lady who had welcomed them – probably the owner from her demeanour – was doing the rounds of the tables, lighting the candles. So romantic a setting; it could have been designed for celebrating engagements, wedding anniversaries, any notable family occasion. This was their own anniversary, even if not quite the date, of their first visit to this wonderful area by some two years. Two twin years, and now a celebration of their potential third child.

As Roberta picked up her knife and fork to start demolition of the lamb, his next question slipped out. 'What if you hatch another set of twins?'

Her cutlery clattered down. 'Oh lor, Andrew! I couldn't, could I? Not two sets!'

'We'd better check soonest. Though we are at least prepared, logistically. What was that you said about taking some more extreme precautions? Bit late now.'

The candlelight could not disguise a rising colour. 'I think the gardener's shed had an effect of unintentional proportions, don't you?'

'Inspired by the thought of that mattress being dumped; a sort of celebration?'

'Or that I did a virtual character change and *you* thought I was Andrea? Gave me a bit more welly than usual? Like you did earlier. Maybe I was a virtual Hazel today?'

'Roberta! What are you suggesting? That we – I – need stimulating to make it?' He shook his head. His veal escalope was perfection. 'I don't think so. All I need is you, just you. No one else. Not an Andrea, certainly not a Hazel. I married you, R, because you and I fell in love, or to more accurate, you fell and I loved you.' He didn't feel like adding anything about her seducing him.

'So you did. So I did. You're sure there isn't an interesting mental picture in your mind of some other. . . when. . . ?' She was being quite diplomatically vague given the surroundings but he knew exactly what she was driving at. They finished their platefuls simultaneously, though she speared the last carrot from the vegetable dish and munched reflectively. 'You know what I mean?'

'I know what you mean. Do you really think I need what you're suggesting, R?'

'Sorry,' she said. 'But a girl needs reassurance occasionally and we do seem to have some more erratic moments now-a-days. Forgive me, dear.' The waitress came to clear the plates. There didn't appear to be any pressure on them to move through the courses in anything other than their own time.

Outside a pale three quarter moon had risen to show a silvery ripple on the vastness of the black waters below in the bay. Roberta's Italianate features were still alluring, the curl of her hair around her neckline and the dip towards the mystery of her cleavage now shadowed by the candlelight.

He reached across and picked up a hand, selected a finger and moved the ring. 'No one else, love. Not as I love you. I'm the lucky one, knowing you. Loving you. Being father to our children. Others pale in comparison.'

'Even Andrea?'

'I . . . ' and he stopped. He couldn't deny her. He couldn't say he didn't love her, because that would be untrue, though it was in an entirely different way.

'Ah. And Hazel?'

'She's only a child, R.'

'A twenty year old female child, Andrew, with all the appropriate and evident attributes and as transparent a need as any girl. I'm sure there's no lack of inspiration there, despite the situation.' She took a deep breath, but saw the waitress coming across with the dessert menus and let the moment go.

A quarter of an hour or so later two more polished plates were taken away and the coffees arrived. It was now totally dark outside, apart from the distant moon with a minimal reflection on the blacker waters below and the pathway lights. They really shouldn't be any later, or else Hazel would worry.

If she didn't say it now, she never would. 'Andrew, my darling, perhaps I should let you into a secret idea of mine,' and she spoke softly, just a trifle tearfully, for less than two minutes.

'June, love. I've had another call from Alain.'

'What a surprise. So?'

'The pressure's off. He'll wait. Said some quite complimentary things about loyalty, I'm really rather pleased. Let's go out for lunch.'

'You'll upset Mary.'

'She can come too.'

'Mary? Out to lunch? You must be mad, girl. She won't want to do that!'

'Why not?'

'It's just not her. Not what she does.'

'All the more reason.' Andrea jumped up. 'I'll go ask.'

'Go out to lunch?'

'Yes. I feel like celebrating. It'll make a change from sandwiches, and give you a break. Please?'

'Well, if you're sure.' Mary started taking her apron off. 'So long as we're not too long. Where do you normally go, the Royal?'

June kept her amazement to herself, picked up her coat and followed Andrea out of the office. Andrea's little car seemed crowded with the three of them and arriving at the Royal in giggles were typical office girls on an outing. They took a table in the corner and got the waitress to fetch the drinks. Mary stuck to a tomato juice; June had her usual lime and lemon, Andrea merely a white wine spritzer for last time she'd been here she'd overdosed on Chardonnay or Chablis or something. They ordered.

'So why the celebration then, Andrea?' June slurped at her brimming glass. 'After a phone call from Alain?'

'I'm going to take the job. It feels right.'

'Without consulting Andrew – or Roberta?' Mary seemed quite at ease, surprisingly.

'I'm my own girl.' She swirled the glass round, held it up and looked at the bubbles. 'He said nice things, like he knew what I could do. I like him.'

'Like?'

Andrea closed her eyes and saw Alain's grin in her mind's eye. 'Yes, like.'

'More than Roberta did; he rubbed her up the wrong way.'

'True, but it's just him. I don't mind. He's given me an

opportunity I'd be silly to turn down.'

Mary nodded. 'Reckon you're right, lass, but you'll be missed. In more ways than one.' She had no allusions about the physical attraction between the girl and her daughter's husband, knowing full well that it was just that, not a potential for strife. And anyway, Roberta was made of far sterner stuff than some, though if Andrea were out of day-to-day reach – then maybe it would be no bad thing, far less contentious.

'So when will you tell him? Before or after they get back?'

Andrea stared at her glass, twirling the stem. 'After. When I've talked to Andrew.'

'My father'll try and get you to stay,' June said, intelligently. 'He won't want to lose you, and knowing you, you'll melt. I know, I've seen you.'

'What are you saying, June? That I say yes to Alain now and present Andrew with a *fait accompli?* So I don't melt?' She grinned, wryly, for June had a point.

Mary smiled back at her. 'Depends on how strong-minded you are, Andrea. June's right. You'll need to work some notice out too, so you don't leave them in the lurch.'

'I wouldn't do that, leave them in the lurch, I mean.' A very emphatic statement and Alain would just have to understand. 'Hopefully Hazel will be quick on the uptake. And you know what's what as well, don't you, June?'

She nodded. 'To some extent. But it isn't what I want to do, not now. I think I'm best away from computer screens. Too close to home. The home that was.' Her mood changed. The situation she was in, pushed firmly back to the back of her consciousness whilst busy with the affairs of the Manor, came rushing back into focus. Her marriage, William's lack of interest in her as a woman – female – his love was for technology, not for cuddling her, his wife – and she felt incomplete, abandoned like a discarded doll. Her eyes pricked and she wiped a hand across her forehead.

'Hey, hey! June?' Andrea's hand left the glass and reached across. 'I'm sorry, I didn't think. . . '

'Aye, lass. We'd best get back.' Mary stood up. 'Thanks for

the invite, Andrea. Makes a nice change. Not that we should make a habit o'this.'

Andrew went and paid the bill. 'A lovely evening,' he said, 'thank you so much. Lovely setting, I'm sure we'll come back sometime.'

The owner, manageress, whatever she was, made the right noises. 'Thank you so much for coming. I do hope you had an enjoyable evening.'

He nodded. They had indeed, there was a nice calm feeling to the place and it certainly had helped them both.

Roberta was waiting for him outside, a divine picture of feminity in the shadows, ghostlike in her floaty pale blue and so much an enigma. He adored her. She took his hand, and they walked the steps down to the car park, close but silent. At the car she swung round and lifted her face to him.

'Kiss me?'

Hands pressed to her cheeks, mouth on mouth, lips on lips. Two minutes? Three? Five?

A whispered affirmation from him then, deeply felt, sincerely meant, so simplistic but so true.

'I know, *oh, darling, I know*.'

'So why suggest this idea?'

A little shrug. 'Just me. I don't know.' She let herself sag into his arms, lent her head against his shoulders. 'I trust you, Andrew. Whatever you decide. I'm never going to let it come between us. Never.' The sound of another couple leaving the restaurant above them broke into the moment and they stepped apart. The magic of the evening would stay; the consequences of her declaration had yet to be discovered.

Hazel was wide-awake, the twins fast asleep. 'Had a nice evening?' she asked, putting her book down and getting up from her cosy armchair. 'The twins have been fine. And I had a visitor.'

'Oh?' Roberta had a momentary twinge of anxiety. She had no reason to fear the decision to leave the twins under Hazel's care, but with stories of kidnaps and young people being molested floating around the news from time to time, well, one never quite knew . . . Hazel was smiling.

'Your friends – you know the ones who came up on our first day? Sheila came up – and left you this.' She produced a small painting, unframed, and passed it over to Roberta. 'Sort of keepsake, she said. They're off to Spain or somewhere, Malaga? Said to remember the times on the hill. What did she mean?' Her eyes were wide and curious, guileless; nothing that would have told Roberta she'd guessed the significance. The painting – oil on a piece of hardboard – was a landscape with a young woman in a white dress sitting on a rock in the foreground. Extraordinarily, the grey pillar of a triangulation point occupied a left of centre position behind the girl, with the hills and water beautifully captured in a shimmer of a background. Amazing.

'She gave you this?' Roberta ignored Hazel's other query. She handed it over to Andrew, who first held it at arm's length to catch the lamplight before turning it over.

'She's signed it. And added something. Looks like '*Find your way, seek* – er – I think it's – *look for guidance from the* – I can't quite make it out, is it *triangle* – here, you look.'

Roberta screwed up her eyes and held it closer to the lamp. '*Triangles of love*, Andrew, plural. Oh lor.' She swiftly turned to the other girl. 'Hazel, I think it's time you were horizontal. You've had a tiring day. Go on, shoo. We'll sort the rest; I'll look at the twins. See you in the morning. Thanks for looking after things. Night night.'

She was indeed ready for bed and went without further demur. Though the puzzle remained, it would keep. Tomorrow was nearly here and she'd been promised a day out on the hills.

'You know what Sheila meant?' Roberta had quickly checked the twins, shed everything and curled up beneath the bedclothes before Andrew had returned from the bathroom. 'That woman's psychic.'

'It's a fabulous painting; whatever else she is, she's a good artist, though the pillar's a bit intrusive.'

'Precisely the point, love. Triangulation point. Old fashioned concept, taking bearings from three points to determine heights and so on. Don't use 'em nowadays, do we, – not now we've gone all digital and satellite, much less romantic. That's what she's driving at, remember *ménage de trois?* Reckon she's got you weighed up to a tee, boy. Three girls? I thought the only other one was your Andrea. Who's the other?' A rhetorical question, for she believed as well as he did it could only be Hazel.

Andrew sat down, rather heavily, on the bed edge. 'I don't hold with this; too eerie by far. She can't know anything creepy about us – but what does it matter? I've no aspirations to get involved with anyone else, R; you know that, despite what we talked about earlier.'

'Do I? Perhaps our Sheila knows more than I do!' and her voice went a little higher pitched than normal. Startling Andrew, she flung herself out of the bed and he heard her padding down the stairs to return a moment later with the painting, to scrutinise the figure. 'I'd say that was quite like our Hazel, wouldn't you?' firming it up in her mind. 'Where is it, anyway? It's not up on *our* hill, there's no trig point up there, is there? And what's that funny figure on the front? – it looks like a hiker.'

'We'll ask around. If Sheila painted it, then it must be somewhere local. I can't think it's purely from her imagination, except for the inscription, that is,' Andrew was adamant.

Roberta propped the A4 sized painting up on the chest of drawers, crawled back under the duvet but stayed knees up and with her back against the headboard, staring at it. 'I'm sure that's Hazel.'

'She hasn't got a white dress.'

'Oh, but she has. Well, sort of pale grey, actually. The linen one with the brown selvedge?'

'That's only a skirt.'

'Hmmm, so you *do* remember what she wears? She was wearing it the night they came up. And the white Aran sweater.'

With that recall a weird shiver went down his back, as though icy fingers had touched his spine. 'No, Roberta; don't start. There's nothing in it. Sheila only put her into the picture because she remembered her – what did she call her, as *"a beautiful colleen"*?

'Which she is, my husband. Young, softly beautiful, and very very desirable. Isn't she?'

'Yes,' he replied, shortly. 'But she's also our *joint* responsibility and I wish you'd stop pushing her under my nose as if she were some sort of vestal virgin. What is it about you, Roberta, that you constantly need to have a go at my susceptibilities? I thought we'd managed to get matters straight earlier on. That I'd try and be a male figure to her and so on without actually waking up irrepressible emotions and that you'd enjoy watching the by-play?'

Roberta slid down and covered her head with the duvet. 'Sorry,' came a muffled voice. 'We'll just have to see what happens tomorrow. You will take care of her, won't you?'

'Can you see me doing less? No, she'll be all right. Enjoyed your day?'

'I did. Did you?' She moved the cover back. 'Because it meant a lot to me, my love. What we need to keep us going, memories for the future.'

'I shan't forget. Apart from a panic attack, yes, I enjoyed my day. Go to sleep, love.'

'Mmmm mmmm.' She slid back under the cover and within minutes he heard her breathing deepen to slumber. He switched out the bedside light but stayed awake for a while, wondering about the day ahead. How would he manage with another challenge?

'Are you sure you'll be all right for the day, love?' Their breakfast was just a messy pile of plates on the drainer and the time was moving on.

She stared at him, eyes narrowing down, saying nothing.

'Sorry. At least give me credit for asking. Only I'm a bit bothered, in that the mobile doesn't work so well here so you might not reach me if there is a problem?'

'And what good would it do anyway if you're five miles away from the car up some hill even if *your* mobile worked? Be sensible, dear. I'll be ultra careful with them, they're our children so don't worry. Just you have a good time and make sure you look after her – you're just as vulnerable. Make sure you keep an eye on the weather. Go and find your trig point. Hazel, you look after him, don't let him run away with you or do anything silly. Go on with you, I'll be fine. I'll enjoy having a day with these two on my own, really.'

After the sound of the car had diminished and the quiet of the valley returned, she turned on her heel and went back indoors. Abby was playing with her grey bear, walking it over the blankets of her cot. Chris just lay there, sucking his thumb, but his eyes picked up on her approach and he scrambled to his unsteady feet, grasping the cot edge then holding out podgy arms to be picked up.

She laughed at him. 'Who wants a cuddle, then?' She reached down and heaved him up, getting an arm round her neck. 'My, Christopher Hailsworthy, you're getting heavy. Today you're going to show mummy just how well you can walk. Let's get you strapped into your chair for your breakfast then I can get your sister organised. Back in moment, Abby dear.'

Abby looked up and gave her mother a big smile.

'Oh, how I do love you two little children!' And it was true, she loved them deeply, never doubted for a single moment that she always would. Ever since she'd become pregnant she'd become a much happier, a more fulfilled, much rounder person and her love for her Andrew deeper than ever, despite his other girl. She'd come to realistically accept she couldn't own his soul any more than he could hers. Their marriage was solid, theirs a partnership indissoluble; no point of being jealous over the understandable human feelings awoken by others that couldn't be simply ignored or pushed into the background. If she'd had feelings for some other male, would he have accepted it? Hmmm. Probably not. Well, she hadn't, so it was academic. Alain had tried but she hadn't felt anything, though yes, Andrew had gone a bit sultry over it – and did that contribute to the episode in the gardener's shed? She pulled a face; the experience would stick in her mind almost as firmly as that first ever evening with her skirts rucked up round her waist. Some clients had eyed her up and down. Andrew had eyed some clients in turn, for as the expression had it, one or two were very much in the 'eye-fodder' category. Nothing came of it or ever would. But Andrea, she was different. He'd had sex with the girl and admitted it but never hinted he wanted to make more of that relationship. Funnily enough, she'd come to terms with their imprudence, accepting it for what it was, genuine human response to a perceived emotional demand. And she knew she'd be labelled as 'odd' by many another, who'd have chucked their partners out for far less than that. What good did that do? Wrecked lives, expensively. Much better to be sympathetic, or was that empathetic? She lifted Chris into his chair.

'Just let me get Abby, darling, and then we'll have a lovely sticky breakfast. Won't be a mo.'

And today, she'd thrust him into a potentially explosive situation with another girl who – sadly – had a not dissimilar problem in her life as Andrea had had, though from a different slant, certainly. Andrea's had been a claustrophobic home life and a strange attitude to her sexuality that had kept her aloof. Until she'd met that someone she could look up to – Andrew – and the rest of it, as they say, was history. Well, hopefully history. Mind you, his situation had made him equally – if not more – vulnerable. Poor Sam; she'd come out of it okay in the end, though it had been touch and go. Hazel's problem was a less than effective mother and no father figure and a stultifying adolescence, trapped in her own weird grey world of dumb make-believe. Now the girl was raring to go and rampant with it. Watch out, Andrew dear. And she'd have to accept whatever transpired. As she'd told him last night, explaining what she thought he ought to do for the girl as well as what she'd done. Whoops. Put it out of your mind, Roberta, girl, and get on with the day.

'Up you come, Aubrietia. Did you know how you were christened, my darling little girl? No, I didn't think you did. Well, I'll tell you one day. You'll be a little terror amongst the boys, I know.' Roberta carried her through and fitted her into her chair. 'The sooner I can get you two doing things for yourselves the better. We're going to have a real good go at getting you fully mobile today. Races across the grass. Now, what do you want for breakfast? Sloppy cereal and sticky honey fingers?' She'd have to have something herself too, her tummy was murmuring. Would she have the same nauseous starts to the day as when these two were being constructed? And what would they think to competition? At least it had to be a companion for one of 'em. No twins – if that showed up she'd swear she'd have an abortion and start again. Then thought once more and denied the notion utterly. No way. She'd not demean that excitingly frenetic quarter of an hour in the shed. If twins then twins. And sterilisation.

Andrew found his way through Bantry with a little difficulty, for the roads were rather narrow and traffic had the usual *laizzez faire* attitude so different to home. If someone doubled parked in their Bedfordshire home town the way that van had done in front of him, there would have been a fair old expression of road rage.

'You know where we're going, Andrew?'

He nodded. 'The map's down there if you want to check. Out onto the Cork road and turn right, can't go wrong. First place is Durrus; I had a good look at the map earlier. Then I think we'll take the coast road,

'I'm not much use with maps; I've never needed to be. This is rather an adventure and I'm loving it. I owe you, Andrew.'

He took a sideways glance at her. 'We owe you, Hazel, for being such a super nanny to the twins. I reckon we'd have had rather a struggle without you. It's Mary you have to thank – if she hadn't brought you to our notice when we started the B & B lark we'd not have known. Shame you had be devious though, that could well have backfired.' The vehicle in front turned right and gave him the clear road, past the huge new Marine hotel and the entrance to Bantry House. 'Enjoying the experience?'

'Totally.' She took in the aspect of the harbour with all its boats, the reach of the wind stirred ripples of water stretching way out into the bay and ignored the reference to her former state; it was far too miserable a thought. 'It's very good of you to give up the last day to me.'

He smiled at her. 'My treat. I'm looking forward to it. Provided the weather holds.'

There were a few clouds drifting inland and a mass of grey on the horizon, though the sun was giving of its best at the moment. The road widened and there was the turn-off. 'New territory for me. We didn't get down here last time.'

Hazel hesitated, before taking took the plunge. 'You weren't married then – to Roberta, I mean. Was it different?'

'Hmmmph.'

It was if he'd snorted in a cross sort of way and she pulled a face. 'Sorry.' Had she overstepped the mark, gone beyond the boundary of her fragile new relationship with him?

They were heading into the village and he pulled over into a lay-by opposite the few shops. 'I'm going to get a couple of bars of chocolate, seeing as we came out without a packed lunch. A weakness, Hazel, and Roberta doesn't buy them for me – at least not often. Back in a moment.'

'Wait! I'll come with you.' She unclipped her belt and slid out. They crossed the road together. 'I apologise for that question, Andrew.'

He reached for a hand. 'Hazel, love, your turn will come. Until then, dream. I did, and it happened.' He swung her hand up and touched to his lips. 'Let's have a look at those gardens after we've been shopping.' He nodded at a sign at the end of the paving. 'Might as well while we're here.'

He bought three bars, a packet of biscuits and a couple of small boxes of fruit juice. She sorted through the postcards and bought two. Then they paid for entrance to the gardens and walked through into what was obviously someone's particular pride and joy. They ambled along the paths in silence, taking in the odd collection of 'artefacts' that stood as focal points at every turn. She felt rather surprised at this decision to spend time walking alongside a landscaped valley streambed, however pretty and well cared for it was; she'd far rather be out on the hill and said so.

Andrew swung round on her and acknowledged his concern. 'We'd be on our own up there, Hazel,' giving her an option to back out as well as stating his position.

'Yes. So we would, and what's wrong with that?'

'You don't mind being alone with a bloke with a reputation for having an eye for the ladies?'

She hadn't seen it that way, despite her silly thoughts that other evening before Roberta had talked to her, but his question gave her a tiny little frizz of excitement; was she that hazardous a female? Like an Andrea? *That was it. She had been his weakness.* No wonder he was on edge, in case it happened all over again. But no, she couldn't be in the same league, she was far too young to be an attraction for him, especially with her stupid 'I'm a dim wit' approach of a couple of years ago.

'Roberta didn't mind me coming with you, for after all she suggested it. What's the matter, don't you want to? Take me up the hill, please, Andrew. Don't you want to?' repeating the query before she added, in a very grownup way, 'If I had any doubts I would have said long before.'

He still wasn't absolutely sure, despite smiling at her innocence. Yes, he fancied getting out onto the hill, taking advantage of the territory. Yes, she was good company and so on. Problem was he didn't know her capabilities, her stamina, or how she'd behave or how indeed, whether he could, would, in such an isolated and evocative place, stay immune from her undoubted charms. Suddenly she had become an unknown quantity. Roberta, dear Roberta, what have you done?

'Okay, Hazel. Let's go up a hill.' He took her hand and swung it again. 'Let's see what it's like on top of the Sheep's Head.'

She was grinning at him. 'Funny name for a hill. Why that for heaven's sake?'

'I have no idea, unless there were always lots of sheep seen from the sea. All I know is that there's a way-marked path around the whole peninsula, which makes it easier in one way and a problem in another.'

'How come?' He still held her hand and she liked the dry firmness of his hold.

'If we follow the path it might not take us where we feel like going; if we don't we're technically trespassing – I think. Whatever, let's go. Time's pressing.'

They walked back across the road to the car and drove on.

She sat still, wondering if she'd come up to his expectations. Maybe it was that he couldn't be sure she would manage to keep pace or have the stamina to do the mileage, which was why he'd hesitated, rather than because she was a girl in an Andrea guise and no Roberta. This was a challenge. She'd never been on a long walk before, let alone in rough country. She could but do her best. He turned right, away from the coast and the road started to climb, twisting upwards towards the skyline. Then there was a car park area ahead and Andrew swung the Volvo onto the empty gravelled area.

'On our own.' He grinned at her. 'Not quite like the Lake District. Place would be swarming, scenery like this.' He got out of the car and stared around. To the south was Dumanus Bay, beyond that the run of blue-green hills towards the lighthouse and the distant waters of Roaring Water Bay. To the north, hidden by the loom of the hill they'd tackle, would be

221

Bantry Bay and the Beara; and tucked away beyond Bantry, Glengariff and where Roberta would be with the twins.

Behind him he heard the car door open. She came up behind and stood close.

'It's so beautiful up here, wonderful views.'

'Yes.'

'Perhaps I'd better change, if we're going to walk.'

'Change?' He spun round. She was fine as she was, in his view. Good to look at, nice to talk to, a charm of a girl.

'I brought my shorts.'

'Only if you want to. The ground doesn't look too bad. I'll go and have a look up there.'

To leave her to decide about changing out of her skirt, he walked up the track to a beautiful polished slab of black rock that looked – and was – obviously like a seat. On the front were carved the words: 'Water and Ground in Their Extremity' – how completely in keeping with the spirit of the place and from someone, a wonderful thought that imprinted into his soul.

On the other side of the road a statue in front of a large cross, the Virgin Mary nursing a wounded man – Christ? It stood out in glaring white, a constant reminder of the staunch faith of the community. He turned and looked back at the car. She hadn't changed. She was still wearing her off-white linen skirt and the Aran sweater and she waved at him.

They made good progress on the first mile, for the 'ground' was, indeed as he'd said, not too bad. She did not feel at all out of place in her skirt either, because as Roberta had said, it meant she could move just as well and keep her cool. Those shorts were too tight anyway. The newly bought fell-walking boots were very good if somewhat strange to her feet more used to slip-ons and the thicker socks not too bad. She was quite enjoying this. Mind you, she didn't quite see where they were going because the path kept winding about.

'We come back this way?'

''Spect so. Always looks different when you walk the opposite way. You okay?'

'Yep, fine, thanks.'

'Good.'

The cloudbank had thinned out and the threat of rain dispersed. He checked his watch. Not quite eleven. Plenty of time. They might even reach the end of the peninsular and still get back in time. The marker posts weren't too intrusive and certainly helpful considering he'd an unknown quantity in Hazel; they wouldn't, shouldn't stray and get lost, not that the patch suggested they were at any real sort of risk. The views were spectacular, both ways. They could get quite drunk on all this amazing scenery.

An hour later and they were even higher; and then, looking towards the top of the next rise he saw it, the little pillar he'd spotted on the map. The trig point. Instinctively he knew it would have been his personal goal, his pinnacle of achievement, ever since Sheila had given them the painting and thrown the challenge at him. She knew, that witch of a woman, what a temptation a young girl like their Hazel would be out here on the hill in a flirty skirt. Roberta had seen it too, and added her unspoken weight to the challenge. Sheila would have to have been up here to paint the scene and that knowledge was unsettling.

'See it?'

'What?' She shielded her eyes from the brightness. 'Where?'

'Top of yon hill. Straight ahead. 'Bout another ten minutes.'

'That pimple on the ridge?'

He nodded. 'Then we'll take a lunch break.'

She laughed. 'A bar of chocolate each?'

'I've survived on less.'

'You've done a lot of this hill walking, Andrew?'

'Fair amount, over the years. My first wife didn't much care for it, but I managed a week on my own every now and again.' Should he tell her? Why not, for she probably knew anyway. 'It was a walk that brought into me Roberta's world, Hazel. Life changing.'

'Tell me.' That soft smile she had and the welcoming eyes were fascinating, so difficult to resist and deeply dangerous.

'When we get up the top. Come on.'

Fifteen minutes give or take and they reached it, perched on a slab of rough concrete set into the rock. Intrigued, Hazel ran her fingers round the peculiarly shaped verdigris coloured metal let into the top of the concrete pillar, walked round and saw the painted sign on its western face.

'Like the marker posts.' Then abruptly she realised and focused her thoughts. 'This is on the painting. The one Sheila gave us!'

He nodded. 'And, my dear girl, look at what you're wearing. White, well sort of.'

'Bizarre! Why would she do that?' Hazel flopped down on a patch of grass. 'I think she's weird. Spooky.' She stretched out and closed her eyes.

Andrew looked down on her recumbent figure for a reflective few minutes, reminding him of another girl, another place, another age, as his thoughts swung around and around and finally clarified. Then he sank down onto his haunches alongside her; an absolute charm in every way, that linen skirt a beautiful foil to the rising shape of her thighs and the Aran provocatively lifting with her steady breathing. And she hadn't missed a step on the way up; she'd been great. She'd come such a long way since they'd first taken her into their lives and he was so intensely proud of her. Time passed. Minutes maybe, but immeasurable. His mind swung around. Samantha, June, Peter – Peter, he must get in touch. Andrea, Hazel.

A sudden surprising confirmation of the idea came, swelling up inside him as a surging intensely delightful orgasmic pain. That she was, could have been a dream of a daughter, a superbly incredible thought, was absolutely true; spoken of in idle conversation but essentially, that was where she lay.

'Hazel?'

She opened her eyes, lifted her head, cupped a hand over

to take away the sun's glare and gazed up at him, at his vivid stare. He reached forward, took hold of a hand and gently pulled up her towards him.

'Andrew? What is it?' her query turned to concern and then to delight as his other arm came round her and she was close, so close and her pulse rate started to climb.

Roberta looked at the clock. Mid-day, gone. They would be way up the hill by now, probably parked on some rock or other for lunch. Lunch! They'd not packed a picnic – oh how stupid of her! Glory, but they'd be starving! Oh heavens! They should have said. Oh, well, nothing she could do about that now. She wouldn't explore the illogicality – she had been too not thinking, silly woman. And it obviously hadn't occurred to either Hazel or her husband. The twins, tired out from their enforced route marches round the garden were now happily flat out and snoring. Well, sort of. Standing on tiptoe at the end of the lawn she could just about make out the distant run of hills and presumed that's where they were. She'd have loved to be with them, but she owed this day to Hazel. All sorts of weird thoughts were going through her mind, conditioned by her knowledge of the precarious nature of Hazel's hormones and her interpretation of Andrew's attitude to legs in skirts. She should have put the girl in jeans, far less provocative and… and why oh why did she always reduce her to a mere sex object? She wasn't. She was a pretty, shapely girl with a lovely disposition who adored her kids and did all sorts of things that she, Roberta Hailsworthy, wife of Andrew, really should have done as a proper mum. But she *was* a proper mum. She'd just spent an entire morning encouraging Abby and Chris to toddle on their own and make intelligent noises like 'mummy I love you' and 'daa-daddy' and 'look, burrdee'. And worn herself out, let alone the horrors. Stop calling them horrors, R, and also stop wondering about what those two are doing up on that hill. Think about tomorrow and packing up and going home to

225

another pregnancy and the reactions she'd get from dear mum Mary. Abruptly she spun round and went back into the house.

The wooded valley below muffled much of the sound, but the eventual noise of a vehicle in its low gear approach up the steep hill not only woke her up but triggered an alarm in her mind at having stupidly dozed and that added to the muzziness of disturbed sleep. The twins! Wriggling up from the untidy slumped position in the large old armchair, peering at the ancient clock to discover it was gone four and hearing happy sounds from the room next door, the mixture of thoughts made her head spin; going home, being pregnant and how has he coped with Hazel? Or was it from waking up suddenly? And please no, she didn't want another black out, so she let her head hang down and sat still while the brain got back into gear. A car crunched into the driveway. Abby was saying 'mum mum mum' and giggling. Chris was singing – or at least making better noises than his usual holler. The old clock was ticking and her heart was pulsing at a much faster rate. The car doors slammed, footsteps crunched on the pebbles.

'Roberta! Darling, we're ho-ome!' Andrew's voice sounded distant, fading away and the carpet seemed awfully close . . .

SIXTEEN

Mary answered the phone; the girls were out in the garden somewhere. Afterwards she sat down, her forehead propped on the cheek of her hand, letting the sweep of emotion run through, feeling the sting of tears. Her heart pounded, a twinge of nausea from the sudden pain within and the shock bringing a fear for her own stability and indeed, fallibility.

Andrea came in from her late afternoon stroll round the autumnal estate. 'Mary? Whatever's the matter? You look awfully grey; can I get you anything? Are you all right?' She put a solicitous hand on Mary's shoulder and the elder woman reached up to grasp and hold.

'It's Roberta. She's had a blackout. Andrew's phoned. Taken her to the hospital. She's . . .' and the tears rolled. 'She shouldn't have, not at her age, not with the twins.'

'Shouldn't have what, Mary? Surely she's just had a funny turn, nothing serious. Not Roberta.' Andrea's mind went into freefall, trying to run through the scenarios, the logic – there wasn't any – and the logistics, they were due home anyway, Hazel would manage the twins, Andrew was awfully good at the reassurance bit, she should know, she'd experienced his attentions; so what, she wondered, would be at the root cause and in moments, intelligently, twigged. 'She isn't, is she?'

Mary nodded, sniffed, rubbed her eyes and reached for a hanky. 'She wasn't planning to. She never said, neither. Andrew didn't know, not afore they went. Silly girl. Silly, silly girl.' The sigh was peculiarly appropriate. 'Best get on, nought we can do 'till he rings again.' With some effort, she stood up and Andrea realised how much she was showing her age.

'Where was he taking her?'

'Bantry, I think he said.' Mary shook her head slowly in that disapproving side-to-side habit Andrea had seen before and wiped her eyes again. 'He said she'd blacked out before, at some Abbey or other, thought it was nought serious. Reckon she's worried the lad; he sounded a bit fraught. T'aint the first time he's taken her to hospital neither.' Again that so expressive sigh. 'Poor man, all my girl's done is give him trouble. Oh, Andrea, lass. Best tell June. You go; I'll put the kettle on.'

June was far more matter of fact, not that she had any familiarity with these things other than something one of her office friends had experienced.

'She's suffering from high blood pressure, I bet. If she's stressed it affects the brain, so it switches her off to regain stability. It's called fainting. You wait; he'll ring up and say it's just a scare. She'll be fine if she takes care of herself. I'm sure she will. You see.'

It was almost midnight and long after they'd had a somewhat sombre supper that the phone rang again. Neither June or Mary had thought to go to bed. Andrea had gone home, but only after making sure she would be told what was what, assuming he did ring that night.

June took the call. Mary had dozed and hence only just aware of the ring.

'Dad?' She listened carefully, 'So she'll be all right? Thank heavens.' She was doing her own little bit of head nodding, taking it all in. She'd been right, then; her guess correct, high blood pressure. 'Staying in overnight? Just as well, p'raps. Hazel okay with the twins?' She smiled at the phone. Dad and his girls! 'Yes please. Just so we know. Give her our love, won't you? Yes, dad, I will. Now you just take care of her. 'Bye dad, sleep well. Love you. 'Bye.'

Mary waited.

'High blood pressure. Possibly something about a thyroid.

228

They're doing tests. Dad says she's being difficult, wants to discharge herself tonight; he won't let her. She'll be all right to come home, though, provided she does as she's told. She never said about being pregnant?'

'Reckon she wanted to judge the moment. No doubt worried about what he'd say. Didn't tell me either. I know my girl, so I knew she was, only just though. Weren't planned, like.' A bit of colour in her cheeks and neck suggested this was a confidence not easily expressed.

June could understand that, but not to tell your own mum? 'I'd best phone Andrea. I promised.'

'Aye.'

As she spoke to Andrea she could sense the girl's relief and wondered, cattily, if that was more for her father's sake than Roberta's, but at least she'd sleep more easily, whichever way.

'Best get to bed, Mary.'

'Aye, lass. Thanks for being so common sense about things. Take after your father, you do.'

June flushed. Compliment indeed, and hugged the old lady. 'Thanks, Mary,' and had never felt so more at home and comfortable about things for a long time, not since before she'd first heard about her dad's *affaire*. It would work out. It had to. He couldn't do without her, not now.

Three days later and they were all home, safe and sound, well, sort of. On the first full day Andrew drove Roberta into town to see her old friend Doc Mac, pleased for her that he was available, for she would feel so much more at ease and confident in him than with another younger and likely far less tolerant member of the Practice. He waited ages or so it seemed before he was invited into the consulting room.

'Andrew – if I may call you Andrew – I'm pleased to say that Roberta's not in too bad a shape, but there are some aspects that could cause a modicum of concern.'

She was sitting in the opposite chair, hands clasped in her

lap, eyes bright, a wee trace of a smile, and he loved her, the flow of her hair, the way her long neck gave way to the shape of her, those lovely legs, sleek under the linen skirt, the slender crossed ankles. And pregnant.

'She needs to watch her pace, should take a fair amount of rest, and I'm going to put her on some drugs to control the blood pressure – as best I can, given her pregnancy – and we're going to check a few other things. Nothing, I can reassure you, that should alarm either of you. It's early days yet, but I don't foresee a long-term problem. These things happen.'

'The baby – er -?' and hesitated.

Mac smiled. 'Roberta's already asked, Andrew. I doubt twins this time. Should be fine. I'd like to see her again in a fortnight, sooner if anything else occurs, not that it should. Just take care of her.'

On the way home, she asked him the question she'd dreaded, put off until she knew it wouldn't go away.

'You don't mind, do you, Andrew? About me getting pregnant again? It's not too late, you know.'

'What do you mean, R?' as if he hadn't realised.

'Well, you know, getting a termination.' She sat hunched up in her seat, scared at the whole concept and of the way he might react and what she'd do or say if he said yes, kill the child.

The turn off into the dead end lay-by was coming up where he'd taken Andrea that day and he swung smartly left, drove to the end, switched the engine off and turned to face her.

Her hands were twisting together; she looked small, defenceless, a frightened little girl.

'No.'

She bit her lip. 'Do you still love *me*?'

The emphasis on the *me* was too strong.

'I love *you*, Roberta. And the child in your womb. Planned it – he, she, – may not be, but I've loved you and that's what it is. A love child. *Our* love child. So *never, ever,* suggest anything other than taking the best possible care of yourself so we make sure it happens as . . .' and couldn't finish because his emotions got the better of him.

She saw the tears run and felt ashamed she'd ever doubted him, felt so badly over the way she'd messed about not telling him straight out and the way their beautiful holiday had trailed off to such a stupid end. All the bright bits, all the wonderful days and the scenery and the lovely people, and their own loving and the caring and . . . she'd all but forgotten Hazel.

'Let's go home, darling. The twins. I'm sorry I ever doubted you.'

He swallowed, took his hands away from the clenched grip on the wheel to wipe his eyes, to take a hankerchief out to blow his nose and then to reach across to touch her own clasped hands.

It took a few days before life really felt anything like normal again, by which time memories of the sojourn in Ireland had sadly faded away into a misty background. Andrew made damned sure Roberta did as she was told, put her feet up for an hour after lunch and dinner, took her pills on time, and kept an eye on her when she met the avalanche of clients who, despite June's professionalism and enthusiasm, had waited until she was available again before confirming their orders.

June couldn't be concerned; Roberta had passed on some of the comments she'd had back from the clients.

'The Fosters were very taken with your ideas, June. They're worry muttons, though. Just wanted me to say how well planned the designs were before confirming the order. And the Andersons were the same. So you've done well. A flair for it, it seems. Well done.' She'd paused, and assumed June would have guessed correctly what was coming. Now:

'Want to stay? *Can* you stay?' for Andrew had indicated something of the way his daughter's thoughts were running and it was a very mixed blessing.

231

June's feel for the Manor was growing on her and the two or three e-mails back from William in the last fortnight had strange undertones that even technoletters couldn't disguise. He'd found another woman, probably another geek, she was sure of it, and in a peculiar way she was quite glad. Not for her to sever the final strands of a bad marriage, largely because it was far too close to home. Her dad's experience wasn't quite the same, but *two* divorces in the same family? Peter – brother Peter in far off Romania, holding Mum's hand and doing a jolly good job by all accounts – had actually encouraged her. 'Never liked the bloke,' he'd e-mailed, and that was that.

'I can stay. If dad's okay with it.' Silly question, of course he would be. 'And if Andrea goes . . .' and that was a *big big* mistake. Because Andrea had worried over her announcement and held back, despite another animated – *passionate* – plea from Alain, and now she'd let the cat out of the bag.

'*Andrea? Going?*' Roberta all but squeaked and June worried. She wasn't supposed to be stressed, her dad had said. 'Who said she was going? June, what's been going on?'

'Sorry, Roberta.' Lips clenched, she thought hard and quickly but had to be honest. 'The film company's guy Alain; he's been in touch. Seems he's losing his p.a. and wants her as a replacement. She's flattered but very mixed up over it, doesn't want to let us down. So didn't want to say anything until you came home and she could discuss. Please don't let on, for my sake!' Which was true, and it sounded all very straight forward, said like that. The complications of how Andrea was attracted to the man and given both her and Mary to understand she'd go were another thing. Or how the girl showed what feelings she obviously still had for her father. So how contradictory and mixed up was that?

Roberta sat down. So it was about to happen after all. 'Your father won't want to see her go. Any more than I do, I suppose. But we can't stand in her way, not if there's fame and fortune beckoning. Just as well we've got you about the place.'

'And Hazel.'

'Ah yes. And Hazel.' That bloody silly blackout she'd had had prevented her from discovering how that last day's hike across the Sheep's Head Way in Ireland had gone, latterly it hadn't seemed overly relevant apart from Hazel behaving far more of a grown-up girl than ever. 'What . . . ' but thought and restarted her query differently, 'has she said anything about her trip away?'

'Not really. Other than she enjoyed it, the twins behaved a lot better than she'd hoped, was sorry you weren't too well. Did she help you cope?'

Roberta was totally honest. 'I couldn't have managed without her. But maybe something happened out there that I can't put my finger on; she is a different girl. Has your father said anything?'

June woke up. If something had happened, then Roberta might rightly be concerned. Certainly Hazel seemed a good deal more mature with a deeper edge to her personality, more refined, more self assured, much less hesitant. And this was a youngster with an e.s.n background?

'No, he hasn't. Should he have?'

Her question took Roberta's memories back to that lovely evening spent watching the light changing over Bantry Bay from the Wave and Sky restaurant, how she'd thought to push Hazel's development towards becoming a fully fledged adult one step on by getting her husband to flirt with the girl, in order for her to get a feel for the real world. And worried about it, to the point, now she understood, to where her hyped up emotions may have stressed her into that last blackout. Like the earlier occasion at Jerpoint where she'd felt something much the same. But there her mind had cleared itself of one dilemma, only to have another one take its place. She should have allowed herself to have more faith in him.

If he'd had any opportunity at all, it would have been up on that hill. She'd made her own play that time two years ago, up on a hill and, boy, it had happened. And Hazel? Had it truly happened for her? This stupid business over her blood pressure, was it all her own silly fault, messing about with other people's emotions? And, as June had asked, should he have said anything specifically?

'Maybe not. She's growing up, isn't she?'

'Yes, and I think you should be proud of her. I know your mum is. Shame she's got no dad about. I wouldn't be without mine.'

'June, you do say some lovely things. I wouldn't be without your dad either. Let's go and find him, get some tea organised. And thanks again, for keeping the Barn alive while we've been away. Consider yourself hired. Design Consultant. Hailsworthys and Daughter. Come on, girl.'

She didn't raise the subject again. Andrew had heartily concurred with appointing his daughter to the team, sorry only that her marriage had been the sacrifice. Hazel went about her job of keeping the twins in order in her usual unassuming way, without demeaning Roberta's true role as mum in any way. Andrea kept her head down, no doubt waiting for the opportune moment to announce her departure. June, as happy a girl as she had been for ages, emphasised her role by clinching a superb deal with a holiday home company. Mum Mary fussed over her girl far too much, but she surely did appreciate the comfort. The days went by. The autumn rains set in, the garden looked greyly dismal in the mornings, and the clients kept coming.

Roberta's blood tests came back and Doc Mac called her into the surgery.

'Have any trouble sleeping?'

She had sometimes, especially if they ate later than normal.

'Fall asleep during the day?'

She laughed. 'Fat chance! Though if I sit down after lunch I could doze off.'

'Couldn't we all. How's your energy level?'

She pulled a face. 'I manage.' She thought she'd begun to show, maybe wishful thinking but her skirts were tightening.

'Well, the blood pressure's under control. Not sure if there's anything else lurking in the background. We'll do another blood test in a couple of weeks. Now, let the practice nurse have a look. I'll see you again in a month.'

She went home moderately happy. At least the threat of 'twins again' had gone away.

Alain kept up the pressure. Andrea almost dreaded the lunchtime phone calls, which seemed to be his regular time to plague her. She knew she was dithering, and couldn't bring herself to face up to making the decision. Well, she'd actually made the decision, hadn't she? But not told the only man who could persuade her otherwise. Then the moment came. He'd come into the office, propped himself up on her desk with his feet on the other chair and looked at her.

'I missed you, out there.'

'I missed you too.' They went back a fair old way and could say these things. 'Shame about Roberta.'

His eyes bored into hers. 'Shame she's pregnant or shame she had a couple of blackouts?'

'Being unwell out in Ireland. And I'm very happy for you both, having the third.'

'Puts a slight strain on the logistics, or will do eventually. Did I hear you right about training Hazel up on this thing?' as he tapped the top of the screen.

'Sure. She'll be great.' She took a deep breath, 'when I leave.'

'Leave? You can't leave, Andrea?' His voice rose, sounded ever so slightly cross, His hand came down and cupped her chin. 'Why?'

'Alain's offered me a job. P.A. His current model's gone maternal.'

He frowned. 'But why ask you? Surely there's plenty of secretarial staff in his outfit? I can't lose you, Andrea, not after all this time. You don't want to go, do you?'

She caught his hand, took it down to the desk. 'I do and I don't. I've got to look at the long term, Andrew. You and I are who we are. That's something we'll never lose, neither of us. I have to move on, reluctantly, but I do. You've got Hazel.'

235

She noticed the change of expression, fleeting, but there, and wondered.

'Ah, yes. Hazel. Another one who may ultimately wish to move on.' He eased off the desk and stretched. 'At least I've got June.'

'And Roberta.'

'And Roberta.' Then he grinned. 'She won't ever be a candidate for the 'moving on' league. Least I sincerely hope not. Look after Hazel, Andrea. She's special. Very very special. When do you want to go?'

'Only when you and I agree I can be spared. Alain will wait – that is, unless Steph starts to hatch. Thank you, Andrew. For absolutely everything.' She stood up and wrapped her arms round him. The kiss lasted and lasted and her heart rate climbed. Another time, another place, and this, in her mind, could well have had a historically inevitable outcome, for it was just them, what had happened in their ordained togetherness and hence precious and exceedingly unique. 'Keep Roberta safe, Andrew. She's special too, you know.'

They broke apart. Sadly, she thought he rather spoilt the effect as he wiped his lips and had to say it, 'I'm not infectious.'

The grin came before another restorative embrace and this time his hand softly cupped a breast. 'Maybe not infectious, Andrea, but very catching.' The hand wandered down and ended on her bottom. 'I want to talk something through with you. Can you spare an hour later?'

She collected the hand and brought it back under firm control. 'Sure. When and where?'

There was no need to suggest somewhere specifically private; their passionate fling from way back had moved into a deeper and mature relationship well outside the physicality of sex, though the actuality of those few encounters had left a depth and a value far beyond what many would understand.

'If it stays dry, we'll potter round the garden? After tea?'

She pulled the chair back into place and sat down. 'Right,' and thought to ask, frowning at him, 'Was that why you came to see me?'

He nodded. 'If you fancy being Mother Confessor. I can't burden Roberta with my queries on this one, or daughter June. Not until I've got it straight in my mind.'

'Sounds intriguing. No, don't go on. Let me finish this. See you later,' stared at the screen and resumed typing. She heard the door close and took a deep, deep breath.

SEVENTEEN

'I don't believe you!'

He shrugged. 'Haven't you noticed the difference in her?'

Andrea hesitated momentarily. Yes, she had, but hadn't interrogated her thoughts specifically. What was it that he was saying, that the experiences of Ireland and his newfound attitude were responsible and not purely just the 'being away'?

She ignored the question and posed one of her own. 'What's Roberta going to say? If – when – you tell her?'

'She put me up to it in a backhanded sort of way. Thought Hazel needed to experiment with her femininity.' He remembered very clearly her explanation, probably edited, of what had happened out there on the first evening when the two girls had gone out for a walk. At the time he'd taken it without any reaction, treated the whole affair as a casual matter-of-fact thing, part of Roberta's wish to continue her education of a naïve teenager and now very glad he had.

'What's her mother going to say? You can't merely waltz in and tell her you're going to take her daughter away permanently, can you? Though it is certainly high time she made her own way in the world; most parents would be overjoyed to find their youngster was about to fly the nest.' Reflecting on her own situation, ironically almost an identical one, she swallowed her self interest and carried on, 'At least you haven't got her father to worry about, and I suppose his absence really started the whole thing off. Glory be, Andrew, but you don't do things by halves, do you? First me, then Roberta, now Hazel. Good job June's a proper daughter else she'd be a target as well. And with Roberta's third on the way!

Just as well you've got the Manor. A girl in every bed. Well, not me, not now. I wish you luck.'

'So you think it'll work?'

'No idea. If it does, maybe Alain will come and make a film of you all.' She glanced sideways at him, admiring that so determined look that came every now and again. If that's what he wanted, then so be it. 'Yes, why not? Go for it. She deserves it, that's for sure.'

'As you did?'

She grinned. 'I suppose so, though you didn't class me as a daughter then, now did you! Losing my knickers to you was rather a rite of passage. I'm sadder in some ways, much happier and wiser in others but a lot more grown up than I once was. Thanks.'

'Don't mention it. An enjoyable exercise. But I don't like the sadder bit.'

'Turn of phrase. As was your 'exercise'. Glad it was enjoyable.'

'As I recall, you'd didn't argue.'

She reached for his hand and squeezed. 'No more I did. We've been great together, Andrew. So have you got used to the idea I'm leaving?'

'Sort of, sadly. At least you won't be entirely out of reach. As you say, we've grown up. And now I've another young lady to look after.'

'You love her?'

He nodded. 'I love her,' knowing she'd take the statement quite the right way.

'Lucky girl. Don't upset Roberta. She's your life, Andrew. As are the kids. Are you sure you can manage the whole thing? It's asking a lot of everybody, including June. Just to satisfy your whim?'

'More than a whim, Andrea. Were you a whim?'

She considered the question, recalling that odd evening. Going round to his place, *on a whim*, merely because she was bored, because he was a challenge and then, ultimately, the evening after Samantha had walked out, she'd felt sorry for him and he'd ended up making love to her. Took her virginity in fact. On a whim? No. Certainly she'd never, ever, regret their fling – yes, fling, – because time had moved on.

They'd walked right across the garden and the old beech cast its ancient protective shadow across them. She managed her skirt carefully to sit down on the bench he'd installed, near where she'd collapsed the day her father had died and where Mary had found her. He moved to stand in front of her, looking down, no doubt getting an eyeful of her cleavage. If she hadn't gone round that night would she still be virginal? Would she have had the chance of this job and in its train, taking part in the filming of the – to her – strange television programme and hence meeting Alain? Was that on a whim?

'Sit down, Andrew. Stop looking down my front.' She watched the expressions chase across his face, irritation, wry amusement, and then a strange feeling of something more. 'Please?'

He sat down alongside her, hunched up, staring at his feet. 'All Sam's fault. Blame her. Not regretted things, Andrea? Have you?' and turned to look at her; reached for a hand.

'You brought me alive, Andrew,' and his grip was warm and comforting. 'Gave me something I hadn't had, but we've had a few close shaves since, haven't we? Roberta's been extremely understanding. How a woman could have watched her husband flirt like you do I really don't know. And now she's encouraged you to flirt with Hazel? So what did happen to bring all this on?'

'In Ireland?'

'Yes. And did what happened cause Roberta to flip? Because if it did, that's not very much like you. You're usually more protective of her than that.'

He drew his hand back, put fingers together close into the prayer position, tucked his chin into them. He felt her freed hand come up and stroke the back of his neck, her thumb massaging. And this girl was leaving him. She should have been with them in Ireland then maybe she wouldn't have had the job offer. Wishful thinking.

'Do you really want to leave?'

The hand went. 'Stop it Andrew. You asked me to come out here so you could get Ireland and Hazel off your chest. Don't complicate things.'

He wouldn't give up. 'Don't go.'

'I might leave now, if you don't stop pestering me. And I am leaving, Andrew, because I need to move on, you need to move on and Alain needs a good organiser. I've finally made up my own mind and I don't want you trying to change it. Now tell me what went on.'

His head went down again, looking for the inspiration that would clear his mind and immediately he saw Hazel, stretched out on the grass below that trig point, the way she came up to him and . . . the retelling of that part of the defining moment would be cathartic. He'd have to explain very carefully.

'Don't tell me you . . .' the look she gave him, the tone of her voice too suggestive only because she'd been down one particular road with him, but she would be very surprised if she got what she'd believed was the wrong answer.

He became defensive. 'She's become a lovely person, Andrea. Of course not. *No. I did not.* No I wouldn't have, not ever. Certainly not after the way I now feel about her. No, I don't think Roberta's black-outs have anything to do with it.' How could he express himself to this particular girl with whom he'd had an entirely different relationship to the one growing between the – as described – his and Roberta's protégé? He had to try. 'Who does she remind you of?'

'Hazel?' Andrea, deeply relieved he'd denied any wrong doing, became aware of how serious he'd turned and thought for quite some time to try and get it right, working through all the possibilities before she drew only one inevitable conclusion. 'In a strange way, maybe Sam? A younger, perhaps livelier Sam, but not dissimilar. Not that I really knew your ex-wife all that well other than when she and my mum got together.'

He nodded. 'Exactly. It surprised me. All of a sudden, there she was, a youthful re-incarnation, and I hadn't seen it. Until then.'

'What? Up on a hill, in Ireland? How weird!'

'That's what the painting was telling me. It kind of triggered my thought chain.'

'The one you have in the office?'

He'd had it framed and hung it where it was a constant reminder of the day. *The* day.

'So what does it tell you?'

'That I can't escape the obvious. That's what happened; Hazel is a younger Samantha. However, she's on a different plane because she's been so vulnerable, hence the daughter aspect, you see? I loved Sam, Andrea, she gave me June, and Peter. Then we drifted. There was a hole, a big hole. I tried filling it . . .'

'. . . with Roberta?'

'. . . and you.'

She slipped an arm round him. 'So you did. I wasn't complaining.'

'Neither was I. We were different, An.'

She jerked at him, startled. 'An? My mother's name for me.' Then she chuckled. 'Shows how far we have come, Andrew. Don't ever stop loving me.'

He kissed her, lightly, on the cheek. 'I couldn't,' he said, and went back to his dilemma. 'So how can I explain my need to bring Hazel closer into our family picture?'

'Simply tell her about Sam. Roberta, I mean. And I'm sorry that I thought the wrong thoughts.'

He grinned. 'Understandable, apology accepted. But to tell her that Hazel's another Sam? I couldn't. Not while she's in this fragile state.'

'So what *did* you tell Hazel?'

The moment she'd come into his arms, up by that trig point, he would never forget, because precious didn't come anywhere close. Between sea and sky, the two of them alone and yet together. Words not said, not needed. Melded together. Water and ground in their extremity carved into rock, carved into his soul. She the purest of clear water, he the ground on which she'd rest. Sheila's words, *Triangle of love.* But was there a missing person? He and Hazel were only two. A quandary. It couldn't be Roberta, that wouldn't fit and Andrea was moving on. Who, then? He pushed it to one side.

'Told her she'd become part of me.' His eyes misted, for at that saying she'd nestled into him and asked *'like a daughter?'* and he'd said yes, like a daughter and he knew he could never renege on that statement. 'Told her she had become, out of the blue, as precious as a daughter.' He had to wipe an eye and Andrea looked at him and her feelings for him swelled and swelled.

'Then you *have* added to the harem.'

'Not a harem. And I haven't told Roberta.'

'Hasn't she asked?'

'She flaked out, remember, and then it didn't seem to matter.'

'But Hazel's changed. Hasn't she noticed?'

'Not to remark on it, not to me at least. Hazel's still working things out for herself. You don't suddenly acquire a new father figure and take it for granted. But she's a lot more refined and, I think, a lot happier underneath. I've not dwelt on it; there's been no need, because we both understand each other and where we are.'

'I'd agree there. And I'm looking forward to training her up in the office. Because I *am* going, Andrew, but I won't lose touch. No way.'

They walked back across the grass arm in arm. Roberta was in the sitting room with her book and another mug of tea; she'd seen them on the bench together and though curious, it didn't bother her. He was like that, enjoying heart-to-hearts every now and again and always told her afterwards what it was all about or what conclusions had been drawn over the discussions – it could have been over anything. Andrea was leaving and she'd obviously got round to saying so. Just as well because she couldn't have kept it from him much longer. Another change in routines and more upheaval. Rather sad in many ways but a lot better for the girl in the long run. She'd miss her. Just as well they had Hazel. And June. Poor June. She felt for her, because she'd been through it – well, not quite the same, but the end result was. Stupid bloke, that William, he didn't deserve a girl like June. She was a chip off the old block – not that Andrew would like being called an old block. She smiled at the phrase, replaced her marker in the book and left it on the chair seat as she got up and stretched. Her waistband was getting tighter by the day and the stretch marks were coming back. Motherhood! Some small consolation that she'd wasn't nauseous this time round. Maybe 'cos there was only one in there. It was time to light the fire; darker and cooler evenings with autumn well on its way. Mug in hand, she returned to the kitchen. Mum Mary was doing something with a pan. Her turn to cook dinner. Would Andrea stay?

'Mum, what're doing?'

Mary reached for the jar again. 'Can't you smell, lass? Curry. Chicken version. How many's?'

Roberta laughed. 'For dinner? I was going to ask the same. Maybe Andrea will stay seeing as she's been out chewing the cud with Andrew. Where are they? I thought they were coming in?'

'P'raps back in the office?'

'Maybe. And June?'

'Still in the Barn. And Hazel's doing your job,' Mary added, darkly. 'Bathing them lusty children o'yourn.'

'You mean your grandchildren!'

'Aye, but it's still your job. You go on up for a while. I'll have words with Andrea.'

Mary found Andrea and Andrew as she had expected, in the office, leaning over the computer screen together, the girl's arm round him. 'Time you two called it a day. Stay for dinner, Andrea?'

She withdrew her arm and stood up. 'Yes, Mary, that would be lovely. My mum's out tonight – joined a book club – so I would only have had an omelette or something. May I go and freshen up?'

That didn't really need an answer. She left to go and use the downstairs wash and shower room. Andrew also straightened up and switched the computer off.

'While I've got you on your own, Mary, there's something I need to say. I've decided to approach Hazel's mum to ask her if Hazel can live here permanently. Not just as an au pair or nanny, but as part of the family. Sort of adopt her.'

'Lord help us, lad!'

He could see he'd startled her. 'I know. Think what you like, Mary, but I've really taken to her. As a daughter. Since Ireland.'

'Bless me! I knew she were different when she came back, even more than after the do she had with Roberta that day. What more's been said then, lad?'

So out with the explanations again, a clearer and more precise description the second time round after his first faltering version for Andrea. 'It was out on the hill above the Bay, Bantry Bay. Once we'd come to the top after a hike up into the hills; she'd flopped down on the grass, stretched out by the trig point and suddenly she got to me. Everything; in looks, mannerisms, even what she wore that day. Just like Sam was in the very early years. And she knew it too, that was the eerie part of it. We came together exactly like father and a reunited much loved daughter. So that's what happened. Roberta doesn't know exactly how I feel. She may have guessed, but I've not said. She had that black-out and I haven't had a chance since. I wanted to bounce the situation off Andrea first because I value her views.'

'Then you'd best sort it, lad, and quick. It doesn't do to keep any secrets from your wife, especially in her state. But thanks for the explanation, I knew there was summat. And I'm right glad for the lass but heaven knows what her mother'll say. Or her own father, if he ever turns up. Ee, lad. You're a rum 'un. First one girl then another. Still, best daughter than paramour.'

Andrew laughed. 'Paramour? How very eighteenth century! She's not married, Mary. Turn it round, but I'm certainly not a sugar daddy. Perhaps I might have been tempted if she'd been a few years older *and* Roberta hadn't come into my life, because she's sure turned into one delectable young lady. Roberta, I know, may have had thoughts. But no, Mary, not that way. What I am sure about is that she's come to mean an awful lot more to me. Call it a sort of affection if you like, for I guess that's what it is. Blame Ireland. Has a magic all of its own. Especially on tops of hills, and by a trig point of all places. Some symbolism there.'

Mary sniffed. She had a very expressive sniff.

Andrew laughed. 'Come on, Mary, I can smell burning curry.'

Later on that night he had the perfect opportunity although he lacked the courage to come right out with the situation. Roberta, poised as was her wont on the stool in front of mirror to comb out her hair (and often managed to get him involved for mutual satisfaction) asked the question.

'Are you happy with Hazel's progress, love?'

'Ah. I wondered when you'd ask. Are you?'

She spun round and looked at him. 'I asked first.'

'Um. The short answer is yes.'

'That all? Merely *ah um yes*?'

So he had to commit himself. 'That day on the hill, you know; when I had to rush you off to Bantry?'

She pulled a face. 'How could I forget? You've not been very forthcoming – something to hide?'

In all honesty he could say 'no', there wasn't anything he wanted to hide, especially from her but he was running away from how to explain. He'd spoken to Andrea, and to Roberta's mum, nonetheless was still unsure of how best to approach his strange change of attitude to the girl. But he'd had a few open heart talks with Roberta before; so what was different now?

'You met Sam. Can you think of her now, how she looked and so on?'

'What's she got to do with Hazel?'

'Think of Sam as a younger girl.' How he wished he'd got instant access to those old photo books so he could show her, but they were all buried in the Manor attics along with more of his surplus gear now the family house had been sold.

He watched her frown and the worry lines appear on her forehead before what he'd said dawned on her.

'*You think Hazel's like Sam?* In younger years? Surely not!'

He nodded. 'Whatever the trigger, it struck a chord. Echoes of a past love, R. You know what they say, emotive feelings can be stirred from similarities,' and the old memory surged back into his thoughts.

They'd gone for a walk along the Dunstable Downs, left the ageing second hand car in the Zoo car park and explored. Gone through the strange Tree Cathedral with the plantings reminiscent of a church nave and cloisters and strolled out onto the open pasture. Watched the gliders wheel and circle above them, listened to the skylarks, disturbed the tall grasses and seen the pollen drift away in the light summer breeze. Looked at each other and the unspoken thoughts made close-held hands tighten, the search for a secluded hollow below the hawthorns led them down a bank away from casual eyes. Samantha, a lovely slim and deeply pretty girl in those far off days had stirred him beyond measure. Their earliest tentative and clumsy lovemaking had been behind the sand dunes away on the coast beyond Sheringham, his inward smile at her itching in her seat on the way home, complaining about sand in her knickers. She'd been the adventurous one.

But that particular lovely warm and sunny day on the Downs she'd worn the floaty skirt in a sort of cotton muslin; the shape of her legs and thighs clearly visible against the light. A pale coloured lightweight sweater emphasising her shape and the picture of her stretched out on the grass . . .; echoes of the past, his deep passion for her . . .

Hazel, in all but name. Why he'd had the flashback at the sight of her in white, stretched out so provocatively on soft grass and of the same age when his blood had run hot for Samantha. She who'd born his children and with whom he'd shared his life for twenty years. Now they'd parted, divorced, gone down different paths for the want of some lasting stimulus to the maturing marriage.

Could he continue this explanation to Roberta without becoming childishly or emotionally upset? Even now he could feel the tightening of his chest.

That afternoon. Lost in the incomprehensible need to make her his. Writhed and thrust, surged into her, made her scream with the mutual exhilaration and . . . June had been born exactly right . . . *That afternoon on the grass was déjà vu. The wheel spinning. What goes round . . .* But he hadn't, had he? Not taken her, made her the woman she might have wanted to be, wittingly or no? Would it have gone that way? . . . No, it would not. No recriminations. Instead he'd offered her kinship, a far more meaningful gift.

Roberta was staring at him. 'Echoes of a past love! Past love? Don't tell me you're re-living the past you had with Sam, darling? Please, not after we've been together three years, loved, had two lovely children, another one coming; you're not suffering withdrawal symptoms now, surely?'

'Haven't you got fragments of the past locked away somewhere in your mind, R? Times with your father even? Or in the early days with Michael? We can't erase things on our hard disc completely – traces will always stay.' Then he said what everyone says sooner or later and instantly regretted it. 'Don't worry, darling.'

'Don't *worry!*' she all but screamed at him. "course I worry. You're telling me you think Hazel's like a young Samantha, who you obviously shagged at every opportunity offered in those days and I let you loose on a remote Irish hilltop with her! I must have been mental.' She'd gotten herself so suddenly worked up, gone red in the face and straight away it worried him.

'Roberta, darling, calm down! It was you who wanted me to flirt with her so she could find out what it was like to have a man after her! I didn't want to get involved, remember? I only agreed to because she means so much to us – and I nearly didn't take her up the hill. She insisted.'

248

Her muscles had gone all tense and her head was beginning to go fuzzy again, just like Jerpoint and the afternoon they'd come back. This was *not* good. 'Androo oo . . . '

He caught her easily as she drooped down, a head flopping with her arms like an abandoned glove puppet, swept her up and laid her on the bed, loosened her nightdress buttons at her neck and then lifted her legs to stuff a pillow under to raise them. Within a minute she'd come round, fluttered eyelashes like any well trained Jane Austen character and smiled wanly.

'Teach me to get worked up. Sorry, love.'

'You weren't faking?'

'Nope. Did I take my pill?'

'I hope so. I haven't checked up on you. At least I know what's happening, though I'd rather it didn't. And I'm the one who should apologise. I should have explained before. D'you want me to go on or would you rather I left it?'

She eased herself further up the bed and leant on the pillows against the cushioned bed head. 'If you're into the mood of the moment, dear, you'd best carry on. I'm okay.'

'I'll get you a drink if you want?'

'In a while.' She closed her eyes. 'You just carry on. Just tell me what happened.'

She'd come up into his arms and, as in all the best magazine romances, stared into his eyes. Hers the dark grey and hypnotic, searching, wondering, beautiful. He had to, with the softness and yet youthful firmness of her so close and warm, seal the just parted lips with his kiss. 'I couldn't help myself. She'd walked up that hill with me, not missed a step. As though . . . ' *As though she'd been his. And that was what made it perfectly normal and happy and wonderful.* '. . . she was my daughter. June used to walk like that, unconcerned, effortless, used her muscles, her body, looked every inch what I'd always thought a girl should be. Diana, Athena, goddess like. Hazel has the same knack. Haven't you seen her, R, holding those kids of ours, walking, so poised? Like a dancer? Sam used to be the same. Till she thickened out after Peter's birth and lost interest in walking.'

He'd told her then. Told her she was such a beautiful person, like Samantha had been, like June, and I'd have been proud to own her as a daughter. 'I kissed her, R, but I didn't flirt, didn't attempt to make love to her. No *Liaisons Dangereuse* in this. Because I'd like to think we could adopt her. As a daughter. That's what she means to me. Why she's changed. Why I feel so much involved with her.' *She'd kept her arms round him for minutes, her head resting into his chest, and had cried out of sheer sheer happiness, kissed him again, and as they'd started the return journey from the place neither of them would ever forget, held his hand, kept glancing at him and he'd felt literally on top of the world. Sheila's 'triangle of love' wasn't a tug of war, it was cementing a relationship. Bless her.*

'Oh.' Roberta opened her eyes. What could she say? 'So no more flirting?'

'No more flirting. She doesn't need . . . perhaps better to say doesn't 'want' . . . anything like that for a while, not while she'd adjusting to having a more meaningful father figure in her life. I've filled the gap, my love, and I love her. As a daughter.'

'Goodness.' She blinked. This husband of hers kept on surprising her. 'I'm not sure about the 'adoption' bit. She's still got a mum and she's a smidgen under twenty. Though I think I get your drift. Goodness,' she said again, realising she'd as good as said 'okay' in her response. 'I think a sort of grown up 'god parent' might be a better – or easier – concept to deal with. Oh, Andrew, dear man. Come here.'

He took the five steps back to the bedside from his 'lean on the wall' position and her arms came up for him.

'I love you,' she said simply, and pulled him down. 'You've done a lovely thing for the girl. And thank you for being so good to me. Kiss me?'

She'd asked, back at the car, what Roberta would say, and he'd said, don't worry about it, because she's very understanding about people and relationships, far more than you'd realise and she probably feels the same way as I do now – and didn't she help you understand things a few days ago? – and Hazel had blushed and gone all coy and said that was before and it didn't matter now, and would he forgive her for being all foolish and far too girlish the other evening. Then they'd kissed again and got into the car and driven back to the cottage in companionable silence and found Roberta collapsing on the floor. . .

He kissed her as requested before shedding the rest of his clothes and sorting out the duvet to cover her before rolling in alongside and switching off the bedside light. 'Godparents, plural,' he said to her. 'Hmmm. Yes. Don't mind that. Me *and* you.'

'S'right. *Me* and you. Lucky girl, isn't she?'

'Yep. So are you.'

'Egotist.' she said sleepily after a few minutes thought.

No answer to that. His worries at an end, he'd gone to sleep.

EIGHTEEN

A ndrea took the plunge. She rang him first thing the following morning.

'Do you need me to fill in an application form or anything?' she asked after she'd heard the expellation of breath and that *''Good girrrl,'* almost as though she'd obeyed an instruction like some pet dog – or bitch in this case, not that she ever wished to be known as a bitch for it wasn't in her nature to be bitchy.

'Gracious no. Personnel or H R, as they love to be called nowadays, will no doubt need to absorb some details, but I have my own right to hire. And fire,' he'd added, with a chuckle in his voice. 'I am extremely grateful and very very pleased,' he went on in a much more serious tone, 'that you've come to your senses. Steph will want to personally vet you to make sure you're fully suitable in her eyes, but I'm sure you'll take that in your stride. When can you come over?'

'I'll have to clear it with Andrew, Alain, and I can't leave until Hazel's been trained up. Probably another couple of weeks?'

A sigh down the phone this time. 'I guess I'll have to live with it. Now, the cast 'n crew showing – have you cleared that with your boss?'

She hadn't, being infinitely more concerned over the decision to leave. 'Sorry, no. I'll ask them today and come straight back. When?'

'Sooner the better. It's all cut and spliced, figuratively speaking. The series is slotted in for the beginning of November – six programmes to end on a pre-Christmas note. You'll love it.'

'I'm sure we will. Is there anything else?'

'Just get that young Hazel sorted, Andrea. I'm a verrrey happy chappy. Sooner the better. More overlap with Steph. Oh, and what about another lunch? I promised?'

'So you did. When I get back to you?'

'Fine. Speak later then. 'Byeee.'

She tackled Andrew straight away, as soon as he walked into the office.

'Cast and Crew? What, a sort of pre-publication thing? Sure, I don't see why not. Best check with Roberta though I'm sure she won't mind – love it in fact. And getting Hazel trained up must be a priority. I'll have to work out with Mary when we can let her off twin's duties.'

'Can June help as well?'

He frowned. 'She's already said she doesn't want to be office bound if she can help it.' Reflectively he added, 'Maybe we'll have to hire someone else for one department or another. See what you're doing, An, making me all stressed out.'

That 'An' again. She loved it because it made her feel more part of his life than ever before even if it was a prelude to a separation. She'd make damn sure Alain didn't call her that. Special for just him and her mum, rather like the way only he alone called Roberta 'R'.

Roberta, found in the Barn carefully arranging a new set of curtains into their folds and feeling an awfully lot chirpier than she'd been for days, stretched her back, rubbed her hands down the side of her skirt and pulled a face at Andrea. 'Do I really want to be seen making a fool of myself? Not that I've got much option, I guess. When does he want to hold this shindig?'

'I'm not sure it's a shindig, Roberta,' Andrea said carefully, 'because that smacks of lots of booze and a knees-up. Rather more sedate a do, I fancy. A few film or telly big-wigs perhaps and hence the odd bottle of spirits. I don't honestly know, but I'll soon find out. So it's okay with you?'

She got a nod and a 'yes, it's okay' before the other question came at her. 'Andrew. Did he talk to you about Hazel?'

Oh dear. Andrea gritted her teeth. Was she going to upset things? Cautiously she replied, 'He mentioned something about a changing relationship? Inspired by Ireland?'

Roberta gave her a sideways glance, a bit like the proverbial 'old-fashioned' look but happily didn't delve any further. 'We're looking to give her more of a guardian style level of support, Andrea. As though we'd been appointed godparents? What do you think?'

With considerable relief, Andrea nodded her head. 'That seems awfully good of you both and I'm sure she'd welcome it. How will her own mother take to the idea?'

'Don't know. Andrew's thinking on how best to approach her. If she'd been a much younger child it might have smacked of adoption. Or kidnap,' and she giggled.

'I rather think you'd have created some very unwelcome publicity if that had been the case. She's her own person now and an adult in law, so what does she think?'

'Welcomes our support. Never having had a proper father to look up to; and though it comes rather late on, it must be better than nothing. And she's rather taken to my husband as replacement father figure.'

Andrea really wanted to say, yes, I know, but daren't. Instead she smiled and thought how consistently well she got on with Roberta considering the common but uneasy relationship they'd shared. But it had taken on a different and deeper meaning as time had moved on and that difference came out clearly in her reply. 'He's an easy man to take to, Roberta. We both know that.'

'So we do, my dear, so we do. Let's go and have tea.'

'Can I have the morning off next Wednesday?' asked Andrea the following morning when Andrew joined her in the office at his usual ten o'clock time. 'Alain wants to introduce me to Steph, his present p.a., and allow me get the low down on a few basics before she leaves? I should be back by lunchtime.'

'Don't see why not. Better to take the whole day if you want, but can you start to take Hazel through *our* basics here before then? Mary will take care of the twins after morning tea break until lunch, then again from two until four. That'll give you approx two hours morning and afternoon. And June will pop her head in some afternoons if there's no clients in the offing, just so as she's aware of things. She's out this morning, delivering samples to the Petersham's.'

'Of course I will. She's going to be fine. And I'm sure it will do her good. Boost her confidence no end.'

He spun the other chair round and sat frontwards like the Cliveden Keeler girl photo, facing her. 'I had words with Roberta.'

'And?'

'She's taken to the idea rather well. Unofficial god-parents, she described it as, really rather sensible. But there's something else about Hazel that's bothering me.'

'Ah?'

'She came out of school without much at all in the way of qualifications and seeing as we've kept her isolated up here for what, nigh on three years, she's not managed anything else. No college, no evening classes. Just us and the kids. Oh, I know Mary and Roberta have passed on things but it's not the same, is it? If she takes to the computer, can we get her to put in some time at the College? Get some NVQ's or something?'

She thought. There was some chance, certainly, that it might work. She'd done a fair amount at the College in her day and it would be a lot better equipped now. 'I don't see why not, Andrew. Will she want to?'

He wriggled off the chair and stood up. 'Find out what's best suited, An, if you would, and then *you* ask her. I'll go and have words with Roberta.'

When he had gone, Andrea did a very unladylike thing. She pulled her skirt edge up, kicked her shoes off and lifted spread legs onto the desk in front of her, lent back rather precariously against the spring of the office chair and stared first at the dark screen, seeing a very indecorous mirror image of herself, and then up at the high ceiling with its ornate coving, a relic of former glory. In this room, on this chair; that was the last time she'd experienced intimacy of any sort and that not a pleasant occasion, merely a mechanical relief of need. Since then she'd flirted, attempted silly seductions, made it perfectly clear she would if he'd asked and got absolutely nowhere. As time had gone on, the highly charged emotional feelings between them had generally wasted away. Oh, true there were moments when the atmosphere had become slightly more explosive; however the ignition spark just hadn't happened. That time in the old lay-by was as close as it came and Roberta had uncannily deflated the memory. Her thoughts and her eyes came back down and she tugged at her hemline so the reflection he'd love to see didn't show. Love to see? Or would he? Roberta was his and his alone. So why was she hell bent on maintaining this thing of hers? Especially since she was leaving to get within another male's purlieu and he with a few 'come hither' signals floating about. She leant forward and rubbed hands down the inside of her thighs, moved her legs a fraction and nearly fell off the chair as it kicked backwards. Then she straightened up, pulled the chair back under her and livened up the screen to start the day's work, having thus diminished any girly thoughts down to near nothing and for keeps.

Hazel appeared ten minutes later.

As he went across to the Barn, his mind surging with echoes of Andrea's thoughts about Hazel's education, a customer's car pulled in to the car park, a lovely deep maroon Jaguar, personalised plates. He hovered, the only polite thing to do as they'd obviously seen him.

He offered the conventional greeting, not knowing who they were, Roberta hadn't said, but then she didn't always. It came as a pleasant surprise to hear the Irish burr. 'From Waterford, you say?'

'Indeed. We have a house over there on the Surr River. You know the country?' The man, in his late fifties with a nice open look about him, sported a well cut jacket, his shoes were polished and his companion – 'May I introduce my wife?' – knew her fashions too. A pleasant smile, eyes a smoky sparkle under the mass of deep chestnut hair, the deep green costume with a loose wide leather belt, a warm and firm handshake. 'Siobhan is Irish born. Hence the connection. We're here on a mission. Your reputation has spread.'

Andrew inclined his head, acknowledging the compliment. 'It's not me you need to see. Roberta, my wife, is the expert. Had you an appointment?'

Siobhan took over. 'Our apologies, no. We came on the off chance, not having too much time left before our return to Ireland. If . . .'

'No, that's not a problem, I'm sure Roberta will be pleased to show you round. This way?'

They found her tucked away in the tiny office space she'd created after the re-hash from the filming, a sanctuary with a cosy armchair, a low table and shelves full of fabric sample books. Here she retreated to marshal thoughts and gain inspiration; where some of her best concepts came into focus and she did not welcome intrusion.

'Roberta – Mr and Mrs Drivas; they've come on spec, on their way back to Ireland.'

An incipient frown and a potentially curt reply disappeared. 'Ireland, you say?' and eased out of her chair. 'We've only just come back from West Cork ourselves. It's good of you to find us, what can we do for you?'

'Siobhan and Donald, please. We're only too pleased if you can spare us some time – whereabouts in West Cork? It's a lovely part of the country – we have a lovely small cottage we retreat to when the chance occurs way behind Balllickey. Well, more up in the Borlin valley actually. Know of it?'

'Yes, we do. Perhaps not well enough. We've only been across the twice, but it's been our delight. Great place to regain one's sanity.' Andrew caught Roberta's glance; she had that misty brooding look suggesting her mind was drifting back to memorable days; then she smiled at him.

'Just what I need. A link with *auld Ireland*. Why don't you come across to the house for coffee or something? Then you can outline what you've got in mind. I'd love to help.'

Siobhan's smile produced the loveliest dimples. 'What more could we ask? If you're sure we're not intruding?'

Andrew was positive. 'Of course not. All Irish customers are very welcome,' and could well have nearly added *'especially delightful ones like you'*.

Coffee was served in Mary's best traditional way in the sitting room, where Andrew's thoughts went back in time as they so constantly did. This was a reprise of Roberta's hospitality those three years ago and they still served Taylor's, this brand 'Lazy Sunday' – if his taste buds were in tune, though they did occasionally use some others. The home baked chocolate and ginger cookies were fresh from yesterday's baking. Donald looked very at home, legs crossed, relaxed, Siobhan demurely with slanted knees in *that* self same chair. Roberta stood with back to the fireplace. Too early in the day for the comfort of the fire, but the rug was still the same. Why?

'I'd like some advice, Mrs Hailsworthy, because our place hasn't had a revamp for some time. We've been abroad for a few years; now we've returned, probably for good, it would be nice to look for some comforting concept to see us into old age!' Siobhan's smile again, lovely.

'Please call me Roberta. And my husband's Andrew. How *did* you find us?'

'Ah. Wheels within wheels. An old friend of mine passed on your name, she works with Alain?'

Roberta exchanged looks with Andrew. *Alain.*

'So what had you in mind?'

Donald re-crossed his legs and held out his cup for the refill Andrew offered. 'If we let you have some good photos and sizes, sketches and a few basic thoughts, could you come up with your own new ideas, sketches, colours and fabrics and so on? We don't want to change the furniture so much because that's old, comfortable and suits the house, but the walls, curtains and so on . . . possibly some re-covering?'

'You could always come and stay with us for a while if needs be,' Siobhan interjected, 'it would be lovely if you could. And the little cottage might be grateful for a freshen-up as well?'

Roberta's face gave it away. Andrew could see her mind working. He knew she'd love to, it was just that in her present 'condition' he didn't fancy letting her go. Tread carefully, old son.

After he'd seen them out of the front door and watched them walk across the gravel towards the car, Donald with his confident strides, Siobhan with the fascinating sway of the Irish green of her skirt, he closed the heavy old door with its satisfying clump and went back to her.

'You want to, don't you?'

She nodded. 'I'd love to. Nice people. Very pleasant. They didn't mention children. Pity they didn't appear before we went to Ireland ourselves.'

'True. How long would it take, d'you think?'

She shrugged. 'They only talked about two rooms. Two days max.'

'Want to?'

'The twins?'

'I suppose we'd manage.'

'You wouldn't mind? Perhaps I could take June with me? Leave you with Hazel.' She grinned. 'Could I trust you?'

He met her eyes. 'You know the answer. But I don't want any more dizzy spells and I'd worry about you.'

'I'd be all right with June. And they seem very steady people. I'm sure I'd be okay.'

'I'd love to come too, you know that.'

'I'd love you with me, darling, but let's be sensible. You'd have nothing really to do other than ogle Siobhan.'

'Or go for some lovely long walks.'

'True.' She looked across to the window. The big old beech was turning a gorgeous shade of golden orange in front of the blue of the mid-day sky. Yes, it was a lovely day for a walk and she felt wonderfully happy and inspired . . .

'Is Andrea all right in the office? She's got Hazel with her?'

'She has. And yes, I suppose so. Why?'

'I want you to take me up the hill, Andrew. Just you and me. Now. We'll take some sandwiches. It's a lovely day out there.'

His heart surged at her comment. Why not? Surprising, she'd never actually been out with him on his favourite local walk and that phrase, 'take me up the hill' struck a chord, a very deep melodic chord.

It hadn't taken very long to make sandwiches, cut some slabs off the latest fruit cake and put some coffee in a flask. Mary had been surprised but rose to the challenge. June had swept back into the yard at the psychological moment and raised her eyebrows.

'Going out? For a walk?'

'Yes. What's wrong in that?'

'Nothing, dad. Just – well, surprising, in the middle of the working day?'

'One advantage of having resident staff. Boss's perks. Look after the shop. Andrea's in the office and the twins are asleep – for the moment. Hazel's with Andrea but she'll go back to the twins if they wake up. Shan't be over long, I don't suppose.'

'Back for tea at the latest, June,' Roberta added. 'My fault. Put it down to the strange fancies of a pregnant mum.'

'I thought that was eating fads, not out of character actions?'

'Not out of character, June, done this before, but not here. Come on, Andrew.'

She dragged him across the grass towards the stile and June returned to the house, shaking her head. Fathers!

NINETEEN

The ground was hard under foot, the edges of the recently drilled fields clearly defined but the summer grasses hadn't yet fully died back and lay matted and tangled between the stiffer stems of hemlock, suckered blackthorn and trailing bramble. Amidst the scrambling vines carrying clusters of the red berried woody nightshade and the blacker ones of buckthorn a few plump blackberries still hung amongst the decaying remnants of earlier ripenings. Roberta reached through and picked a few of the less squashy ones.

'Should have come up here before. They're quite sweet. Try one?' She popped one into his opened mouth. 'What are they?' and pointed.

'Sloes. Blackthorn berries. Think gin?'

'Oh, yummy.'

'Only in gin with plenty of sugar, love. And you need lots. Mary wouldn't thank you if you lumbered her with doing that.'

'Spose not. Shame.' She picked a few more blackberries and nearly lost her balance.

'Watch it, don't want a tumble. The bench is up here.'

'Bench?' She wiped purple fingers on the grass. 'What bench?'

'Where I was when I first saw you. Fall off that horse.'

'From up here?' She hadn't really thought too much about it. 'Oh!' He'd just appeared, as if from nowhere and the where-from had never truly concerned her.

'Is that all? – a life changing moment and all you say is '*oh*'.'

They trudged on up the field edge for another half mile

and there it was, half buried in this summer's accretion of lush grasses. He'd last been up here, when, late spring, just before the filming? Four months? A lot had happened in the meantime.

'You saw me from here?'

'Yep. Turn round, look across the fields. See, through the gap?'

'Oh yes. The lane. And the Home paddock. I can just make out the Manor roof. Goodness, it's a fair way down. How long did it take you to reach me?'

He pulled a face. 'Not sure, three minutes, five? Straight down the field edge, across the ditch. I didn't run.'

'Why not?'

'Cos I might have fallen myself. Better to reach you and able to help than not reach you at all.'

She tucked an arm into his and reached up to peck a cheek. 'Glad you did reach me.'

'So am I. Could even say I was glad you fell off.'

'Rotter. But you're right. Regret it?'

'Not one iota. Life changing moment. But then, I've said that before. And this is where it all started, well, sort of. Poor old bench. Don't know that it's safe to sit on now.'

She pushed the grass away and gingerly sat on the side with most of the slats still in place. It held, surprisingly. 'There. Don't think we'd both manage it though. Pity. We could have had our sandwiches here.' She rose and they continued on up the slope.

He looked at his watch. 'We've only been gone three quarters of an hour. We'll get to the top of the hill first. I seem to remember an old gamekeeper's hut. You okay?'

'I'm okay. Loving it.' The early afternoon sun was behind them and cast long shadows, glancing off the hedgerow's golden leaved hawthorn and giving the pasture land in front the same glow of autumn. In the valley below the russet brown of the chestnut's leaves stood out against the bronze of the beech and the bright yellow of the sycamore. Another week or so and it would have likely all gone, swept ahead of the winter winds.

'You sure you want to go to Ireland?'

The tone of his voice pulled at her and she stopped. 'You don't really think I should?'

'As I said, I'd worry, that's all.'

She prodded the toe of her walking boot at a molehill and thought for a moment. 'Then I won't. Let's send June. She knows the way I work. So long as the Drivas people don't mind. Oh, knickers!'

'Pardon?'

'Well, if it wasn't for Tertiary here,' and she patted her tummy, 'I'd be perfectly alright. And we'd both have gone.'

'You're not having second thoughts?'

'About our child? *No!* No, that I'm not. You loved me and this is proof. Not that I need it, 'cos I get that every day.' She walked on and he followed, watching her hair bounce around on the collar of her Barbour.

At the top, where the pasture gave way to the wood edge, she waited for him. 'Will you ever give up looking after stray women, Andrew?'

'Stray women? You mean the Andrea's and Hazel's of this world?'

'And me. I was one as well.'

'Not the same, Roberta. You weren't a stray, more like someone who, at the time, needed help. It went on from there. And I think, to be fair, you saw I needed help as well.'

'Did you?' She ducked under the overhanging hazel branches and into the wood's shelter.

He followed her lead. 'As events turned out, yes. Not that I knew it at the time. Infatuated maybe, but I think we've moved on.'

'Have we?'

Infuriating woman. He took a long stride and caught up with her, grabbed a hand and pulled her round. She had that tantalising grin, almost a smirk.

'This is for real, Roberta. I married you, remember. For better etcetera. And it has been for the better. An awful lot better. Don't knock it.'

The smirk went; replaced by the coy wistfulness he knew and loved, shook her curls at him, gently pulled him towards her and offered her lips.

'I'm not. But I am all mixed up inside.'

'Why so?' A windblown branch lay awkwardly straggled on the side of the path, but adequate as a seat. He eased down and let her cuddle up beside him. 'Is that why you wanted to come out here? To talk about us?'

'Mmmm. Because it's a beautiful afternoon and I wanted to be alone with you.' A rabbit suddenly bolted out from underneath them, from where it had played doggo but couldn't stand the strain, to streak for a burrow not twenty yards away. Roberta squeaked. He laughed.

'Not as alone as all that, but I take your drift. Are you bothered about something in particular, R?'

'Your sudden pash for Hazel, what might happen when Andrea goes, my silly fainting fits, poor June's failing – failed – marriage. And mum's not as bright as she was. I wouldn't want anything to happen to her, she's been my rock for so long.'

They stayed quiet, the sun's slanting beams of light flashing through the branches of the laurel pheasant cover at the wood edge and making the leaves appear to drift and dance. He held her hand loosely, lightly massaging her fingers, one by one.

'Surely I made it clear about Hazel?'

'Still a pash. You scarcely looked at her before Ireland.'

'Oh, that's not really true, is it, love? I've always liked the girl, ever since she first came! Okay, Ireland's magic showed her in a new light, allowed me to see her properly, put her into perspective. I can't help it if she reminded me of Sam. That's something neither of us could change. We will have to allow her more chance to become her own person, though. She'll have to get out there, not stay with us like some eighteenth century governess, obliged and beholden until the day she dies. I'm sure of that.'

Roberta heaved a sigh, a large intake and expellation of

breath. 'So that's all it is? Not a secret yen to have it away with her, as a challenge to prove your manhood?'

'I rather thought that's originally what you wanted me to do, Roberta. Give you some sort of kick, me taking on the servant girl. Sorry. Not me. She didn't warrant that sort of attention, not that she isn't an incredibly desirable young lady if you look at real definitions, especially since you took her in hand. So you're as much to blame as anyone.'

She studied her feet, scuffing them about in the detritus of leaves below. "Spose so. She just struck me as needing some masculine attention. Sort out her hormones. I wasn't going to play Sappho again.'

'Again?'

'I told you. I had to.'

He hadn't remembered and didn't want to know. The thought both appalled and aroused him and he got up to stretch and consider her comment. Roberta alone with Hazel up in that wood that evening no wonder they'd come back hand in hand. No wonder she'd shifted the emphasis over towards him. At least the girl now knew what made the apples grow. 'Lordy me. And if I had?'

She gave a careless shrug. 'I'd have taken it in my stride, I suppose. Academic, though, isn't it?'

He nodded. 'Yep. As I'm supposed to take your actions in mine. Oh, Roberta! And she's not come back at you?'

'No. Happily. I rather think you taking her onto the Sheep's Head and finding a different aspect to her attractions sorted that. She's been an awfully steadier girl since. That thing of Sheila's helped.'

'Back to the trig point again. Finding your position in life.'

'Mmmm. Where are those sandwiches?'

'I said the old gamekeeper's hut, didn't I? 'Bout another half mile.'

'Okay.'

They trudged on, Roberta kicking the old leaves about like a five-year old. The hut, a small and dilapidated structure of mould green shiplap with rust red corrugated iron roof, sagged into its sheltering Horse Chestnut bole. As far as he could recall, it did have a couple of benches and a sort of table.

She peered through the half open door into the dim dustiness of cobwebbed depths. The table, no more than an old scullery bench, still sported an old china mug and a bent spoon. One bench lay on its side; the other held the remnants of a cushion. No window, the only light came from the cracks in the planking and the hole in the roof, below which lay a matted heap of decaying twigs, as though a rook or pigeon's nest had fallen through..

'Yuck. No way. Doesn't look as anyone's been this way for years. Not eating my sandwiches in there.'

'You'd have been grateful if it had been raining.'

'If it had been raining, we wouldn't have been here.'

'True. Back to our tree bole?'

'What's wrong with that lot up there?' She pointed. Through the thinning line of trees beyond was a small stack of old fashioned rectangular bales.

'Then we'll go and see.'

The straw had been there since last year, judging from the grass beginning to grow through, but the edge of the stack had been quarried and the remaining two bale depth enough to allow a makeshift parking place out of the draught. Andrew emptied his capacious pockets of the lunch bags and shed his coat.

'Phew. Glad to get rid of that weight. Old Barbours are all very well, but heavy.'

She sat alongside, hers more modern and lightweight and she'd not closed the zip.

Despite Mary's rapid and impromptu sandwich making, it was none the less effective and they munched happily in comparative quiet.

'Almost as good as being on holiday.' Andrew bit into his tomato and the juice went everywhere.

'Hey, that splashed me!' She wiped a cheek.

He laughed. 'Sorry. Happy?'

With a full mouth, she merely nodded, waited until she'd

swallowed before adding, 'of course. Despite you frowning at me. Wasn't my fault, you know. Time and place, need. Caring.'

He knew to what she referred and had to forgive her. Caring. His key word. Despite the social and moral stigma, sometimes you had to slip away from convention and codes of conduct to fulfil the obligation, get that crucial step further on.

He tactfully moved on to her other mentioned concern. 'Andrea. I care about her, R. And worry.'

'That I know. Bet you you'd have taken to her big time if I hadn't happened, Sam or no Sam.'

Where had he heard that before? It was very clearly a possibility he would have, too. He had taken her in the truest biblical sense and the prompt, that spark of ignition, had been from a desire not purely based on lust, although that had naturally reared its unlovely head, but from his conception of the girl's need. And his, damn it.

His turn to sigh. 'Maybe. Probably. All right, yes. Maybe I would. I don't know. Hypothetical.'

'But you did.'

'Don't rub it in.'

'You enjoyed her.'

What could he say to that? 'Is enjoy the right word?'

'I don't know. You tell me.'

Thinking back and that not a desperately good idea; actually, in a strange way, he hadn't. Biologically, from what he could remember, maybe, though nothing like the way he and Roberta loved. That was something else, every occasion a new adventure. Slowly, hesitantly, he tried to put it into perspective; how the mood and the magic had never been quite the same, totally unlike that which continually existed between him and this girl in front of him, her cake poised and her mouth open to show those perfect pearly white teeth, the tip of her tongue, the pert shape of her under the cashmere.

She put the cake down and brushed the crumbs away, then eased her coat off her shoulders to carefully spread it out on the bale below her. 'Judging from that hut and these ever so soft straw bales, no one comes up here from one blue moon to another. And it's a lovely day. What was that about mood and magic? Can you run it past me again, lover boy?'

The jaunty way she walked, clutching his hand warmly and firmly, swinging her coat in a free hand as they made their way down the pasture towards the bottom gate, said it all. He'd never been all that forthcoming about his feelings over the other girls before; somehow she had at last achieved it, delving into the sensibilities to drag it out of him and by heavens, she didn't half feel the better for it. And the consequences – well, not quite like an Irish hillside or the gardener's shed, but still to remain way up the list in the 'favourites' file. Straw bales, soft but bloody prickly. June's situation and her mother's state of health had been temporarily forgotten.

They got back in time for tea. The four house-bound women were sitting around the kitchen table and, judging from the sudden silence as they pushed open the door, had been talking about them.

'You're back,' said June, unnecessarily.

Her father grinned at her, looked around behind him in humorous jest and replied. 'Yes, I think we are. Anything left in the pot?'

Roberta hung her Barbour up behind the door. 'And any crumpets, Mary?' She loved Marmite on butter dripping hot crumpets and her appetite was rampant, as rampant as her stimulating husband had been; now topping up the teapot.

'Had a good walk?' asked Andrea, aware of the increased vibrancy emanating from Roberta and guessing.

'Yep.' Andrew pulled up a stool as his mother-in-law went to ferret around in the freezer for crumpets. 'Lovely day out there. Anything happen?'

'Not a lot,' June replied, 'other than the Drivas people called. Confirmed their offer of a residential consultation.'

'And Chris was sick. Ate too much lunch. Oh, but he's all right now,' Hazel added hastily as she saw Roberta's face change. 'And Abby's fine. I left them playing on the rug for a few minutes.' She nodded at the intercom device that listened into the nursery. A few gurgles and squeaks could just be heard, fair indication a lively battle was in progress. 'I'll pop back once I've drained my mug.'

Roberta nodded. She'd go up but the crumpet idea took precedence. Mary had slotted them into the toaster.

'How did the training go?' Andrew posed his question into the mix and Andrea picked it up.

'Well. Very well in fact. Isn't that right, Haze?'

Hazel pulled a face. This abbreviation wasn't entirely to her liking but the inference was she'd been accepted. 'It's a lot easier with a good tutor. Computers aren't as frightening as maybe I'd thought. It's good. I'd best go. Excuse me,' and she left to go upstairs to see to her charges.

'And I'd best go as well. Mum's expecting me to go out with her tonight. Hazel's right, Andrew. She's fine. Another day or two and you can relax.' She stood up. 'If we can confirm the preview showing for Friday evening, folks? Should be fun.' The toaster popped. 'Best go before I'm tempted. See you tomorrow.'

Roberta munched happily. Andrew reached over and stole a piece from her plate. Mary smiled and dropped another pair into the toaster. June sat quiet, watching her father. He looked a lot more relaxed than of late and she was glad for him. The Irish holiday had done wonders for them all and Hazel now even more of a different girl. The old Manor had such a remarkable ambience and it certainly appeared to have a fantastic mind-settling effect. Her father, settling down with Roberta; Hazel coming into delayed adulthood, Andrea's life beginning to blossom in a far better and less introvert way, and her own feelings crystallizing. Yes, she'd have no qualms about a divorce now she'd got a permanent job here, her father and step mum wouldn't push her away. She'd live a little, go out more, become adventurous – and if by another sheer coincidence, Roberta asked the question.

'We'd like you to go to Ireland, June, and look after the Drivas contract. Your father won't let me out of his sight and I'd worry if he was worrying. So we thought it would be good experience for you; I know you'd do a good job. How about it?'

'Me?'

'You.'

'On my own?'

'Well, yes, except you'd be with them. Donald and Siobhan, I mean. A nice couple, I'm sure you'd get on fine. I'll ring them in the morning and talk it through.'

She couldn't believe it. Go to Ireland, on her own, be entrusted with a plum job she knew Roberta would have loved to do. 'Are you sure? I mean, with all that Ireland means to you both? Not that I don't want to give it a go, but . . . '

'No buts, June. We'd love to let you have a crack at it. Do you good. And before Andrea goes.' Andrew looked at his eldest daughter. Radiant, that was the word. Good. Very good. Just what she needed. Get her out of the doldrums. 'Settled then.' He reached over and grabbed the last half crumpet from the plateful that Roberta had been steadily demolishing. 'I'm in the office for half an hour or so. Then dinner?'

Mary had been sitting quiet. 'Stew's in the oven, lad.'

'Lovely. Roberta?'

'I'm away up to see the infants into bed. Then a shower and a change. Remove some of the afternoon's souvenirs. After that . . . '

'Quiet evening, I think. A few c.d's over coffee and liqueurs. Do some reading. Let the day slide away.'

June eased her chair back from the table, leant across and gave her father a kiss. 'You get nicer by the day, dad. Thanks.'

'So we did the right thing?' The usual pre-sleep de-brief.

'Seems like it. No regrets?'

She clasped her hands behind her head, having smoothed her hair out across the pillow.

'Not really. It's not that I don't fancy going back to Ireland, but this is nice and cosy and it's coming up to winter time. And you're right about the dizzy spells. The last thing I'd want out there. Good for June's morale, I could see that.' She lapsed into silence.

Andrew leant across and smoothed the covers over his wife's recumbent shape. October. Three months down the line. Six months to go. Seen from this point in time, an age. April then. Spring time. At least it wasn't Christmas. Easter, more like. Would she carry the child successfully, not have too many problems? After all, she was pushing forty. Goodness, they were getting old, another few more years and he'd be heading towards fifty. Fifty! With a son or daughter who'd barely be five. Son? Daughter? Which? Did it matter? He'd already got two of each. A girl would be good. But then Chris would love a brother, because step-brother Peter he'd not even met. Peter! Maybe he should make more of an effort and try and get him to visit next time he was back in the country. He'd e-mail Sam; tell her what was going on. She'd always sounded interested. Had she been told anything about June and William? He couldn't remember. He turned over and thumbed the bedside light off. Roberta was already asleep; he could tell from her breathing. A good day, a very different but rather good day it had been; rash, conceivably very rash, making love out there. Daft. Good though. Her idea. Two of a pair, they were. That's what made them so special. She stirred and he put an arm carefully over her, tucked himself into her shape. Lovely and warm. Cosy. Relaxing. His love.

TWENTY

The wind woke him up, whistling in its eerie way through the gaps in the shutters. And the sickly smell of the damp concrete. The sleeping bag wasn't doing its job, so bloody cold out there. Christ, but he'd be glad to get out of the place. All right for mother, kipping in the old Merc motor home. This was one last visit too far; being supportive and showing you cared was all very well, but sixty-four kilometres from civilisation and no creature comforts. Dedication, that's what it was. He tried turning over and very nearly fell off the bunk, rolled back and shivered. Was that a vestige of dawn showing? As best he could, he pulled the cotton cover close round his chin and tried to empty his mind.

He must have dozed. The room's delights – a crappy table and the wash basin now vaguely visible against the dull green painted wall, the chair with his rucksack and the oddly out of place rug all forming a pattern of weird familiarity. Another time, another place. Pillar to post. The life of a travelling charity dogsbody. How he'd changed! So had mother. Hard as the proverbial, tough old thing she'd become. Loved her though. God, but she'd got guts, standing up to the fat old git who'd try to elbow her out of the store. Given him what for! The kids loved her too. See the way the eyes lit up when she patted them on the head after they'd swallowed the pills. Time to get up.

He sluiced his face quickly in the cold water, tipped a handful over his head and scrubbed to kill off any overnight bugs, dried himself, rubbing the coarse towel vigorously to get the circulation going. He rolled up the sleeping bag, crushed it into the rucksack, laced up the straps and looked around. Nothing left. His boots stood to attention by the table leg; he shoved each foot in turn into the unyielding leather and bent down to lace them up. Outside he heard the motor generator cough itself into life as Albert started the system going. Tea in twenty minutes. The door groaned its protest, grated on the rough concrete floor; he closed it behind him with no regret, doubted he'd ever be back. Crummy place, this, but these orphanages were always hidden away as if to ensure no one knew they'd ever existed. At least three – or was it four – lucky kids would escape from a short and dismal existence today.

'Good morning, Peter. I won't ask if you've slept well. Your eyes are bloodshot again. I'd better do some of the driving today.' His mother, stepping out of the motor home door, looked as perky as ever, how she managed it was a continuous miracle. Mind you, she'd lost more weight and looked positively skinny. Scrawny even.

'Sure thing.'

They made their way across the yard to the low rise building that acted as administration block. Albert's generator was fouling the damp morning air with its diesel fumes, but at least there'd be breakfast. Maybe the power would come back on today, maybe it wouldn't, but no longer their concern. Going back to civilisation after three weeks out here wasn't soon enough.

Taking the only kids back who could understand what was happening to them was the best bit, seeing the way they responded to a bit of t.l.care. What outfit so lacked the elements of common humanity and understanding that it closeted its unwanted brats out here was incomprehensible.

They ate the bowls of porridge, the rye bread toasted and spread with the best bit – the black cherry jam – slurped the hotter than hot tea from chipped enamel mugs, patted Albert on the back and made his ancient creased face contort into a smile, before summoning courage to cross the yard and bang on the orphanage front door. Olga – Peter's name for the unsmiling matriarch of the place – had the four all lined up and ready. One boy, three girls. They'd squash onto the bunks in the motor home, happy to start on the adventure. Would their parents ever have dreamt what would have happened to their offspring? Doubtful. Likely dead anyway, victims of disease, depravation, disaster of one kind or another.

Andrew woke before dawn. Before he'd dropped into an unsettling night's sleep he'd thought of Peter. And his son was still in his mind now, in these wee small hours. Out there in the wilds of Eastern Europe, looking after Sam, an odd parallel with the way June could probably see herself as looking after him. With the way their lives were going it was high time to reinforce the admittedly fragile ties, get to know each other better. Two years Peter had been with the Charity now, three if not four since last seen; long before Sam and he divorced. High time to get in touch. Maybe e-mail the Charity's office to get an update. What else to do? See what needed to be done for Alain's preview thing. Check out Hazel's progress. Have a look at the order book. And they were coming up to the half-yearly figures. Problem with being an accountant, you couldn't forget your role. Not that they were struggling, far from it. Amazing where all these clients came from with pots of gold to spend. Like the Drivas people. She was nice. And Douglas he could latch onto – a gentleman and pleasant with it. He'd best get up.

Roberta kept still. She'd been awake for some time as well, knew from the restless movements he had been too; her instinct told her something was on his mind. He'd not attempted to cuddle her. When he'd crept out of the bedroom she relaxed, spread herself out and managed to ease back into a doze. Far too early to get up.

He made himself a coffee and took it into the office. Once the system had woken up he logged on and brought Sam's e-mail address forward. How best to say what was on his mind? That he would like to see her again, or at the very least find

when she was coming back into the U.K.? That he'd woken up
to the idea he'd not seen Peter since goodness knows when and
that a shortcoming maybe should be remedied? Something had
to be said.

She came back to wakefulness, startled at her clarity of
thought. That's what was bugging him! The chance remark. So
okay, no reason why not – high time, in fact. She bounced out
of bed, flung the cosy wrap over her shoulders, padded down
in search – and found him in the office.

'Morning, love,' he said almost absentmindedly, putting an
arm round the nakedness of her thighs under the dressing
gown. He was staring at the screen, at an e-mail not yet sent.

She bent down over him and read.

*'High time we caught up. Is Peter still with you? Hope the
project is going according to plan. Be good to see you when you're
next back. Lots going on here.*

No signing off greeting, not yet, so that's what he was
cogitating over?

'What's in your mind, darling? You tossed and turned last
night. Conscience pricking or what?'

He leant back to take her hand and bring it round him.
'Sorry. I've been remiss. Cosseting June, taking Hazel on board
and abandoning my son. Wondered about which version
you've got in there,' and he patted her tummy, 'thought it
might be good for Chris to have a brother and woke up to the
idea he's already got a half-brother he's never seen. Hence this.
What d'you reckon?'

'As long as the *'good to see you'* bit hasn't got a hidden
yearning? Not back-tracking?'

He pulled her tighter and chuckled. 'Not in the way your
mind's working, love. But she's still been very much part of my
life; we're still best friends, I hope. But Peter will have changed,
and yes, I'd very much like to catch up. Send it?'

'Send it. It's fine. Let's just hope they're somewhere where
they can read it. Come on, I'm hungry. And getting cold.' She
reached over, eased a captive hand away and typed: *'Love and*

best wishes, A & R.' and clicked onto 'send'. The message hovered and went. The yellow bar 'Your *message has been sent.'* appeared.

'That's it. Wait and see. Come on, breakfast,' she repeated as he cleared the screen.

'Yep. Thanks love. You're a very understanding woman. Glad I married you.'

'Glad you did too. Never a dull moment.'

The old Mercedes might have looked tatty round the edges and rather a lumpy thing to drive but it ate up the miles on the indifferent roads remarkably well. Saying *'au revoir'* to Albert had made the old guy screw his eyes up to suppress emotion; he'd been good to them, eased their way through some difficult moments and Samantha had slipped him quite a few notes out of their remaining hoard of barterable currency. Sterling and dollars went quite a long way in this neck of the woods. Now he and the barrack block of an orphanage were behind them.

A tense moment at the border but a mixture of smiles, more showing of authority's paperwork with crinkled notes inbetween pages and a suggestion that the mission had support from on high did the trick. The four kids in the back remained silent and their little faces showed the apprehension; pushed from one crummy situation into another during all their remembered moments, Peter felt for them. Working with the Charity these last nearly two years had changed his outlook on life; that was for certain sure. A voice from the back sounded urgent; he turned round to give a reassuring smile. The darker haired little girl – and the prettiest – was holding her hand to her crotch over the coarse linen of her almost denim-like skirt and had a screwed up expression.

'Sam,' he'd changed from calling her 'mum' in front of their 'clients' ages ago, 'the dark dot wants a pee. Can we heave-to for a while?'

Samantha saw her chance and pulled the truck onto the

broad gravel edge to the concrete road. No traffic on this stretch to speak of and the dark gloom of the endless pine forest muffled what sounds they made. She switched the engine off and the silence floated down. Peter dropped out of the cab, went to the rear door and beckoned the needy one towards him, reached for her little frame and swung her down. 'Over there,' he said and pointed at the scrubby bushes. The chubbiest one also scrambled towards him and he laughed. Once one wanted a pee they all did.

Twenty minutes later, after they'd all taken their turns behind the bushes and Sam had dosed them up with warm ersatz coffee from the big flask they were back on the road. Two hours down, three to go.

Two more stops, one in a little village where they managed to find some fresh baked bread, a selection of sausages, a chunk of tangy cheese and some very good orange/red sweet apples the kids loved; finally towards the end of the day's lighter hours they entered the town. The Charity's base was only a mere two miles further on; Peter was doing the driving on this last stint and Sam had taken the chance to catnap, her head jammed up on the big pillow she never went without on these missions.

The kids had been very good. Overawed maybe from the length of their journey, the young boy had stretched out and slept most of the way; they'd wondered if he wasn't feeling overly great. The pretty dark haired girl who seemed to respond to 'Solly' as a name (or was that a corruption of 'Sorry'?) kept the other two amused. She was the bright one. Another strange place for them tonight; tomorrow the tedious process of getting their documentation sorted for ultimate acceptance into the adoption chain. They'd have a future, unlike some. Some you couldn't help above day-to-day care before the slow decline to dementia.

At last, the aged school buildings; he swung the old truck into the yard alongside the miscellany of other vehicles and let the engine die. Sam stirred.

'Home sweet home, Sam. Mission achieved. Let's hope supper's on the go.'

From the opened back door facing the yard emerged the Base's resident nurse and the local Doctor. The usual routine; ensure the newest additions to the community weren't going to bring in any problem infections.

'Okay, kids. Off you go. Go and get scrubbed up and ready for supper.' Did they understand? He made the wash and eat gestures as Dotty and Doc Benjamin encouraged the four to scramble out. 'Right, mum.' They were on their own. 'Let's go. Good job done?'

She nodded. 'Good job done. Thanks, Peter.' She reached for a hand and squeezed. 'As usual, couldn't have done it without you.' She nearly added *'chip off the old block'*, a cliché not entirely appropriate but it made her think of how Andrew would have handled this and many another trip. Rounding up the more suitable orphaned children might well have appealed to his caring side; she knew that was one of his stalwart qualities and to be fair, she'd have loved his support. But then she'd been the unthinking one so it served her right. Donald had actually told her so once. Showed how much he understood her. She couldn't wait to get back to him.

Peter squeezed her hand in return. 'Good team, us two.' He nodded towards the little posse of refugees and their mentors going through the door across the yard. 'Those four seemed a decent enough bunch. Good note to end on?'

She smiled at him. 'You'll be glad to go home?'

'It can get to you after a while. Yes. It'll be good to take a break. What'll you do?' as if he didn't know the answer.

The smile deepened. 'Yes, Peter dear. I'll go back to Donald. Keep in touch?'

Though it would be a few days yet before they went separate ways, he knew what she meant. She'd return to the rambling old farmhouse in Surrey and let Donald, his new (newish) stepfather cosset her until the urge to go adventuring and the Charity's entreaties sent her out on another mission to help the uncared-for in some other outlandish place. He'd have to seek another casual job somewhere to support himself for three months at least before the Charity would let him go abroad again. If he did; something was telling him it was time he put some roots down.

Between them they unpacked their kit from the old truck based motor home that had done sterling service these past two months before they lumped it round to the office block and spent an hour and a half on a de-brief with the director of local operations. Then free to go. Just as they were about to leave, Patsy, the indefatigable doyen of the office there, caught them.

'I've an e-mail forwarded from HQ for you, Sam. From an Andrew?'

'Andrew?' her stomach pulled at her as it often did when the past flicked back into focus.

'D'you want to read it on screen or shall I print it out?'

'Print it, please, Patsy. We'll wait.'

Two minutes later and Patsy handed Sam a single A4 sheet. 'Don't think there's a panic, Sam. You want to reply?'

Sam read and then handed it wordlessly to Peter.

'High time we caught up. Is Peter still with you . . . be good to see you . . .'

He looked at her. 'Mum?'

She felt, stupidly, tears pricking. After all this time, all these miles, all these countries, after marrying again and after all that she still loved him.

'Peter,' she said, 'When we get home, go and see your father. Tell him I still love him.'

The office was so memorable. The comfortable aura of familiarity. The crisp light oak and aluminium desks, the recently installed new computer monitors, the deep fuchsia coloured carpet, the limestone paint, the beautiful modern prints Roberta had chosen for the walls, the bookcase, the modern design of the lighting, and her own office chair. The chair she might miss most of all. Here she'd made her home after the debacle of the Brewery's demise and she dreamt and moaned and laughed and sworn and done all she could do to live the life she loved. And now she'd thrown it all away. Given him up, abandoned her aim after all her aspirations, her moody swings between loyalty, passion, stupidity, longing and fierce protectiveness. These last few weeks or so had truly been difficult, no doubt about it; the changes brought on by her father's death, the filming, Hazel's emergence from her chrysalis of dull sub-normality, June's advent – and the discussion she'd had with her own mother. And Roberta pregnant again. What was that she'd said about burning boats? Ah, well, all behind her. New job, new life.

The usual plethora of rubbish e-mails were easily dumped. Why didn't the originators of all this garbage realise most internet users had become so savvy over this waste of space? Talk about saving energy! She was never in the slightest bit tempted to explore the variations of the subject boxes nowadays; always the same automatically generated endeavour to appeal to greed or self-infatuation. Who in their right mind needed potentially spurious pills to boost their flagging sex life? The remaining dozen or so seemed genuine – and there, amongst the customer's replies and the new enquiries sat one from Samantha's Charity. She recognised the name. She'd print it out for him, easier than hollering down the corridor even if he were in the kitchen.

'*Samantha Hailsworthy* – she still used her former married name professionally despite the divorce and her new marriage and Andrea realised something of the significance of that decision – *to Andrew Hailsworthy. Thanks for yours of yesterday –* yesterday? He must have been in the office on a Sunday? – *and the enquiry. Current project now wrapped up, we're coming home tomorrow, flying out of Bucharest. Heathrow approx 11.00 hrs Wednesday. Peter with me. I'll call you. Yae, Sam.*

Yae? Looked like a Gaelic greeting or something a hippy might have dreamt up. Intrigued, she spun the chair round and headed off in search, clutching the print-out.

'Morning, Mary. Andrew?'

'Good morning, Andrea. They're all in the Barn. Did you not see the Jaguar? Customer conference.' Mary, a little behind schedule this Monday morning, hadn't liked being late and wasn't in the best humour. The cycle up this morning from her little cottage – she still went back there every now and again – had taken more out of her than usual and she still had the beds to do. Hazel would no doubt want her to look after the bairns again. What was going to happen when Andrea left she still wasn't sure about. 'When do you leave us?'

'Don't know yet, Mary. I'm going to see Alain day after tomorrow. Maybe I'll work something out then. Hazel about this morning?'

'Aye, lass,' replied Mary, heavily. 'Once I've done upstairs. After coffee?'

Andrea saw the way the wind was blowing. 'Whatever suits, Mary. I'll fit in with you. See you in a bit.'

She hadn't seen the Jaguar Mary spoke of because she'd gone in the front way. A well polished maroon XJ6 with a single digit number before the 'DVS' on its number plate sat in the rear yard. Smacked of discreet money. Lucky for some. In the Barn, there were a middle aged couple with Roberta, Andrew and June; all in earnest and jocular conversation, broken off as she pushed open the door.

'Ah, Andrea. Come and meet the Drivas's. Future clients, from Ireland. Siobhan, Douglas, Andrea is our Office Manager – but only for a few weeks longer, I'm afraid. She's leaving us for the brighter lights of the film and television world.' Andrew beckoned her forward and slid his arm round her. *Any excuse.* 'She's been invaluable.' *And how.*

Roberta frowned, ever so slightly. 'Did you want something in particular, Andrea?'

'I've brought this across for Andrew.' She smiled at this Siobhan and the handsome guy who must be her husband. Lucky her. 'Nice to meet you both,' and made no comment about her imminent departure. Andrew had really no reason to mention it, now she felt uncomfortable, handed the sheet over, smiled again and turned to go.

Andrew scanned the message. 'Andrea, wait.' Giving the sheet back to her, he added, 'acknowledge this, will you, and add *'yes please do, you'd be welcome.* And sign it *'A E Y'.* Thanks.'

She caught his eyes. A quick flick as if to say, don't hang about. And she intuitively guessed the *"as ever yours",* so *Y A E* – *"yours as ever".* Hmmm.

An hour later, the Drivas people had gone and they foregathered as usual for coffee break.

She'd sent the reply as requested, still curious over the relevance of the mnemonic. Perhaps merely a blast from the past. Would Roberta be party to this? She doubted it. June was all dancing eyes this morning. What was going on? Surely she had a right to know, despite the reinforced declaration about her leaving.

'June's going to Ireland at the end of the week, going back with the Drivas's; we've landed a contract to refurbish their country house near Waterford. Roberta would have gone, but in her condition maybe not wise.' He was looking straight at her, as though he expected a reaction, a criticism or at least some comment.

'Sounds lovely.' What more could she say? 'June, you lucky girl. I'm envious.'

'It's only for three days or so. I'll have to fly back to Luton.'

'Still a nice opportunity for you. Roberta, aren't you sorry at missing out?'

'Of course I am, but it'll be good experience for June.'

Silence then, apart from the burbling Aga and the kettle's gentle steaming. Andrew was looking pensive. Mary, in the big armchair, looked asleep. Roberta also seemed in a brown study. The sudden trill of the phone brought them all back to life. Mary got up, collected the mugs and took them to the sink. Andrew reached for the phone, Roberta leapt off her stool, muttered 'I'd best see what Hazel's up to,' and June merely stood up and stretched.

Andrea watched Andrew's expression as the voice on the end of the phone carried on; an indistinct murmur.

'Yes,' he said to the phone, 'that's absolutely marvellous. Of course, it's not a problem. How could it possibly be? I'm thrilled. Yes, do let me know. Whatever. No, of course not. Yes, I will. Thanks for phoning. Look forward to that. Have a safe flight. 'Bye.'

A flight? So that was Samantha, she'd bet her best knickers on it. The e-mail she'd sent must have reached her. Now what complications?

'That was Sam. Phoning from Romania, of all places. Not a bad line either.' He was beaming at them. 'It's my comment about Peter. He wants to come and stay.'

June sat down again. Peter? Brother Peter? Coming here. after all this time? 'Dad? What comment?'

'One thing led to another, June. I won't go over it all, but I sent an e-mail to Sam – your mother – asked about Peter; they're coming home and she suggested he came to see us. She's going back to Surrey, of course,' and June thought he sounded disappointed, 'but maybe she'll pop up for a day, who knows. It'd be good to see her again. Wouldn't it?'

'Yes, dad, it would. How would Roberta handle it?'

'Better than you'd think, my lass,' Mary suddenly interjected. 'There's no ill-will there, not that I's aware of. Your Peter, eh? What age would he be now?'

'Year younger than me, Mary. Twenty-two.'

'Used to be a bit of a free-loader,' said his father,' though I rather think working with the Charity might well have changed all that. We'll see. He'll be coming here on Wednesday. He can have the end room, can't he?'

'Reckon.' She paused. 'Reckon that B and B conversion ain't earnt its keep, Andrew.'

He grinned at her. 'Maybe not in commercial terms, Mary, but we'd be hard pressed to manage all these comings and goings without it. Perhaps we'll have to start on the attics!'

'Hmmph. I'd best look for another girl, then. If young Hazel's taking Andrea's place, what'll the twins do for company?'

283

'I don't know. I'll go and talk to Roberta. You two okay?'

A chorus, 'Yes, we're okay,' and a giggle. Mary grinned. She suddenly felt much much better. If Andrew's Peter was coming to stay, that'd put another man in the house, and a good thing too.

'Peter?' Roberta looked totally bemused.

'Yes. My son.'

'I know who he is,' she retorted, tetchily. 'I had the impression you thought he was a bit of a . . . ' she nearly said 'waste of space' but stopped herself in time. This new attitude of her husband's and the e-mail she'd helped him dispatch put a different complexion on things. '. . . a young man who looked for the easy option,' she finished it off in a far more polite a manner.

'I don't think working for the Charity, especially on the shoe string budget they had for the Romanian project, would appear to be 'an easy option', R.'

'Perhaps not. Sorry, love. Of course he'll be welcome. And yes, it'll be good to meet him after all this time. June I love, so why not her brother?'

Hazel had kept quiet, brushing Abby's hair and encouraging her to fall asleep while Chris amused himself pushing a wooden car round the rug, but she spoke up and asked the same question as Mary had. 'How old is he?'

Both Roberta and Andrew turned to her and she went bright red.

'Twenty-two.' Andrew caught Roberta's eye and winked. 'Only a little older than you.'

'Oh,' she said. 'Is he staying?'

'Yes,' replied Andrew, gravely. 'He's staying. And knowing him of old, probably for some time.'

'Oh,' she said again. 'That'll be nice. Does he like children?'

'Given that he's spent the last three months sorting out Romanian orphans for possible adoption, very probably. Why?'

'I'll need some help with the twins if I'm going to be working in the office.'

'So you will, my girl. So you will.'

TWENTY-ONE

'Glad to be home?' Her ears were still suffering from the flight, pressurised cabins or no.

He nodded. 'Aren't you?'

Samantha pulled a face, wrinkled her mouth and sniffed. 'Yes and no. Shan't be sorry of a rest. And it'll be nice to eat decent food again. And sleep in a cosy bed; though after a day or two it might pall. I enjoy the challenges.'

'That I know, mother dear. Which is what took you away from dad, remember? Do you still think it was all worth while?'

'Maybe, definitely if you think of our achievements, Peter. But as you know, your father found a new lady friend who he married as soon as my back was turned. And gave her twins. Your step brother and sister. Be nice to them, Peter.'

He turned away from her because, very very strangely, he felt suddenly emotional. It had been far too long since he'd seen his father, yet alone spoken to him. June he'd e-mailed a few times, but hadn't plucked up enough strength of mind to make real contact with his father. But his father had asked after him and it had touched a tender spot. After the last few months spent in Eastern Europe and seeing the sadness and courage expressed by tragically abandoned young lives, a total change from the squalor and misery of strife torn Africa, he wanted his own brand of human contact. Mum was fine, if a little hardened to life, but who else? No girl friends and not much contact with his mates from college who'd scoffed at his decision to go abroad and work for free. So if dad would have him for a while, maybe they'd work something out. He picked up his rucksack.

285

'I'll be off, then.' The flight had been in on time, there hadn't been too much delay on recovering the baggage and out here on the vast chilly concourse there was no incentive to linger.

'Give my love to your father.'

He raised his eyebrows. 'Really?' Tell him I still love him, she'd said it before they flew home. So there must be some embers glowing there somewhere; watch out, Donald.

Samantha pulled another face. 'We lived together for twenty years, remember. Go on; call me once you're installed. Oh, and kiss June for me. She's had her problems too. If you fall for a girl, Peter, make sure she's the right one. Your father'll know. Thanks. For absolutely everything.'

She turned away and Peter saw the shoulders droop and then straighten. Poor mum. He shouted after her, 'Luv you!' and she turned and waved.

'His flight was on time, R. So I'll need to meet the twenty past four. Shouldn't take long. Back for tea. All right?'

'All right,' she replied, gravely. This sudden turmoil amongst the already turbulent times might be too much, however, there wasn't anything she could do to change things other than becoming a completely selfish person, which she was not. 'I hope he's going to enjoy his stay.'

Andrew caught her drift. 'You're worried it'll mess things up?'

'Just let's say the reputation you've woven around him doesn't fill one with optimism. I know it's been years and people change, I know he's your son and therefore I'm a step mum, I know we've got June here, but forgive me if I'm just a teeny bit concerned?'

'If it doesn't work out I promise you I'll do whatever's necessary.'

'Like chuck him out?'

He grinned. 'He's probably bigger than me. I'll get June onto him.'

She smiled back. 'We'll see. Go get him, Daddy. At least Mary's dying to meet him and Hazel is sprucing herself up, so watch this space.'

'Hmmphh.' He went out to the car, smiling to himself. Dinner this evening. Perhaps he should have tried harder to persuade Andrea to come back, but after her day with Alain she'd wanted an evening to herself. Or else she'd used it as an excuse, who knows.

The rail station foyer was as crowded as usual at this time of day. Would he recognise his son after four years? Would Peter recognise him? They hadn't agreed on a 'wave a red carnation and carry a copy of the Times' routine. Pot luck.

The outpourings of passengers increased with the last arrival, the push and shove and jostle of commuters all trying to be first to reach the car park and hence save twenty seconds on the way home. He wasn't looking for brief cases and laptop bags, but something maybe scruffier, like a rucksack or duffle bag. Did they still have duffle bags nowadays?

There. Couldn't be, surely? Tall, well, he'd always been big for his age. Not blonde hair exactly, but certainly a lightened brown, bleached out, wavy. Tanned from months in the open air, lined forehead, smiling. Denim jeans rather washed out, an oversized brown sweater and heavy brogues. And a rucksack. His son, Peter.

'Peter!'

'Dad!' They clapped arms round each other and squeezed. 'You don't look a day older! Fit, I'd say. It's been far too long. I'm sorry. Good to be here. On your own?' He looked around, but saw no obvious accompanists.

'On my own. You look the part, Peter. And different. My, but it's good to see you. Had a good trip?'

'Not bad. No long waits, happily. Mother sends her love.'

'She all right? This way, down the steps.'

They moved off, through the swing doors and down into the car park area. 'The Volvo – over there.'

'My, my! An improvement on the last tub that I remember.

Business must be good, or does this belong to my new step mum?'

'She used to run an MGF – open top. We traded in both my old car and hers for this. Family commitments, you know.'

'Ah yes. New step kids. I'm looking forward to meeting them – they're now, what, two? Quite an adventure for you! And yes, mum's fine. Tired, of course, but it won't take her long to spring back. She did mention coming up for a day.'

'Did she? Hmmm.' He thumbed the key and the car doors clunked into 'unlocked' mode.

Peter opened the back door and unshouldering his rucksack, slung it in.

'Hey, mind the upholstery! This isn't a Charity battlewagon!'

'Sorry, dad. Too used to clapped-out Mercedes trucks. Mind you, the last one was jolly reliable. You know what we were doing?' He slid into the front passenger seat. 'Rescuing orphans?'

Andrew nodded. 'Tell us all about it over dinner. You've changed, Peter. Did it affect you?' he asked, as he eased the big car out of the passenger pick-up area. 'Will you go back?'

Peter stretched long legs out. 'Yes. And yes. There's a lot to be done out there – and elsewhere. Too many unloved kids. Desperate shame. Mother's great with them.'

'I can imagine.' He eyed his son's sideways profile; the strong set of the jaw, the determined look that now seemed locked in place, and felt both humbled and proud. This was *his son* – and without the decision that his Sam had taken to go off and meet new challenges, this wouldn't have happened. Recollections of the young girl he had fallen for flooded back, then the *déjà vu* picture of Hazel, up there by the trig. point. 'Did we tell you about Hazel?'

'Hazel? No, I don't think so. We didn't exchange all that many e-mails, dad. Your last one was good. I'm glad it's brought me here. So who is Hazel?'

'A girl Roberta's mother found to help us. Started as a,' and he chuckled, 'bit of charity work, supporting and encouraging a youngster who appeared to be a bit simple and hence with not much future. She helped on the early bed and breakfast front, later she took over as a sort of nanny, which was great – helped Roberta out tremendously – but then we had the television filming crew around . . .'

'Television?' Peter interrupted.

'Didn't we say? Oh, sorry. We've obviously got a lot of catching up to do. Briefly – Hazel showed up so surprisingly well in front of the camera that Roberta thought there was more substance to her than was immediately evident, so cutting a long story short she's become part of the family. Well, sort of,' realising he'd still some work to do on that front, but bring her fully into their world he would, come hell or high water.

They'd left the town behind them and Andrew allowed the car to come back to an amble, as Peter took in the run of the lanes and the vibrant autumn colours.

'Very pleasant out here. It's all coming back. You sold the old house.'

'Thank goodness. At a sensible price. Any regrets?'

Peter shook his head. 'Distant memory. You're sure you can cope with me in this Manor of yours? I don't want to be a burden. I can always go back to mum's for a while. And if the Charity doesn't want me back I'll have to find another job.'

They turned into the lane. 'No hurry, Peter. Day at a time. This is us,' and the gateway and the drive and the gravel and the swing round in front of the steps and the Manor's welcome. And Roberta, there on the threshold in that familiar and much loved linen dress. Clever girl.

She'd tidied herself up, thought about how best to give a good impression, thought 'like father, like son,' and slipped into the old favourite that had worked its magic so long ago. Good she could still wriggle into it, showed how trim she'd kept, though yes it was getting tight, a mixed blessing. Pottering around the front rooms of the house, tidying, moving vases about, plumping up cushions, straightening a lop-sided

289

picture, thinking, worrying, would Peter's visit be a pain or would it work? Mary had taken a philosophical view, told her not to worry, June would help smooth any wrinkles out. She checked her watch. High time they were back.

Through the window the skies were greying down, prelude to a gloomy evening. Not the best light for showing off the Manor; it would look all dull and dreary and she wanted to try and show her husband's son a welcoming home. Andrew had impressed on her that was what he sought, a restoration of good relations. It was up to her. The new wife. The step-mother, not a wicked witch. Come *on*, where are you? Then the noise of the car, the swish onto the gravel; she opened the door and nailed a smile into place. Pray heaven he was a male version of June.

There he was. Tall; a shock of weathered light brown wavy hair brushed well back. Firm featured with an open uncomplicated grin. In scruffy jeans and a cosy looking sweater, he hoisted a rucksack from the back and advanced up the steps.

'Hi, I'm the long lost prodigal son. And you must be Roberta.' The rucksack got dumped on the top step and she was enveloped in a masculine odour of strength in a truly lovely hug.

She struggled and he let her go, caught her cheek with a light kiss. 'Dad's a very lucky man.' he said. 'You're gorgeous. Can I have another kiss?'

A bemused Andrew stood at the bottom of the steps. 'Hey, hey, steady on, Peter! She's not some Charity volunteer to be thrown about!'

He laughed. 'Apologies if required. But seeing as I haven't had the chance before . . . '

She held him at arm's length. 'Glad you approve. And you *are* a male version of June. You'd best come in. Tea's on the go and you can meet Mary and the others. There is a distinct air of anticipation awaiting you. Curiosity maybe. Whatever. Come on in.'

Andrew could see the hall was having the same effect on his son as it had had on him that first time ages ago when he'd escorted Roberta back after the precipitous tumble off her horse. Welcoming, warm, evocative, absorbing.

'*You live here?*' The same unbelieving statement June had made on her first introduction, the same glance around, taking in the feel of care and comfort so carefully expressed in deep pile rugs, well polished antique furniture, the paintings on the panelled walls, the traditional brass and crystal pendant and the marvellous flower arrangement of autumn bronze chrysanths that Andrew knew were Roberta's joy. Here he had shed his shoes and Barbour that day and entered his paradise, Roberta's world, never to leave. Now Peter was experiencing the same enchantment.

Roberta's deep brown eyes smiled, sensing the magic was working, 'We do. And welcome, Peter, we're very pleased you felt you could come. It's so nice to meet you after all this time.' In her voice perhaps the slightest hint of criticism, the suggestion he might have made more effort to visit before. His sister had come unannounced, checking up on her father's misdeanours – as she had then thought they were. Now she was part of them. Would Peter be the same?

'Thank you,' Peter replied formally. 'It's good of you to have me. I hope I'm not going to be an inconvenience.' Had the surroundings overawed him?

'An inconvenience? No way. Leave your bag here. Let's go on through to the kitchen, it's cosier.' Andrew took his arm and Roberta led the way.

Hazel had tucked herself into the corner, away from the door. Mary stood by the Aga, arms folded. June had been told to stay put in the kitchen too, although she'd been sorely tempted to ignore her instructions and rush out to greet him on the steps. Roberta held the door open and ushered him in. He stood, uncertain, before June launched herself at him, hands flung round his neck, almost as if she was the long lost girl friend.

'Steady on, girl.' Hands up and onto her shoulders, gently eased her down. 'Lovely to see you, sis, – and looking brilliant. Life with dad suits you?'

'Couldn't be better. Oh, but it's lovely to see you again, Pete; here, say 'hello' to Mary, Roberta's mum, and Hazel.'

His eyes swivelled round. Mary, buxom, gentle smile, hands now down on the table, watching the lad's reactions. Hazel, hesitant, stepped forward to offer a hand that he grasped with both his, held hers as softly as a bird and the thrill went through her.

'Sit down, all of you. Tea's made. Peter, do take the stool. Hazel, the cake, please, love . . . ' Mary took charge and the spell broke, the chatter started, questions posed, half answered, mugs re-filled, cake crumbs fell unheeded to the floor and any reserve he'd had dissipated within the next half hour, or was it over an hour they talked?

Roberta ultimately made her move. 'Peter, we've organised a proper Manor dinner for tonight. You happy with that? It's what we do. Might be a change for you, forgive me, but it's our way of making the welcome home special. That okay? Smart as you like but not to worry if you can't.'

'Fine, Roberta. Lovely. It's really awfully good of you all. You're spoiling me.'

'Not at all. It's what we do,' she repeated, 'gives us an excuse.' The last one had been Hazel's coming out dinner – and how that girl would sparkle tonight, she could see it in her eyes, the desire to impress. And Peter was a younger Andrew. Heigh ho!

Mary took the lad upstairs and showed him the end room. ''Tis the only one left,' she told him. 'June's in there, Hazel's next to the nursery, your father and Roberta's room is that one. All rooms en-suite. This suit you?'

'Nursery! The twins? Can't I see them? Where are they – Roberta hasn't . . . '

'Nay, lad, they'd be all over you. Fast asleep, happily, 'cos they's had a tiring afternoon. Don't fret; they'll be swarming about shortly. Make the most of the peace and quiet. Do you care for little people?' She paused and chuckled, realising how silly the question was. This young man spent his time looking after tiny people a good deal less fortunate than the two little residents here.

'Nursery? Down there?' He moved softly down the corridor and Mary couldn't, wouldn't stop him. The door opened quietly, he stepped into the room, and saw Abby with her mouth open and hands curled up, Chris with a thumb half out of his mouth, on his side, both still as Mary said, fast asleep.

His father's children. His step sister and brother. Roberta's gift to his dad. Beautiful.

Mary noticed his reaction. This son of his father was out of the same mould. Thank the Lord, he'd bring happiness to the Manor, she could feel it in her bones.

He'd made the best effort he could. The trousers had seen better days; the shirt wasn't ironed but at least clean. A priority, a visit to the shops for some better kit. No point in asking dad for a loan of any gear, nothing would fit. At least he'd made best use of the shower, bloody marvellous to have somewhere like this for the first night back in the UK. This morning – only this morning – he'd been in the Charity's stay-over place, basic, basic, basic. But here! His hair combed and he'd managed a decent shave. Feeling clean was half the battle.

A tap on the door. 'Peter? It's June, can I come in?'

He reached across and pulled it open. 'Of course.' She looked – and smelt – wonderful. A dream. 'June, you look great! And that's an understatement. What it is to see a decently dressed woman.'

'But mum . . . '

'Did her best, true, but you don't go out of your way to impress in places we get to. No point, and could antagonise. Mind you, women in trousers aren't always right either. Dodgy, sometimes.' He changed topic. 'Isn't Dad's Roberta a lovely girl too? I think I can see what brought them to all this. And it's not just her looks – I love those dark eyes – but there's something about her. Vibrant, I'd say. I gather she's pregnant. Is she keeping well?'

'Mostly. She's had a few dizzy spells, 'cos her pregnancy's brought on high blood pressure – or the stress of coping with the filming and Hazel's new role, and Andrea's leaving. Oh, yes, you've still to meet Andrea.' She'd closed the door to the corridor, but her voice dropped still further. 'Dad's . . . ,' and hesitated. How much should she say? 'He met her at the Brewery when he did a big job for them, and I think . . .' Now she was beginning to colour up. Damn!

Peter laughed. 'I think I can guess. The old man's still got a spark in him! Don't fret, sister mine, because I won't worry.' He looked at his watch; the one mum had given him that had seen a fair few miles. Eight o'clock, Roberta had said. Just like a country house Dinner. Best bib and tucker, best manners, best smile. 'Then let's go. I'm looking forward to this.'

The ambience was every bit as persuasive as that first time, only his role had changed. Then, an already married man with an unexplainable hesitancy in his mien, now, the master of all he surveyed. The cliché was true, as far as it went, with Roberta his wife, Peter and June his own children, Hazel his declared protégée and Mary his mother-in-law. The candles flickered and the reflection sparkled on the glasses full with the best burgundy Mary had brought out of the cellar. Only Andrea was missing, but she was no longer within his purlieu. She had finally opted out.

He raised his glass. 'Welcome home, Peter,' he said without thinking, 'here's to a new chapter.'

Glasses clinked, decorous sips taken, smiles all round. Roberta lifted the tureen lid and the drift of rising steam from the casseroled venison started the juices flowing. It had been Mary's inspired idea, this dish, and she knew it would work.

'How did you know this is my favourite?' Peter politely asked, accepting his plate.

'Is it?' Roberta, ladling out the next portion for Hazel, smiled. Happy choice, Mary.

'Mmmm. Mind you, out in the sticks anything hot is sometimes a bonus. This is a real treat. It's a lovely room, Roberta.' Traditional, deep carpeted, antique mahogany table, the houseplant thriving in the Doulton urn, velvet curtains drawn against the autumn's dark, the gilt brass multi-armed lighting pendant casting a golden glow, comfortable chairs with firm cushions; apart from what they were wearing, it could have been the nineteen thirties.

'Thank you – we think so too, don't we, darling?' The inference was obvious; Andrew knew her thoughts had returned to his first formal visit too.

'It's seen a few momentous occasions, certainly. Eh, Hazel?'

Bringing her into the conversation was his intent and she rose to the challenge, as she had in her dressing. The lemon yellow dress gave a good contrast to her dark hair and the pendant lay snugly in its mysterious shadowed valley. Not a hint of excess make-up, but a fascinating suggestion of dark eye shadow to emphasise the deep grey eyes now fixed on him. And she knew she could still call him Andrew.

'As when I abandoned my old life? I couldn't have asked for more.' She turned towards Peter to explain. 'Your father – and Roberta – have been fantastic. Once just a kitchen help, a sort of Cinderella – now . . .,' – and this was the crunch point – '. . . I'm like one of the family. Since Ireland,' and once more she sought Andrew's gaze, 'when I found out what it was to be a cherished girl, loved for my own sake. So I'm a sort of adopted daughter, not an unwanted brat.' The colour was rising, she could feel her cheeks warming, but this must be as good a time as any to declare herself. 'If you and your mum have been rescuing orphans, Peter, then you must know how I feel. Your father – with Mary and Roberta – have rescued me. Put me back on track.' Andrew had used that word, explained all about the significance of the triangulation point and how symbolic he thought it was. And then there was the painting . . . she pushed her chair back, laid her serviette on the seat, and with an 'excuse me, back in a mo'' comment, skipped out of the room.

Andrew, looking straight at Roberta with a slightly puzzled air, wondered. Had he over reacted in his inclinations? What was she doing? True, that day had affected him very strongly and they'd all been under the spell, the spirit of the place, but time had dulled the sharp edge of its attachment. Peter crossed his legs and eased back on his chair, unperturbed. June knew what Hazel was after and Mary just let it flow over her. A minute passed in absolute silence before she returned.

'There,' she said, holding it out so Peter could see, 'what d'you think? Does it look like me?'

Sheila's painting, with the sea, the sky, the gorgeous colours of the hills and the focal points; the girlish figure in white against the geometric shape of the mapping point.

He reached out. 'May I?'

'This is all very well, folks, but Mary's casserole is going to get cold. Why don't we save this until later when we can have coffee in the sitting room?' Roberta, though in tune with Hazel's ideas, didn't want her occasion hi-jacked.

'Oh. Sorry, Roberta. Of course,' and she retrieved it from Peter's grasp and laid it, picture side down, on the side table. She smiled at him, a warm, 'I think you're nice' smile, and reached for the vegetable dish. 'Carrots?'

He'd lit the fire in the sitting room on his own while the others helped clear the table and sort the kitchen out. Mary had excelled herself; the meal had been fantastic. A lovely, lovely occasion that he hoped would start to make up for the lost time and ground since last he'd sat down to a meal with his son. Ages ago, likely before the last term at University. Now Peter had matured, obviously become very grown up with the experiences he'd had, and probably had put a lot of his degree – in Geography and Economics – to use. At least that was something, and likely a good deal better than having a 2.1 in Media or Sports Sciences that might, he thought somewhat cynically, be considered an easy option to explain the spend of tax-payer's money on a three year jolly, student loan or no. He gently stirred the sticks and added another few small logs.

There, that should do. A favourite place of his, this, squatting down on the rug in front of the fire. Here it was he'd first made love to her, his wonderfully tantalisingly seductive girl; where she'd first . . . the door opened and there she was, a vision, wearing the dress she'd worn on his first night alone with her.

'Andrew?' The unasked question; because they were so close each knew the other's thoughts.

'Roberta.' She came within reach and he lifted a hand to lay it against a warm thigh.

'Don't say it, love. I know. And I could wish we were alone, but we're not. So behave,' and she stopped any potential explorations with a smooth down of the skirt of that familiarly beautiful blue dress. 'Let Hazel expand if she wants to. Good for her.'

The door opened again in front of the giggling girls, with Peter carrying in the tray of coffee mugs and percolator. 'We had a battle over mugs versus espresso cups, and we won.'

Hazel's face was flushed, and Andrew was unsure whether it was warmth, too much burgundy or the mood of the moment. 'Mary's not best pleased, but she's bringing the mints.'

The percolator only just went the rounds. 'I'll refill it,' said Mary and disappeared back into the kitchen. June had brought the painting in from the dining room and propped it on the mantelpiece.

'Don't leave it there long, June. We don't want to spoil it.'

She felt the marble top. 'It's not warm yet.' She peered closer at the girl in the painting, 'Clever. Very good artist. You sure it's Hazel?'

'From all the chat we had with Sheila – the artist – as good as definite. It all fits.'

June readjusted it so Peter could see. 'What do you think?'

He had sunk into one of the armchairs at the side of the room, not wishing to either get too warm or hog the place, for after all, he wasn't a permanent resident, but he had to struggle up out of the chair's welcoming depths to get a better look. 'So what is it about this painting, then?' Everyone seemed to be quite worked up about its significance, but blowed if he knew what it was all about.

It was Roberta who explained, despite the fact she was least involved. 'This Sheila is an Irish girl we met the first time we went to Ireland. We reckon she has the gift of second sight or something – she told me I was pregnant before I knew myself, then this last time declared my husband had 'been good to me', and here I am, preggers again. Then she'd written on the back something about *'triangles of love'* and *'seeking guidance'*. Your father worked it out. At first we jumped to conclusions,' and she caught Andrew's amused smile, 'but when it came down to it, the clue was the pillar.' She paused and gave him a chance to think.

'You took Hazel with you?'

Hazel piped up. 'Yes and a good job too. What with fainting fits and the twins getting livelier by the day.' She certainly wasn't going to explain everything that she'd learnt that week or so away, but discovering how lucky she was in determining she now had a surrogate father – and mother – was uppermost in her mind. 'Your father and I went on a hike into the hills together on the last day, and we found that pillar thing,' 'The trig point,' Peter interjected, and she nodded. 'It was the picture,' and she pointed to the painting on the mantlepiece, 'with me in it. So it all fitted in, and here we are.'

'So the triangle . . .?'

'I thought it was Sheila's way of telling me to find affection for Hazel – to find our way. As a daughter, purely that.'

'With the emphasis on the *'pure'* you understand,' added Roberta. 'I don't want her straying into uncharted waters just yet.'

'That was the other thing. Words carved on a black chunk of rock we found. *'Water and Ground in their extremity.* Very emotive.' Andrew heard Mary coming back and leapt up to open the door. 'So that's what we mean about doing the same thing as you and your mother. Rescuing waifs and strays. Well, a waif.'

'It's what is known as 'caring', Peter. What your father does. Sometimes too well.'

'You'll meet Andrea tomorrow,' June interjected, and he wondered quite why she got mentioned at that precise point.

Mary started refilling the cups. 'What was it like, out in Romania?' she asked, managing to turn the conversation round.

'Grim, in a word,' he replied. 'How long have you got?'

TWENTY-TWO

A ndrea slept in that Wednesday morning. She didn't have to get to the Studios until eleven, Alain had told her. 'Take your time. Come for coffee. Takes me an hour or so to sort out the debris, then I'll be ready for you. Can you stay all day, 'cos I'd love to lunch you in the dining room. Where all the famous people have eaten. We'll have the Bond table, provided no-one else is around.'

'The Bond table?'

'Yes, where Roger Moore, Sean Connery and all that lot used to sit. Good view of the rest of the place.'

'You're kidding.'

'No I'm not. You can pretend you're the other Samantha.'

'Um. Oh, all right.'

The security guy on the gate checked her name against his list, got her to sign in. 'Park on the left, miss, where the 'Visitors' sign is. Someone will meet you in the reception area. Please stay there until they do. Here, pin this on you.' He handed her a rather large badge, prominently marked 'Guest'. 'Privilege badge, mostly it's the simple 'visitor' one. Guess we may be seeing you again, then?'

She smiled at him. Make a good impression and life becomes easier for all. 'Guest' indeed. And yes, he'd be seeing her again. Should she risk showing off? 'I'm Mr Perlain's new P.A.'

'Alain's P.A.? Steph leaving then?'

How much did she say? Diplomacy, girl. Remember who you represent. 'If she hasn't said, then you don't know, right?'

'Ah,' and he tapped his nose. 'Right you are, miss. We'll get on fine. Glad to meet you. I'm Dave.' He thrust a big hand out.

'Andrea. And thanks for the welcome. I'd best get on.'

'Right oh, miss. Hope you enjoy working here. Your boss is a great guy.'

Which presented a comforting start. She parked up, walked across the tarmac, pushed open the door and there he was, sunk down into one of the enormous grey leather armchairs that filled the entrance hall. Marble, mahogany and brass, huge photos of the stars past and present in serried ranks around, posters of some of the latest big movies on the large board in front of her, all combining to overawe her. He climbed out of his seat.

'Andrea.' He held out a hand.

'Alain, this is awesome!' She took his hand and was tugged towards him, to have the Gallic greeting.

'Lovely to see you,' the simple phrase but said with meaningful undertones. 'Glad you're impressed. Come and meet Steph.' He held onto her hand and they walked up the broad staircase, along another passageway between yet more photos and posters to a panelled door.

He opened it one handedly and ushered her through.

More grey armchairs, a desk, marble effect wall paper, a couple of decent sized plants – real as far as she could see – another desk, and Steph, brunette and comfortable, rising to meet her.

An hour later and it was time for lunch, down endless corridors, across a courtyard, into a huge panelled room overlooking a beautifully landscaped area with exotic plants and a water lily pond. Her head was spinning with what she'd been told, what went on.

'Here. The Seat. Only for special guests.' he grinned at her. 'Make the most of it; you'll likely be on sandwiches from now on.'

Stephanie had joined them and she too grinned. 'He's pulling your leg. We have a very decent dining room of our own. This is the luxury suite. But yes, make the most of it.'

Andrea loved it. The place, the easiness and friendly attitude, and the sense that no one was too unimportant to be ignored. Steph had shown her the basics of how the office ran, nothing she couldn't grasp. The rest would be mastering who was who and their place in the scheme of things. And lunch was superb.

'And so it should be,' Alain answered when she'd said so. 'We aim to please. This afternoon we'll do the grand tour. Not that you'll remember too much first time round, it's vast.'

And it was. In and out of massive studios, through workshops, design rooms, special effects guys who teased her with an automated owl, underground chambers, seeing 'the back lot' and its scattering of sets in varying stages of construction and destruction, the vast lake where sea scenes were shot – and introduced to dozens of people who she'd never remember first time round. By the time he'd given her tea and some beautiful crisp biscuits and Steph had shaken her hand and said 'glad he's going to be in safe hands' she was totally bemused.

'Oh, you'll get used to it,' he'd said, piloting her back to the main door again. 'You'll get your car pass and security badge the next time you come. After a while folk'll get to know you and it'll be fine. You'll see. I'll call you tomorrow for an update on the cast and crew showing at your place. It is okay, isn't it?'

'Sure,' she said, beginning to fall into studio vernacular. 'They'll love it.'

'I knew they would. The show's going to be great. Roberta's going to be swamped with customers after this.'

'Hope she can cope.' She had to be concerned, knowing there wasn't too much slack in the organisation. 'Thank you for a wonderful day.'

'My pleasure,' he said. 'It's been a wonderful day for me too. And you've made a good impression on Steph which is most of the battle. Well done, *my* girl.'

She laughed. 'Wait until I've had my first pay cheque. Then I might accept the '*my*' girl bit.'

She got another cheek to cheek kiss; he took the badge off

her and let her go. Dave was still on duty and she got a parting wave.

Her mother, not unnaturally curious, probed into every detail of her daughter's visit.

'And you're happy about going?'

'I am.' Then she became reflective and it truth were told, more honest. 'Some bits of me. Most bits, really. Little niggles, maybe, about how others will see me. And I won't have the same freedom I've got – had – at the Manor. Small fish in big pond again, shades of the days when I started at the Brewery. But Alain's nice; I think I'll enjoy working with him. Yes, I'm sure I will. I'll be able to give you a guided tour, mum, once I've settled in.'

'That Alain; he's not married?'

'Not that I'm aware. No, don't think so.'

'What age is he?'

'Mum!'

'Well, you never know.' Her mother had a smile on her that could have been classed as mischievous. 'Stranger things . . .'

'Please, mum. Leave it. Don't prejudge me – or Alain. It's bad enough me leaving Andrew behind. I want to make a go of this and I can't keep on thinking about relationships.'

Her mother sighed. 'All right dear. So long as you're happy. Tea?'

Settled comfortably into the Manor's sitting room, they talked long into the evening. Peter's tales were fascinating, a lively mix of humour, sadness, success and failure, the difficulties and the brighter sides. Eventually Mary began to nod off, excused herself and went to bed in her little downstairs room. Hazel jumped up, making a comment about the twins which caused Roberta to half rise out of her chair and say 'I should go' but Hazel waved her down, smiled and added 'I need to go to the loo anyway.' June's eyes stayed on her brother, seeing how much he'd matured and turned into a really nice bloke, someone she knew both her mum and her dad would be proud of, as she most certainly was after hearing his stories..

'Will you stay with the Charity, then?' she asked at a suitable moment.

'I thought you said your contract was up?' Andrew eyed him, liking what he saw and wondering just what would happen.

'It is. Two years, and that's at the end of the month. Mum wants me to take a breather. Not that she will, I don't suppose. She'll take a month or six weeks off, then I guess they'll ask her to do another stint somewhere. She's very good, dad.' Peter lifted his gaze as he put his coffee mug back down onto the little table and his eyes caught Roberta's. 'Sorry, Roberta, but honestly, she did say to tell dad she missed him.'

Andrew's emotions surfaced. Torn, between the woman he loved and the woman he had loved and in a peculiarly disturbing way began to realise the ties he thought had been well and truly severed were still in place, like a hidden rope in the water between a tug and its tow, suddenly snapping out of the waves when the towed ship slowed down. Strange analogy.

He thought the past was buried under water but here it was, surfacing. Water and ground in their extremes. God, but that Sheila had hidden some deep messages in her painting. Suppose it hadn't been Hazel? If not, who? Suppose the triangle had been him, Sam and Roberta? He stood up.

'Time we were all in bed. Tomorrow's another day.'

Peter looked at his watch; the one mum had given him. He'd seen his father's face change and wondered. Mum had remarried; Roberta had married his father; so there was no going back. Time had moved on. 'She's very happy with Donald, dad.' he said, trying to smooth things over. Maybe he should have kept his mouth shut. Roberta's eyes were wide open and staring at his dad. Oh lor.

Andrew moved across to the door. 'Put the lights out when you come. I'm going up.' and they heard his footsteps up the stairs.

'She is happy with Donald,' Peter repeated. 'Shame if dad takes it the wrong way. Sorry, Roberta, but I couldn't not say.'

'That's okay. I know your father well enough. He'll mull it over for a while and then he'll be back to normal.'

'Perhaps its dad's way of dealing with the things,' June said, sensing the change in mood. 'You know, he can be both placid and yet forthright. That's not to say you aren't, Peter,' she added hastily, 'but dad's had a lot more experience of life.'

Roberta pushed her chair away from the table. 'Stop this, you two. You'll have us all going maudlin, talking around this hypothetical psychology. Water under the bridge. Come on, bed.'

June caught Peter before he went into his room. 'You shouldn't have said that.'

'Perhaps not, but she did say *Give my love to your father* and when I queried it, she added 'I *did live him for twenty years*' and it's only right for Roberta to know. Mum also told me to give you this,' and he took hold of his sister firmly round the waist and kissed her. 'You're lovely, my sister. William needs his head testing. 'Night 'night."

Andrew couldn't rest. Roberta knew; he kept moving from side to side, from on his back to back on his side. Finally she put the light on again. He lay there, arms down by his side, turned his head and looked at her.

'You still have thoughts about her?' she asked and in reality, couldn't censure him

He sighed. 'I suppose I do. Peter's brought it all back to the surface. I can't help it, love.'

'That's because you are who you are, darling. Why I fell in love with you, remember? If you'd been a hard hearted guy, one of the love 'em and leave 'em types, you'd have likely shagged me rigid, given me the twins and then swanned off to Andrea if not back to Sam, if she'd have had you. But you didn't. You haven't even,' allowing herself a get out clause and ignoring Andrea, 'as far as I know, had any other girl since me.

We still work well together, we love each other, you're a smashing dad to Abby and Chris, you're taking Hazel on, and now you're giving a lot of thought to Peter. Sam won't be missing you in that way, I'm sure. You just care about her because of all the things she's done with Peter. Bloody marvellous woman; I know I couldn't have done half of what's come her way.' She reflected on her thoughts, staring up at the shadowed ceiling. 'If she wants to come to see you, Andrew, I don't mind. It's up to you.'

He snuggled up closer to her. 'Thanks, love. I love you.'

'I love you, too. Now go to sleep. It'll be a lot clearer in the morning.'

Samantha, feeling one heck of a lot better after her long soak in the bath, rubbed the mirror clear of the condensation and tried to take a good look at herself. She rubbed the glass again with the towel. It was no good, the moisture kept coming back, so she slung her robe over her shoulder and padded into the bedroom. Donald was reading the latest Ian Rankin, but pushed his glasses onto his forehead as she appeared.

'You're a sight, Sam. A lovely sight.'

'Hmm.' She dropped the robe and did a slow turn in front of the long wall mounted mirror. 'Skinny and wrinkled. Brown maybe, but I ain't as sexy as I once was. Pass me my nightie.'

'You don't need a nightie. You've been gone far too long. As far as I'm concerned, sex is oozing all over you.'

She laughed. 'Not all over, love, but oozing may be right in some places . . . '

Some little while later, with his hands still firm on her bottom, she transferred her weight onto one elbow and used the free hand to push her hair away from her eyes.

'Feel better?'

'Not bad for starters. I missed you.'

'I missed you too. Rather a lot. It's going to take a while to catch up.' She caressed his face and let her head droop to kiss him. 'I might not go back, Don. I think I've had enough.'

'Sure?'

She flexed her thigh muscles and felt him stir again. 'Except it's quite exciting to come home to this. Ah!' He'd gone right back, as easy as that. But why didn't she feel quite so motivated and desperate now? When they'd first met, that time during her long leave, she'd not known anything like it, not since the early days with Andrew, bless him. Now, well, it was all right, but not quite the same and so her thoughts strayed, even as he rolled her over and got much more physical. Wonder what Andrew's like with Roberta?

'So if you don't go back, what will you do? Though it'd be good to have you around all the time.' It was long after that golden glow moment that he asked the question.

'Really? I might get boring again. Look what happened to Andrew.'

'You don't need to think about your former husband, surely? Didn't he leave you?'

'You know as well as I do it was mutual. Look, forget it. I'm thirsty. I'll go and get a drink. Want something?'

'No thanks. Don't be too long.' He'd reached down and collected his book from the floor, picked up his glasses and was immersed in his story before she'd even tied her dressing gown's cord back round her waist and left the room. Was she all that unimportant? *He* should have got out of bed and fetched *her* a drink. What would Andrew have done?

Andrew woke before Roberta, not surprisingly after a troubled night. He kissed her forehead, grateful that it was her he found in his bed. He'd dreamt many stupid things, all wrapped up in a mixture of Sam's first home coming, doing old Stephen's tax returns, the mad pash with Andrea, an odd excursion into the old small barn that had something to do with spiders rather than mattresses and best of all, a gorgeous resurrection of the day out with Hazel, the vision of her up on the hill. Last night's chat was coming back. Roberta didn't mince her words; sometimes her occasional crudity annoyed him.

A sleepy murmur. He kissed her again. Yes, she was the only woman he wanted in his bed, ever, despite the downside of re-awakened memories.

'We need to get on.'

She wriggled closer and flung out an arm to capture him. 'Not yet?'

'Sorry love. Can't concentrate. Too many things going on in my head.'

'Peter again?'

'Hmmm, and Hazel and Andrea and the thing Alain wants to stage.'

'Oh, all right. I'll play mum for a bit. See you downstairs.'

He found Mary already busy. Breakfast looked like being far more formal than usual with all the plate settings round the table – they were going to run out of seating space at this rate. He counted mats. The conventional five now augmented by one. Peter. And the twin's chairs, of course, and another space would be needed in a few months' time.

'Far cry from two years ago, Mary.'

'Aye, lad. 'Tis good to have your Peter here. How long's he staying?'

'Not sure. I'm not going to ask.'

'Nay, neither you should. Summat'll turn up. Alus does. Roberta up?'

He nearly repeated her 'aye'. 'Yes. You okay with all this, Mary?'

She gave him her usual matronly smile. 'Wouldna' have it any other way. Mite lonely when there were just my girl and I. The place teks to folk far better.' The breakfast bowls were being dished out. 'When will you speak to Hazel's mum?'

That question was not one he could answer off pat. He'd put it off, chickening out, but after his promise to the girl there was an obligation. 'What's the best time?' he asked.

'Reckon 'bout tea time. She works mornings. That new man of 'ers don't get back 'till gone six as far as I knows.'

'Has she asked after her daughter?'

'Not recently. What the eyes don't see, you ken.'

He nodded. And Hazel hadn't expressed any idea of visiting her mother either, not since they'd got back from Ireland with the notion she'd become part of the family. A thought struck him and he chuckled. Stranger things had happened.

'What's that, lad?'

'Oh, just a thought. Nothing of consequence. I'll go and round up the troops for breakfast.' The bacon – in the oven – smelt beautifully and his appetite was growing.

'Aye, do that.'

After an enjoyable chatty time over breakfast, he wandered off into the sitting room to listen and lie in wait. As soon as Andrea's car crunched onto the gravel, he shot out and cornered her before she could enter the house. She got her normal 'luverly to see you' kiss before he took her by the arm to escort her up the steps. 'Peter's here.'

She gave him an enigmatic look. 'So?'

'Er, well, he's quite different. Don't . . . ' she'd put an arm round him and stopped him.

'Andrew, you're worried about us?'

'Er, well . . .'

'Don't be. I'm going to be the perfect secretary girl, for what time I've got left. You've not asked about yesterday.'

'Sorry, no, I haven't. How did you get on?'

'Very well. A thoroughly enjoyable day and I know it's going to be fun. Very different.'

'So glad you're going.' Not a question. A bald statement.

His voice sounded flat and she knew it had hurt him and that saddened her. 'Andrew, dearest Andrew, it's me. What I am. We're not in the 'never going to see each other again' scenario; I love you in the best way possible; and that's never going to change. You've got Roberta, and Hazel and June. And I'm always going to be part of you. Aren't I?'

Standing on the Manor steps, feeling something of the chill at ten o'clock in the morning of a dreary and damp day talking about an adjustment to a relationship that had meant so much to him was bizarre. Yes, of course she would always be part of him. Not of the triangle though. He wrapped his other arm round and hugged her. Lovely girl. 'We'd best go in. Come and meet Peter.'

He could sense the mutual approbation. Andrea no doubt seeing a younger, maybe more virile version of himself, Peter the undoubted assets and attractions of a girl his father had latched onto, and if the 'like father, like son' quote was true, well, there she was.

'Andrea, how good to meet you. I've heard about you, of course. I gather you're an indispensable part of the business or perhaps not so indispensable after all. You're going to Pinewood or somewhere?'

She'd put out a hand and Peter being Peter had used it to tug her within kissing range. Cheek rather than full on, thankfully, his father's thought.

She pulled back, diplomatically. 'I've been very lucky. Your father's been very good to me. So has Roberta, of course. But it's good to see you. How was Europe?'

Tactful, thought Andrew. His son, not un-naturally, was happy to elaborate. Andrea appeared to be interested, too. She was a good listener. He withdrew, left them to it and went in search of Hazel. Another action to deal with. Upstairs, found with the twins, and though it was high time she was back in the office with her tutor, Andrea's preoccupation with Peter would have delayed that girl's start on the routines anyway. Not to worry.

'Hazel, I need to see your mother, to establish how we can confirm your permanent move here. That's okay, isn't it? What you want to do?'

Hazel's eyes didn't leave Chris; the little boy was standing, teetering, in the middle of the carpet, holding onto his latest toy, a plastic telephone that did all sorts of noisy things. Abby was happily sorting through her growing collection of furry animals.

'Yes,' she said. 'Though Mum won't know I've gone. Chris, don't drop that, please. Sad, isn't it?' She turned her gaze. Thoughtful grey eyes and with a depth to them that he loved. 'Wish she hadn't lost track of my biological father, though. Can you believe he's still out there, somewhere?'

'If he surfaces?' and there was the water analogy again.

She shrugged, reached out to rescue the telephone just before Chris let go. 'Come here, Chris. Sorry, Andrew. He won't know me, not after all these years. I doubt I'd recognise him either. You're my father figure now. Bit late in the day, but better late . . . ' She grinned at him. 'Don't tell my mum that. Else she might start fancying you. When do you want to go?'

'Mary suggested about teatime.'

'She's right. Want me to come? I need to clear my room there. Not that there's much left.'

She sounded so matter of fact about it that he felt slighter easier in his mind. A hurdle that needed clearing, one that he'd put off, one that could have just been left to fall over on its own accord but also one he needed to remove from his thoughts before the girl would be truly on her way to being her own person and part of them, their family.

'Tonight?'

'If you like. I've nothing on.' She chuckled. 'In the diary, I meant.'

'I know what you meant. And there was something else that crossed my mind. Daughters don't normally get paid – other than an allowance.'

She chuckled again. 'I wondered when that would surface. Would you really stop my pay?'

'No – but we might not give you a rise. In lieu of the training you're going to get.' He kept the smile in his voice.

'Training?'

'As in go to college. Day a week or evenings or whatever. Get you some qualifications. Talk it over with Andrea. Sort of make up for lost time.'

'Do I need to?' Chris had latched onto her skirt and was still standing there, sucking his thumb. She gave the telephone back to him and he promptly sat down and started to push buttons. The 'phone made a peculiar ringing sound and the red light flashed. 'Dring -ing', he said. 'Dringgg-innn.'

Andrew would have picked him up, but Roberta's voice echoed up the stairs. *'Coffeeee!'*

'No, you don't need to, but it seems a logical move. As I said, talk to Andrea. Are you coming down?'

'In a while. I'll see if these two want a nap. I'll go down to the office once Mary's free?'

'Good girl. Speak later then.'

During the course of that strange day, Roberta got a splendid order from another hotel group, June finalised her arrangements with the Drivas couple to leave for Ireland at the end of the week, Andrea worked out with Hazel what qualifications might be right for her and Mary started thinking about another 'young lass for the kitchen'.

Andrew showed Peter around the estate during the rest of the morning. 'How much did your mother say about us splitting up?' he asked as they approached the little barn.

Peter gave him an old-fashioned look. 'Nothing specific, dad. Just the bare bones of the story. At least it didn't start because of another woman, did it?'

Andrew had to laugh. Given that Sam had once suggested he 'played away' and now he reckoned it that had been merely a ploy to allow her to slide away without tears, he couldn't really comment. 'She and I just got bored, Peter.'

'So no juicy stories? What's with the Andrea girl? She's a doll.'

'Met her at the Brewery. Did an accountancy job for them, before they went bust. So we took her on.' He hesitated briefly. 'I have a lot of time for her.'

'I thought so,' Peter responded, dryly. 'She has that look about her. What's this place, then?'

'The old barn.' He opened the new door. 'The film company did it up for us. It was in a bit of a mess. I thought we might make it into a visitor tea room or something. What do you think?'

'What was it before?'

'Roberta's former husband had it as a sort of workshop. And where he played away with the secretary girl.'

'Lucky girl. Lots of atmosphere.' He screwed up his face in a cynical expression. 'He didn't appreciate Roberta then. Stupid man. I think she's gorgeous, dad. Lucky you.'

'Mmmm. I know. But what about you? No girl friends?'

'Out there? A few East European ladies who would have loved to have got hitched. Not my scene. No, no girl friend, not at the moment.'

Andrew took the opportunity. He closed the barn door behind them and as they walked back down the path, asked 'So what do you want to do next?'

'Find a job? I suppose the Charity will call me here in the next day or so to tie up loose ends. I don't know. Something will turn up.'

'You can't stay here for ever, not that we're in any hurry to curtail your visit.'

'Don't worry, dad. I know that. Just grateful – and rather pleased, actually – that you let me come. It's great. Lovely place,' and with a grin, added, 'lots of lovely girls.' They walked round the corner. 'Hazel's a charmer. She got a boyfriend?'

Andrew shook his head. He didn't particularly want to go through her background with anyone, not even Peter. 'Just say she'd lived in a world of her own until she came here. Roberta and I – we – have treated her much as a daughter lately and now she's blossomed.'

'I'll say.'

The client's car was turning out of the drive. The big Barn would be Roberta's to show off. 'I'll leave you with Roberta, Peter. I need to catch up with the office. See you at lunch.'

Hazel was in the chair, Andrea leaning over her. Both girls swivelled round.

'Hi. She's got it all taped, Andrew. I can leave with a clear conscience. And she can always call me if there is a problem she can't solve. I reorganised the filing system while you were away, made it streamlined – and she's on top of that too.' Andrea stood straight. 'With June helping Roberta, Andrew, you've got it made. What will you do with your time?'

'Go back to accountancy?'

'No Breweries left.'

He laughed. 'Just as well.' He thought of Peter's comment, 'something will turn up'. 'No doubt lady luck will throw something my way.'

Hazel sat quiet, watching the screen. 'Look, there's a new e-mail.' She moved the mouse, clicked and brought it forward. 'From the Charity. For Peter. Shall I print it?'

Andrea looked at Andrew and winked. 'See what I mean? And after barely a week. Can I take the rest of my holiday entitlement before I go? If so, don't expect me in tomorrow! Okay, Haze. Print it.'

Andrew wasn't sure about this 'haze' nickname any more than she obviously was, the girl screwing her nose up. He frowned at Andrea. 'Hazel. Well done. Bring that with you. It's lunchtime.' He took Andrea's arm. 'Come with me,' he said and marched her out of the office.

Out of Hazel's hearing, he asked her to refrain from using the abbreviation. 'She doesn't like it, neither do I.'

'You call me An.'

'That's different. 'An' is a term of endearment.'

'Despite me leaving you?'

'Yes. More so. When will you go?'

'End of the week. We've the cast and crew showing on Friday, remember.'

'So we have. Do you want a party?'

She moved her head from side to side, in an 'up to you' gesture. 'Might be nice. Tell you what; bolt it onto the film show. Then they can pay for the booze.'

'That,' he said, 'is a splendid idea. Your parting shot. Organise your own leaving party. Let's go have lunch.'

TWENTY-THREE

Later that afternoon Andrew took Hazel to see her mother. Other than dropping her outside the house he'd not actually been near the place, Mary did most of the communicating. The end of terrace house sat comfortably enough amongst its neighbours but had an air of dejected despair; peeling brown paint on the window frames and dandelions growing in the dirty gravelled path. He sensed Hazel's spirit shrinking; curling up within her, back towards the dull grey wimp she'd been when first he'd seen her. He put out a hand and rested it comfortably on her knee as the car came to a halt. Her hand came down on his and held him there.

'You okay?' Such a simple question but with a great depth of meaning. Back to the hill and its trig point, back to the moment when it had all come clear; becoming a part of him.

Her grey eyes again. 'Now I am,' came back from her, also words with intense meaning.

'Right then.'

They walked up the less than twenty metre path hand in hand like lovers comfortable in their togetherness. She paused, looked at him again before turning the broken plastic door knob and letting the panelled door with its cracked etched glass lights swing back. A waft of stale air, uncertain smells of bodies, cooking and old carpets enveloped them.

'Mum,' she called. 'It's Hazel. I've brought Mr Hailsworthy to see you.' She pulled at him. 'Come on in. She'll be watching the telly in the back room with her pot of tea. I shouldn't,' she added, meaning don't accept an offer of a cup.

Hazel's mother looked an amorphous lump, of indifferent age and character, sitting wide legged like that in a dishevelled grey frock, sprawled out, a cup on a chipped saucer balancing precariously on the arm of a cretonne covered armchair of dubious vintage. The television was flickering and quite loud.

'Don't get up,' he said, unnecessarily. She wasn't going to move, he could see. 'I've come to ask if Hazel would like to move in with us at the Manor permanently. We've plenty of room and it would mean she didn't have to concern herself about travelling back and forth? My wife's expecting our third soon and we really need a proper full time live in girl.' All of which was perfectly true but didn't put the facts into perspective.

The woman stabbed at the remote and the sound died. She didn't even look at him. 'Yeah. Sure. Then I gen let thy room. Sure shy's what ye want? Bit slow like, that 'un. Be nay bovver? Ye teak care o'eer. Good lass,' she ended, surprisingly. Underneath the unkempt exterior there would be some concern about her daughter's future, he hoped, expected, though it might take a bit of finding. Perhaps she was so sure of her daughter's position at the Manor she didn't care. Whatever her mind set was, it hadn't surfaced.

'I'll be emptying my room now. You'll know where I am, if you want me.' Hazel stooped over her mother and offered a kiss on her brow.

Andrew stood back. It had been much easier than he'd thought but had to wonder how on earth such a lovely girl like Hazel could have been the offspring of this woman. True, her hair was clean and not too untidy; her skin wasn't as wrinkled or patchy as it could have been, but the dress, her posture and her speech! How could any man take to her? No surprise she worked as a cleaner. No surprise Hazel's father had disappeared off the scene either, and he wondered what manner of man lived with her now. He didn't want to find out.

Hazel beckoned him out into the hall way with her head. As he left the room the television's sound returned with increased decibels.

'Stay here. I won't be a moment.'

'Don't you want a hand?'

She shook her head. 'I'm not letting you see upstairs. Bad enough down here. Now you can see why I acted the way I did.'

He nodded. 'Don't be long.'

'I won't.' She'd brought two carrier bags with her, just two, and ran lightly up the single flight of stairs out of the hall way where they stood. He heard movements above, drawers opening and closing, the careful shutting of a wardrobe door and then she was back, clutching the two bulging bags and a tatty golden furred teddy bear with a pink ribbon round its neck. 'I couldn't leave Terry. Loved him since first I can remember. All done. I'll just say goodbye.'

The television's noise didn't alter, she was barely gone a minute.

'That's it. Let's go.'

Back in the car, he sensed her tensed up emotion, and touched her knee again. 'Brave girl,' he said. All she could do was nod.

Fifteen minutes later they were back on the Manor's gravel. 'Thanks, Andrew. I owe you.'

'It's a bit sad, my love.'

'S'pose so,' then turned to him in surprise having realised what he'd actually said. 'You called me 'your love'. Do you? Love me?' A tentative questioning voice and he felt for her lack of parental affection. She still had some miles to travel before she became totally secure in her attitude but she'd get there. He was positive she would.

'Yes, Hazel, I do. Very very much.' Her very strong prescience about their relationship had got to him and he couldn't deny her.

A happier light hearted giggle. 'It could be misconstrued.'

'True. But you and I know where we are. As does Roberta. That's what matters. I'm just so glad it's all worked out. Take your stuff upstairs then come down for supper.

317

Peter read the note again. Andrea had given it to him, folded, in the middle of the afternoon.

'Sorry,' she'd said. 'It came this morning; Hazel printed it out but we both forgot to let you have sight.' Her face had remained void of any interpretation; that she knew of the contents was obvious but in her anticipatory role of P.A. wouldn't make any comment, had turned her back on him and walked away.

'Hope you are recuperating. Congratulations on the excellent report, you'll be pleased to know all clients are successfully placed. Can you call the office? We have an offer on the table. Regards, Richard.'

Richard. The Director of Operations. Mum's boss's boss. How come he'd emailed? Recuperating? Guess that's as good a word for it as any. An offer? Another assignment? Would that be with mum – she'd as good as said she wanted a longer leave period – or was there someone else's hand that needed holding? Only one way to find out. He'd borrow the office phone if Andrea would let him.

She was there, busy typing away, skirt hitched up over lovely knees and a bust line to drool over. Beautiful hair, too.

'Sorry to interrupt, Andrea.'

She swung round. 'Not a problem. What can I do to help?'

'This e-mail. I've been asked to phone the office – the Charity's London office and I wondered if I might use the phone. My mobile's on the blink, too much dirt or wet I guess.'

'Of course. I'll be in the kitchen. Help yourself.' She brushed past him, a lovely smile, and her scent lingered. Dad's delight, he thought, not realising quite how near the mark he was.

The reception switchboard girl took some persuading. 'And you are? Sure it's Mister Bennett you need? I'll see if he's free. You may have to speak with his secretary. One moment.'

Then he was speaking to the man himself.

'Richard here. Thank you for phoning in, Peter; sorry to interrupt your leave but I think you might consider it worth

while.' The gist of what was then said near blew him away –
him? After a mere two years – less – and they wanted him to
consider *that* job? Would he come to town for an interview – *a
formality, you understand* – and meet the team?

He put the phone down, carefully, and walked down the
corridor into the kitchen. They were all there, three of them and
looking curious, even expectant. June must be upstairs with
Abby and Chris, but at that moment she reappeared.

'They've gone off to sleep. Reckon I tired them out. Little
angels; how are you so lucky, Roberta?'

'All these doting Aunts they have. You're looking extra
chipper, Peter. What's up?'

'You'll never guess.' He knew them well enough, even
after this brief stay. 'Mum's Charity – they want me to run –
manage – the volunteer staff office, in London. Full time.' He
pulled out the remaining stool and perched on it, legs stretched
out. 'They think I know what it takes.'

'And do you?' Roberta's question had a tense ring to it, as
if she was conscious of the importance of the moment. Mary's
face was impassive, June's mouth dropped open and Andrea
merely smiled.

Peter looked down at his feet. It was a daunting prospect,
being a decision maker, putting people into grim, uncertain and
potentially dangerous situations or telling an enthusiastic person
with a heart in the right place but no essential stamina for the task
that they couldn't go. Was he the right person for that job? Richard
seemed to think so. Had his mum anything to do with this?

'Yes,' giving Roberta and at the same time himself, the
answer. 'Yes, I reckon I do.'

June, from her position by the door, crossed over and
hugged him. 'Lucky you.'

With an arm wrapped round her, he grinned at them all.
'Maybe it's luck, maybe it's not. It'll take some time to get used
to the idea. At least it's a job. In London. Where do I live, sis?'
He looked up at her. 'Digs?'

She moved away and sat back on the chair. 'Talk to dad.
He'll be thrilled for you.'

Roberta frowned. She had an instant idea but needed to discuss it with Andrew first. 'He should be back shortly.' She caught her mother's eye and saw the almost imperceptible nod. Mary had read her mind.

Andrea stood up. 'Time I was on the way home. Congratulations, Peter. I guess it could be a well deserved position. And a very responsible one, too.' She echoed June. 'Lucky you.' She picked up her coat and slung it over her shoulder. 'See you guys tomorrow.'

She heard the car coming back up the drive, stood in the gloaming at the side of the gravel and waited. Andrew saw her in his headlights and pulled up alongside. The window slid down.

'Hi, Andrea. Everything okay?'

'Very. I'm just on my way. You've got a surprise in store.' She grinned at him. 'See you tomorrow.' She peered in at Hazel. The girl looked happy enough. 'So you've left home?' knowing her question would not be taken the wrong way.

Andrew answered on Hazel's behalf, not wanting this to turn into an inquest.

'She is old enough, Andrea. Roberta and I are very fortunate to be able to help, you know that. So another step forward?'

'Great news, I'm very glad for you,' she said across Andrew to the smiling Hazel. 'See you in the morning. Oh, and I nearly forgot to say Alain's coming tomorrow.'

'Tomorrow? But it's not Friday?'

'No, but he wants to see you before the event. Didn't say why. 'Bye.' She turned away towards her little car and Andrew took the Volvo round the back.

'You all right with Andrea, Hazel?'

'Of course.' She unclipped her belt. 'I think she's lovely. I can see why you. . . ' and very nearly committed a *faux pas*, suggesting something about the relationship she thought might be in place but wasn't sure. '. . . think highly of her,' she substituted.

Andrew laughed as he got out of the car. 'Hazel, you're as bad as my wife. Just you be careful, my girl, remember I'm *in loco parentis* now, and despite your age, I'd still tan your backside if you step out of line.'

She blushed. He must have read her mind; something she may have thought of as sexy a few weeks ago was now very different. They walked across the yard towards the back door and their hands met and clasped. His touch, the evening, the glow of the Manor's lights, the repartee and the knowledge she was loved for being who she was made her heart brim over. Unconsciously she squeezed his hand; he turned to her at the door and dropped a kiss onto her hair.

'Welcome home, Hazel, love.'

Ten minutes later and they'd heard Peter's news. Andrew was immensely pleased; all he'd said and thought about his son's lackadaisical ways over the past couple of years or so was forgotten.

'Does your mother know?'

'I expect so. Richard will have discussed this with her, I'm sure, and for all I know she may have put him up to it, though he won't ever say. I'm sure she'll be pleased.'

'Will it affect her?'

'Only in so far she'll have to find – or rather *I* may have to find someone else to hold her hand, metaphorically speaking. If she goes out again. I'll talk to her tomorrow, before I ring the office again. Then I'll have to find somewhere to live in town, that's the downside.'

Roberta's eyebrows were twitching; Andrew knew the signs. 'Well, no doubt something will turn up.' He looked at Mary, still holding her own counsel. 'Should we celebrate?'

'Reckon,' she said, with a smidgen of a smile, wondering when the suggestion would surface. There was a very good parcel of smoked salmon in the freezer she could something with and the latest boxful of vegetables from the farm shop would see them well on their way.

'I'll throw summat together. Give us a hand, Hazel?'

'Sure, Mary, love to. I did a pretty good paella while we away, mostly on my own.'

'*All on your own*, Hazel. She did your tuition credit, Mary,' Roberta chimed in.

'Aye, she would that. A goodly girl, aren't you, lass? And glad I am that you're where ye are now.'

'We all are. Now spare the girl's blushes. I'm off upstairs to change. When's dinner then?

'Gie us an hour, lad.'

'Fine. See you in a bit.'

They drifted off, June and Peter took themselves into the sitting room to talk over his and their mum's roles and how he saw the future, Mary with Hazel as disciple started on the dinner cum supper. Andrew climbed the stairs and Roberta wasn't far behind. She looked in on the twins, happily still asleep but the idea she was neglecting them wouldn't go away. The sooner they found another girl to help Mary the better.

'All falling into place, darling. Couldn't be better.' He started undressing to get into the shower. Roberta sat in front of the dressing table mirror and stared at her reflection.

'Guess not. I had an idea.' Her face was showing changes once more. Pregnancy.

'About the flat?'

'You guessed?' Would she still be as attractive to him after number three was born?

'Hmmm.' He eased out of his shoes. 'Do you think it's right, to let him have the use of that place – I mean, a penthouse flat in Eaton Square is pretty well out of reach of any Charity worker's salary. Won't it do more harm than good? Can't we support him in other ways?'

She hadn't seen it from that angle, just wanted to offer a helping hand, for this was Andrew's son, brother to June who she'd come to love as the sister she'd never had. As Andrew was giving affection to Hazel as another – another – daughter. He was lucky, he had two already let alone the extra one he'd recruited on top of the Sheep's Head. Three girls. June, Abby and now Hazel. She could possibly feel left out – but she didn't. She felt blessed instead. The tertiary one for her was on its way and she stroked her tummy. Yes, it was beginning to bulge.

'He could stay here and commute.'

'True. Though we're running out of bedrooms. No bed and breakfast facilities.'

'I'd have to give the interior décor courses a miss anyway.' The last one they'd held was a mere memory from before the filming. Pity in a way, but not as necessary now the reputation was spreading, and she thought of the Drivas contract and the reminder June would be away after the do on Friday night. 'Will June be all right?'

'Sure she will.' He'd finished undressing and headed for the bathroom door. 'You showering?'

She chuckled at him. No, it would only lead to a delayed return downstairs. 'I can read your mind, my lad. I showered earlier. Go on, I'll change and see you downstairs.'

The dress she chose was another special memory one, from the time he'd first taken her to London. Maybe its last outing. Another milestone. She dressed carefully, brushed out her hair and put the hairpiece in place. The necklace was the one he'd given her, the scent from the last birthday. Different parts of her life were coming together, aspects of their world forming that lovely whole. Recollections of the ten days in Ireland. Jerpoint and its mystique. Garanish and the Edwardian splendour of the island gardens and how he'd loved her there. The hill and way she'd seduced him again. The beautiful evening overlooking the Bay. Hazel's rapturous glow when she'd come alive in her newly found feminity; accentuated by Andrew's acknowledgement of his true devotion for her. Now Peter was here, another stray piece of the jigsaw in place. What more could she want? The shower had stopped; she slid into her heels and left him the space.

After dinner they retreated to the sitting room. The curtains remained undrawn; Andrew went to close them and was struck by the mysteriously beautiful light outside. He peered across to the left and saw the nearly full moon behind and silhouetting the branches of the beech. The skies had cleared so maybe there would be the first frost of the autumn.

'It's pretty bright out there. Almost magical when you see it like that.' About to complete drawing them across, Roberta stopped him.

'Leave them. No one's worried.' She was still in euphoric mood; with a lovely meal and wine and company and conversation and now this, the gathering of the clans around *her* fireside, as she'd asked herself earlier, what more could she possibly want?

'I'm going to walk round the garden,' Hazel suddenly announced. 'It looks so lovely in its silver light.'

'Put a coat on, dear. It'll be cold.'

'I'll join you if I may?' Peter's eyes hadn't left her all evening. There was something about the girl that fascinated him and she certainly knew how to dress. It was difficult to imagine this glowing persona was the same girl his father had described earlier and he wanted to find out what made her tick, her history and where she thought she was going. Something about her? Very much so, an aura, an inner radiance. 'Find the right girl,' his mother had said. Would he need to look further?

'Sure.'

Roberta had been right. It was cold. Hazel snuggled into her fleece and folded her arms across as they walked slowly round the skeletonised flower beds and through the shrubbery towards the beech tree's bench.

'You like it here?' He'd shoved his hands in his pockets; thought his sweater would be warm enough but out here, yes, cool. The air was crystal cold and scintillating, totally different to Europe – or Africa for that matter.

'Love it. Wouldn't be anywhere else. Your father's a lovely man, Peter.'

He looked sideways at her, saw the sincerity in her face

and heard in the tone of her voice that she meant exactly that. She was getting at him, this girl.

'He's a lot different. Reckon Roberta's worked her own magic.' What more could he say?

Hazel nodded. 'She's lovely too. But it's Mary I owe. She first brought me here, and it all went on from there.'

'So what changed you, Hazel?'

'*Who* changed me, Peter. Roberta, first. Then your father.' She might have said '*fell in love with me*' but that wasn't strictly true, not in the way he'd take it. Instead she just said, 'saw I needed some love', which was true. 'He has the capacity to care, Peter, just as your mum does, and maybe you do too.' The same latency she'd felt in his father was with him in an intriguingly different way, the impression that she'd be safe and yet excited by knowing more of him.

'Hmmm. Okay. So we seem to have established a family trait. Little did mum know what she was starting.' She was matching his step, pace by pace, across the silver lawn.

'If she hadn't gone, none of this might have happened.' She swung her arms round her.

'Want to go in?'

'Not just yet.' They'd reached the bench and she sat down, carefully smoothing her skirts under her fleecy coat. Peter sat alongside. She shivered and rubbed her gloveless hands. 'Well, not just for a moment. It's so lovely in the moonlight.'

Peter took his hands out of his pocket and reached for hers to enclose them in his warmth. 'We don't want frostbite.'

'Don't be silly,' she said but didn't resist. A moment of silence, then as one hand withdrew, the next thing she knew was that he'd put an arm round her shoulders. It felt like a totally new experience and she very nearly stiffened up, but Peter was like an Andrew and he was warm and his sweater was cosy and rather comforting. There was a glimmer of a feeling somewhere deep inside her, not unlike the time up on the slopes above the cottage in Ireland when Roberta had . . . had shared her love. She nestled into him and he half turned towards her.

As Andrew thought they'd been out rather too long for a cold night, he went to the window and looked out, across the ghostly lit lawn.

'What is it, love?' The firelight flickered shadows of flame on the walls.

Mary was fast asleep, June was dozing; Roberta got up and joined him. He pointed with his head, silently. In the moon's glow they could just see the two on the bench, a girl who had come a long way with them and the son of his first love, Samantha – who still had a firm place in his heart. Two shadows in the shadow of the beech where he had once pledged his love for this girl alongside who was now his truly beloved wife. The triangles were coming together.

She reached for a hand and lightly squeezed.

TWENTY-FOUR

Friday. The end of the week, the end of an era. A chapter's ending, the turning of a page.

Roberta struggled with the concept most of the day, musing over her precious design layouts, a stroke of fabric here, a twitch of curtains there, a slight adjustment of a vase and the repositioning of an occasional table. But it was no good. She could feel the deep set emotion building, welling up inside her. Last night's dinner had had a tinge of a wake about it; the knowledge that things would not carry on *ad infinitum*, there was change in the wind and that wind was blowing relentlessly towards her. June was packing her case; the Drivas couple would be calling for her after ten this evening and she wished, fruitlessly, that she was doing the Irish trip but the dice had well and truly rolled away from her. She was pregnant and that was that. Andrea would not be driving her little car onto the Manor's gravel on Monday; the empty parking space would remind them all she'd gone, gone into a new and demanding life that would, she was sure, lead her into marriage. Hazel would be swinging her precious young legs on the office chair; Andrew would be looking down over a different shape and guiding a different hand. And Peter? Ah, the moonlit garden had evidently produced its own brand of magic. His eyes never left the girl, her coyness and lowered eyelashes told their own tale. Love under the moon. So be it. His living here while working at his tailor-made job in London would see its own result; Andrew's son and his quasi adopted daughter who she'd lifted out of the doldrums – what a happy state of affairs. Samantha would smile. Mary was rightly cock-a-hoop.

She came to the end corner and her little hideout, her refuge. The comforting softness of the big old armchair absorbed her; she tucked her feet up under her and let her head sag back onto the cushions.

Andrew found her asleep. He stood, uncertain, poised to turn back and leave her, knowing about the strains of the day and the evening ahead, for he too had an odd mixed up feeling inside. It would do no harm for her to take this time to rest her mind, but she woke; a sixth sense or telepathy between them, for they were twin souls?

She held out a hand. 'Darling. I'm sorry, I fell asleep.'

He smiled. 'So you did. No problem, but it's nearly teatime. Are you coming across?'

'Teatime? Heavens, I must have been really asleep.' She unfolded legs that felt numb and rubbed her ankles. 'Pins and needles. Silly me. Have you missed me? Good job we had no clients today. Sorry,' she said again. She held out a hand. 'Give me a pull, gently.'

Cautiously, she put feet to the floor and stood up, holding onto him. 'When do they come?'

'The technical guys and caterers; about six thirty. Alain said he'd be here at seven. Celebes at half past.'

They'd run through the 'cast and crew showing' logistics yesterday when Alain had come over, they'd talked at length about the film, the broadcast, how it might affect them, whether there would be any follow-up, and finally, importantly, about Andrea's new role. Andrew had become a good deal easier in his mind after Alain's explanation; how she would fit in, how good she'd be, what the future held for her; how could he not welcome this opportunity for the girl he held in such esteem?

'I'd best get changed. Have a shower, try and get in the mood.'

'You're feeling the same? Sort of sad?'

She nodded. 'I could cry, my love,' and she lent against

him, burying her head into his chest, putting her arms tight round him and feeling his close around her. Then the tears did come, soaking into his sweater; he felt her shoulders heave and heard the muffled sobs. What else could he do but hold her, let her cry, feeling his own emotions rise and engulf him.

'Roberta, darling girl,' and his own voice sounded strange to him, 'it's not the end of the world. I know it's brought change, but we're still together. Always will be.' They stood, enmeshed as ultimately Roberta's spasm of emotion ebbed away and she moved a hand to rub her eyes and brush the tears off her cheeks.

'It's been a strange summer.' She lifted her head to gaze at him, the faint smile, the quizzical raised eyebrows. 'And you've been so good to me, living with my foibles. I'm sorry I thrust Hazel at you, love.'

He had to chuckle. 'The girl's come a long way. She's okay. And now she's got Peter.'

Her grin came back at him. 'Was that why you invited him here?'

'No, it wasn't, but I can say it was a good move. Don't you think they complement each other?'

'Yes, perhaps they do.' Then a striking thought. 'Sheila. Had she more of a glimpse into the future than we realised?'

'I don't know that I want to go there, R. Certainly it was a magical afternoon on the hill, but the symbolism of it all might be beyond me. Just a lovely place, time, circumstances, mood, the girl – yes, I saw Hazel as another Sam, but then as a daughter, but now as a . . .' He stopped. Daughter-in-law? The waymarked track he'd led her on had taken another turn and reached the pointer to different path. That's how life was mapped out, bearings taken, distances estimated and a journey they all had to travel. 'Did you feel anything at Jerpoint?'

He felt her stiffen. 'How did you guess?'

'I had my moment, you had yours.' His was up by the trig point, several days later, but equally momentous.

'I think that was when I knew we'd never part; something happened to me, I no longer worried. Maybe the Abbey had a friendly spirit? Then the getting back on track I talked about?'

'We've done that. Reached our point. Brought others to theirs.'

'I love you, husband.'

He grinned. 'Just as well. 'Cos I love you too and . . .' his hand rested on her tummy.

Her third and last child. Another of their triangulation points reached; and mysteriously somewhere down inside her womb, to bring her happiness and contentment, she felt a tiny, tiny movement.